Why You Must

 A San Francisco Saga

Susan Gee Rumsey

Published through: lulu.com

Cover and Text Design by: Susan Gee Rumsey

A CIP record for this book is available from the Library of Congress Cataloging-in-Publication Data

ISBN-13: 978-1-387-73286-9

Don't die with your music
still inside of you.
— Dr. Wayne Dyer

Contents

1.

Juli Ponders the End of Her Marriage

That first night your husband failed to return home as promised and didn't call to say he'd be late, you were a young wife, worried and sick with anticipatory grief for what you feared must have happened to him. Years later, after a score or more such "nocturnal omissions," you think to yourself: he better be dead and chilling on a slab at the City's morgue or at least be lying unconscious and sprouting tubes in the ICU at S.F. General. Because nothing short of death or coma is going to get him off the hook tonight.

Midnight, David had said. Right after the show. Okay, not right after. More like, after the cast and crew have hosed themselves down and struck off across Geary Street to the Curtain Call to spend an hour or more in witless drinking. Meanwhile, you wait six blocks away in your tiny, dingy downtown studio apartment, the best that two would-be artists can afford in this glamorous Baghdad-by-the-Bay. Turns out you were not so "ready for the '80s" as you thought. After five years of marriage, your home is still furnished in

College Dorm Classic: cinderblock-and-raw board bookcases, an eternal Indian-print bedspread suspended curtainlike from the ceiling to serve as a room divider, and a fusty foam mattress on the floor that you curl like a giant rubber taco and lean upright in the closet during the day. Assuming you get around to it.

One o'clock in the morning, you start to wonder: what to do? An hour ago, you turned down the oven to avoid cremating your tuna casserole. Now you turn the stove off entirely, remove your canned food collage from the oven's stained and burnt interior, cover the casserole dish with foil, gently used and saved from last week, and transfer what was to have been dinner to the fridge before the stove cools sufficiently to allow the resident roaches to scuttle back in. You think, I can reheat. But even before the clock ticks up to two, and the oven goes stone-cold, you find yourself wandering aimlessly around the apartment — from the single mid-size room you inhabit, to the bathroom with its raucous, inadequate plumbing, to the kitchen so small that a person standing at the sink must step aside in order to open the oven door.

You light yet-another cigarette. You're already on your second pack of the day since you got home from work. Now the ashtray overflows with bent orange-and-white Marlboro butts sunning themselves on a berm of gray ash. The place stinks. You stink. You carry the offensive heap from the living room/bedroom to the kitchen and dump the mess into the garbage. You rear back from the filthy cloud of ash that puffs up at you from the trash can's dark interior. You go back to pick up butts you lost on the way and to use your hand to wipe spilled ashes from the low coffee table — a fresh start. With the ashtray empty, the visual evidence of all your hours spent alone is gone, and it becomes easier for you to deny your true circumstances: that last call at the bar was now nearly an hour ago, yet there is still no sign of that man you married.

Damn the Theater, anyway! When the two of you moved to the City nearly seven years ago — you, the writer, and he, the actor — you knew the stage would prove a demanding mistress. You just didn't realize how insistent she'd be. Nowadays, it seems, he is always with HER. And though you're glad he's working (even if it's only bit parts and background) and though you're glad of this gift of free time you've been given in which to write your Great American Novel (even if you never get around to doing it), you nevertheless feel the sting when your friends tease you about your "phantom spouse," who never shows up for you on Friday night field trips into North Beach and who's never home when they drop by your apartment.

"But he's in Theater," you explain. "He doesn't have evenings free, especially not weekends."

"Yeah, yeah," they smirk, "we get it." But you notice that men sometimes raise an eyebrow and give you an expression that says, Okay if I'm not your type, but you don't have to go so far as to invent a husband to put me off.

And that incident at the bus stop earlier today left you feeling more confused than ever. At five-forty, you returned the manuscript you'd finished proofing to Tweedledum, one of two production editors you support at Raker & Ho. You shut off your IBM Selectric typewriter and tidied up your desk. By six, you had grabbed your purse and hurried past the receptionist, also packing up, to head for the Muni stop at

Battery and Green. Leaning against the sign pole and damply enveloped in bay fog, you raised your chin and inhaled a sweet-sweet sugar wind blowing in from across the street. You looked toward the tiny, decrepit, garage warehouse that is home to an old-fashioned fortune cookie factory. For months, you've watched them operating their ancient Rube Goldberg-style machine that rotates and presses into the wee hours, folding cookies around an infinity of futures. Tonight you wondered which fortune was yours.

Then it began: a young woman joined you at the bus stop. When you realized she was staring at you, you pretended to be lost in your own thoughts. But her attention was irritating. Moments later, she spoke.

"Aren't you David's wife?" she asked. You turned and, before answering, took her in at a glance: younger than you by five to ten years, nice looking in an overly made-up way, big hair curled, fluffed, and shellacked into place. You are glad to note the big white bow at the collar of her Dianne Feinstein blouse has slipped to one side and is coming undone.

"Sorry, you must have me confused with someone else. I don't know any Davids."

"No, really, I feel sure we've met before. After one of the A.C.T. shows. Judy, isn't it?"

"My name's not Judy. Besides, I'm single."

The young woman's smile melted. She frowned, wrinkling her brow with a look of consternation. "Oh well, then. I'm the one to be sorry. I apologize for interrupting you."

"No problem," you replied blandly. "I have a common face."

You turned away. Your bus arrived, wheezing to a stop. As

you worked your way down the aisle, holding onto the sticky overhead bar, you glanced back and were relieved to spot your nosy temporary companion still standing at the bus stop. But she was watching you go. You didn't like that.

The incident continued to gnaw at you as you shopped at the Cala Foods on Polk, then trudged back up and over the Bush Street hill. You had surprised yourself with your spontaneous lie. You generally thought of yourself as a person who was truthful to a fault. Yet, without any premeditation, the lie had come. Unbidden. To protect you. You had refused to yield the truth to a stranger whose relationship to you — and to David — was unknown. As you stood in the kitchen that evening, assembling a dinner no one would eat, a feeling came to you: today is the beginning of the end.

Hours later, you realize the cigarette smoke in your apartment has congealed into a poisonous miasma. You wrench open the window next to the fire escape and squeeze through to sit on the milk crate that is your version of a deck chair. In your attempt to make yourself comfortable, you accidentally knock over a green plastic pot containing the withered, broken stump of a long-dead coleus your mother gave you a couple years ago as an apartment-warming gift during one of her blow-through-town shopping sprees. You watch crumbles of dirt plummet to the sidewalk below and wonder what kind of natural talent enables you to kill every single plant you touch. You feel like Midas's loser sister. You remember reading that coleus is supposed to be a hallucinogenic — you wonder why it never occurred to you to try smoking it.

The iron bars of the fire escape landing feel wet and slimy and numbingly cold on your bare feet, but the pain is good. To think that something hurts more than your stomach and your heart. You flick cigarette ashes overboard and watch them sail to the street two stories down. The City's resident fog bank has crept all the way into the neighborhood you jokingly refer to as "Lower Nob Hill," blanketing all the rich creeps two blocks above you and all the wino-bum degenerates two blocks below you. You watch soft-focus traffic lights at the corner of Bush and Leavenworth changing from red to green to yellow to red. You watch the oncoming traffic, noses pointed towards the bay. You watch for David.

It's nearly four when you see a cab pull through the intersection, veer to the loading zone curb across the street from your building, then stop, its hazard lights flashing. You watch David get out, thinking how strange he should come home in a taxi, considering that the theater and his after-show hangout on Geary are only blocks away, down the hill. But, of course, it's so late, nothing's been open for hours, so you suppose he must have gone to someone's place after the show. You panic. You crush your cigarette to death on a wet iron bar, scramble back inside the apartment, force down the warped front window, click off the overhead light, slide into bed. You don't want David to know you've been waiting up, sick with anxiety and angry for hours, so you pretend to be asleep.

You lie on your slightly damp foam mattress on the floor, breathing hard and listening hard for the mechanical grindings of the Otis elevator across the hall, bringing Orpheus home. It takes forever, but at last you hear the squeaking cable, the cage door slam shut. His key attacks the front door, rattling the Schlege deadbolt before catching and turning it. You hold your breath. He stumbles in.

Drunk? Stoned? Both, most likely. You realize, in roughly seven years with this man, you have never once seen him entirely straight. You wonder if wherever he's been tonight, whatever (and whoever) he's been doing, has left marks on him. One night, you remember, he came home with a sprained ankle that he said he got while getting off the bus. You asked him why he was on a bus when the show was just down the hill; he shrugged a reply. Another night, his back was covered with bruises and scrapes; he said he fell. He appears, from time to time, with welts or abrasions. His body hurts him. He offers no explanation.

Tonight he goes straight for the bathroom, flips on the light, slams shut the door, vomits loudly. For reasons you don't understand, the sound of his throwing up makes you laugh. You wrap your pillow around your head to muffle your snickering and so you can't hear the barfing. Stillness follows, then you hear him running the shower. You know he will be in there awhile, so you get up out of bed in the dark to take off the jeans you're wearing and to slip on the sweatpants you normally sleep in. Then you get back into bed to wait some more.

It feels like hours before David emerges from the bathroom. And there you are in bed, once again pretending to be asleep, your back a barrier against his side of the mattress. For a moment the room is flooded with light from the bathroom, and in your mind's eye, you see him backlit, just the shadowy silhouette of a man. He flips off the light and shuffles toward where you are huddled in the dark.

When he pulls back the sheet and lies down, you feel the heat and damp of his naked body next to you. You remember the last time he hurt you in bed, and you think: don't touch me! He doesn't. Instead, he curls and rolls away from you and begins to sob deeply with his face buried in his pillow.

Oh god, now what? You are torn between fury and fear and pity for this pathetic, despicable man you still love. You know you should ask him what's wrong, but you also know whatever answer he gives you will be a lie. And you don't want to hear it. Not tonight. Not anymore.

He is shaking. You wonder whether you should pretend to wake up now and try to comfort him. But the shaking grows rhythmic, so it becomes clear to you: he is jerking off. This disgusting man, lying right next to you ... is beating off. So you wait and continue faking sleep, till he shudders down and passes out.

As you wait, you wish yourself far, far away. You slip into your nighttime mindscape and fly west, up and over the City's hills, to go walking on Ocean Beach, out beyond where Playland-at-the-Beach used to be. Fog is here as well, and the sand feels cool and soft and soothing beneath your bare feet. Not like the iron bars of your cage of an apartment. A quarter moon casts a shiver of sparkling highlights on the waves. The vast ocean comforts you with its deep, steady rhythm.

Here you are content to be alone. You wander along the beach, looking for doors — that most common human-made object to wash onto shore. Here you are free from the demands of your urban existence, including your so-called marriage. You are safe within your dream. You promise yourself: the next door you find lying on the sand, carried in on the tide, you will open it, step over its gritty threshold, and escape through its portal to wherever that may lead.

2.

David Weighs
His Options

Night after night of carrying a tea tray with an empty pot or brandishing a blunt stage sword, speaking such lines as "You rang, madame?" or "The better to serve you, m'lord," was not what you had in mind when you decided to go into acting. But what *did* you have in mind? Did you ever actually decide on a career in the professional theater?

When you think back twenty years to the green lad you'd been in high school — that first time, as a sophomore, you auditioned for a show — you remember mostly what a charge it was to get to hang out with the cool drama kids. Where else could you have fit in? Though you were tall for your age, you weren't athletic. You didn't play a musical instrument, so no band or orchestra for you. And while you were smart enough to be an egghead on the debate squad or run for student government, you were painfully shy about your shabby, ill-fitting school clothes and the crummy trailer you and your alcoholic mom called home. You were also dyslexic, something no one understood back then, in the pre-enlightenment of the mid-'60s in America.

Especially not in rural California, where *The Grapes of Wrath* — essentially, the story of how your relatives two generations ago made their way across country to the Salinas Valley — was excluded from the public library because it aggravated the local powers-that-be. Of course, by the time you graduated from Salinas High, Steinbeck had received a Pulitzer Prize for that same novel once banned and burned in your hometown, as well as a Nobel Prize on general principles. None of which helped you in the least with your sorry inability to spell your own name correctly or take down a phone number without messing it up. Incidentally, you don't recall having received any invitations to join the yearbook staff either.

But those drama kids, even though a lot of them were misfits, too, they were a community of misfits. They hung together, partied together, stuck up for one another, and more or less created their own world of "The Theater," in which everyone literally had a role to play. Naturally, you wanted to be part of that — you wanted to be tight with them. They were a tribe, a clan, a family. You'd never really had that, people you belonged with (and belonged *to*), people who accepted you and to whom you didn't have to prove yourself. People you weren't ashamed of knowing.

Also, it must be acknowledged, the Drama Club had a reputation for attracting hot chicks who, in turn, had a reputation for being easy.

High school. You were another, different sort of person in those long-ago days before Nam, before the relentless Asian sun burned you an old-man neck, before the fetid jungle rotted your leather watchband off your wrist, before you had lived night and day with the certain knowledge that someone somewhere was always out to waste you. Years later, you still kick yourself every time you remember how, on your own and right out of high school, you actually walked into the Marine Corps Recruiting Office and signed up. The act was intended as a dramatic gesture to proclaim your despair when the girl you thought you loved married someone else. What a dick you were!

Right away in Basic, you realized you'd made a terrible mistake. No more sleeping in, no more hanging out, no more, "I dunno — whatta *you* wanna do tonight?" From now on, or at least for the next three years, someone else would decide what you would do tonight. And you often think back on that morning your drill sergeant decided to impress upon you how essential it is to *not* refer to your gun as a "gun." First, he ordered you to drop your pants and lie spread-eagle on your back in the dirt, so he could stand, boots and all, on the tender flesh of your inner thighs while he lectured you regarding appropriate military nomenclature. Then he had you run the track twenty times, holding your rifle in one hand and your exposed cock in the other hand, chanting, "This is my weapon, this is my gun! The one is for killing, the other's for fun!" Having completed this aspect of your training, you shipped out to Southeast Asia. As soon as you got to Nam, your killing and your fun began in earnest.

Boot though you were, you proved yourself a crackerjack marksman with your "weapon." So, of course, the Marines made you a desk clerk and sat you down to a rusty Royal, where you used two fingers to pound out endless forms in quadruplicate. Thus culminated the heroic gesture of your joining in the first place. Most of your time in country, you didn't see a lot of action from base. However, you did learn how to remain stoned around the clock, while on duty, without anyone ever catching on. And you did learn how to have a kick-ass R&R in Bangkok with the boom-boom "angels" at the Thai Heaven Club. They loved you: so cherry as you were back then and never, ever a cheap Charlie. Fuck all those boring temples and tiresome floating gardens! This is how you discovered you could smoke your way to safety and find freedom between the legs of someone you'd just met. All the thrill of combat — then victory, and the only form of death you looked forward to!

It would have been impossible to explain all this to your new, fresh-faced young friends at the suburban state college you would later attend on the G.I. Bill. Already you were years older and years wiser than these babes right out of high school. None of them had ever been shot at. You gravitated, naturally enough, into the drama department. There you struggled with the same difficulty you'd had in high school of not being able to memorize your lines. Fighting to overcome the problem, you wrote out your every speech in longhand, over and over and over and over. This mostly worked, but still you died each time you had to call for a line. Once, during a dress rehearsal of the big spring show, you had to go onstage with book in hand. After that, you noticed, the two professors who directed shows at Cal State Hayward didn't cast you in the big speaking parts. The time had come for you to receive your formal introduction to a professional lifetime of toting trays and wielding spears. But even a nonspeaking role was still enough to grant you membership in the exclusive club of college drama students and to gain admittance to their cast parties after each show.

Juli was the first girl who seemed to understand what you'd been through, what you were still going through. She talked to you like you were a human being, not a retired baby-killer. You were careful those first couple years to never come on to her. Anyway, at the time she was going steady with one of the big campus stars, and she attended every opening, every closing, as well as most of the performances in between. Well into the 1970s, she was still sporting huge Twiggy eyes, and you remember your first glimpse of her: how she wore the smallest pair of red velvet hot pants you had ever seen. Velvet on velvet, just the memory of which got you hard. She was braless, too. But you wondered why she bothered to cover her nipples with bandaids.

You remember the final cast party for *The Taming of the Shrew*, yet-another men-in-pantyhose production. You were wandering around the Castro Valley tract home shared by half a dozen college actors, searching for the dope room. You made your way down a long hall to the back of the house, to Petruchio's bedroom, which had French doors that opened onto the backyard patio. And there she was outside, alone, sitting on her red velvet butt on the back steps, smoking cigarette after cigarette and grinding them out on the cement with the heel of one of her knee-high, suede boots and kicking the butts into the hydrangeas. When you sat down next to her, she didn't scoot over to make room for you. She let you get real close. Then the two of you talked awhile — about what, you don't recall, that was nearly a decade ago — and after a few minutes, you leaned in and kissed her full on the mouth. Then you pulled back quick, half-expecting her to slap you or yell at you or at least make a face. Instead, she looked at you thoughtfully, smiled, and kissed you back. Afterwards, she stood up and said it was time for her to go: she had to be at work in the morning.

Trying to hold onto her a few moments longer, you asked her where she worked. At Bennett's, she said, the photo-processing plant on Industrial Boulevard. You winced: you knew the place. That plant processed every roll of film from every wedding, graduation, vacation, and stag party taken by every amateur photographer in Alameda County. Running 'round-the-clock shifts, it was one of the few employers in Hayward that could accommodate college students with their ever-changing quarterly class schedules. As far as you could tell, half the students at Cal State had worked there at one time or another. Even your current, live-in girlfriend was working there, on the breakdown crew that sorted the thousands of rolls of film as they were brought in from the public drops in drugstores and grocery stores. You hoped Juli worked a different shift or a different section or both. You were tempted to ask, but decided against it. Better not get into the subject.

A few minutes later, you heard her arguing with Richard, big-man-on-campus Mr. Theater, his trained voice projecting down the hallway, hers whining and pleading.

"Richard, please, just run me home quick. It's only fifteen minutes out of your evening. I have to get up and go to work in the morning."

"Juli, you knew this when you came to the show tonight, why didn't you drive your own damn car? Ask someone else for a ride. I'm not leaving my guests at my party in my house. I have important people here tonight."

You sniggered a little at that, having observed Mr. Theater

long enough to know which of his big-breasted party guests would be "important" enough to chat up as soon as his girlfriend left for the night. You hated having to approach two people in the middle of an argument. But since they were blocking the hallway, you had no choice but to try to squeeze past. As soon as you emerged from the shadows, however, Richard looked up from Juli and focused his attention on you — you, someone he ordinarily ignored, as he would any male actor relegated to the nonspeaking parts — and asked, "My good fellow, would you mind terribly squiring m'lady to her domicile?"

"No sweat," you replied.

You could see, by the sour look on her otherwise pretty face, that Richard's official girlfriend was less than pleased at taking second place to her boyfriend's professional and puerile interests. However, the way you saw it, his loss was your gain. Potentially, at least. Moments later, the two of you stood outside on the sidewalk of this quiet, tree-lined street. You opened the passenger door of your car for the night and, bowing deeply, gestured for her to enter.

"Nice car," she commented as you climbed in behind the wheel.

"Thanks," you replied, not mentioning that the vehicle belonged to your live-in girlfriend, who, you recalled again, also had to get up in the morning to go to work.

You were a good boy that night and made no further advances, but all the same you felt encouraged. More than a year later, after Juli and her boyfriend had had yet-another fight and were taking a break from one another, you took that opportunity to make a hard pass at her. The second time, it worked. Far better than you had imagined.

Now, of course, years later, she is impossible to get rid of. After college and your big lymphoma cancer scare at Letterman Army Hospital on the Presidio in San Francisco (ultimately revealed to be a case of cat scratch disease), you and Juli moved to the City, to Haight Ashbury, to become Artists. For months, you would knock around aimlessly, auditioning occasionally when you heard about a show being mounted in some storefront or church basement. Then, a year and a half out of college, at Juli's urging, you applied to the acting school at A.C.T., the American Conservatory Theater. To your surprise, you were accepted. And Uncle Sam — bless his heart! — paid for your first two years of training, while Juli kept you on track, insisting on rehearsing you at home, filling in for your scene partners.

But then, you had some ... late nights in the homes of your scene partners. Whereupon Juli started making serious noises about leaving you. So you took her to city hall and married her.

Since completing your course of study at A.C.T., you've managed to secure a few acting jobs — a couple student-penned scripts at the Conservatory's playhouse, a handful of days as a film extra (courtesy of the Brebner Agency), a TV commercial for orange juice in which you rode a cablecar up and down California Street, a voiceover for an audio-tour of the local museum of modern art, and even a non-fucking part in a film by the great porn director Alex de Renzy. But these days you don't know how to respond to Juli's questions about why you don't push yourself to go further. No, you don't have a game plan. No, you aren't interested in moving to L.A., Minneapolis, or the Big Apple. No, you don't want to try applying again for A.C.T.'s third-year program, the one that gains you entry as an apprentice into the hallowed repertory company. What was the point when they were already willing to call you for a menial walk-on whenever someone flaked?

Because, whenever you inadvertently confront your own feelings — one of those painful exercises that, as an acting student, you were forced to tackle daily — you have to admit: nowadays, you really don't care. Not about acting or theater, not about your wife or your friends, not even about yourself. In short, you can't seem to get yourself to care much about anything anymore. And when, at A.C.T., you were instructed to recall the best moment of your life and the feelings of exaltation that accompanied it, the memory that always arose was the day you got discharged from the Marines, boarded that Freedom Bird, and flew back to the world — the day you had your life handed back to you.

Unfortunately, your ennui and general indifference to your own existence have become ... problematic. Because somehow, as a direct result of your being Juli's guest at the Christmas-in-January office party at that snooty publishing company where she works, followed by a bartending gig at yet-another A.C.T. fundraiser several months ago, you find yourself rather seriously involved with a not-so-young woman who's not only the supplier of the acceptable wines served at A.C.T. fundraisers, but also the fag-hag friend of one of your wife's bosses. And though everyone at the Conservatory seems to know your business at least as well as you do, Juli remains blissfully unaware (thank god!). That may change, however, because you fear you may be falling in love with Barbra. Worse, tonight during your regular biweekly visit to her Ocean Beach condo, Barbra leveled an ultimatum you can't ignore: it's either me or your wife — you must choose or else we're done.

You suspected from the start this woman has the power to break whatever's left of you. You are afraid. Yet you find yourself still going to her. The danger — it turns you on.

But you know only too well how much you suck at making important life decisions. You'd so much rather get stoned and shelter in place. It was well past three this morning when Barbra picked up the receiver of her super-phone with all the "speed-dial" buttons, gave it a quick blast of Lysol disinfectant, and coolly called a cab to take you "home" — a word she pronounced with a decided sneer.

At that point, you were already reviewing the lie you'd told your wife at the start of the day to excuse your absence at the end of the day. Now the moment had come for you to begin augmenting your story to cover the actual time elapsed and to sidestep future scrutiny. You replay in your mind the conversation you had with Juli as she was getting ready to go to work this morning:

"Walk-on tonight?" she asked as she sat on the coffee table to pull on her clunky Frye boots.

"Yep," you replied from your bed, with a heavy sigh of resignation over your going-nowhere career.

"Tray or spear?"

"Tray."

"Oh, I'm sorry. *Uncle Vanya* has a butler?"

"Dream on. It's just a regular servant. Those period pieces always require some anonymous groveler to maintain the status of the toffs."

"So: 'round midnight?'"

"Probably. But, you know, afterwards there will be alcohol and, quite possibly, drugs involved."

"I'm shocked."

So, as your wee-hour cab speeds across the city, from Ocean Beach to Lower Nob Hill, you stare out the window, watch lights flash by, and ruminate on what would make a good cover story to explain your extra missing hours. What a relief it is when you arrive "home" to find Juli already asleep and dreaming. You ignore the stink of another one of her lousy tuna casseroles and immediately turn your attention back to your main concern: the gauntlet Barbra has thrown down before you.

What to do? you ponder as you lean against the hallway wall to yank off your own Frye boots (identical to Juli's, but larger), then fumble at your belt and let your jeans drop to the floor. You owe this woman you married, you suppose, but you'd rather not. Do you still love her? Yes. No. You don't know. Do you still want the life you have? No. Yes. You don't know. Conflict and confusion twist your stomach, till suddenly you find yourself kicking aside your pants and running for the bathroom to vomit up the night. You flush the toilet, reach into the shower, grab and turn the knobs. In Nam, you spent hours in the shower, running water hard on your back, your chest, your head. You peel off the rest of your clothes, step into the tub, and open your mouth to let the shower fill it again and again, washing away the sour-bitter taste of alcohol and stomach acid.

You have no idea how long you were in the bathroom, but as you emerge, it suddenly occurs to you: you have to get up in a few hours to go work the phones in the Time-Life boiler room in the Financial District. You better get some sleep, if that's even possible. Fortunately, delivering a pre-scripted pitch in your best trained voice, then not-listening to people's lame-ass excuses for not-buying yet-another set of glossy art and history books is a job you could do even in your sleep. You long to quit, but know the loss of your one steady paycheck would be just one more thing for Juli to get upset about.

You feel a surge of resentment toward your sleeping wife. Barbra would never want you to waste your time and talent hawking books. She would never allow you to squander the energy you should be saving for your art. You are starting to get some perspective on the choice Barbra presented to you. Lying in bed, you feel your chest swell with emotion, painful nostalgia for the poor country boy who never had a chance, till you are forced to turn away from your slumbering, unsuspecting wife, bury your face in your pillow, and sob it all out before you explode from the pressure of this whole stupid mess you call your life.

3.

Barbra Takes Revenge

Y ou can't help yourself. It's simply too delicious to make these calls to the wife a dozen times a night. Not to mention, it's so easy, once you set the number to speed-dial.

You love imagining how her schedule is being interrupted — how she was in the kitchen, cooking dinner for someone who isn't coming home tonight, or napping on the sofa after work and having an uneasy dream about a man who's lost interest in her, or sitting in the bathroom trying to squeeze one out. You relish the sense that you can influence her life, that you are able to have a real impact on somcone. It feels like when you were a kid, shaking up the ant farm your silent father had given you for your tenth birthday, after the little buggers had been laboring away for months, then watching them all race around, panic-stricken, as their homes were destroyed. What fun!

Loren dropped by for a visit this evening, just back from the Big Apple and another one of his Great American Literary Acquisition junkets. He obviously has something he wants to tell you, only he can't seem to get around to spitting it out. A new wonderful boyfriend, no doubt. Someone handsome, dreamy, and eager to suck cock. A bathhouse buddy, perhaps, with his hair in his eyes, gym towel slung coyly over one shoulder. Or a twenty-year-old secretary by day/faux-lumberjack by night, with plaid shirt, steel-toed boots, and tiny, neat mustache, someone he met clubbing in the wee hours. A book editor might not make the really big bucks in terms of salary, but the Wide World of Publishing can offer him the opportunity to make some really big buck in the back of a meat truck.

The tea kettle is screaming on the stove, and you head for the kitchen to silence it. As you pass the phone, you take the opportunity to pick up the receiver and, after first giving it a short blast of Lysol (to kill the germs that have settled there since your last call), you speed-dial your rival for the third time since sunset. As soon as you hear the line connect and the phone at the other end begin to ring, you set the receiver down on the table. Minutes later, returning to the living room with a serving tray (tea and baked goods for Loren), you pause briefly to listen to the line. The constant whine you hear tells you that the ring was answered, then the phone hung up. Score one for your team. You smile over your tiny psychological win in the effort to demoralize your opponent.

Loren accepts the tea and looks up at you with an expression of consternation. You note that his beautiful, Midwestern, corn-fed face is marred tonight by jet-lag, fatigue, and, most likely, too much indulgence. His suit seems strangely too big for him, reminding you of that weird guy, David Byrne, with the Talking Heads band.

"Do you have to do that?" he asks, nodding in the direction of the phone.

"Lapsang Souchong, your favorite," you respond. "And yes, everyone should have a hobby. Here: I also made scones for us."

"No, thank you, Barbie. You know I don't do carbs. But, please," he pleads, "these calls you make — they're so mean-spirited of you. This woman hasn't done anything to you."

"She's holding back someone with a huge talent."

"Not another actor? I'm sure his onstage talent isn't the only thing he has that's huge."

You smirk into your own teacup, acknowledging the truth of this remark. Huge, indeed, you think.

"One of these days, honey, technology is going to trip you up. Pacific Bell will develop some kind of system for identifying a caller's number. And then some wife you've been torturing will have your number. And then you'll be found out. And then won't that be embarrassing?"

"That will never happen."

"Just you wait and see, Barbie Blair. Just you wait and see. Besides, I'm pretty sure this guy is living with one of our editorial assistants. They could even be married."

"Oh, Lorie, you're always so worried about respectability and how things look, aren't you? Well, you can euthanize your concerns. David and I had a talk last night, and I put my foot down. He knows where his best interests lie."

"Blackmailing him to extract a commitment? A very creative come-on, I must say. Hope you get what you want; hope it makes you happy after you get it. You need a man who will stick by you. We all do."

I suppose so, you think. Then you remember how, once upon a time, ages and ages ago, you had imagined the man who would stick by you was in fact this very man who now sits on your sofa, delicately blowing a cooling breath across the hot surface of his steaming cup of smoky Lapsang Souchong.

You and Lorie had been made for each other. Or so you once thought. Anyhow, that's how your mother always put it. Growing up in agricultural Northern California, walking the dirt-road miles between your father's farm and his father's ranch just to play together, never minding whose house you ended up in for dinner, riding the same yellow bus into town to get to school, then dating for real, going to prom — it seemed your destiny to spend your lives together.

You and he even have the same birthday, January 22, though he's a year older. And because he was forever one year ahead of you, you'd always known he would leave for college before you did. You'd hoped for no more than a year apart, but your lackluster grades could only gain you admittance to the regional junior college. You'd have to wait two more years before you could apply to Berkeley as an upper division transfer. By then, he'd nearly be done and graduated.

Your mother did her best to comfort you. She said your grades were plenty good enough for a girl. She herself had been a college student for a couple of years right after the war. Back then, she said, most young women went off to college to find a husband and get their MRS Degree. But, as she explained it, you didn't have to do that, because you were already promised. All you really needed was something to occupy your time for a few years, while you waited for him to come home and collect you. So you may as well keep going to classes, but you didn't need to.

Before he headed off to UC Berkeley, Lorie had given you

his high school class ring, a tacit promise to return for you. Of course, his ring was much too large to stay put on your finger. But after you wound part of a skein of sock yarn through the ring, around and around, then painted it over with clear nail polish, it fit you perfectly. You worried, in that first year when you were a senior in high school and he was gone to college, a freshman, the months apart would be unbearable for you both. But every time you missed him and felt anxious, you would turn his class ring on your finger, the same finger you knew would one day carry his wedding ring. This gesture, even performed unconsciously, soothed you.

When he came home for the summer of 1969, however, he was different. Moody and angry over nothing. You thought it was all that upset at People's Park. The demonstrations, the legions of tactical squad police beating up students, the National Guardsmen sent in to stop the violence, the helicopter tear-gassing of the quad and the student union, that poor man shot where he stood on the roof of some building on Telegraph Avenue, the main drag to the campus plaza. How could there be riots about a vacant lot no bigger than your mother's vegetable garden? People were dying over this dirt. You'd never been to Berkeley, but every night you watched the network news on television. As the clips sped by, you scanned faces in the crowd for that one special face — the man you loved.

You remember: you were so afraid for him. You twisted his lump of a class ring on your finger and silently recited, in your head, the kind of prayer that is learned in early childhood and later directed toward God by a nineteen-year-old atheist: "Please, God, don't let him die!" Because what if the worst occurred, and Loren never came home? Now, fifteen years later, you realize this is exactly what happened. The Loren you kissed goodbye in his parents' gravel driveway at summer's end 1968 was not the same Loren who avoided your gaze ten months later after you rode down to Berkeley with his parents to pick him up.

His parents were so relieved to have him back, if only for a couple months, they never seemed to notice a thing out of the ordinary. They thought it was normal for a college man to spend his entire summer shut up in his childhood bedroom, reading late into the night. After all, he was going to be a writer, and a writer has to read. They loved him and were proud of him. Everything he did was wonderful. Only *you* noticed the change in him, that something was wrong with him, and after a while, your mother noticed something was wrong with you.

"Did he … try something with you?" she asked one night after Lorie had taken you to the movies in town — your one real date that summer — then returned you to your parents' home, chastely kissing you on the cheek and begging off from coming inside. Too tired, he said.

"No, ma, not Lorie," you reassured her, knowing instinctively it wasn't normal for a boy, especially after he's been away for months, to *not* try something with the girl he's supposed to be engaged to.

"That's our Lorie," your mother exclaimed happily. "You could hardly be in safer hands."

You wondered: has he met another girl? He hadn't mentioned anyone. He didn't ask to break it off with you. He hadn't wanted his ring back. In fact, he never even mentioned the ring, though when you took his unresponsive hand during the movie, he couldn't have failed to notice that big lump on your finger.

As autumn approached, he returned to Berkeley as a sophomore. But this time, instead of living in the southside dorms, he would be sharing co-op housing on the north side of campus with four other guys. When he announced at Thanksgiving time he had decided to stay in the Bay Area over the Christmas-New Year's holiday break, you decided you would drive down and surprise him. And your mother encouraged you in this: "Some boys, once they get a taste of the wide world, don't want to come home. Looks like, if you want him, you're going to have to go and fetch him."

So, two days before Christmas and wearing your very best fetching gear — the adorable little red wool coat trimmed with real black rabbit fur, given to you by your mother as an early Christmas present — you drove the five hours to Berkeley. Then you spent most of another hour searching for a parking place on the hilly residential north side of campus, climbed down out of the cab of your dad's beat-up old truck, hoisted your suitcase out of the truck bed, and headed straight for Loren's house, a block and a half away.

A party was in progress at the two-story, brown-shingle, Craftsman house, and the front door stood wide open. A boy was hanging over the front porch rail, barfing into the hydrangeas. You walked gingerly past him, carrying your suitcase. In the living room, kids were making out. You stopped to look them over, checking for Loren. You were startled to realize at least one of the face-sucking couples was comprised of two boys. You'd heard about this, of course, but so far as you knew, there were no homosexuals in rural California.

You didn't feel comfortable interrupting the smoochers to ask where Loren's room was, but when the drunk boy who'd just finished decorating the landscaping staggered in, you asked him. He indicated the second story of the house with a heavenward fling of his hand and croaked out, "First door right!" A strong sense of foreboding overcame you as you climbed the stairs.

First-door-right was slightly ajar and swung open when you knocked lightly on it. The revealed room was dark, except for a desk lamp. No one was sitting at the desk. You heard a moan and turned toward the bed, where a blanket-covered hill rose and fell, rose and fell. You stood transfixed, your mind struck blank and shut against what you anticipated you were about to see. Then Lorie shouted, "Oh god!" Which made you gasp. At once, the blankets slipped away, revealing the bare backs of two boys, their faces turning to look in your direction. One of them, the one on the bottom, was Lorie. You dropped your suitcase, turned, and fled.

"Hey!" Loren shouted after you. But you were already halfway down the stairs. Out the front door you ran — then stopped. Standing on the porch of Loren's co-op housing, you suddenly realized you were in a strange city with no place to stay and none of the clothes and other things you'd brought with you. There was nothing to do but return for your stuff. You forced yourself to go back inside the house.

As you reached the bottom of the stairs that led to the second floor, you heard someone above demand: "And just *who* the fuck was that?!"

Then you heard Loren reply: "I *told* you, man: that was my girlfriend! ... No, I *don't* know what she's doing here!"

"*Girl* friend? Well, aren't you one mixed-up faggot?"

At the top of the stairs, the boy who was not-Lorie appeared, scowling, wearing only faded, patched Levis, barefoot and shirtless. In one hand, he swung a pair of army boots; in his other hand, he clutched a letterman jacket. He scrambled down the stairs, took one look at you standing there, and said, "He's all yours, honey, and a Merry Fucking Christmas!" Then he was gone out the front door.

You made your way up the staircase. Loren stood in the doorway of his room, wearing his bathrobe. He looked at you, wearing your mother's well-meaning, but sadly naïve Christmas gift. His face was ashen. Without saying a word, he turned and gestured over his shoulder to wave you inside. Without saying a word, you followed him, shutting the door behind you. The talk you and he would have that night went on till dawn and was the most intimate thing you two had ever done together. Or would ever do.

For the remainder of your visit, you slept on Loren's mattress on the floor, while Loren slept on bare box springs. The last of your three nights in Berkeley, you waited till his deep and regular breathing let you know he was finally asleep. Then you crept over to where he lay on his box springs, illuminated by the street light shining in his window, and you watched him sleep. He looked so innocent and content, it broke your heart. Before you left Berkeley to return home, you used a steak knife from the household's community kitchen to saw the yarn off his class ring before giving it back to him.

That night, after your long drive home, you told your mother he'd met someone else and the two of you had broken up. All four parents were sorry, but they accepted the new situation. They believed a nice girl like you, even if she wasn't all that pretty, would certainly have no trouble finding someone else. It took months for the callus on your finger to soften and finally disappear from where his ring had been for so long.

The funny thing was, after that terrible night, you and Lorie felt like better friends than ever. You knew each other so well, and though the romance had never taken on his side, the friendship you shared was real and deep. His secret bound you to him, and you swore to keep it. He never really went home again, except for brief duty visits to his folks. After graduating with a BA in English, *Summa cum laude*, he moved across the bay to San Francisco, a city with more to offer him.

And you, after two years at your local JC, decided to transfer to UC Davis instead of Berkeley, pledged to the Kappa Kappa Gamma sorority so you would have a place to live and instant friends, and earned a degree in viticulture and enology — the study of growing grapes and making them into wine. But once you graduated and had no prospects for either a good job or a marriage proposal, it seemed the natural thing to move to San Francisco, where good jobs were to be had and where your best friend in the world lived. Your best friend who, all these many years later, was now sitting in your Ocean Beach condo, drinking tea with an expression of imminent confession on his face.

"Oh, shit!" he exclaims, clinking his cup into its saucer and transporting the pair over to the nearest end table. With the back of his free hand, he is already brushing dribbled Lapsang Souchong from his necktie. You rush to the kitchen, grab a dish towel, wet one end, and return to Lorie, now holding up the fat end of his tie as if it were a fatally injured squirrel he'd hit with his car.

"Dammit, anyway, tea stain on silk. And this was one of my favorites," he says in a plaintive tone. You see this is his peach-colored silk tie with the pattern of scarlet ovals and asterisk stars that up close looks like a fleet of red flying saucers in a Martian dust storm.

While he holds out his tie, still attached to his neck, you are already daubing and rubbing with your damp dish towel. "Oh, don't worry, sweetie, you can always get another."

"No, I can't. I got it in Greenwich Village fours years ago, and the guy I bought it from died last year. His shop went out of business months ago."

"Last time I checked, you already had too many ties for any one man to wear in a lifetime. Maybe it's time to retire this particular tie and pick a new fave to spill your tea on."

You keep wiping and daubing, but when he doesn't reply, you ask the question that's been nagging at you since he arrived:

"So, Lorie, why did you stop by tonight? Something you want to tell me?"

He bites his lower lip in that special way you still adore, smiles a tight little smile, shakes his head. "No, sweetie, there's nothing really. I just wanted to let you know I'm back from New York, and I'll be staying in town awhile. No more travel plans for the foreseeable future."

"Good idea to give it a rest. Hate to say, honey, but you're looking a little green around the gills."

4.

Loren Gets Down to Business

At home, you stand undressed at your bathroom sink, alternately pouring club soda over your favorite tie, then blotting it with a wad of paper towels, trying to lift out the stain. When you've done as much as you can, you hang the tie over a towel rack and hope for the best.

Turning to leave the bathroom, you catch sight of yourself in the full-length mirror on the back of the door. So you stop to examine yourself, looking for that "green around the gills" Barbie referred to. Your old friend can be catty, but she's hardly ever catty at you, so you tend to take her seriously on this point.

There was a time, as recently as only a year or two ago, when you really enjoyed the sight of your naked self in the mirror. No longer. You used to be so cleanly athletic; nowadays, signs of deterioration are setting in. You thought it was just the usual drag (so to speak) of time, the fact of your having passed from your twenties into your thirties, heading at breakneck speed toward your forties. Your forties! You never imagined you would get so old. Now you're beginning to wonder if you will even make it as far as the Big Four-Oh!

You'd been hearing, for a couple years, about a new "gay cancer" going around, but never supposed you'd be one to come down with it. After all, you can't "catch" cancer, can you? STDs, sure, but not cancer. Yet, there was no arguing with those nasty, purplish spots on your left thigh and the angry assemblage on your chest, which started out as just a single blob, but now looked more like a bunch of small rotten grapes. Thank god, both outbreaks were in places you could cover up most of the time, instead of on your face or hands like some poor bastards.

At first, you thought they were funny-colored freckles or, later on, maybe moles — some benign skin anomaly. You ignored them. Later, you applied a few dabs of zit cream before you left for the baths. But one evening in the sauna, after you'd sweated off the acne coverup, some guy at the other end of the bench leaned toward you and said quietly, "Those spots on your chest — better have them looked at." You thanked him and did nothing about it. Except quit going to the baths. But his words nagged at you. Months later, you dropped in at the Free Clinic in the Haight, where they sent you to UCSF to have your spots biopsied, then gave you the news: Kaposi's sarcoma lesions.

Now, instead of ignoring them, you find yourself obsessing on them every night when you undress — feeling them, pressing on them, examining them up close with the magnifying glass that came with your two-volume, slipcase edition of the *Oxford English Dictionary*. They don't hurt, but they definitely don't enhance your sex appeal.

So now, they're proposing to remove the spots, but there's not a thing they can do to take away what's really wrong with you. And it's funny, but you realize you felt almost relieved to hear the diagnosis of AIDS, that immune system thing that, only a couple of years ago, was called GRID — gay-related immune deficiency. At least now you have an explanation for all your stomach troubles, the nighttime sweats and chills, the diarrhea, even the general weakness and overwhelming fatigue that made you give up your workouts at the gym. And here you had thought all your tiredness was simply the result of stress from working too hard. Okay, partying too hard.

One good thing: at long last, you are thin enough to be considered hot. And you didn't even have to spend weeks making yourself puke to get here. But, of course, you can't in good conscience do anything now with your newly acquired hotness.

Whenever you survey the living room of your beloved lower Pacific Heights flat — from the expensive, roll-top desk positioned in the bay window to overlook Fillmore Street, to the floor-to-ceiling, built-in bookshelves filled with all your favorite volumes (including a number of first editions), to the Barcalounger in one snug corner, where you sit reading each night (that you aren't out partying) before you go to sleep — you remember what a big deal it was when your folks loaned you the down payment and you managed to secure a mortgage on the rest. Making that commitment really took a bite out of your party funds. But, for the first time ever, you felt like a grownup instead of a college student on perpetual spring break. That was only five years ago.

At the same time, becoming a homeowner in the City

has locked you into a job you no longer want to do. You're fed up with having to babysit everyone else's genius — you have stories of your own to tell. Except you know, only too well, that no one is going to pay you to stay home and write your stories. Worse, even if your Great American Novel were to be accepted and published and marketed, the royalties wouldn't cover even so much as, say, this most recent business trip to New York. Sickening, yes, but you've been in the biz long enough to know the truth. No work of fiction ever sees its way into print unless the publisher feels assured of not only a return on their investment, but a serious profit margin as well. After all, how else can they afford to pay *your* salary?

Which, thank goodness, Raker & Ho is quite generous about. Not to mention, all those perks.

A deep, choking sob escapes you. You lean into the full-length bathroom mirror and press your forehead to the cool glass. How much longer will you be able to work? As soon as the treatments start, you'll be too sick to drag yourself into the office. By then, no amount of blemish cream will improve your appearance. And, once you stop working, how much longer will you be able to stay here? As little as editing pays, you're well aware: disability pays even less. How will you cover your mortgage, your taxes? Will you ever write your novel? Will you live long enough to see it in print? to attend your own release party? to sign copies for your adoring fans?

Until a week and a half ago, when you got your diagnosis — right before you left for NYC, thanks a lot — your time on Earth seemed to stretch out before you nearly to infinity. At the very least, another half-century. Plenty of time for writing. What did it matter you'd spent the past ten years advancing other people's creativity? The time would come for your own creative output to bloom. Besides, you were still collecting worldly experiences so you'd have something to write about. What would a green boy from outside Fort Jones, a place no one has ever heard of, have to write about? Moreover, through your work at Raker & Ho, you were actually studying the process of literature — on-the-job training, as it were. Or so evolved your elaborate self-justification.

But just as you were getting to where you wanted to be — having acquired enough life experience to have something to write about, as well as enough education and maturity to be able to communicate those experiences on paper — the alarm on your internal clock went off: time's up! Everyone out of the pool.

No fair.

Your imaginary evil twin, your alter-ego Nerol (as you like to call her), wishes both of you had received your diagnoses after you'd come back from this most recent Manhattan junket. Then you might at least have had the pleasant memory of one last fling to comfort and sustain you as you settled down to the hopeless business of trying to get well from an illness everyone knows kills anyone who gets it. Some go quick, others slow; some leave quietly, while a few are dragged out screaming. Literally. But eventually, one way or another, they all die. Of course, if you'd had your fling, you wouldn't have known at the time it was to be your last. But at least you would have had it.

Too late now.

You smile to recall all your memories of New York! New York!, going back to your very first trip, when you were only a little more than a year out of college. How thrilling to be a part of it — sent Back East two or three times a year to represent your West Coast publisher at the home office. You'd put on your vagabond shoes, harvest a tasteful selection of silk ties from your now-vast collection, board a plane, and when you disembarked, people treated you like Someone Important.

You'd met with agents, who took you to lunch. Or dinner. Sometimes even to bed. You spent hours at the Strand, picking through its eighteen miles of books. You made it a point to visit the Manhattan settings for much of the fiction you love, such as J. D. Salinger's *Catcher in the Rye*, E. L. Doctorow's *Ragtime*, Dashiell Hammett's *The Thin Man*, and, of course, Truman Capote's *Breakfast at Tiffany's*. You took the ferry over to Long Island to inform your next reading of F. Scott Fitzgerald's *The Great Gatsby*, afterwards wandering back to your hotel past the World Trade Center with its extraordinary Twin Towers, which will stand forever as the world's greatest city's own monument to itself.

Back then, you were young and healthy, in need of little sleep in a city that never sleeps, so you prowled the wee hours as well. In this post-Stonewall era, there are bars and discos and bathhouses, like San Francisco, but oh, so so much more. With plenty of studs eager to meet a well-built, fresh-faced, straight-acting Youngman in his twenties, visiting from the Wild West by way of Frisco and eager to take a big juicy bite out of the Big Apple. You were well aware you appeared to be offering the ever-attractive challenge of potential conversion. Though any man who got you on your knees soon realized he'd been preaching to the choir.

But on this last trip — your last for a while ... maybe

forever — you were as chaste as a Jewish granny on a shopping spree after her grown son has pulled her credit cards. At least, a bubbe who'd ventured into the packing district at 4 a.m. to put a little something down on layaway (get it: *lay*-away? Heh-heh!). You shut your eyes to re-live the memory of that disco on wheels, its flashing lights and pounding, throbbing music, men crammed together, shoulder to shoulder, butt to butt, chests and groins sweating, snorting poppers, stomping to the beat. No harm in a bit of partying. Dancing is good, it doesn't always have to be foreplay.

Alas, you were even more tired than usual, so you returned early (and alone, of course) to your hotel room with its too-big-for-just-one bed. You lay alone on the anonymous sheets and jerked off. Then you passed out and had strange dreams.

You dreamed you were back home in Northern California, living with your parents. You must have been in high school, because you dreamed you were still dating Barbie, and everyone acted like the two of you were getting married. You dreamed you had it all to do over again — and you dreamed you did it differently this time. You got married to Barbie. You had kids, a boy and a girl. You took over running the family ag empire, third-generation lands now owned by your folks and Barbie's, as was your assigned destiny. But the funny thing was, even though you did everything differently, it all turned out the same. Except your soul, not your body, was dying.

And in your other, different life, you also hadn't written anything. Instead, you inflicted your unfulfilled dreams on your son and daughter, aware that those dreams had nothing whatsoever to do with who your kids were. Even Barbie, a haggard, worn-out version of herself, was disappointed in you. Only she refused to admit it. But no one was more disappointed in you than you were in yourself.

It seems life is a one-way street. You can't flip a U or even pull over for very long. You made your choices; now you have to live with them. Even on your way out for good, you still have to live with those choices. As long as you can manage to do so.

Filled with new resolve, you step back from your image in the glass, cinch up your silk bathrobe, exit the bathroom, and trudge to the kitchen for a glass of Chardonnay from one of the two bottles Barbra sent home with you. You must admit: her job grants her access to a lot better "office supplies" than yours does. Then you wander into the living room, to the bay window and your desk — a solid-oak roll-top so big and expensive, you swear the store must have charged you by the pound, but you didn't care, you wanted to have the perfect stage on which to do the writing you never do. And there awaits your typewriter, the cherry-colored IBM Selectric you named Big Red. A little dusty, you note as you sit, pulling off its black vinyl cover, which you drop to the floor.

A sheet of paper is already rolled into the legal-size platen, left over from god knows when, so all you need to do is flip the rocker-switch and turn Red on. He fires up with a satisfying hum. You don't know yet what thoughts you have lurking within, but you are determined to find out.

Suppose you live only another year? If you can manage to write just one page a day — one good solid honest page of copy, each and every day — you'll have your novel dicked by the time you die.

You stare hard at the page and read the single typed line already there: "Gay is more than sex."

Since you can't remember having typed these words, you encounter them now as though God Himself, or one of his intersex angels described by Milton, left them as a message especially for you.

Because the observation was so true: before you'd ever had sex (with someone besides yourself), you were gay. And now that you will probably never have sex again — surprise! still gay. Ergo: who you choose to have sex with says nothing about who you are inside. If you'd stayed in the boonies and married Barbie and raised a family and become a gentleman farmer, you'd still have been gay, that's just the way it was.

You've met a few men, generally older, who'd married women and had kids. Typically, they were trying to keep themselves in line — "managing their condition," as your doctor might have described it. Oftentimes, you met them in hotel bars or at conferences. A visit to their hotel room or yours proved their condition was not in remission after all.

You felt sorry for them, aware they'd come of age in a time that offered fewer options. But you could hardly feel smug about your own liberation, since you'd never even come out at work. You wanted to; you just couldn't bring yourself to do it. And it hurt you, because concealing who you really are seems the same as pretending to be someone you aren't. Your stance isn't honest, and you know it. Now here was this ... disease about to out you.

Twenty minutes later and touring the kitchen for a second glass of wine, you pass your stereo and consider that perhaps your inability to commit words to paper tonight is due to the excessive quietness of your flat. A little night music might limber you up. You power-on your stereo system, lift the turntable cover, and squint at the LP already in place. You have noticed at Tower Records that audio cassettes are taking over, but at this point in your life you have no interest in replacing your entire vinyl collection with tape, even if cassettes do take up less room and don't weigh a ton. You flip the switch and watch as the turntable spins and the needle arm lifts, swings, and descends with a bump onto the record.

Sitting back at your typewriter, you sing along with the recording: the 1972 movie soundtrack of *Cabaret*. A glance at your kitschy starburst wall clock tells you it's early still, just past nine, so even if your terrible voice annoys your neighbors, they won't start hammering on the ceiling for at least another fifty minutes.

"Start by admitting from cradle to tomb, isn't that long a stay! Life is a cabaret, old chum!" you bray, leaning back in your desk chair and kicking out your legs, Liza Minelli-style. "Only a cabaret, old chum! And I love a cabaret!"

You know all the words to all the songs from so many Broadway musicals. And you love to sing along. But this is one private pleasure you never share with any of your friends, straight or gay. Even Barbie doesn't know you do this. It's just too … faggoty. Only your neighbors, two night nurses (female) at the Saint Francis burn center, are familiar with your complete repertoire.

By the time the needle has found its way to the center of the record, you've lost interest in your own thoughts. You drain a third glass of wine, slip on some chinos and loafers (no socks), and head out to the Alta Plaza Bar and Grill, three blocks away, for a nightcap. With its live jazz, kindly lighting, sleek interior, table linen, and cherrywood bar, the Alta Plaza remains the

City's classiest, most respectable gay bar. Many nights there, you've met doctors, interns, researchers from Pacific Medical Center. It occurs to you such a medically oriented group might offer some welcome opportunities for useful conversation not available to you elsewhere. But tonight you don't care who you meet. You simply need some company so you won't have to be alone.

5.

Juli Attempts Open Marriage

O pen marriage." For years now, you've heard about it on KGO Talk Radio, read about it in the Pink Section of the Sunday *Chronicle*, seen it mentioned in various lifestyle magazines. It could work, you think. Maybe it could work. Better than no marriage, at least.

You wince to recall how your jealousy and possessiveness cost you your steady boyfriend in college. You are determined not to make the same mistake again. Not now, when you are married to this man, and the stakes are so much higher. It occurs to you that the difficulty of balancing freedom and intimacy in a relationship is one reason why people in theater, particularly (and the arts, generally), prefer to live together without being married. No wonder marriage more or less fell out of fashion in the '70s.

So: Open Marriage could be a solution, giving everyone something of what he or she wants without forcing anyone to sacrifice all. Only there have got to be some ground rules. No more telling you he'll be home by midnight, then showing up at dawn. You suppose he has a right to other intimate relationships — after all, that's what the Free Love Movement of the '60s was all about — but don't *you* also have a right to some peace of mind? Don't you? What about fairness and equality?

The morning after this most-recent of David's late-nights, you woke, feeling like total shit, waited till he opened his eyes, shoved a cup of coffee into his hands, then laid into him and grilled him till he confessed:

Yes, there was someone else.

Yes, he thought he might be in love.

No, he didn't want out of his marriage with you.

No, he wasn't going anywhere.

So ... what was *that* supposed to mean?

This wasn't the first time you'd cornered him about a likely involvement. But it was the first time he'd frankly confessed to one. For years, you've insisted his lies upset you even more than whatever he was lying about. However, now that he has, in effect, called your bluff on that point, you are not so certain about your preference for truth. You realize truth changes everything. You realize truth demands that you make decisions and actually *do* something about your relationship. You can't simply cold-shoulder him with the silent treatment for a few days and call it even. Now that you are defenseless, your response is to cry till you throw up, then cry some more.

That morning after you'd grilled him awhile — long enough to realize this particular round of marital negotiations was going to require more time than you'd considered at the outset — you called in sick to work. Then you made him call in sick as well. And when he protested he could lose his job, you countered with the minuscule probability that anyone in the

Time-Life boiler room would miss him on a Friday. In fact, you said, his colleagues will probably be glad he's gone — more chance of getting the commissions that would have been his.

Then the two of you spent the day together, something you hadn't done for a couple years. The two of you had breakfast at the tiny, old-fashioned lunch counter in the Arcade Pharmacy on the corner of Bush and Leavenworth. The two of you walked up Leavenworth and over the hill together, down to Aquatic Park, below Ghirardelli Square, west and away from the madness of Fisherman's Wharf, through Fort Mason to the Marina Green, and finally to Crissy Field within sight of the Golden Gate Bridge, gateway to the Pacific Ocean. Being next to the ocean always raises your spirits — even just the smell of it, the feel of it. It was as if an escape route away from all your problems had been prepared and was waiting for you.

The two of you ambled alongside the bay, not speaking. The two of you sat on a public bench, overlooking the water. He tried to comfort you. You pushed him away. Then you flung yourself onto him and clung there. Crying again. Getting snot on his denim jean jacket. Finally, at the point when the two of you seemed in danger of getting too much fresh air, the two of you retraced your steps to Aquatic Park and caught the Powell-Hyde cable car back up and over the hill to within a few blocks of your apartment. And there in your apartment once again, as you paced in a tight formation the length of your low coffee table, you haltingly suggested a few ground rules were needed between the two of you as the basis for any ... understanding.

In his protected position on the other side of the coffee table, David sat on the floor as a little girl might — knees bent and together on the carpet, lower legs and feet splayed out, the opposite of akimbo. His hands rested in his lap, palms up, and he silently stared at them. His refusal to look at you was starting to make you angry. You suspected him of not listening, you thought he'd checked out on you. But when he finally spoke, it was surprisingly clear, not only had he been listening, but he'd evidently been thinking quite a bit about this issue that lay between you.

He proposed *she* would get every other week. You considered this idea. Projecting the arrangement forward a few months, you realized immediately that, depending on when the new schedule started, you'd be choosing between getting your husband on Christmas or getting him on New Year's. It was a double-bind setup between two equally unpleasant options: knowing you'd have a date for New Year's Eve, but would be alone on the year's single most important togetherness holiday — versus having your spouse with you on Christmas, but knowing he was looking forward to ringing in the new year with someone else.

The other fifty-one weeks, you supposed, it didn't make all that much difference. How much time did you and David really spend together, anyway? A couple hours each day? Most of the time, you were at work and he was at A.C.T. or at Time-Life or at some little film or TV commercial gig, courtesy of Brebner's. Or he was off with his friends (or so you thought), while you wandered around the apartment, wondering why someone as creative as yourself (or so Kitty said) never did any actual writing, aside from journaling. Maybe now you could get started on that novel. Now that it seems you actually have something to write about.

But already you knew you would miss having a warm

body next to you in bed at night. More significantly, you would miss the illusion of a predictable future, the security of being able to pretend to yourself there was someone in your life you could count on. Someone watching your back.

No one was watching your back. No one ever had. You'd grown up with minimal guidance and minimal support, always conscious of working without a net. Your parents weren't bad people. In fact, they were probably as good as they could be, but they were babies themselves. You realize this now. They met, got married, had you, then your dead brother, then split up.

Unexpectedly, the memory comes to you of a conversation between your parents that you overheard when you were four, maybe five years old. It was evening. Your mom and dad were sitting at the kitchen table of the flat they'd rented on Harrison Street in Oakland, across the San Francisco Bay and only a block or two from where your dad still lives in the house he inherited from his parents, your grandparents. Your dad had come home from his job as a delivery van driver for Lawrence Berkeley Lab in the hills above the University of California campus. Outside, through the window over the kitchen sink, you could see it was already dark. You realize now it must have been late fall or even winter.

On that long-ago day, as on every other day in your life up to that point, your mom had been home with you. And, for the past six months, with your baby brother as well. She was trying to talk to your father about how much they would need to save up in order to send both you and your brother to college someday. Your father was saying they didn't need to worry about sending you to college, only your brother.

Because, after all, you were a girl and would just get married. A college education would be wasted on you. Better to save up for your brother, the boy.

So that was how you learned, at age four or maybe five, an important difference between boys and girls: boys went to college, then out into the world to become something special; girls grew up, got married, and never amounted to anything. Girls weren't worth educating. From that time on, it became your unwavering ambition to attend college. Already you were in nursery school; you had been reading since age three, and, if anyone inquired, what you liked to do best was draw pictures. But a year later, after you entered kindergarten and grownups started to ask you what you wanted to do when you grew up, you told them: I want to go to college.

So you did go — first to the university, later (after your car accident made commuting impossible) to the nearby state college — even though neither of your parents helped you financially, and you always had to work at two, sometimes three, jobs. Your mother let you live at home (she and your dad were split up by then), but she didn't give you any help otherwise, because she didn't have it to give. And your frugal father, who did have it to give, gave you no help at all, because no one had told him he should, and he somehow couldn't figure it out on his own. Or maybe he still didn't see the point of sending a girl to college — all that money wasted, just to get a husband.

Nevertheless, you managed to push through and finish your degree: a BA in English, with honors. English majors — the "aristocracy of the unemployed," as David's friend Bill liked to say. What to do with that degree? In college, you'd made a little extra money typing term papers. And while you were typing them, you usually made small improvements as well, in spelling, punctuation, and grammar, so you thought you'd make a good editor. An editor — that was a useful profession, wasn't it? After you and David moved to the City, you tried a couple local dailies and a handful of book publishers, mostly textbooks. Except no one was interested in a twenty-three-year-old, totally green, wannabe editor.

So, when the West Coast office of Raker & Ho offered you a position as receptionist on their front desk, you jumped at it. And, months later, when Raker & Ho's two production editors, Tweedledee and Tweedledum, asked you to serve as their shared proofreader and sometime copyeditor, you were only too happy to oblige.

Nevertheless, you always felt destined for much more in life. There was greatness in you, you could feel it. You simply hadn't been called to perform the right labors that would reveal your greatness. Growing up, you'd never wanted to be a teacher or a nurse or a ballerina or any of the other careers approved for little girls. And having witnessed firsthand the heartbreak of parenting, you decided early on that being a mommy wasn't going to define you, either.

Early in your relationship with David, you believed the two of you would rise together. It was your destiny, you thought, the reason fate had brought you together. Perhaps he would win an Oscar acting in a film for which you had written the screenplay. Something like that. Why is it, then, you always have energy for his career, but so little for your own?

Except, how was this new arrangement of "Open Marriage" to fit in? How could you and David be great and famous together, if you spent half the year apart? Would he become great and famous alongside someone else? And if yesterday was in fact the beginning of the end, if you split up like your parents had, then what? What would become of you? You remember only too well how difficult life was for your mother after she walked out on your father, taking you and every last thing in the apartment along with her. In the newly impoverished circumstances of your single-parent home, you sometimes reminisced on all the dinners you'd refused to eat back in the days when you were all together. Would finishing your boiled carrots have kept your family intact?

David says he wants to be with you, says he doesn't want to end the marriage. Yet he also says he doesn't want to give up this Barbra woman. You cannot understand what he is doing. You imagine there is a choice to be made here, but he refuses to make it.

"Well, then, what *do* you want?" you ask him. "You want an … open relationship?" You are afraid even to say the words.

Open Marriage had been such a big thing in the 1970s when you were in college, and you had to admit you found its ideals appealing: two people living together in The Now, with realistic expectations; having mutual respect for each other's personal privacy; engaging in open, honest communication characterized by sharing, self-disclosure, and honest, productive fighting; enjoying flexibility of roles, as well as equal power and responsibility in the relationship; benefitting from open companionship; and always, always being able to trust one another completely.

In short, the two people in an Open Marriage would be free to come and go from their relationship, supporting one another, but not telling each other what to do. They would be free to have important relationships outside their marriage (even other sexual partners!), then be free to return to their marriage, which would somehow magically self-repair after each mutually sanctioned lapse. The theory was that a marriage would be all the stronger if the two people chose, freely and on a daily basis, to remain in the relationship. In theory, the concept appeared sound (though only if you casually ignored all your own feelings of betrayal); in practice, however, the arrangement seemed like total bullshit.

David shrugged noncommittally in response to your question. You chose to interpret his gesture as a yes.

"But we can't have an Open Marriage without ground rules, David. If you tell me you are coming home at a particular time, but you don't do it, where does that leave me?"

David stared at his hands in his lap as if he was just noticing they belonged to someone else, so you added, "I worry about you, you know."

6.

Why Bill Can't

Today, first time ever, you saw a man holding to his head what looked like a black milk carton with an antenna, and he was yelling into it. He was standing on Market Street in the Financial District, just as you emerged from the subterranean Montgomery Street BART station, and he seemed like a pretty ordinary, '80s kind of guy in his expensive suit, white shirt, silk noose, and wingtips. But he was shouting crazy stuff, bawling out random nonsense. Once you tuned in, however, you realized he was delivering buy and sell orders for some kind of high-level transactions. Which had to mean he was talking on the phone.

Holy fuckola! You hurried off to the old part of the Financial District just south of Market for a happy hour meet-up with your old buddy David. Meanwhile, your mind was careening forward in time to some apparently not-so-very-distant future in which, you realized, the jig would be up on the tactic you routinely employ to repel panhandlers and street crazies. Because, although a decade of working in Social Services has provided you with formal introductions to nearly every nutjob loser in the City, you've learned how to sidestep them all after-hours by employing the simple strategy of talking aloud to yourself. With emphasis on a-LOUD.

Each evening as you leave work to walk home through the Fillmore, especially if it's after dark, you stuff your hands in your pockets, tuck your chin into your chest, and immediately start reciting, at the top of your lungs, whatever transitory, idiotic, stream-of-consciousness bullshit happens to be running through your head. All the bizarre, insane, irrelevant, inconsequential, totally inescapable thoughts that inevitably come to you — you just shout them out. And if you are actually upset about some damned thing, especially if you are angry, so much the better. This subterfuge — insofar as it *is* a subterfuge — works like a charm. Every crazy you pass on the sidewalk, even the aggressive down-and-outer who was your 10 o'clock interview that morning, veers away as surely as if the two of you were negative magnetic poles being pressed together. But, after all, you learned how to do this by observing these same wacko clients.

You sigh with pre-nostalgic regret for your tried-and-true, soon-to-be-outdated strategy for survival on the mean streets of San Francisco. Dammit, technology is changing everything! Even a Luddite like yourself can see it coming. One day, you can tell, it's going to take a lot more than yelling in public to no one in particular to make others want to leave you alone. Pretty soon, people will just think you're talking on the phone. The times have been a-changing, and you will be left behind.

You round the corner at New Montgomery and see the venerable Sheraton-Palace, which first opened a few years after the Great Earthquake of 1906 and has just recently been declared a City landmark. Across the street, you spot the House of Shields, a place that you had always thought was members-only. You give its enormous front door a good hardy yank and enter a pre-War-to-End-All-Wars drinkers' paradise.

At once, you are greeted by a vampire in a tuxedo. You remember that a vampire cannot enter your home unless he is invited in, and you wonder if the reverse is also true — whether you must be invited inside by this resident vampire. You suddenly feel acutely self-conscious in your plaid Pendleton shirt and square-toed Frye boots that have been your civilian uniform since you got out of the Army nearly fifteen years ago. You silently curse your old friend for insisting you meet him here. You hope he isn't late as usual.

You speak your friend's name, and the vampire conducts you to the magnificently carved redwood bar, where, fortunately, your old friend is perched and waiting, wearing a sport coat and turtleneck sweater over Levis — formal dress for struggling actors — posing like a Hugh Hefner impersonator at a second-rate sex party. He greets you with a controlled smile, then turns at once to the vampire.

"Eddie, would you please find a table for us ... out of the way?"

Eddie the vampire, old enough to be your grandfather (or even your grandfather's grandfather), offers a dip of his head, which you understand to be a residual bow, and escorts you to a small, round, dark corner table. A moment later, drinks arrive without your having ordered anything. Since you are here at your friend's behest, you do not question the underlying process, but merely wait to learn why the pleasure of your company has been requested.

"You know," David says as he lights his Marlboro with flourish and puffs out the match, "you're always saying how lonely you are. But if you would lose that Deadhead look and simply spiff up a bit, you could probably get laid all you want."

"Is that why you asked me here — to rag on my ass for my devotion to classic hippie sartorial aesthetics?"

"No, of course not. I was merely observing. But you must admit: that was then, this is now."

"I admit nothing."

David laughs. "That's the spirit!"

"So?"

"So?"

"So — why are we meeting like this?"

"Right. I have a favor to ask. It concerns Juli. Lately, she's been ... upset."

"Oh?"

"Yes. Our marriage is ... in transition. We're opening ourselves to other relationship possibilities."

"You mean: you're seeing someone else. Again. How would this one be different from any of the others?"

You are surprised to see David has the decency to look uncomfortable.

"Just take my word for it — this one is different. And Juli is aware of the situation. Which makes it ... awkward. But Juli herself suggested we try an arrangement of Open Marriage."

"Better than nothing, eh?"

"Oh, probably. But at least it gives me some time to sort things out."

"I thought 'things' were going great for you."

"Yes and no."

"Must be going pretty well for you to be tanking up at this trough."

"This is quite an establishment, alright. Here since 1908. It was a men's club and didn't let women in until just a few years ago. Except whores, of course, they're welcome everywhere. Secret passageway under the street still runs to the Palace. Barbra set me up here with a tab so I'd have somewhere suitable to conduct business."

You note the name of his new patroness and bite back the urge to ask what sort of business he might wish to conduct here. "And what's the favor?"

"Starting next week, Juli and I will be on a schedule of alternating weeks, and I'll be staying ... elsewhere. I'd appreciate it if you'd keep an eye on her so she doesn't do something stupid and hurt herself. You're in Social Services — you know how women are. Besides, she's always liked you."

"Sure. But how do you suggest I keep an eye on her?"

"Just call her now and then to see how she is. An occasional five-minute call, that's all I'm asking."

"I can do that. If you think it would help. But what I don't get is why you bother going to all this trouble. If I had someone like your wife at home, waiting for me, I'd never leave the house."

"Yeah, well, you can say that, because you don't know her the way I do. She comes off as all sweetness and light, but she's actually the needy, controlling type."

"Don't tell me she objects to your dating other women?"

"Only the ones she knows about." But he adds, "Can I help it that I'm oversexed?"

Having settled what to do about his "needy, controlling"

wife, David shifts the conversation to some new wargaming system he's excited about. You know he'd much rather talk about orders of battle than either his acting career or his adventures in the sack. The two of you have been playing board games and simulating the great battles of history since high school. This man is your oldest friend, yet you are starting to realize you don't much like him. Or rather, you like him alright — you just don't respect him.

When you met, he was fourteen and you were sixteen, two teenagers growing up in Salinas in the early '60s who shared an interest in history. Neither of you was athletic or had a car or was especially popular or interested in school, but you both were willing to spend entire days in adolescent male camaraderie, moving cardboard "troops" around a paper game board on your bedroom floor. Back then, you were throwing six-sided dice; nowadays you're up to ten sides or more. You still remember your friend as a skinny kid — all elbows, knees, and knuckles being raised by a single mother in a double-wide, rental trailer. He was so poor, he thought you were rich because you lived in a tract home. He was so poor, when he first started coming over, he thought your mother was the maid. No wonder he now relishes the right to occupy a table at the House of Shields.

Within months of that first game you two played, you would acquire your driver's license, followed by your first car, for which you paid all of fifty bucks scraped together over a year of saving up weekly allowances, plus birthday and Christmas money from relatives. After that, you too could pack the car with friends on a Friday night and drag the long straight backroads alongside stenchy fields of Brussels sprouts, or take your girlfriend to the Saturday-night drive-in and steam up the windows making out, or drive around, alone and aimlessly, on a Sunday morning in a town empty as a backlot movie set. The price of underage freedom was then 30 cents a gallon. You dug behind couch cushions for the spare change that had escaped your father's pants pockets.

David meanwhile, two years behind you in high school, started hanging out with the drama kids. Theater never appealed to you, but you admired the tight social circle of these greenhorn thespians, and you welcomed their recreational dope when David started showing up at your wargames with a joint or two stuck in among the cigarettes in the pack he kept stashed in his sock, hidden under his pant leg. The two of you would take a break from gaming, wander a couple suburban blocks to the nearest always deserted public park, sit on a damp bench under trees in a remote corner of the park, and pass a doobie back and forth, always keeping an eye out for local cops cruising the area.

It was good times, especially after you graduated from high school and before you were expected to have constructed any sort of life for yourself. But it was boring. So naturally you ended up getting into trouble. Your girlfriend told you she was pregnant, so you did the right thing, married her and joined the Army to support wife and child. You were nineteen. But she lost the baby. Or maybe there never was one (she was such a liar!). In any event, you soon lost her, when she fell in love with some other guy and took off with him while you were still in Basic.

You had no time to worry about your destroyed personal life, however, because you were already on your way to yet-another agricultural armpit — Fort Leavenworth, Kansas, where you were treated by local authorities to a demonstration of how they entertained themselves on a Saturday night: by tying a big Black queen to an office chair and beating him senseless. The worst thing was, they expected you to enjoy the show. You couldn't wait to get the hell out. The memory of that man slumped there in his torn red prom dress, one high heel missing and nylons shredded, blonde wig on the floor, has stayed with you for nearly two decades.

That was the nadir of your then-twenty years of existence. After several months of assignment at Leavenworth, however, your luck started to change. In your company comprised of thirty-seven guys, thirty-six were shipped out to Nam; but you — you got sent to Heidelberg, Germany. You wondered if the Army still thought you had a pregnant wife. Or maybe two lucky stars converged overhead. In any case, even the Army couldn't ruin so cherry a tour of duty as that. As soon as you got to Germany, you celebrated by going on a major drunk with your new best buddies. That night ended with you and another guy passed out in the back of a beer truck and getting driven into the factory on the outskirts of town. You thumbed your way back to base.

For the next year and a half, you spent your every leave visiting — and getting stoned in — as much of Europe as possible: Austria, Italy, France, Holland, Belgium, England, Denmark, Norway, and Sweden. In Stockholm, you visited a comrade who was CO and AWOL, which would later earn you five years of unfriendly interest from the U.S. government, especially the Internal Revenue Service, till eventually they nailed you for a minor tax evasion: $75 of undeclared income from the wargaming figures you sold to make rent in Frisco. After that, you would be left in peace.

Back in the barracks in Germany, you achieved minor, low-key notoriety for having invented an organizational tool designed to save valuable time and energy each and every Army day: you created a false cardboard bottom for your military foot locker and glued all your socks, underwear, and toiletries to it. Your real stuff you simply chucked underneath the inspection-ready cardboard cover. Eventually, when you were discharged, you would sell, at a profit, this same cardboard false bottom to the next guy coming in. Never mind that the glued-in-place underwear was visibly dusty and nowhere near his size.

In the meantime, you arranged for an apartment off base and a German girlfriend, who turned out to have a German boyfriend, who objected to the amount of time she was spending with you. In January of 1969, you experienced Jimi Hendrix live at the Jahrhunderthalle in Frankfort. Then it was time to go home.

Returned to California, you stopped in Salinas to see your parents. Your mom was glad; your dad yelled at you. He was angry to learn you had no intention of accepting the job he'd managed to secure for you at a local seed company, a deal he hadn't bothered to run by you first before making the arrangement. You tried to look up your old friends, but except for two working in their parents' businesses, flipping burgers or repairing shoes, everyone had fled the valley to scatter in all directions. You went to visit David's alcoholic mother, still living in the trailer park, and learned he had joined the Marine Corps after getting himself jilted by a young woman he imagined was his One True Love. Now he was in Vietnam. You thanked her and left town before the weekend was over.

The drive north to San Francisco took two and a half hours in your shitty car that your parents had been babysitting the three years you were away. You'd already been accepted to S.F. State; within weeks, you would start classes. That summer you crashed with friends you met at a Grateful Dead show at the Family Dog out near Ocean Beach. Sometime that fall, you moved into a walk-in closet in a Mission District flat shared by four other people. It was still 1969 and already your hair was nearly down to your shoulders.

The following year, David, raw out of Nam, phoned you from your parents' home in Salinas, then weeks later arrived unannounced at your flat in the Mission. He was clearly changed from the eager geeky high schooler you'd man-hugged and pounded on the back as you left for the Army. He still wanted to wargame with you, but the balance between gaming and getting stoned had shifted. Instead of firing up a joint for a toke or two between moves, the gaming had become a way to occupy yourselves during an afternoon of getting wasted.

And David turned out to be different in other ways that took months, even years, to be revealed. When he first arrived in the City, he crashed with you, sleeping on the scratchy communal couch for several weeks till two of your four roommates approached you with separate concerns about him. Bonky was upset because he'd caught David leaving his room, and now part of his home-grown stash was missing. Sheila was upset because, one afternoon when she thought she and David were simply sharing a friendly joint, he suddenly came on to her, hard and fast. Just basically jumped her. "Not cool," she said, "not cool at all."

When you promised both your roommates you would talk to David, Sheila clarified her wishes: "No, man, he needs to L-E-A-V-E. I am *not* putting up with that shit. Especially from someone who isn't even paying rent."

She was adamant, and you couldn't afford to jeopardize your own living situation and relationships, so you agreed: your old friend had to go. But, most of the time, he was gone somewhere else, anyway. A few days later, when you managed to corner him for a heart-to-heart, he had news for you:

"Got into Hayward State on the G.I. Bill!"

Hayward State, a California State University campus in the same system as San Francisco State, where you were matriculating, was located on the far other side of the bay, high in the hills. No way could David live in the City and go to school in Hayward.

"That's great," you said. "When are you moving out?"

"I'm out already. I just stopped by to give you the good news and say adios."

Since the "problem" of your old friend seemed to have been solved without any unpleasantness, you let the matter slide and never had a talk with him. Years later, you wonder if confronting him back then would have made any difference now. Of course, certain knowledge of an alternate future, even if it were possible to obtain, would be only a booby prize. By the time David finished up at Hayward State and moved back to the City to attend the American Conservatory Theater's dramatic arts training program, still on the G.I. Bill, he no longer needed to sponge off you — he had Juli to sponge off.

And by then you were well aware of what a lying, thieving womanizer he was. One good thing about not having a wife or a live-in girlfriend is you can still be friends with this man and have him over, but you don't have to worry about his trying to get into her pants. You do have to secure your stash, however.

"So, whaddya say?" he is saying to you.

"Huh?" you reply, startled out of your reverie.

"I thought, in your profession, you were supposed to be such a good listener. But I don't think you heard a word I've been saying."

"Sorry. Tired, I guess."

"Well, that's my point. I have a little something here to fix that." He holds up what appears to be a tiny envelope origamied out of a dollar bill.

"Blow?" you guess.

"Couple lines of this, and you'll forget all about being tired." David waves the teeny envelope back and forth in your face in the hypnotist's classic gesture of mesmerizing. "We could go to your place and pull an all-nighter with Marita-Merkur."

"Tempting as your offer is," you respond, "I really have to get up and go to work in the morning. I can't sit up till dawn chasing you around the Balkans. Besides, uppers don't agree with me. I get too wired."

"Oh, well then," he says, slipping the itty-bitty envelope full of marching powder into his breast pocket, "more for me."

You stand up to indicate you are now departing.

"Taking off?" he asks.

"Yep. It's that time. Thanks for the drinks."

"Remember to call Juli."

"You got it."

Back on the street, slightly unsteady from a bellyful of booze and nothing to eat, you head back to Montgomery Street BART. Up ahead, between you and the escalator entrance to the underground station, you spot that homeless alcoholic guy who's missing both hands because years ago he passed out on the railroad tracks — not once, but twice. You remember him from the days when he was panhandling near your old apartment at the corner of Haight and Masonic. You'd never had him as a welfare client, though, because he was too wrecked even to apply for assistance.

You are within 200 feet of him, when suddenly you feel his attention fasten onto you. You ball up your fists and stuff them in your pockets, tuck your chin into your chest, and raise your voice:

"Goddam sonovabitch piece of shit! Just WHO the FUCK does he think he is, anyhow?! Lotta nerve, asking ME to fix HIS situation cuz he's ready to jump ship and move-on-UP to something better — self-serving-jerk-asshole-CREEP!"

At which point, your double-amputee, clearly on the verge of extending his pitiful stumps in a plea for spare change, recedes into the shadows of the doorway where he is camped. You breathe a sigh of relief and congratulate yourself on another successful repulsion.

7.

Why Juli Can't

Come Monday, after the longest of long, terrible weekends at home, you find yourself back at work. But you are distracted, still trying to understand your new "understanding," your redefined relationship with the man you were so accustomed to referring to as your "husband."

In the span of three days, the laws that govern your planet have changed. You are baffled to find your workplace still standing, seemingly unaffected by recent marital-seismic events, your coworkers carrying on in a parallel plane of existence, unconscious of you, as if this day were no different than any other. What you had expected to see was the entire neighborhood collapsed, in ruins, emergency crews sifting your building's wreckage for manuscripts by prestige authors.

You enter Raker & Ho's newish glass building that crouches on the edge of the Financial District, within the massive shadow of the Embarcadero freeway. Only a few years earlier, the neighborhood had been littered with dilapidating light-industry and warehouse buildings providing shelter for a hodgepodge of small businesses. Like the fortune cookie factory in the ancient garage across the street. But the process of urban renewal is well advanced; this building where you work is proof of that evolving reality.

The elevator opens silently onto the fifth floor, revealing a polished, black reception desk that bears a strong resemblance to the alien monolith in that Kubrick film, *2001: A Space Odyssey*. You trudge toward the hallway that leads to your cubicle, passing the receptionist, greeting her with a wave, glancing automatically at the clock on her desk, which faces out to the reception area: 9:25 a.m. Only a couple years ago, you sat there — in that very seat, doing her very job. So you are well aware she is required to be at her post no later than 8 a.m. sharp, or Hell sends out an invoice, demanding payment. You, on the other hand, though you are the lowest of the low in the editorial food chain — an editorial assistant — you get to wander in any time up to about 10 a.m. With impunity and only the public-facing reception clock making a tacit appeal to whatever Puritan work ethics you and your editorial colleagues may still harbor.

Of course, if it happens you are needed at the *other* end of the day to proof and mark up galleys or to stand at the copy machine for hours or whatever, then you will be expected to stay till your production editor is assured of meeting *her* deadline — even if she waited to flag you down just as you are struggling into your coat, making ready to dash out the door. Then phone calls home will be made, evening plans cancelled, Chinese take-out sent in, No. 2 pencils raised and at the ready. Then you know you probably won't be leaving work before 9 p.m. At which point, the $1.50 an hour raise you got when you were hired from temporary in Reception to permanent in Production starts looking kinda paltry. Meanwhile, the new receptionist left hours ago. With a clear conscience.

As soon as you reach the aquarium where you live, throwing down your purse and coat, you continue speeding along the hall with its stinky new carpeting, and hang a sharp right into the Formica-clad lunchroom, where the Eternal Coffee Pot dispenses a bottomless supply of local dark roast. Coffee fuels this place diurnally; alcohol fuels it nocturnally. You fill your giant Wonder Woman mug with life-sustaining brew and turn to watch Gretchen from Accounting tape a note to a computer that has mysteriously appeared on a corner table in the lunch room since you were here last week. Looking over Gretchen's shoulder, you read the note. It says:

"I am an IBM PC — a 'Personal Computer.' I am your friend. You may touch me, if you wish."

Gretchen laughs and says, "Pretty cool, eh? Brand-new model, just out. And tiny — only 50 pounds. Not like those monsters that fill an entire room or even a whole building. My boss said to set up this little baby for the folks in Editorial to play with. Whaddya think?"

You stare, then reach out tentatively to the typewriter-looking keyboard and tap a few keys. Characters appear on the screen, but nothing happens. An underscore mark keeps blinking and flashing in place. You turn toward Gretchen, mystified.

"What do we do with it?" you ask.

She moves to assist you. "Good point," she says. "I should boot it up for you people, so you won't have to make like Aladdin and guess how to 'Open Sesame.'"

"Okay, yeah. But after that, what's it good for?"

"Oh, I dunno. We run our spreadsheets on one just like this. Legal will be cranking out contracts. I guess you'll be inputting manuscripts."

"'Inputting'?"

"That's what they call it."

"But the authors already send in their manuscripts typed. We make our changes right on the page in pencil. Then the edited copy doesn't need to be retyped till the compositor creates the galleys. It seems redundant to retype a manuscript after it comes to us. More work for no good reason. I don't see much future in this — at least, not for Production."

"I get it. But I'm just following orders here. I think you can play games on it, too."

"That's something, anyway."

You wander out of the lunchroom and back down the hall toward your cubicle, watching the tilt of coffee in your cup, feeling uneasy. Your discomfort is a sensation you've grown all too familiar with since that film actor Reagan became president of the United States.

But you can't blame him for today's dyspepsia. Today you are simply … tired and worn thin. The workaday world is relentless: you get up, get dressed, go to work, work all day, come home, eat dinner, stare at the TV for an hour or two, go to bed, then get up a few hours later in order to repeat the cycle all over again. Like the instructions on shampoo bottles say: "Wash, rinse, repeat." Come tomorrow, you will wash-rinse-repeat another four days, just so you won't have to do it for two days. And, it turns out, two days are just enough to give you that taste of the freedom you've been missing — and, like any addiction, make you crave more.

In your college days, you worked two, sometimes three jobs, while carrying a full courseload of 12 to 16 units each quarter. You were desperate to get your degree. You got used to firing yourself out of a cannon each morning to hit the streets at a run.

That was long ago. You were younger and had more energy back then. You had goals and optimism, too. You still secretly believed yourself capable of achieving whatever you set your mind to.

Or: whatever to which you set your mind.

Or: to whatever your mind was set.

Or ... whatever.

You'd been working since you were fourteen and had already gotten a foretaste of what your elders always insisted was "the Real World." Which was why, at first, you tried so hard to stay out of it. You graduated from college with your little degree, then attempted freelancing. You took the editorial tests distributed by textbook and commercial publishers; you applied for their freelance projects. A little bit of writing, a lot of proofreading — these tasks were the occupational refuges of the good English major who'd learned her lessons well.

Even in the vigorous halcyon days of West Coast publishing in the 1970s, freelance work could be spotty. It soon became clear, unless you were working on a project right this very minute and had your next project waiting in the wings, you were essentially "unemployed." The very thought made you too anxious to focus on the work at hand. And simultaneously dried up all your creative impulses.

You tried applying for regular jobs in publishing. But there never were any. Every substantial editorial position seemed to be held by right of inheritance. No one ever left a job except by dropping dead, pitching face first into his or her typewriter. After you'd exhausted the full spectrum of apparent publishing possibilities, you set your jaw, signed with a temp agency, and accepted the humiliation of offering yourself as a college-educated file clerk who could type 65+ wpm. When a series of bland stints with public relations firms and the credit card divisions of various banks led to a temp gig with a publishing house for which you'd already done a bit of freelancing, you jumped at the chance.

That year, nearly three years ago, their regular receptionist — the same gal you'd greeted this morning as you came in — was going out on maternity. Shortly thereafter, when all of the local publishers went from paying their freelancers by the hour to paying them by the page, you realized you'd inadvertently done the smart thing. Better to sell out to the 8-to-5 than to become a wordsmithing bracero unable to afford to give each manuscript the time and attention it needed, if not deserved. In this economy, literary excellence would always take a back seat to market profitability.

But today — today is still Monday. So your goal for the day is simply to get through to the end of the day. You work diligently toward that goal so you can draw a line through one more square on your desk pad calendar. One down and four to go. But at least Monday offers this consolation: tonight the theaters will be dark, and David won't be on call to fill in for anyone anywhere. All day you've been looking forward to your evening with him. You think about what you will cook for dinner.

Hours later, you are caught by surprise, most unpleasantly, when Irma, one of your two supervising production editors, appears at 5:50, ten minutes before your intended departure, and informs you: you will be staying late.

You nod, biting your tongue to keep from crying. She explains: one of their prestige authors must have his copyedited manuscript back in his hands by the end of this week, so the work must be photocopied and packaged tonight, then sent out first thing tomorrow morning. She explains: the project *would* have been complete and on its way by now, except that *you* were ill on Friday and no one else in the office was available to do the job. You wince from the glancing blow she has delivered. You nod and chew the inside of your cheek.

You chew harder when you see which "prestige author" is responsible for your ruined evening: your old college creative-writing professor. The same one who broke the news to you about your complete lack of "special great talent in this area."

In singles and pairs, your coworkers pass your glass cubicle, leaving for the night. You watch them go, offering an occasional wave, feeling like a lizard in a terrarium when it's closing time at the zoo. Until, at last, there you are: on your own among the rows of quiet cubicles, photocopying 700 pages of copyedited manuscript.

It takes forever. Sticky, yellow Post-it notes flag most pages, communicating extended editorial comments. These notes must be folded out (sometimes peeled off entirely) and copied separately, so Production can retain its own record — after which, the notes must be replaced just so. Pages with corrections must be copied again. Everything must be legible, of course, so you have to double-check it. Since each page must be handled individually, you'll be lucky to have this job done by nine tonight, manuscript photocopied, wrapped, and ready for tomorrow's pickup. Already the tiny copier alcove has grown so hot you consider stripping down to your underwear.

By the time the photocopying is within sight of completion, it is a little past eight and you are lonely and in need of company. You call home (again), but there is no answer — you leave a message. For your future self, most likely.

Then you call your best friend, Kitty. An unapologetic night owl, she is a sure bet for company any time after 3 p.m. and before 7 a.m. She starts her day around the time little children are getting out of school and office workers are beginning to eye their wall clocks seriously. What's more, she never seems to mind interruptions. She picks up on your second ring. In the background, you hear her two TVs blaring away, each with its own VHS tape player running different movies. In years to come, you will realize your old friend was the original multi-tasker before the term had even come into general use.

"Hey, where were you this weekend? That man of yours come home again with his underwear inside out?"

Whew! You realize: no hiding from old college friends to whom you've been confessing for years. And fiction writers, as you know only too well, make a habit of remembering every detail of character they come across. Hey, it could be useful one day.

When your hesitation affirms her intuition, Kitty makes a sound into the phone receiver that begins with an exclamation one might make while driving past a particularly ugly traffic accident and ends with a fart noise.

"I can't tell you what to do," she says, sounding both

exasperated and disgusted with you. "But if it were me, I would kick his rotten ass straight to the curb. You have to *decide* what you want in life."

You want to tell her the full extent of what happened this weekend, how you and David had discussed a new arrangement to save your marriage. But before you can get a word out, she has already dashed ahead.

"So, let's talk about what's important," she runs on. "How's your writing going?"

"Great. I have the entire manuscript for a book on writer's block."

"What?! Oh wait, no, I get it: you just bought yourself a new journal and all the pages are blank — right? Very funny. Let me rewind that question and play it back again: how's your novel coming along?"

"It's not."

"What's the problem?"

"Dunno. Lotta things. Too tired after work. You name it." You don't want to go into how all your crying and throwing up over the weekend made it so hard to concentrate. "Sometimes my only alone-time at home is when I'm in the bathroom...."

"Whatever it takes!"

"No, but seriously...."

"I *am* serious."

Your protestations of having no alone-time at home sound lame, even to you. Especially after this weekend's realizations. You try a different line of self-defense.

"I just don't have anything important to say."

"Sure you do. Write about whatever's twisting your tail — there's your subject."

"Okay, well then, I'm too upset to talk about it."

"I can believe that. But maybe writing it out would help you get a handle on your situation."

"Guess I was hoping for some inspiration, at least," you offer weakly.

"You know better than that. If you wait, inspiration never arrives. You have to be already working. Then when inspiration does come, you climb aboard. After all, you survived Dr. Bug-Ass — I thought you had more grit."

"Oh, hell."

"Thatta girl."

You don't know how to tell your old friend what you've known in your heart for years now: when it comes to writing, you just don't have it. No "special great talent," that's what Old Bug-Ass said.

"Speaking of coincidences," you begin.

"Were we?"

"Absolutely. Wait for it: guess whose manuscript I am Xeroxing right this very minute?"

"Whose? Oh, *mal de merde*! Surely not the good doctor himself?"

"The very same."

"Unbelievable. How is it? Another Third World political manifesto lightly disguised as important contemporary fiction, I assume?"

"So it appears. But, frankly, I'm only an extension of the Machine, making copies as requested. I'm not reading the thing. Just handling the same pages I know he typed with his own pudgy fingers, feeling the grease spots from his lunches makes me sick to my stomach. I can't stand even seeing his name on the title page."

It was one thing to be an English major in the 1970s with academic interests, taking courses about "Literature of the Early Renaissance," "Spanish Literature of the Golden Age – in Translation," "John Donne and the 17th Century Metaphysical Poets," "Shakespeare for Modern Times," etc., etc., ad nauseam. It was something else to be an English major with writing ambitions. Not only had you not stood the test of time — obviously — but it seemed most likely that in time you would fail utterly. In fact, you felt you had already failed. Even before trying.

A lit class can be a lively party, so long as most of the students have read their assignments and the instructor knows how to engage them. By contrast, the atmosphere of a college creative writing class is more likely to resemble a wake. Except there, in the creative writing class, one is *required* to speak ill of the dead. Which includes every dead-on-arrival draft you and nearly every other student in class wrote all quarter long. Here your lifeless "art" would first be dissected, using Academia's two classic surgical tools of theory and criticism. After the autopsy, your late, dearly beloved draft would be laid out for public viewing.

The instructor referred to by most of his students as "Dr. Bug-Ass" had a singular reputation for instructional brutality. But since he was the only game in town, the only instructor who taught creative writing at your institution, each one of his classes started out with at least a couple dozen students. By midterm, however, the class would have shrunk down to a baker's dozen. And by the end of the quarter, the group could easily fit around a table in the school cafeteria. Or into a public phone booth. Only the impossibly hardy and thick-skinned survived. Or that particular quarter's handsome Young Turk chosen to be teacher's pet.

Course procedure was the same each week: lame student efforts to write short stories were mimeographed (oh, that wonderful smell! a cheap high, now fondly recalled) and distributed to everyone in the class, then read before the next session, so they could be "discussed" in person. Discussion began with everyone sitting in silent attention, waiting for a pronouncement from Dr. B. Every class for every course included Dr. B's one Young Turk, who became increasingly arrogant under the grow-lights of the professor's approval, while all his other classmates withered by comparison, their literary efforts revealed as laughably naïve, even pathetic.

Nearly everyone in class was afraid to speak for fear of expressing the wrong opinion. The unspoken, but universally understood, rule was: a story can be liked by the class only if Dr. B likes it. Silence reigned at the start of each "class," but eventually the professor, surveying his students with undisguised contempt, would begin to dissect whatever story lay before him on the coroner's table of his podium. And as soon as he proclaimed his opinion — nearly always negative — the rest of the class would fall upon the story, along with its author, and tear the carrion to pieces.

A cruel system, it seemed. But, like most everyone else, you justified it by reminding yourself: this man was a world-renowned author, who'd come here to America from a Third World country where he'd been oppressed not only for his writings, but for his sexual proclivities as well. He, unlike you, had seen the world and knew what he was talking about.

If he said your story or anyone else's was a waste of good paper and typewriter ribbon, he must be right. Besides, the publishing world was a harsh place, he was always saying that, so probably he was simply trying to toughen you up. For your own good.

Oftentimes your problem was — he explained with a weary sigh — you were trying to tackle subjects you knew nothing whatsoever about. And because your experience in the world was so limited, many topics you might wish to write about should in fact be avoided. "For god's sake," he exclaimed in his strongly accented English, "write from your own experience! And try, if you possibly can manage it, to find some universal themes." Then he would close his eyes, remove his black-plastic frame glasses, and massage the bridge of his nose to relieve the pain of the headache that you, his students, were obviously causing him.

As it happened, your story that day had focused on a subject you felt strongly about, but had no personal experience of: a soldier fighting the "conflict" in Vietnam. So you boldly raised your hand and asked: "Well then, since we have no experience in the world and don't know anything, what should we write about?"

"As I have been telling you all this quarter: write about what you *do* know about and what you feel strongly about."

"For example?" you pressed, though already you had a premonition you were pushing to your peril.

He shrugged dismissively. "How am I to know what you know about, after you are being coddled in American suburbs for twenty years? Why don't you write about how it felt to get your first period. Or write about your weight problem."

This was one of those times in your life when the overhead fluorescent lights suddenly became unbearably bright and hummed like a million bees about to attack. All the air in the room seemed to have been sucked out, and the resulting vacuum made your head feel in danger of exploding. For a moment, you became functionally blind, deaf, and mute. As the hour ended and everyone left the classroom, you continued to sit there, having been turned to stone.

Fortunately, all this happened on the second-to-last class session of your final term. You missed the last session the following week, but stopped by Dr. Bug-Ass's office to drop off your final paper, a story you had worked on joylessly over the weekend about an infant who strangles in its bedclothes. After all, you wanted ... you *needed* credit for this course. You hoped he wouldn't be bothered to hold office hours so close to the end of term. You hoped you could simply stuff your manuscript, concealed within its manila envelope, into his in-box by the door, then disappear before anyone saw you.

As it happened, however, there he was — door wide open. He waved you in with an uncustomary wide grin. Finals were the following week, but he didn't give finals. He was clearly in an expansive mood.

You handed your story to him. He immediately pulled out the manuscript and skimmed it, quickly shuffling pages. He laughed. "At last! After convulsing all quarter, you have finally identified a Universal Theme. Something, maybe, you know about. Good work!" Then, to your surprise, he reached over, gave your bare thigh a squeeze, just above the knee, and held on for an extra second or two. You had time to notice that his fingernails were cut square with beveled edges, not filed to curves. Immediately, you regretted having worn hot-pants to campus that day.

You thanked him, replying with something lame and regrettably self-revealing about how you really hoped to do well in this course, because you thought maybe you wanted to work with words professionally. At which point, he examined you quizzically, screwing up his face briefly in order to bring forth a thought.

Then he sighed and told you, almost ruefully it seemed, "Miss St. John, I know you are eager to 'express yourself.' But, let me assure you, at this green time of your life, there is nothing much to express. Like all other members of your race and sex, you have been spoiled with the softness of your upbringing. And if you had any special great talent in the area of literature, it would certainly have revealed itself by now. Why don't you concentrate on giving some nice young man a few coming-of-age experiences that *he* can write about later?"

He winked to indicate he understood (and intended) the inherent naughtiness of his suggestion. And, ultimately, he gave you an A for his course. But you knew the grade was only for show — a booby prize — since, as he already told you, you had no "special great talent in this area."

It still hurts you to remember all this, though it happened a decade ago. What amazing survival instincts your friend Kitty must possess to have known, after the very first session, that she should drop out of Bug-Ass's creative writing class and never look back! While you were sitting through two quarters of humiliating biweekly sessions, she was setting out, uninstructed, on an actual writing career. Now she has two books in print and keeps to an eclectic schedule that looks down its nose at the dull conventions observed by the rest of the world. You ache with envy.

By contrast, you are continuing to muscle your way through each day, barely surviving the bad air and fluorescent lights on the strength of your determination and with the support of endless strong coffee. Yet you have nothing to show for your persistence. No wonder you find yourself on this Monday night sorting the photocopied pages of a probably altogether forgettable work (and getting paid only a $1.50 an hour more than the receptionist), when what you really need is to be home with the man you married, checking to see whether you still have a life there and already knowing in your heart that you most likely don't.

It's nearly midnight by the time you have copied and reassembled the manuscript, boxed it in FedEx packaging, switched off the Xerox machine, and made ready to jump ship. On your way out the heavy front door, you nearly — heart attack! — collide with Loren McMaster, that cute and flashy young acquisitions editor famous for wearing a different silk tie every day of the year. He is coming in as you are going out. Automatically, you check to see which tie he is wearing. You are surprised to find him tie-less for the first and only time you can recall in the nearly four years you've worked here. Not only is he tie-less, but he is wearing chinos and a black Chorus Line t-shirt, like a regular person. You notice he has loafers on, but no socks. Briefly you wonder if he might be gay.

In Acquisitions, where the big editorial money flows, you know people like Loren McMaster let themselves into the building as early as 4 a.m. so they can teleconference with the company's headquarters in New York City, where the business day has already begun. Once again, you note: everyone in Acquisitions, where books are *conceived*, is male, while everyone in Production, where books are *born*, is female — curiously mimicking the human reproductive process. No wonder, you realize, that authors so often refer to their books as "babies."

Meanwhile, Mr. McMaster stands before you in the reception area, looking shocked. You immediately begin apologizing for having startled him.

"Sorry, didn't mean to surprise you, working late...."

"No, no, it's nothing. I'm the one who's sorry."

His voice, strangely choked, attracts your curiosity, makes you look him in the face. You realize he's been crying. Fascinated, you hold onto the moment.

"Are you ... alright?" you ask.

"Not really," he admits. "But there's nothing to be done about it — just the ordinary tribulations of an all-too-ordinary life."

This man, only a few years older than you, is already a lion in the publishing world. No doubt, in college he would have been just the sort that Dr. Bug-Ass would have chosen to be his Young Turk for a term or two. You want to dislike him for that. Yet, in this moment, he seems so frankly nice and vulnerable and attractive that you feel guilty for wanting to not adore him. You also feel guilty for hating this whole publishing business where success has come so easily to him.

"Sure I can't do anything for you? Make a pot of coffee? Turn on the copier? Call out for pizza?"

He laughs. "That last one would sound good if I hadn't already just eaten. But no, you go. It's clearly been a long day."

"It has," you acknowledge. "Good-night, then."

As you head for the elevator, you wonder: what do all these guys have to cry about when it's their world, their oyster, and they make all the rules?

8.

Why David Can't

N ow that you and your wife have "an understanding" about your only other sexual involvement she knows anything about, for certain, you are free to be with your mistress. And now, just maybe, you have found a way out of this life you got yourself into. Because Barbra is not the sort of woman who will stand for the constant catting around that Juli has put up with for years.

If only your wife had done *her* job of keeping you in line, everything would be fine. It's her fault you do the things you do. And if she'd been more responsive in the sack from the start, you'd never have gotten involved in your nightly, even daily, trawlings.

Lately, you find yourself thinking about pussy all the time. And you must have pussy every couple of days at least or else the pressure builds up so much, you feel your brain will explode. Sometimes it gets so bad, by the time you get to the bar, you first have to go into the men's room, shut yourself up in a stall, and jerk off simply to be able to sit comfortably through Happy Hour with a drink in your hand, calmly waiting for a prospect to wander in.

Can you help it that you're oversexed?

It makes you smile to realize, after all these years, why they call it "Happy Hour." Why shouldn't Mr. Happy have his own hour?

But Mr. Happy is happy only if everything goes as planned. If the right She comes in. If She accepts your invitation to begin the elaborate and highly competitive game of seduction and submission. If She's willing to take a chance on leaving the bar with you. If She's willing to receive you, an unknown man, into her bed at her apartment, her hotel room, her friend's house, her car. Then you can relax, you can finally go home, still glowing with post-coital euphoria, and get some well-deserved rest. What your wife doesn't know can't hurt her. And Juli hardly suspected a thing until, on top of making your usual sexual rounds, you started spending so much time with Barbra you couldn't think up enough lies fast enough to cover your own fully exposed ass.

In the years since you left college, moved to the City with Juli, went back to school, got married, and started taking on acting jobs and whatever else you could patch in, your recreational scenario is one you've played out literally hundreds of times in nearly every possible circumstance in your life. Not only in the bathrooms at bars (Curtain Call, Henry Africa's, House of Shields, Vesuvio's, Specs, etc., etc.), but backstage and during certain classes, on the wee-hours, cross-town Muni bus (plenty of room to stretch out on the backseat, but beware of the quick stops), at work downtown in the Time-Life boiler room (late shift, supply closet), at the houses of (former) friends, in Golden Gate Park, and on the roof in the parking lot above the police station in North Beach. Also, anywhere else you find yourself with time to kill.

One evening when you were home and Juli was cooking dinner, you got The Urge. You told her you were going out for a pack of cigarettes, and you didn't come home till well past midnight. By then, Juli was frantic, crying, but she calmed down after you told her you'd run into an old Marine Corps buddy in the corner liquor store and gone over to his hotel room with him. She wanted to know why you hadn't brought him up to *your* apartment, so nearby; she wanted to know why you hadn't called to let her know where you'd gone. You explained how you were so surprised to see him — someone you'd thought had died in Nam, you told her — and how war-talk could get pretty rough. Also, you explained you didn't want your old friend to think you'd become a pussy-whipped grunt who had to check in with his old lady before wiping his ass.

Begging off in the name of the easily bruised male ego always shuts her up. Besides, you really did run into an old buddy in the liquor store — only she was a fuck-buddy — and things did get pretty rough. That was cutting it close, you realize now, but the thrill of this spontaneous encounter, enacted under such tricky circumstances — in your own neighborhood, right across the street from your wife, with no prior setup to explain your sudden and prolonged absence — more than made up for the fact you'd known this skanky barfly-ho for years.

Nowadays your search for fresh meat and the One Pussy to End All Pussies is pretty much an ongoing pursuit that occupies your mind like a meditation mantra recited over and over and over in your head until stripped of any residual meaning it once might have held. No sooner than you finish one encounter and go searching for your underpants among the tangled sheets on the floor at the foot of her bed, you begin to have thoughts of your next quest. Your next conquest.

All day you've been thinking about her, this Brave New Woman you have yet to encounter. As always, you are excited to imagine the world of possibilities attached to someone you will be meeting for the first time. You pray she will be The One — that woman who will take care of you and all your needs, keep you in line, yet get out of the way to let you be your own man. Every night, she will fuck you blind. Always she will know what you want without your ever having to tell her. She won't raise hell when she hears you've got a late rehearsal. She won't nag you for your check on payday just because the rent is due. You won't have to wait to screw her till she falls asleep and can't object. She'll be the girl you've been waiting for your entire life, the missing piece who will complete the puzzle of your existence.

After years of practice, you've mastered your strategy. This is how it goes:

You walk into one of a half-dozen bars in the city where you are on friendly relations with the bartender and sufficiently well known to be allowed to carry a tab. If you need to buy a round of drinks for the house in order to impress this girl, whoever she is, you certainly don't want the humiliation of being denied within earshot. No, you need to be able to project an image of easy affluence. That's where being an actor helps in a big way. Because, though you were raised dirt-poor among relations who are missing important teeth, you can still play rich. Or, at least, you can play comfortable. What's more, women are susceptible to men in glamour professions. They always love it that you are an actor.

So: you always sit at the bar, not at a table, where you can talk to the bartender and to the cocktail waitresses, who arrive and depart like bees at a hive, but where you can get up and visit a table without looking odd. If you can, you sit facing the door, the better to check out each candidate cunt as she enters. (Your second-choice seat is one facing the mirror over the bar, whose reflection reveals each incoming possibility over your shoulder.) On a sunny afternoon inside an especially dark bar, it takes her a few moments to get oriented as her eyes adjust to the low light. You can get a good look at her in those few moments and notice, among other things, whether she is there to meet someone she already knows or whether she looks like she would be willing to meet someone new. Meanwhile, you sit, looking cool, waiting without seeming to wait. And if you start feeling impatient, you remind yourself: take it easy, she's coming, she's on her way. You can always order another drink. And you always drink the same type of drink — a Brandy Alexander or some other sweet cocktail you can start by offering her a taste of. It's part of the ritual. Like casting a spell.

Of course, your strategy works better with complete strangers — women who've never seen you before and with whom it can be arranged to never see you again. The women you work with downtown, sit in drama classes with, or meet backstage in the theater can become ... inconvenient. So, thank god you live in a city that attracts an apparently endless supply of strangers. And, of course, your gambit works better in bars because you can bet any woman who walks into a bar without having prearranged to meet up with friends is most likely looking for just such a fantasy as you are willing and able to provide.

Women — they always pretend they don't want it, but they do. Look at the way they dress, look at how they act. They're always coming on to you. Are you supposed to ignore that? Any straight guy will grab whatever pussy he can, especially if it's within petting distance. That's simply human nature.

Besides, no one really cares what you do with your dick. All that prudery went out with the Summer of Love, which unfortunately you had to miss in lieu of serving your country by shooting some gooks. But later you made up for what you missed. And then some.

A year or so ago, your old friend Bill tried to talk to you about your complicated life. He suggested you had a problem. But the way you see it, *he's* the one with the problem. After all, you're getting laid — he's not.

But if you think about it (which you try never to do), you have to admit he has a point. On those evenings when you can't persuade any women to do you for free — a pro bono boner — you have to *pay* for your BJ, and that can get expensive. Moreover, now you're in your thirties, things take longer and you run out of steam faster. You require more rest than the constant effort to supply yourself with snatch allows.

Actually, you never really get to rest, and you are just plain tired. You'd like to take a break, but you can't. You'd like to be able to quit — if only for a few months — but you can't. You've tried. When you asked Juli to marry you, that hooker at the

Embarcadero Center was supposed to be your last. But you managed to stay clean for only a month before the old Urge returned and you found yourself checking out women on the street. Two nights later, you were back in some bar, lying in wait.

9.

Juli Makes a Fool of Herself

After a night of sobbing against your husband's chest, you'd imagined a compromise had been reached: David will spend alternating weeks with her. In exchange, he has agreed to see a marriage counselor of his choice with you.

Your marriage counselor turns out to be a fetching young woman with long dark hippie tresses, wearing purple sox with wide, suede Birkenstocks. She is named Marsha. You and Marsha get off to a bad start.

"Do you mind if I smoke in here?" you ask. In most places, the inquiry would be no more than a polite rhetorical statement.

"Yes, I mind."

So much for putting you at ease. Next, she wants a therapeutic statement of intent from each of you:

"Could you please express your goal of therapy?"

David answers first, with scarcely a moment's hesitation: "Our marriage is ... changing, and we are seeking support in this time of transition."

While Marsha nods approvingly at David, you turn open-mouthed toward him, astonished more by his glibness than by his studied tone of sincerity and outstanding diction. But, after all, he does have a professionally trained voice.

"And, Juli," Hippie Marsha prompts, "what is *your* therapeutic goal for coming here today?"

Your mind is completely blank, a perfect Zen slate. Without a ready answer, you feel you have wandered onstage during the performance of a play you never rehearsed nor even read, because you didn't know you'd been cast in one of the principal roles.

"Well?" she presses.

"I, uh ... I ... I want my marriage!" you blurt out, knowing you have just confirmed Marsha's initial assessment of you: a complete idiot and totally lame.

"That may not be a realistic expectation," she replies, gently reproving you, "but I appreciate your frankness."

After that first joint meeting, you and David begin attending individual sessions. You know you are not supposed to ask David what he discusses with the therapist you share. But you can't help yourself and you *do* ask. He tells you he won't talk about it. He tells you he is offended you would even ask.

"Aren't you curious what I tell her?"

"No."

Hippie Marsha had suggested, in one of your individual counseling sessions, that you and David need to establish some ground rules for your evolving marital situation. At first, you moved to defend yourself against what felt to you like blame that you had allowed the relationship to get so out of hand and that you ought to have "made" him behave better. Then you started to tell her about your past efforts to come to some agreement about how you should treat one another — to establish the very "ground rules" she was now scolding you for having neglected. But then you realized: here is a therapist-sanctioned opportunity to impose some predictability on your domestic scene. Maybe it would be to your advantage to endure the chastisement you were paying her for and to do as she says. Or, at least, to *try*.

At home at first, David seemed to acquiesce to whatever you asked for. But then the time came and he went, just as he pleased, just as he'd always done, heedless of whatever ground rules you hallucinated the two of you had agreed upon. Eventually, you quit asking questions.

His first departure was the hardest to accept. The two of you had never discussed the matter of procedures — the exact process by which you would separate from one another each week that he would be staying with Barbra. Should you make yourself scarce while he packed for his week away? If you were home, should he kiss you goodbye and say something kind to reassure you he'd be coming "home" in a few short days? What if someone phoned, looking for him? Should you take a message, then call him at Barbra's? Or give the caller Barbra's number? What if you had an emergency situation in the apartment or something put you in the hospital? What sort of circumstance would be important enough to bother him at the home of his mistress?

Without any ground rules, as suggested by Hippie Marsha, David had never even seen fit to acknowledge that this first period of sanctioned infidelity was approaching.

But, suddenly, on a Monday morning, while you were trying to scrap yourself together for work, you noticed he was vigorously jamming clean underpants into his attaché case. You called attention to this obvious gesture of forethought and preparation:

"So ... I guess this means you won't be coming home tonight?"

"That's right."

"And I won't see you or hear from you for the rest of the week?"

He grunts his assent.

"And you won't even call me to let me know you're alright?"

He does not dignify the question with a response of any kind. Moments later, he is out the door, and you are alone.

10.

Juli Leaves Town

Y ou catch the airport bus from Dulles and spend the hour-long ride into Washington, D.C. with your forehead pressed against the window, smudging the tinted glass. Wrought iron and iron gray — these are your first impressions as the bus pulls through the narrow streets of Georgetown. A light autumn rain had sponged traffic soot from the town's well-oiled bricks and left them shiny. The trees are delicate, finely knit in that dignified section. Stately, three-story homes line these streets, laid out in neat, aesthetic circles like stone daisies. When you step from the bus, you find the air humid and heavy.

Dark wood and thick brown carpeting muzzle the hotel room in which you are to stay for three nights. Two king-sized beds, with matching brown-and-black spreads, together offer enough surface to sleep an extended family of boat people. On the walls hang framed, parchment lithographs, classic scenes of English hunting parties from a previous century. The room announces firmly, "Men only." You read the guest information packet cover to cover — the room service menu, hotel rules, detailed instructions for operating the telephone without assistance from the hotel switchboard. You are unsure how to call home. A minor matter, however, since you have little reason to do so.

This trip to D.C. — to attend, over a long weekend, an international conference of publishing industry professionals on "The Coming Desktop Publishing Revolution" — was set up months ago and presented to you as a reward for all your hard work. But you understood that, in fact, you were being sent as a proxy for your publisher's real production editors, who are too busy doing actual production to take four days out of their schedules to sit with dozens of other overworked editors and listen to how to do much too much work even faster so they can take on even more work. They prefer to stay home, do the work, and offer up their editorial assistant to maintain appearances.

Initially, you were thrilled to learn you'd be sent on this junket. Now you are reluctant to leave home for even a few days of one of your weeks with David. You only wish you could have thought up some way to get out of going to D.C. entirely.

Before you left San Francisco, you tried to talk to David. One night a week ago, you fell asleep around midnight. When you awakened hours later, you found yourself still alone in bed. At first, you supposed he must not have come home yet. But when you got up, you discovered him on the other side of the hanging Indian-print bedspread room divider, sitting on the floor with a TV test pattern for company, smoking a joint and playing a one-sided game of Tobruk, chasing the Desert Fox deep into the African desert once again.

When he glanced up at you, you saw the whites of his eyes were red with nets of swollen capillaries. The skin on his face appeared loose, pallid and waxy like a plucked dead chicken, a supermarket whole fryer. Idly, you wondered if he'd been doing something stronger than mere weed. Instinctively, you glanced around the room for your hand mirror.

"Why don't you come to bed?" you asked. "You look tired. You should come to bed."

"Juli, I feel so old," he said without looking up. He was peering through a handheld magnifying glass at the square cardboard counters on his paper game board printed with yellow hexagons that looked like a honeycomb in a bee hive, but were intended to represent endless flat desert terrain.

"David, for god's sake, you talk like you're getting ready to apply for Social Security. You're only thirty-three."

"Only thirty-three," he echoed.

This business of being old, too old for whatever he wanted to be or to do, is the same complaint he's had about his life for the past seven, nearly eight years the two of you have been together. Worse now than when you first met, a couple of years before that, when he started attending college on the G.I. Bill, the government's compensation for the three years he spent mildewing in the Marine Corps on thirteen-month tours of duty in Southeast Asia. You remember how he sat taking notes in classes with students three, four, or more years his junior. His experiences made him seem worldly by contrast, a grown man among boys barely out of their teens. Of course, all were adults now. But the years he'd been away seem to have stretched beyond normal boundaries. Now, you realized, he believed the distance that stood between his own progress and that of his peers was far too great to ever be closed.

"Only thirty-three, only thirty-three," he chanted with a glazed expression. "And what have I got to show for it? I don't have a house, a car, a washer and dryer, a VCR — not a goddamn thing. I was talking to this one guy after the show tonight. Twenty-seven years old, MBA from Harvard, and he's making $40 grand a year — to start!"

You felt compelled to argue him out of his feelings. "But, David, that's a different world. He lives in a different world than we do. You're smart, too. You could have done that, but you chose to do something different. If all you want is things, then all you need is money. I thought you wanted to be an artist, to work in theater, to live a creative life, to do something fine and special."

He shook his head. "I don't know anymore. All I know is I feel old."

You kissed him then, out of pity, and went back to bed. Whatever David wanted to do, he was always too old.

The night before you left for D.C., you tried again to talk to him.

"David, you know I leave in the morning. And I won't be back till Monday afternoon." You hated reminding him of this, because all along you have been painfully, privately aware that this particular weekend was supposed to have been *your* weekend and that, as soon as you return home on Monday and the two of you go see your therapist for your monthly joint session, he will leave you for a week to go be with her.

"Uh-huh," he replied noncommittally.

You saw it had become his way with you to say as little as possible. Once upon a time, when you were a couple, you would have looked forward to these few days before your departure as a poignantly romantic time to be shared. Now you saw it would be nothing of the kind.

"David," you pleaded, "aren't you going to miss me, even a little?"

"Of course."

"What are you going to do while I'm gone?"

"I'll be at the theater, toting either a spear or a tray. Like always."

That wasn't what you meant, and you both knew it. So you rephrased the question.

"David, are you going to come home on the nights I'm gone?"

No way he could deliberately misconstrue that question. He mulled it over a moment before replying, "No, probably not."

Stabbed in the heart, you felt your ribs contract, then crack under pressure.

"So, you're going to stay with ... what's-her-face?"

"Most likely."

"But it's not even her week!" you exclaimed, knowing you sound like a kindergartener. At which point he looked up at you quizzically, head tilted, with an expression suggesting he suspects you have lost your mind.

You couldn't believe he was telling you this. You couldn't believe you were hearing this from your own husband, the man you'd been living with for years. The veins in your temples swelled and throbbed painfully. The lights in the apartment grew unnaturally bright. You felt numb and light-headed, vaguely nauseous. In another moment, you would lose all self-control and tear apart this entire place with your bare hands. Starting with his face.

"Well — That's! Just! Great! Guess you won't miss me too much, will you? Guess you can't wait for me to leave, can you?"

"Please don't," he said in a low, even voice that pleaded for compassion. "This is hard on me, too, you know."

You stared at him in disbelief. "Hard on you? Hard on *you*? David, *you're* the one who's doing this to *me*. I didn't ask you to get involved with that slut."

He frowned. "Don't call her that. She's not a slut."

"Whatever!"

He sighed deeply. "Barbra's not a slut. She's a bright, successful, professional woman."

"Yeah? So what the hell am I? Chopped liver past its expiration date? David, what about me? Why are you doing this? Why are you hurting me like this? What did I do?"

That was as much as you got out before you burst into tears and began sobbing furiously. David came to you, sat close, held you, tried to comfort you.

"There, there," he crooned, rocking you gently back and forth, back and forth. "Don't be so sad. It'll be alright. Everything will be alright."

"Oh, David," you blubbered. "Are you getting ready to leave? Please don't leave me. I couldn't stand it if you did."

"I'm not going anywhere."

Maybe not. But if he wasn't leaving, if he really wasn't "going anywhere," then why is there no reason to call home on your first night in a strange city three thousand miles away?

You have to talk to someone. You want someone to know you made it to Washington, D.C., someone to care that you'd traveled all this way. You consider calling your friend Kitty, but dread her asking you why you are investing so much time and energy in something that means nothing to you and isn't going to make you a better writer. Or a writer — period. She doesn't understand, you think as you pick up the receiver of your room phone, dial the hotel operator, and ask him to connect you, please, with the West Coast. Not with San Francisco, but with a small town a few hours' drive north into the next state.

As that other phone rings on the other side of the continent, you stand at your wide, rain-splattered window overlooking the city. A Monet impression of the metropolis at night. A perfect movie scene. It would be a perfect movie scene, except it's real, it's your life. Four rings later, your mother answers her phone that hangs on the wall of her faux American pioneer country kitchen.

"Mom! Guess where I'm calling from?"

"Oh, for goodness' sakes, don't tell me you're in D.C. already?"

"I meant to call you before I left, Mom, but I've been so busy lately."

"That's alright, honey. That's good. How do you like our nation's capital so far?"

Your mother never went anywhere when she was married to your father, never got any farther east than Virginia City, Nevada, where they were married. Sixteen years later, in Oakland, California, she divorced him and, years after that, married your stepfather, who straightaway moved her to rural southern Oregon. Nevertheless, she retained unlimited enthusiasm for the concept of travel. There was still so much she wanted to see. Or she wanted her daughter to see on her behalf. In case she herself never made it.

"Mom, I haven't really had a chance to get out yet. It was all fields and trees coming in from the airport. Now it's dark. Also, it's raining."

"Oh, sweetheart, I hope you'll be able to get to the Smithsonian, and to Arlington and the monuments. Washington has so much to offer! I've heard the Kennedy Center for the Performing Arts is wonderful."

"I'm sure it is. But, Mom, this is a business trip. I have a conference to attend. Besides, I have to leave here first thing Monday morning."

"I know, honey, I know. It's just that … there's so much to see. Please try to get out and around a little. Don't be like me. You do what you want with your life. It's the most important thing."

"I know, Mom."

"I'm so proud of you, darling. I just know, one of these days, you're going to be a big success."

"Thanks, Mom. I hope so."

"I love you. You know, you'll always be my bright and shining star."

And that's what you were needing to hear this evening. Now you can unpack and settle in.

11.

Juli Wades into Deeper Waters

You can't help noticing him, because, from the moment you walk into the hotel's cocktail lounge, all he does is stare at you. His eyes follow you like those of a portrait painted by some famous Old Dutch Master.

The conference is officially set to begin in the morning, but tonight the sponsoring organization is throwing a little Friday night, get-to-know-you mixer. Though you've never felt at ease walking alone into a lounge, you force yourself to go downstairs and join the other conferees. Irma would want it that way. In publishing, networking is compulsory. Besides, the hotel charges for TV time.

You accept your name tag from the official greeter, a blonde woman of indeterminate age, with silver lips, pink and purple eyeshadow, and fiberglass big-hair. You smile vaguely around the room and go stand by the bar. Ostensibly, you are waiting for a glass of white wine. Instinctively, you know if you hang on and bide your time, that man staring at you will create an excuse to come over and talk to you.

No surprise, then, when you feel a presence at your back, hear a voice over your shoulder:

"That's a beautiful suit you have on."

You experience a flush of pleasure for having purchased this trendy, dressed-for-success, dark wool skirted suit specifically to make an impression on this trip. It was an outfit you couldn't afford, but how often do you travel for business? And what's the point of credit, anyway? Standing in the dressing room at Neiman-Marcus, you thought of your mother, the shopaholic, and comforted yourself with the absolute certainty that she would never for a moment have allowed a little thing like lack of funds to stand in her way of any item of clothing she really wanted.

"Why, thank you," you reply, turning — smoothly, you hope — in the direction of the voice. You lean forward and squint myopically at his name tag. You left your glasses upstairs. "Thank you ... Joe."

He grins, thrusts out a big, callused hand, and you shake it.

"From New Hampshire," he declares stoutly. "How 'bout yourself?"

"San Francisco, California."

"Quite a place, I've heard."

For the first time you can recall, you are tickled to be able to trade on the secondhand glamor conferred upon those who live in a world-renowned sin city. You regard Joe, noting that his teeth are perfect, large and white. He has a full beard several shades darker than his straight blond hair, almost red, like a pile of freshly fallen leaves. You think his beard might make a nice warm home for a family of little forest creatures.

And Joe seems kind, as if he might be inclined to let them stay.

He clears his throat and touches his chest. He is wearing a sports jacket, wide-wale corduroy, but underneath that — a plaid flannel shirt, unbuttoned at the collar, no tie. Regular L.L.Bean guy. He asks you to dinner.

You hesitate, but tell yourself: you both have to eat, don't you? What harm could there be in two professional colleagues having dinner together, getting acquainted? After all, you are supposed to be networking.

The two of you exit the hotel and march down the street together for a couple of drizzly blocks, maintaining a decent, collegial distance from one another. Nevertheless, by the time you reach the restaurant, an upscale seafood franchise, you are well aware this dinner will involve more decisions than whether you'd prefer surf or turf. Once seated, you force yourself to look directly into this stranger's eyes. They are green and rather nice.

I could do worse, you think. Maybe I'll have the shrimp now, and he can have the prime rib. Then when we get back to the hotel, we'll switch: I'll take the beef, and he can have the seafood.

In the ancient world, all roads led to Rome. In the modern world, all roads lead to bed. During dinner, you sit back and wait for the proposition that must inevitably come at the evening's close, as much to be expected as the terminal punctuation that appears at the end of even the longest, most circuitous sentence.

On your way back to the hotel, you think of David. Dear David, who need never know about any of this. Dear David, who most likely won't care, even if he does find out. Because, after all, what is *he* doing this evening? At this thought, hot tears well up behind your eyes.

You can't do it, you realize. Immediately, you start mentally rehearsing the rejection you must deliver: I'm sorry, Joe, I'm really awfully sorry, but I can't....

"I'm sorry, Joe. I can't. It's not that I don't like you — I do. It's just that... ."

You are standing in the hotel hallway of your floor, in front of your room with your foot holding the door open, and you are fumbling for the right words that will get rid of this man before he crosses the threshold into your room. You stick out your hand for a clasp, but instead he throws his arms around you and hugs you. A big, hairy-chested bearhug that mashes your nose into his tie clip. You can't help noticing, as you pull back, that the clip is a tiny collage of endangered species. You look up, but all you can see is a bushy thicket of facial hair. You push him away, but gently.

"I don't feel I know you well enough for that. I mean, I like you, but well, you know ... a couple hours over dinner, it's not very long to have known someone."

"Oh sure, I understand," he immediately acknowledges, picking up the ball and apologizing with it. You are astonished to see, despite his beard, he is blushing. "I didn't mean to be forward."

He steps back and looks around nervously, as if searching for a hidden camera. "But if you change your mind, my room is number 307 — just upstairs from you, okay?"

"Okay, Joe. If I change my mind, I'll knock on the ceiling to let you know."

"Huh?"

"Kidding. Just kidding."

Your heart pounds crazily as you slip into your room, shut the door, and lean with your back up against it like some horror movie heroine. You are slightly hysterical. You flip the deadbolt and pace briskly back and forth, hyperventilating. It takes several minutes before you are calm enough to try the phone again.

Maybe David changed his mind. Maybe he's home after all. Please, David, please be there, you pray as you wait the interminable length of time it takes to connect you across three thousand miles, to shunt you from operator to operator, to string you along from one line after another, until you hear your very own phone at home ringing, ringing, ringing. You let it ring a dozen times at least before the hotel operator breaks in with the heartbreakingly obvious news:

"Your party doesn't answer. Would you care to try again later?"

My "party." Some party, you think. But what you say, lamely, is, "Oh, yeah, good idea, I'll do that."

Then you remember the time difference. Why hadn't you thought of it before? In D.C., it was nearly midnight. Back home, it wasn't even nine yet. David would still be at the theater.

Pats, the stage manager, picks up his backstage phone.

"No, sweetie, he's not here. He called in sick tonight. Ralphie went on instead. How's D.C.?"

"Great. Guess I'll reach him at home."

You hang up and sit stunned to think he'd actually blow off a performance. Even if it was just a servile extra. You'd had three chances to guess where he was. Now two were gone, and your luck has run out.

The following morning, Saturday, at the start of the conference, you learn about — of all things! — how to incorporate your desktop computer into your production system using a "software program" called Wordstar.

And you side-eye Joe. Whenever he comes within range of you during the conference sessions and at lunchtime, he is friendly toward you, but not overly so. All the intensity, all the eager confusion of last night is gone. Now he's simply another guy. But you have no intention of spending another cold and restless night alone. As gray dawn was beginning to illuminate this gray city only hours ago, you were already deciding it was time you needed to see what all the extramarital fuss is about.

Another no-host cocktail hour follows the first long day of lectures and group discussions. This Saturday evening mixer is a lot rowdier, insofar as a roomful of pallid, repressed editorial types ever gets rowdy. But at least people are actually talking to one another.

You seek out Joe. He is easy to spot in this estrogen-dominant crowd. You find him chatting up a petite brunette from some Texas university press. Glasses magnify her eyes, and her hair is pulled up in a tight bun at the top of her head. You see her future: she will look as she does tonight for the next forty years. She seems to like Joe. You hope you aren't too late.

You wait for a lull in their conversation, a time when both have their noses stuck in their wine glasses. The air around you feels charged with electricity, singing shrilly like telegraph wires strung across a plain, connecting two isolated towns that otherwise would be unable to communicate with one another.

You take a deep breath and step into their charmed circle.

Having successfully invaded their personal space, you nod impersonally, with manufactured politeness, to the brunette before getting down to business with Joe.

"Joe, any special plans for tonight?" you ask brightly.

He glances at his brunette companion, but turns immediately toward you. "No, no, I haven't," he acknowledges casually.

"Well, then," you reply, "I want you to know: I've changed my mind."

His jaw drops slightly. His lips part in surprise. In ways barely perceptible, his whole demeanor transforms. No need to ask if he accepts your offer. Everything about him is already shouting: Yes, yes, here I come!

Now all his attention is focused tightly on one silent, but urgent, compound question: when-where-how?

"Meet you back at the ranch, then," you blithely answer his unvoiced query.

You don't stick around long enough to catch the reaction of the cocktail companion he is about to betray. Instead, you walk away, while your legs can still hold you up, and you hit the street at a dead run, thrilled by your own bravado. The institute hosting the conference is six blocks from your hotel. You jog the entire distance, then wheeze and cough up clots of mucus as you enter the hotel lobby. And, in fact, the lobby seems a good place to wait. He has to pass this way. He can't miss you. You pick a likely chair and settle in.

Less than two minutes later, Joe stands before you, flushed and panting.

"Where?" he asks.

"Your room."

When it comes to ambiance, however, it scarcely matters whose room you choose: his room is the same as yours. If not for the trousers draped over the back of the chair, the manly toiletries next to the bathroom sink, his suit bag hanging in the open closet, you would think you were back in your own room. Realizing this gives you the unpleasant impression you are being studied surreptitiously in some perverse psychological experiment.

"This is just like my room, you know."

"Exactly?"

"Identical."

This is the extent of your conversation as you take off your clothes. You both stand to undress — you with your eyes on the carpet, he with his back to you — and you both fold your clothing with excessive care. He is very hairy. Not at all like David, whose body is pink and hairless as a newborn mouse. When he turns at last to face you, you note he already has a huge erection.

"You're a very attractive woman," he says by way of explanation.

He advances, closing the physical distance between you. He hugs you as he did the previous night. But things are different now. You feel his insistent maleness pressing hard up against your hip. You cannot ignore what you are doing.

"And you're a very hairy man," you reply.

He chuckles. "I like to carry my security blanket around with me."

The joke is weak, but welcome. You realize, in that moment, that movies are the only instruction you've ever received for what to do next. You know which ones you drew guidance from for your first time with David, but tonight's encounter is not the same. The first time with David, you knew him — or thought you did — and you were In-Love. Back then, whatever you lacked in finesse, you tried to make up for with sincere enthusiasm. Or at the very least, with novelty, you suppose ruefully as you clasp this stranger.

An audience viewing this movie you now are acting in would surely presume that you two are well past the getting-acquainted stage. But how mistaken they would be! Who is this man? What does he want from you? Can you give it to him? You feel quite separate from the experience you are having. You can't tell whether or not you are enjoying yourself.

At length, unable to think of a suitable role model among the standard theatrical film fare of the day, you resort to the pornographic section of your cinematic memory bank. Porno pals never know each other, either, but they manage just the same. They never let ignorance nor social convention nor shyness nor a queasy stomach get in their way. Even at a party where they know no one, ten minutes later, they know everyone, as well as the locations of their birthmarks.

Recollections of such scenes now become your Arthur Murray School of Erotic Arts. One-two-three, one-two-three. You and David might do it á la Stanislavsky. With Joe, you have to be content to fuck-by-the-numbers.

The hour you spend in his room seems, at first, like little more than a slightly unusual experience. But, of course, what else can you expect? What other way can you take this man except out of context, a stray thread stuck to the fabric of your life? The encounter — not even to be confused with what might be called "an affair" — is therefore devoid of meaning, an isolated social aberration.

You do it once, twice, first with him on top, then with you. But when he wants to go at it a third time, you've had enough. You suck him off, get up, spit the mess into his bathroom sink. You watch the thick glob of spunk slide like a slug down the side of the curved bowl and disappear into the drain. You look up to see your image in the mirror, parched and dead-white beneath the fluorescent glow overhead. You run a burst of water, rinse your mouth, slap your face. You've had enough.

Back in the bedroom, you dig through your purse for your pack of smokes. But when you stick a cigarette between your lips and click your Bic to light up, he shakes his head disapprovingly. "I really wish you wouldn't. Not in here," he says. You sigh and acquiesce.

Twenty minutes later, the two of you wait for a table in the basement of last night's nearby seafood place. The setting is intimate, as befits the occasion. You order the Captain's Plate, thinking it a good way to try a little bit of everything without having to make a commitment. Joe asks the waiter to bring him a big, rattling plate of slimy, steamed clams in their shells. He slurps them down, sucks their juice, smacks his lips, wipes his dripping beard. You sit quietly, hands folded on the table, frankly in awe of such unabashed gusto.

Joe glances at your hand, eyeing your wedding ring. "Does that ring mean you're married?" he asks.

The question is one you've been expecting, dreading, hoping for, wondering how you will answer. You haven't exactly avoided mentioning David. Rather, you simply talked about other things and somehow never got around to mentioning him. Funny, when you think of it now, how you and this man have chatted for hours and done all you've done together, without ever once bringing up the subject of that other man with whom you are theoretically sharing your life.

On the other hand, you remind yourself, an intelligent, well-educated woman with something going on in her life besides her husband should be able to wax eloquent on any number of engaging topics. Supposedly, only that poorly adapted, house-pet species known as "Occupation: Housewife" is unable to sit still for ten minutes without running off at the mouth about her marriage, her husband, her family, her home.

You think: that housewife is more honest, more forthright in her obsessions than you are. At least she has these things in her life, whereas you ... you have none of them. You can hardly bear to acknowledge your own obsession — how great a proportion of your waking thoughts are devoted to a man who apparently gives very little, if any, thought to you in return. But at least you can muster the courage to answer Joe's question truthfully:

"Yes, I'm married."

He nods sagely, as if you had merely confirmed a basic and immutable law of science with which he is already well acquainted.

"Well," he announces, "the fact that I'm not wearing a ring doesn't mean I'm not married." Having delivered this koan, he offers you a raised-eyebrows look heavy-laden with significance.

This man is starting to annoy you. Really, his teeth are unnaturally white. Probably they got that way from all the nuts and berries he eats back home in New Hampshire. Maybe he chews on maple trees or whatever the hell else they have up there. The clams he is guzzling look like snot. Juice dribbles onto his beard and hangs there in greasy beads. The restaurant is cramped, overheated, full of sickish, fishy steam. You notice he chews his fingernails, his cuticles are ragged.

In college, you took a class in logic, so you are able to reconstruct and interpret the implied syllogism he presents to you:

> *All adults who wear wedding bands are married.*
> *This woman wears such a ring and,*
> *therefore, she is married.*
> *However, all adults who do not wear such rings*
> *are not necessarily not married.*
> *This man does not wear a wedding band —*
> *therefore, he may or may not be married.*

Considering your current pickup status and his guileless nature, you decide to dismiss the possibility that Joe is in fact single, but sometimes wears a wedding band to give the appearance of being married. You suspect he is merely waiting to be nudged into confession.

"All right," you say evenly, feeling exhausted by the need for infinite patience in dealing with this man. "Are you married?"

"Yes."

"And would you like to tell me about your wife?"

"Her name is Beth. I'll show you her picture."

His wife looks fresh and young and hopelessly endearing, a golden-haired snow bunny in her pink ski suit, with two little girls as blonde and precious as herself sitting on either side of her, pressing their fragile bodies up against their pretty mommy.

"My daughters, Tina and Shelley, six and four," he explains.

"Very sweet," you reply grimly. In this moment, you might be two co-workers from the same office out on a lunch break, two colleagues working on the same assignment, now relaxing and exchanging a bit of personal history. Except, of course, for the hour you recently spent banging away at each other, naked and sweating on a hotel bed, with no thought for the grotesque betrayal of your loved ones at home.

"What's the matter?" you ask. "Feeling guilty?"

"I guess so. Don't you?"

You bite the inside of your cheek. "No," you declare. No, you think, I don't feel guilty — just depressed. "No, I've been married awhile, and I want to stay that way. But I guess things like this are bound to happen now and then. I'll talk to my husband when I get home."

"I'm never, ever going to breathe a word to Beth about this," Joe says. He stares longingly at her photograph. "She'd never do anything like this to me. She's not like that."

Not like me, you think. Not low and slutty like me.

"Listen, Joe, my advice to you is: either find a way to not feel guilty about this or don't do it again."

He reverently returns the photo of Beth and the girls to his wallet and says softly, "You're right: I don't think I'll ever do anything like this again." He looks up and through you with large, sad eyes. "In the ten years we've been married, this is the only time I've ever gone out on her."

Oh, swell — and to think you had to be the one who caused this nice family man to stumble, the one who tossed him the apple and spoiled his perfect record. You try to imagine what you should do next. Sympathize? Apologize?

"Joe, I have to get back to the hotel."

Full of clams, he hoists himself up and out of his seat and out of his reverie.

"You want to try it again?" he suggests cheerfully.

You suppose that, as far as he's concerned, it won't count against him if he blows his previously unsullied record of marital fidelity one more time in the course of the same evening with the same woman. After all, same hole.

But you're sick of the escapade, and you're sick of him. You want it over with. You tell him you're tired, you want your sleep, you need time alone. You call it an evening, and the good-night kiss he insists on giving you at your door at the close of your second "date" is anticlimactic in the very best sense of the word.

12.

Juli Gets Out of the Pool

The conference convenes the next morning, Sunday, and you stand in line with the other conferees, your fellow parishioners in the publishing industry, waiting for the promised complimentary coffee and danish as if it were Communion. You feel someone pat your ass.

"Good morning, babe," Joe breathes in your ear.

You turn, he smiles, and for a moment you are blinded by the flash. You return his smile, despising yourself for your hypocrisy. You wonder what the rest of the conferees must think of the two of you, if they've even noticed.

But, of course, someone has noticed. Because someone always notices. There are no real secrets in this world. And, frankly, how humiliating that anyone should have watched such carryings on, dismissing you as trivial and unprofessional.

That wasn't at all how you had intended to present yourself. You had intended to be completely professional, dressed for success, and make the most of the opportunity at hand. Instead, all you'd done was run a long-distance errand as proxy for your bosses, scribble a few hasty notes, and get laid. So much for the pursuit of excellence. Your networking at the conference had involved just one other human being. The skills you displayed weren't at all the ones you meant to promote. Now Joe's salutary liberties are telling you all you need to know about how he views your interactions from the previous night.

By noon, you've had enough of this conference. You need to get out. You don't care where. Never mind the rest of the discussions, you can't focus your mind on them. You need to take a walk, clear your head.

As soon as the conference breaks for lunch, you bolt for the door. Joe follows.

"Juli, can I buy you lunch?"

"No. No, thanks. I've got errands to run."

"Well, let me tag along. I'd really like to talk."

You stop, stare at him, mentally kick yourself. Dammit, anyway. It's not his fault he isn't David. It's not his fault about anything in your life. You even rather like him. You wish you'd just had dinner together and let it go at that. Then you could have been friends. As it is, you pray you never see him again.

"I appreciate that, Joe," you tell him, trying to be gentle, "but I really want to be alone, okay?"

You don't wait for an answer. You turn and walk away. And very soon, though you don't look back, you know he is no longer following. A moment later, you are on the street, moving fast. You've made your getaway. Suddenly you feel buoyant. It's all over with!

You don't know your way around town, you don't know where you are going, but it doesn't matter. You have no special plans. The tourist literature you saw in the lobby suggests greater D.C. lies roughly east and south of where you are. That's enough.

Georgetown is clear and cool that day. Before long, you come to a woody spot and cross a small creek. Soon after, you find yourself in a traffic circle. Dupont, the signs read. Nearly a dozen streets shoot off in all directions like the rays of the sun. You are lost, but who cares? You pick a street, any street, keep going. The sign at the corner says New Hampshire Avenue. Joe's home state. Perfect.

Another traffic circle, then you sight water. The Potomac River. You head for it, looking forward to a walk along the bank. Having grown up on a coast alongside an ocean, being near water is a comfort to you. Or it could be a possible solution: you can always throw yourself in. You don't have to decide yet.

The Kennedy Center for the Performing Arts comes as a surprise. Around the bend from the Watergate Hotel, up a rise — suddenly it is there, so pure, dressed in white marble, eloquent and dignified with its simple classic lines. Theater, symphony, opera, film — the performing arts in all their finery are there. And the walls inside are hung with the artistic riches of the world's masters. Two great halls traverse the building and open onto the Grand Foyer, illuminated by eighteen crystal chandeliers, each one picking up and passing along its light to the next. The bronze bust of JFK — master performance artist on a different stage, the political arena — is huge and awe-inspiring.

You sit on a bench in the Hall of Nations. High up along the walls of that gallery hang the flags of many countries, many peoples. Yet the arts represented within that edifice are universal and eternal. You believe no one understands this better than David. This is what he had longed for, you feel certain, what he had wanted to be a part of. Not some shitty student play in the company's crummy small theater. How far off the track David has gotten. How far off the track you both have gotten.

Is it your fault your relationship has come to this? Maybe you shouldn't have gotten married. Maybe people in the arts shouldn't get married. Even the times were against it. You know this. After all, a couple who marries in their twenties swears a commitment that may have to span five decades or more. Who can predict what may happen between them in that stretch of time? Or even in the span of a few weeks? It's simply common sense to avoid making promises that can't be kept. Better to stay loose. Better to remain free.

You haven't been able to manage … staying loose, accepting freedom. That's been your problem all along. Now you hate the idea of being jealous as much as you hate actually being jealous. Even if you were. Even if you are. Even if you have what feels like reasonable cause for jealousy. Because it's not quite sophisticated nor open-minded, not in this day and age of Free Love and Open Marriage, to grill one's spouse about where the fuck he's been all night.

You remind yourself: jealousy and your inability to contain it cost you your Significant Other in college. On the wall of the first apartment you and David shared, you hung a little plaque on the wall to remind yourself to rein in your "problem." Mass-produced, the plaque was probably nailed to a hundred thousand other walls. It read:

I do my thing, and you do your thing.
I am not in this world to live up to your expectations.
And you are not in this world to live up to mine.
You are you, and I am I,
And if by chance we find each other, it's beautiful.

Well, alright. That's swell. Unless, of course, his "thing" is putting the rent up his nose every so often, when you least expect it. Or, unless "by chance," he finds someone else and "it's beautiful" with her instead. Frederick Perls, whose words were enshrined on that small plaque, had failed to cover those contingencies. Ann Landers covers them daily in the *San Francisco Chronicle*, but her advice to readers makes you uncomfortable. During one of your many moves, when David wasn't looking, you stuffed that damn plaque in the garbage. Right along with his Mr. Natural blacklight posters.

In the Hall of Nations, you sit and search your mind to recall a time before you and David got derailed, a time when everything was easy and painless between you, when you flowed together naturally with loving acceptance. You have to go back quite a ways to find what you are looking for.

Impressions sweep through you — of hillsides and shade-giving trees and a glittering City skylight and star fire, wind, and waves. This day in D.C. is dry and clear. Yet, for a moment, you catch the scent, hear the swoosh of traffic on wet asphalt. You recall a particular evening years past, even before you and David moved in together. You'd spent the day driving in the country. He'd opened his heart to you and filled your imagination with his wonderful dreams, his hopes, his plans for the future.

But you realize now: those were *his* dreams, not yours.

At sunset, the two of you drove into the City, the fog rolled in, and for hours you played together on Ocean Beach, falling in the sand, chasing black waves, wading out into the foamy surf until your feet were numb with cold.

He said you were beautiful. Beautiful. He was the first man ever to tell you that. Richard never had; he only had criticism for you — your long messy hair, your fat arms, your ugly bare feet. But David ... David said you were beautiful.

That night the two of you stayed at the apartment of a friend who lived on the Great Highway near the zoo and the old Fleishhacker Pool that had been closed for years. She was out of town, and you and David had the place to yourselves, making love till dawn. You recall how you'd opened your eyes in that silver-glowing room, where you and David lay together and looked up through the translucent, green-and-white striped leafy tendrils of the Wandering Jew plants hanging above you, swaying in their macrame hangers made of hemp twine. Dawn illuminated the rain-struck windows, and the thunder of surf came soft as a whisper. David's naked back was warm and comforting as he slept by your side. No man had ever satisfied you so thoroughly or appealed to you so completely. No man had ever seemed so determined to win your trust.

But maybe you shouldn't have gotten married. Everyone is always saying marriage was what had done them in. It's your fault, because you didn't want to let go of the good you'd once had together. You feel a twinge as you recall the cast party you went to in pastoral Mill Valley, across the Golden Gate Bridge, a few months after you and David started living together. You'd walked into the communal kitchen just in time to see David brush back a woman's hair from her cheek. A casual gesture. And the woman had smiled and closed her eyes for a moment with pleasure at his touch. Like a cat. You stood frozen in the doorway, unable to remember what you'd come to the kitchen to get. Whatever it was, you didn't get it.

But, in that moment, it seemed the two of you must commit yourselves for always or be lost forever. Just as an unallocated dollar is carelessly spent, just so easily could you and David be lost to one another. At least, that's the way it seemed to you. Then. So you began pressing to get married. And when Prince Charles and Lady Di got married that same summer, it had seemed like a good omen.

Now, when you consider your shared history, you wonder if, in those early months, you hadn't already used up all the good allotted to you as a couple? Maybe when the good has been spent, that's that. Could it be the only way to hold on longer is to let go? Have you become like the biologist's bottled specimen in its medium of formaldehyde — the life lost, but the form preserved for all time?

Once there had been no sadness between you. Once you were a fresh love. But months had passed into years with the struggle to go on living, and hurts had been heaped on top of hurts. David had promised you he'd never hurt you the way other men before him had hurt you. You believed him. But, as it turned out, he had different, more terrible ways of inflicting pain.

Yet he'd said, only days ago — you remember this plainly — he didn't want the two of you to break up. Then you believed him once again, and you clung to your belief. If he didn't want you to break up, there must still be a chance. You couldn't simply turn your back on what had been your life for so long. If you love, then you love. It's not your nature to run away. Something inside always stops you, turns you on your heel, sends you surging back.

By the time you hail a cab and return you to your hotel, it's late. Already dark. You retrieve your key from the front desk and find a message waiting. Joe again. He wants to know if you will dine with him again tonight. You crumple the note and drop it in the nearest standing ashtray filled with sand. You wonder how often the hotel has to sift the sand in order to keep it free of butts. You've already decided how you will handle the Joe situation: you never got that note, you aren't the least bit hungry, you are going home. All you want now is to go home.

Back in your room, you call the West Coast and let the phone ring half a dozen times. It's a long shot, and you're ready to hang up when, at long last, David answers.

"Hello?"

You are struck dumb. You did not expect him to answer.

"Hello!" he says again.

"David! You're home."

"Yes, I am."

"I wish I were home. I've missed you."

"I missed you, too."

"Really?"

"Of course."

The sound of his voice, those words — "I missed you" — are almost too good, too much to bear. Let Joe drag his sorry-ass conscience back to his wife and kids. You are going home.

"David, I need to talk to you. Something happened while

I was here."

"Don't tell me now."

"I want you to know: I understand some things a lot better than I did before."

"Please, not now. I can't hear it."

Silence falls between you, spreads out thinly in the intervening three thousand miles. Not much to say, after all, when you come right down to it.

"David, I'll be getting back into the City tomorrow around one or so. Will you be home?"

"I'll be home."

13.

Juli Learns the Whole Story

A month after you return from D.C. and during one of your marital weeks, you are less than pleased to discover that this time which is supposedly "yours" may not in fact be yours entirely. One night during your week, David stumbles through the front door around midnight (only an hour late, you consider), but half an hour later he goes out for a pack of cigarettes (or so he says) and returns after 3 a.m. You try to remain rational, and, in a level tone (modulated so as to avoid upsetting him), you ask the obvious question:

"And just *where* the fuck have you been?"

He hands you a load of bull about running into old friends again. And tonight it feels so much worse than, say, that other night when he claimed to have run into an old Army buddy in the liquor store, which you so desperately wanted to believe — please, God, let it be so! — and which at the time you *did* accept, in your pathetic, trembly way, because that transgression predated your new understanding of Mine and Thine within the framework of Open Marriage.

At least, you bought his story until he took off his Levis to go to bed and you noticed he was wearing his underpants inside out. Again. And when he pulled the covers up around himself, the air puffed forth a whiff of semen, along with ... the faint scent of Tabu perfume. Which you personally had not worn since 1968.

Turns out a successful working model of this sort of marital agreement is more complicated than merely throwing out a few ground rules to see if they will stick to your therapist's wall. It seems, between planning and execution lies a whole world of acknowledgment, followed by compliance. Then suddenly, it comes to you — the full meaning of the old adage:

> *You have not converted a man*
> *simply because you have silenced him.*

Worse, David's current spate of unexplained, short-term disappearances cannot be attributed to your known rival for his affection. The timing's not right. Not even if he caught a cab both ways. This realization, however, seems likely to lead you down a pathway you'd rather not follow. But you need to know the truth, so you ask, cautiously:

"It's not only Barbra, is it? It's not only Barbra you're seeing?"

When he glances up at you, you think you notice a ripple of surprise wash over his face. Is his expression tinged with a certain respect? Or is that fear in his eyes? Or are respect and fear the same thing for this man?

"No," he admits.

"So," you say, quietly advancing on him, "there are other women you see as well?"

"Yes."

"How many?"

"Dunno."

You can't understand his answer, so you request clarification, "What do you mean dunno? How can you not know?"

"I don't know. I don't keep count."

For a moment, you weigh this idea: he doesn't keep count. You consider the implications, sensing you have left behind simple arithmetic and entered the realm of algebra, which calls into play complex operations with exponents and other such mathematical mysteries. You feel the blood rushing away from your head; a wave of nausea sweeps through you. You take a deep breath to steady yourself. You effort to continue maintaining a low, even tone of voice.

"David. You mean to say you have lost count? Do you even know these women?"

He gives you a piteous look, and you realize you are on the verge of receiving yet-another manly confession.

"No," he admits, "mostly not."

In the hours that follow, you pursue an uneasy game of "20 Questions" that rapidly expands into "200 Questions." As late night arcs into early morning, you begin to form a mental picture of David's life outside this apartment, away from you. This vision so diverges from what you might have imagined on your own and feels so unreal that you forget to be hurt by what it implies for your relationship with him. You press for further clarification.

"So, you go to bars and other places, and you pick up women you've never met before, then you go somewhere, and you fuck them. Do you see them later?"

"Not usually."

"But sometimes you do?"

"Sometimes."

"And do you fuck anyone else? Have you fucked anyone we both know? My friends — have you fucked any of my friends?"

"Some."

"Yeah? Which ones?"

"The ones that let me."

Alrighty, that's putting it out there. And then, although you know better than to ask the next question, you also know you cannot stop yourself from asking it. You steel yourself and begin reciting the names of your female friends, both the mutual ones and those you had imagined were yours exclusively.

And somehow it isn't enough for you to elicit simply a nod or head shake. The narcotic effects of this conversation leave you wanting more and more information. Details, you've got to have details — when it happened, where they did it, what the circumstances were, where you were at the time. In fact, the whole subject has so excited your morbid interest that, without realizing it, you press harder and harder. Until finally he says:

"I don't want to talk about this any more."

"You have to."

"I don't."

"Why not?"

"Because what's the point? Anyone you could name, I pretty much fucked them. You'd just get upset."

"Do I sound upset?"

"Yes."

"Did you fuck them here in our apartment, in our bed?"

"If I had to."

"Why would you 'have' to?"

"If we didn't have anywhere else to go."

"Oh. And where was I?"

"At work. Usually."

Of course. And now you remember that mysterious case of body lice you picked up about a year earlier. The doctor asked if you'd gone camping recently. No, you hadn't. Then she asked if you'd been with any sexual partners other than your husband. No, you said, most emphatically. Then she asked if anyone had slept in your bed that you didn't know about. And you weren't too certain how to answer that one. Suddenly you remembered Kitty mentioning, around that same time, a supposed epidemic of body lice in the City.

No.

"Well, I don't want you to do that."

"Do what?"

"Fuck my friends. I don't want you fucking my friends. I'm not your pimp."

"Right."

"So, does that mean you won't do it anymore?"

"I don't know."

You consider that this conversation is not exactly reinforcing your faith in the institution of marriage. Not even in Open Marriage. You are still stunned by the enormous complexity of the situation. You wonder how all this can possibly work out. It suddenly occurs to you to ask another question:

"Does Barbra know you screw around?"

"No."

"Would she be okay with your being involved with other people? I mean, aside from your wife?"

"No."

"So, she wants to be in a monogamous relationship with you?"

"Yes."

"And she thinks she is getting that. Aside from your wife, of course."

"Yes."

"But you can't give her that, can you? So, why do you even pretend you can?"

David shrugs.

"What are you going to do when she finds out about all your other ... relationships?"

"Cross that bridge when I come to it."

"But why do it in the first place? You could stop. Aren't two women enough for you?"

He looks up from his hang-dog attitude and, to your surprise, declares flatly, "I could never give up the others."

"So, these others, these superficial relationships are more important to you than your marriage?"

He considers this idea briefly. "I guess so."

Which is the end for you, you just know it. But one question still hangs in your mind. You ponder how to present it.

"David, just one thing I don't understand. How do you have time to be married to me, carry on an affair with Barbra, pursue a lot of casual sex with all these other women, go to your job, fill in at the the theater, and still have a life? Don't you ever need some time to just sit and chill and be alone?"

David pauses before he answers: "I try never to be alone."

In the years to come, you will find yourself wishing you had asked, while you had the chance, why David finds his own company so unbearable.

A week later, you are still reeling from your newly enlightened understanding of his worldview. Only months ago, you'd imagined you had but one rival for your husband's love and attention. Back then, you believed you had reason for hope — you could win him back. One woman you can fight — but you can't fight them all. You can't fight every woman who comes along. Your friends, even.

Clearly, the situation is hopeless.

You wonder what comes next.

You suppose this means you are breaking up. Which also means you will be moving, because you cannot afford even this Lower Nob Hill-Upper Tenderloin apartment on your editorial assistant's salary. But where can you go? East and across the bay to Oakland to live with your father? Far north and into the boonies to live with your mother and stepfather? No, you are too old to "go home" again. That would be a step backwards.

Maybe one of your friends would put you up? But they hardly have space enough for themselves, much less you.

Fact is: you're on your own, you're not ready, and it's only a matter of time.

Realizing the end is near, you feel an upsurge of surprising tenderness towards this man you thought had married you. Though you don't know exactly when or how the marriage will end, your new certain knowledge that it *will* end puts everything else into perspective. Each small life-event could be the last such one the two of you will ever share. You want to savor each moment.

At the same time, you are beginning to feel clearer on what you need for yourself. When David first confessed his involvement with Barbra only a few months ago, you were ready to do anything, endure anything to hang on to your marriage. Nearly twenty years ago, your own parents split up and divorced — in your hubris, you supposed you could do better than they had. Now you are starting to weigh circumstances, to measure them and compare.

You are still in counseling with Hippie Marsha. You find her prescient to an amazing degree, considering you never really tell her anything. You decided, early on, you don't like her and you don't trust her. No particular reason, just a gut feeling that keeps urging you to keep it to yourself. Consequently, you are not ready with a prepared lie when she asks you, during one of your ménage à trois sessions, scheduled monthly, like menstruation:

"Juli, do you feel your perspective on your marriage has shifted somewhat?"

"Yes, I do." Dammit! you curse yourself for admitting the truth. Now she'll want details.

"Can you elaborate on that, Juli?"

David looks startled at the turn the conversation has taken. And you yourself wonder: am I about to break up my marriage? You back-pedal.

"Uh, no. Not really. I mean, I haven't thought it through."

"You don't need to overanalyze how you feel towards David right now. Just say what comes immediately to mind."

"Dirty rotten cheating bastard."

"Excuse me?"

"I said: Dirty. Rotten. Cheating. Bastard. He cheats on everyone with everyone else."

"And is this the way you see it, too, David?"

He shrugs. "I'd say that would be an exaggeration." He is as glib as always. But the look which, in that moment, passes between the two of them, your husband and your therapist — this does not escape your notice. And the focus and intensity of the glance they exchange excludes you entirely from consideration for the moment. You ponder what it could mean, already feeling light-headed and sick because, in your gut, you know full well what it means.

Suddenly, your time is up. You and David file out to leave. It's Monday evening again; Barbra's week starts tonight. You suppose David is eager to get back to the apartment, so he can pack a week's worth of clean underwear — the only thing clean about him — and rush back to her.

You and David are walking home from south of Market Street. You've gotten as far as South Van Ness, underneath a massive steel overpass in a world of warehouses and cyclone fences topped with barbed wire. Your counseling session was scheduled for right after your workday, and now it's dark, though not especially late. Consequently, you are surprised when, up ahead, you see three young men turn the corner, walking shoulder to shoulder, coming quickly toward you.

You understand: you are about to be robbed.

No one has said a thing. These men don't seem even to be looking in your direction. Yet, from half a block away, you receive their intention as swiftly and powerfully as if they'd sent you a personal telegram, telling you to watch out for them.

Up to the point when they'd turned the corner and began advancing on you and David, you were still talking, telling your philandering husband how awful he was making you feel. Now you shut up, slow down, hang back.

David, seemingly oblivious to the impending danger, glances back at you.

"What?" he says.

An instant later, they are on you.

You veer toward the street, mysteriously empty for the first time ever on a Monday evening in the City's history. But one thug gets ahold of the backpack that serves as your purse, and you fight him for it in a humorless, futile, dumbshow tug-of-war.

You look back at David and see the other two men are on him. They've knocked him down. He is on his hands and knees.

You scream. The man who's been fighting you for your pack starts punching you in the face.

Now screaming is the only thing you have to do. And because you understand you need to be the best that you can be at screaming, you focus all your attention on being as loud as possible. You draw breath solely so you can scream. Screaming is your whole life. You put everything you have into it. Tonight may be your last night on earth, but you will not leave here quietly — not before you have gotten the entire City's attention. You scream like the ocean, creating a tsunami of pure sound, pulling in vast breaths to power the wave.

You hear David scream, too — a ragged man-shriek of terror.

In a moment, your pack is gone from your hands and you have fallen onto the asphalt. The thief is running away, against traffic, toward the few cars that have appeared. His buddies are steps behind him, all running, a flock of flightless birds of prey.

David, still on his hands and knees, rises to kneeling in an attitude of prayer and supplication. You see the front of his white vinyl jacket, glowing in the dark under the cool, fluorescent street lamps: it is smeared with black liquid ... blood. And the crotch front of his button-up Levis is soaked as well. Astonished, you register that, in fear, he has wet himself. The two of you scream together.

Pity for him, along with sympathetic embarrassment for this unmanning event, shakes you, now silences you. Then you are afraid — was he stabbed? You didn't hear a gunshot.

When you struggle to your feet and stumble to his side, you can see the blood has all come from his nose, pouring down his face and dripping onto his jacket front.

A disabled couple appears before you. She is propped up in a motorized wheelchair, limp and sagging to one side; he walks awkwardly, flat-footed, with a quad cane wrapped in reflective tape. They are smiling, cheerful.

"You alright? What happened?" asks the guy.

"Muggers!" you choke out.

"We figured. Heard you screaming blocks away. We live just over there." He waves a bent, spastic hand in the direction of what appears to be a big warehouse. "Would you like us to call the police for you?"

"No, that's okay, we're okay," David says. He doesn't look okay, but you thank your two broken angels and head home, your usual burdens lighter for having been relieved of your backpack.

At the apartment, you realize your keys are in your backpack, and your backpack is, by now, probably in some Mission Street dumpster. You look to David, in the unlikely event that he could be carrying his own set of keys. He pats himself down, but finds nothing.

"No, really, I had them. In my jacket pocket, I'm pretty sure. They must have dropped out."

You are too upset to do more than nod and lean on the building manager's bell until he answers: a dignified older fellow of the sort who used to be referred to as a "colored gentleman." Daddy Ray, as he is known to his FM radio fans, is wearing an elegant, dark silk smoking jacket and ox-blood loafers. At first, he looks surprised to see you — David especially, blood-splattered as he is — but he recovers quickly and lets you into your apartment with his master key. Then he hands you a replacement key, which you suppose he must have had on file, and tells you, "This will be $2.75. I'll add it to your rent."

Your apartment has lately been the scene of so much unhappiness, but tonight it feels like a haven. You take note of your travel bag, still not unpacked more than a month after your trip to D.C. and still sitting in the hall by the door. For one surreal instant, you are confused about whether it is there because you just returned from D.C. or because you have yet to take that trip, even though you remember having done so.

You watch David shake himself out of his coat, arrange it carefully on a hanger, then hook it on the closet door and step back to admire it. You follow him into the living room where, a moment later, he is rummaging through the orange crate that serves as his chest of drawers here in your Tenderloin apartment. He sits on the coffee table to yank off his boots, then stands to drop his pee-soaked Levis and sodden underpants, step out of them, and replace them with clean, dry clothing. As you watch him do this, you notice that one of the knees in the Levis he'd been wearing tonight had gotten torn out during the mugging. He only has a couple good pairs of pants, so you suppose you are going to need to find a way to mend this ruined pair.

You realize that, for the first time in months, your sinuses are completely, totally clear. Such is the effect of a massive infusion of adrenaline.

You and David look at one another and burst out laughing. Both of you. Oh my god, still alive! We are still alive! You share this moment with your husband in a way you haven't shared anything for a long, long time.

Then you notice David is acting more like a man in a hurry to get out of town than a man whose life has just been spared. It occurs to you to ask:

"David, what are you doing?"

"Packing."

"For what?"

He responds with a meaningful inclination of his head that reminds you today is the beginning of another week with Barbra. Unfuckingbelievable.

"David, we could've been killed tonight. Doesn't that mean anything to you?"

David receives your question as rhetorical and makes no attempt to answer it.

"David, I'm your wife. I need you here with me tonight."

No answer.

"David, if you leave this place tonight, don't bother coming back."

He glances up at you from his orange crate with the faraway look of a man straining to see into his own future. Then he grabs *all* his clean underpants and crams them into his attaché case.

"Don't we keep some emergency money hidden in the apartment?" he asks. "I could really use cab fare."

14.

Barbra Victorious

Years of fishing without a license in other people's ponds have finally paid off: you caught a big one! And he is ... absolutely gorgeous! And yummy. And now every morning, you awaken with the first light, feeling the heat of his body at your back. You cannot believe your good fortune.

But, honey, it was no accident. People make their own good fortune, and you put out a lot ... of effort to make yours. All those calls to the wife. All your patient reeling him in, then pushing him away, then reeling him in again.

Only recently did you present your ultimatum: it had to be either you or that nagging wife of his — he must choose. A week later, he came to you with a compromise. He said he wanted to let her down easy. He said, from now through the end of the year, he'd spend alternate weeks with you. He promised, after the holidays, he'd move in for good. He told you he really loves you. He pleaded with you to accept him on these terms.

Not perfect, but close enough. You even rather respected his wanting to wean her off him. It meant you were right: he's basically a decent guy. Even so, no house key for him till he proves himself and "moves in for good."

How shocked you were to answer the door and find him standing there on your welcome mat — right on schedule, but with the front of his shirt under his denim jacket stained with blood.

"Oh my god! Are you hurt? What happened?!" You grabbed his arm, tugged him inside and kicked the door shut, led him down the hallway into the bathroom, and sat him on the edge of the tub, where he crumpled, passive and pale. And although you have always feared germs, the sight of blood doesn't bother you one bit. Growing up on a farm has some advantages. Plenty of times you've watched animals being sewn up with a needle and thread, or birthed, or slaughtered. You peeled David's ruined shirt off of him, ran warm water into the stoppered sink, sacrificed one of your best washcloths to his injuries.

Turned out he wasn't hurt badly. Bloody nose, black eye, a few minor cuts and contusions. He hadn't gotten shot, thank god. How lucky he was those criminals hadn't decided to use the knife they showed him. He was mostly just upset. You asked him to tell you again what happened:

He'd been seeing his wife back to her apartment after helping her shop for groceries, when five guys stopped them on the street and demanded money, his wallet. He immediately moved to defend himself and his wife — after all, he'd been a Marine — but there were too many of them, and one threatened him at knifepoint. Nevertheless, he tried to disarm his attacker and got punched in the face for his heroism.

"And your wife?" you asked.

"Just crying, upset," he said.

"And then?"

"They ran away," he said with a shrug. The robbery over, he'd collected the dropped, scattered groceries and escorted his wife home. Then he came to you. After all, your week together was scheduled to start that same night.

"Your wife accepted that?"

"She kicked me out."

Which was how you learned David was finally yours, all yours.

The two of you celebrated his newfound freedom and future success by spending your first week together in bed. You called in sick to be with him. And for a few days, he called in sick to his telemarketing job to be with you.

Thank goodness the run is over for that stupid show he was forever on-call to do. His "role" was just a walk-on with one line, and you'd hated the production from day one. Besides, a pretty sight he'd have made onstage: a butler with one black eye swollen shut. For the moment, you've even forgotten to be mad at him for missing his Friday night show on the closing weekend, which on impulse you'd attended in hopes of surprising him, remembering that his wife was out of town at a business conference that entire weekend. Vaguely you wonder if he'd really, truly been too sick to go on that night, or if.... But what the hell, he's here now and he's all yours.

You cannot remember ever in your life being so happy. When Loren calls, you make excuses to get off the phone as quickly as possible. When David leaves for work at Time-Life

Books, you still try phoning that woman he was married to. But the idea of waking her out of a sound sleep or yanking her out of the tub no longer gives you a kick. Besides, at some point, she stopped answering her phone. You realized: you can let it go, you don't need to do that any longer.

You'll be glad when he feels secure enough with you to quit his job hawking books over the phone. When at last he knows he can afford to accept an important role even if it doesn't pay enough to cover the rent. Telemarketing is just so ... beneath him. He needs to concentrate on his craft. In theater. Or movies. Or television. Just so long as he's on his way to becoming the star you know he was meant to be.

After your first besotted week together, when you both reluctantly returned to your respective jobs, you began bringing up the subject of him quitting his. After all, the two of you were living together now as a couple, so there was no reason for him to continue wasting time being underemployed in an area that offered him no opportunity to exercise his true talents.

Hearing your suggestion, he laughed and said, "You forget: I have a trained voice — big advantage in phone sales."

But then he got serious and asked you what you imagined he should do for money until stardom was conferred upon him. You told him you're happy to take care of him. You reminded him how easy it was for you to set him up with a running tab at the House of Shields, where he now always has a place to meet with industry VIPs who can help him in his career. You promised you'd start a bank account in his name and make sure it always contains funds for him to draw upon whenever he needs anything. By then, of course, he already had his own house key — *tu casa es su casa.* Now, you suggested, with no rent to pay, no utilities to cover, and no groceries to buy, all he really needs are decent clothes and enough cab fare to get to auditions.

You watched him consider your offer. Then he said, "I don't know, I have to think about this. You're so generous and kind (at which point, he leaned toward you to kiss the crown of your head), but I'm not sure I can accept your offer. A man needs to be able to hold up his end of the bargain. It's a matter of self-respect."

So you suggested he think about it. Your offer would stand. That was weeks ago.

Today, in the bedroom you now share with this beautiful man, you change out of your suit-and-heels work clothes into something loose, then absently glance at the clock on your nightstand: 4 p.m. You'd knocked off early, claiming a headache, in order to be with him, but he's not here. Even if they'd kept him an extra hour on his part-time shift, he ought to have been home by now. You try to recall whether he'd mentioned having any business after work. Nothing comes to mind. You wander back into the living room to check your answering machine for messages: nothing there.

Suddenly you realize your fib about the headache is real. Your left temple has begun to throb, and the pain is spreading, oozing under your skull. You rub the side of your forehead with the fingertips of your left hand, while massaging the thick cords in the back of your neck with your right hand. Tension.

Now you really have reason to wish David were home, because nothing cures a tension headache like a good orgasm. You suppose you could achieve the same effect by getting yourself off, but that's just so much trouble and you don't feel up to giving your dildo a bath before you start in.

So instead you head for the bathroom and rummage around in the medicine cabinet for those Darvons your ob-gyn prescribed for your painful menstrual cramping. You find the bottle with only two pills left. Enough for now, but you feel certain you'd left better than half a bottle in here. During your recent blissful haze, did you take most of your prescription without thinking? Did David take them? Surely he would have asked before taking someone else's prescription medication?

You stuff the remaining two pills in your mouth and swallow them with a quick blast of cold tap water captured in your cupped hands. Then you replace the last two Darvons with two unmarked generic aspirins and replace the prescription bottle with its useless child-guard cap in the medicine cabinet, reminding yourself to call the pharmacy for a refill. And when you get that refill, you will find a good hiding place for it somewhere else in the condo. Meanwhile, you vow to keep an eye on this little trap with its decoy OTC tablets.

15.

Juli's Lousy Week

Monday: Deep shit and you are in it. Only a few weeks ago, you were boarding a plane at Dulles Airport, eager to return home from your D.C. adventure. Only a few minutes ago, your building manager let you and David into your apartment with his loaner key, following your Frisco urban adventure. For once in your married life, the two of you were united in gratitude for simply being still alive after getting rolled on the street. Now David is gone, again, maybe forever, and you are alone. Again. No backpack, no bus pass, no husband, no nothing. Except the memories of your adventures.

You know you should be exhausted — in fact, you *are* exhausted — but this adrenaline high will not let go of you. You glance at your alarm clock, sitting vigilantly on your pathetic cinderblock-and-board bookcase: 7:50 p.m. You pace in a deflated, deformed circle from living room to kitchen to bathroom to living room, anxious and outraged as a caged tiger. Should you call the police? your mother? your father? a friend?

But what can the police or your folks do for you this evening, when you have become just another statistic to be added to this nation's dreary crime and divorce stats? You settle on calling a friend. You call Kitty. Though the last time you talked with her was B.D.C. — Before (Washington) D.C. — you feel no one else in the world is better able to appreciate the full extent of your loss right now. Especially when you will tell her that your pack contained the fetal manuscript for your "book." She picks up on the second ring.

"Hey! How was our nation's capital? Did you smoke dope with Nancy and Mr. T?" she asks cheerfully. Ugh, you think, momentarily reviewing the continuum of possible answers to her question, ranging from the truth in its raw, unedited state to that truth you feel comfortable with recounting. You hadn't realized, until now, just how much catching up you have to do with your old friend.

"Naw, I just 'said no.' D.C. was great. Or rather, it was stupid. Actually, it was great and stupid. All of the above. But that's old history. Tonight we got mugged. David and I, we got mugged."

"You okay?"

"Not really. I've got a bruise on the side of my face where the guy kept punching me. David bled a lot. I think maybe they broke his nose. But at least they didn't shoot us. One of them showed us a knife, but didn't use it. They got my pack, my Fast Pass, my keys. At least, they didn't get my ID, because I did the old wallet-in-my-boot trick. Landlord gave us a new key. Guess the locks will have to be changed. Guess I'll have to pay for that. My book, the one I told you about, what I've been trying to work on, that was in my pack. Oh yeah, and another thing: David left me."

"Yeah? So: some bad news, some good news — tell me more."

"Okay, but long story. In case you need to go to the bathroom or something."

"No, it's alright, I'm listening. I just went."

"Well, a while back he got involved with someone else, and we tried to work it out, but we couldn't, so now he isn't here."

"Never mind that creep, what about your book? Just kidding — where's the bastard now?"

"With her, I guess."

"And is he coming back, you think?"

"No, I don't. I mean, I don't really know. I told him when he left: don't bother."

"Good for you! You bettah off."

You appreciate the sentiment, but don't feel better off. Not yet.

"Juli, you've been putting up with his bullshit for way too long. The man's a dog."

Sensing more animosity toward David in your friend than sympathy for you, you are moved to ask her a question that's been nagging at you since the night of your long talk with David. He gave you an answer then, but you just didn't trust it.

"Kitty, did David ever ... I mean, did he ... um, ever 'try' anything with you?" Kitty had visited your apartment dozens of times over the past half-dozen years. A few of those times, after you and she had sat up talking and working too late for her to get safely home across town on Muni, she'd slept on your floor on cushions. David had usually been there as well, coming in late after a show and after the bars closed. You'd never noticed him acting in any way that could be interpreted as coming on to her. If anything, he mostly ignored her, even seemed to dislike her. And yet... .

"Well, I, um ... didn't you notice at some point I quit coming over?"

"Uh, no. I didn't. I guess I didn't think deeply about it. What'd he do?"

"Okay, well, there was this one night after you'd already gone to bed. I was still awake and reading when he got home. You were asleep, I guess. Then he came in, sat down next to me, and started kissing me and putting his hands on me. So I told him to stop, and he did. That was it."

"Was that the only time?"

"Yeah. And once he dropped by my apartment unannounced — 'just in the neighborhood,' he said, needed to use the bathroom, whatever — and while we were talking, I got the feeling ... you know that feeling you get the moment you hear a rattlesnake buzzing in the grass next to your leg, right before it strikes? So I told him he had to leave because I had work to do."

"But nothing happened?"

"Nope. That was it."

"How come you never said anything to me? At least about his coming on to you right here in our apartment?"

"Okay, please don't get mad at me for saying this, but I thought maybe you were aware of the situation and had one of those 'open' relationships. Who knew you were such a sound sleeper? Anyway, he said you two had an agreement, that it was okay with you. But I can't stand the man — never could — so it certainly wasn't okay with me. Anyway, I thought, even if you did know and it wasn't okay, what could you do about it? He's such a horn dog."

You are grateful to your friend for repulsing your horn-dog husband, but can't help wishing she'd mentioned it before now. Would you have kicked him out because of it? Maybe, maybe not, but you really feel you would have looked differently at your so-called marriage and come to different decisions. As it is, you now see plainly you've been living in uneasy ignorance for years, unknowingly pimping your best friend to him. You feel like a fool.

"Juli?"

"Yeah."

"Should I have said something to you? I didn't know what to say."

"No, I get why you didn't. I just hate finding out I'm such an idiot."

"You're not. Married people are supposed to be able to trust one another. That's why I'm not married and why I'll never get married, no matter how much some guy tells me he loves me and wants me. You're not supposed to have to hire a private detective to follow your man around to make sure he's telling you the truth when he comes home late."

"I guess."

"It's him, Juli, not you — he's the idiot. Love is not supposed to be this hard. The good news is now you're free to find that out for yourself."

And the bad news is you can't imagine how you will ever find anyone else to love you when you have such contempt and disgust for your own self.

Tuesday: Last night, Monday night, your first official night of being truly, completely alone, you were too jacked up to sleep. The best you could manage was to stretch out on your sticky foam mattress and lie there, fully dressed and jittering, with every light in the place blazing. Shortly after dawn, you are roused by the sounds of the cars illegally parked in front of your building being chained to City-owned tow trucks, hoisted up, hauled away. That's what happens when you overstay your welcome — you lose everything.

Unable to think of what else to do, you shower, dress, and head for work. You must walk most of the way to work because you have no Fast Pass and you won't have bus money until you reach the financial district, where your bank has recently installed one of those new ATMs that lets you withdraw cash 24/7 even when the bank is closed.

You walk into work at five minutes to eight, right behind the receptionist, beating in every other editorial person that day. Then you spend eight joyless hours photocopying manuscripts with all their editorial flags. Several people ask you about the bruise on your jaw. You enjoy their looks of horror when you are able to tell them that gray-green spot is where a mugger punched you last night. Weeks ago, no one, not even the two production editors you support, asked you about your trip to Washington, D.C., the first business trip of your life. It was like it never happened.

Because you started your workday at 8 a.m., ate stale donuts from the break room while camped at your desk in lieu of taking an actual lunch, and everyone feels sorry for you that you were the victim of a violent crime, they didn't ask you to stay late — you are free to leave work at 4 p.m. You rush home and walk in at 5:10, carrying jug wine, a carton of smokes, and a crummy meatball sandwich on a hard roll that cuts up the roof of your mouth. You stay put, wait for David to call. He never does.

⋙⋘

Wednesday: You spend all day proofing the galleys for the first 50 pages of a 350-page manuscript that seems so confused you can't even tell what the book is about. On any "normal" day, you should easily be able to handle 10 to 12 pages an hour. On this day, every time you sit down to the manuscript, your freshly sharpened no. 2 pencil in hand, your mind goes blank. When you glance up at your wall clock, the time is miraculously half an hour later, and you are still on the same page, still holding your pencil at the ready with no idea of where you've been.

You are home by six. David doesn't call. Okay, it's her week, but if he cared how you are, how you are doing after your shared trauma, he would call. He doesn't call. Instead, the Mystery Caller calls, three times, and hangs up each time you answer. The second time, you came hobbling out of the bathroom with your pants around your ankles, only to pick up the receiver, breathlessly answer, and get hung up on. It just kills you. He's leaping around in her bed, soiling her sheets, washing his dick in her sink, and you don't even get a moment's peace in which to take a shit.

⋙⋘

Thursday: You proof up to page 154 of what has turned out to be a social history of U.S. imperialism in the Pacific written by that fucking know-it-all, Dr. Jesus Agonoy-Bugas. The same Dr. Jesus H. Christ! Agony Bug-Ass you knew in college. That bastard. And you thought he wrote only fiction. It just kills you that this season your house is publishing not one but two books by that smug, misogynistic POS. You get home by 6:45. David doesn't call. Someone else calls and hangs up a couple times. You have already figured out your Mystery Caller must be that whore Barbra, still tormenting you, but you can't understand why. She got what she wanted.

You can't see how any of this is ever going to get any better. All you can see ahead of you is a long, lonely life. You wish you had never been born.

❧

Friday: Page 232. Home by 8 p.m. When you retrieve your mail from the bank of boxes in the lobby, you find your building manager's notice of this month's rent, due this coming Monday, along with two new keys for you, one for your apartment and one for the building's front door. You also find an invoice for re-keying your apartment door lock and the building's street door — as well as for making 28 new front door keys for everyone in every apartment. Additionally, he has included a handwritten note reminding you that you still owe for last month's rent, as well as a week's worth of rent for the month before that. You have no idea how any of this is going to get paid. The paycheck you got today is not enough to cover the entirety of this month's rent, never mind all the rest. If you had any savings, you wouldn't be in this mess. Ordinarily, you would have extracted what you could from David. Except, of course, he is not here to be extracted from.

You don't want to do it, but you are going to have to call him at Barbra's.

The building's elevator is stuck again, so you trudge from the lobby up the carpeted stairs to the third floor, let yourself in with your new key, throw down your purse, rummage in the cabinet under the sink, throw back a couple shots of Dutch courage from David's remaining stash of vodka. After a few moments of rehearsal ("Hello, this is David's wife — would you please put David on the phone?"), you call the number you insisted he leave with you in case of an emergency and which you then cross-checked against months and months of past phone bills, searching for the point of origin of David's extramarital diversion.

Of course, she answers. So humiliating. Your hands are shaking, and you have to read your line from the script you wrote for yourself in order to keep from flubbing it after your mind goes blank, as you knew it surely would.

"Hello, this is David's wife — would you please put David on the phone?"

You have only a moment to wonder how David could ever have gotten involved with a grown woman who sounds like a six-year-old on the phone, when David himself comes on the line. He tells you you sound terrible. You thank him; you suppose you do sound awful. You explain the situation. He tells you he doesn't have any money. You are incredulous. Your conversation has become the aural equivalent of a cement-block wall one mile wide and thirty feet tall.

"That's it, David? That's all you have to say: you don't have it? So what am *I* supposed to do?"

Silence from his end. Then he offers: "Don't worry, it'll be alright. Everything will be alright. You'll think of something. You always do."

Coming from him, at this time, in your present predicament, this statement sounds like criticism. Criticism with a subtext of mockery. You slam down the receiver, pick up the entire phone, heave it away from you as far as the cord will reach. The phone hits the floor smartly, tinging in surprise. Its parts separate upon impact, then lie there, spread apart. You crawl on your hands and knees toward the off-the-hook beeping, snatch up the receiver with its curly pig-tail cord, and slam it down hard, again and again with all your might, onto the body of the phone.

Fuck! Fuck-fuck-fuckity-fuck-fuck!

You realize you have hurt your hand, so you stop hitting the phone. You think maybe the phone is broken now, because no sounds are coming out of it. But this could be a good thing — no more Mystery Caller. Also, you won't have to know that David didn't call you back.

However, your rage is by no means assuaged. In frustration, you ball up your fists, pound them against your thighs, hurting yourself some more. Then you press your fists hard against your temples, take a deep, shattering sob, and cry like you are five years old and broken-hearted to have come home from kindergarten and found your hamster dead in his cage. Those stiff little pink feet. You notice your wedding ring when it cuts into your brow, so you yank it off and, with all your strength, throw it away from yourself. You hear it hit the wall on the far, dark side of the room.

As soon as you smell burning coming from the kitchen, you jump up and run for it. You forgot: before you called

David, you put your dinner on the stove to heat — some kind of red-colored bouillabaisse from the deli. Now the fishy stew has overflowed its banks, run down the sides of the pot and onto the stove iron, pooled in the burner pan, charred the pot's interior. The seafood stink in your tiny kitchen is terrible. You flip off the burner.

Meaning to transport the ruined pot and meal from stove to sink, you grab its handle and lift. But smelly fish stew has glued the stove iron to the pot's bottom, giving the whole affair unexpected weight, and the handle is fiercely hot, burning your hand. Howling in pain, you drop the stuck-together pot and stove iron, which hit the floor and separate, splashing globs of boiled-down fish stew across the floor and splattering the wall. You grab an oven mitt and, in frustration, snatch up the still-hot stove iron and lob it hard, like a discus. It hits the wall above the stove and gouges a surprisingly deep hole in the plaster, then falls to the floor again, breaking in two.

Instead of wine with dinner, you decide on wine *for* dinner.

You feel you have come to the end of your rope. You just hope he gets the wet spot. You hope her toilet overflows. You hope his rash flares up and his hemorrhoids bleed. You hope she breaks her leg getting out of bed. You hope the Big Quake strikes this very night and brings this whole lousy, rotten, ugly, stinking City to the ground and everyone with it. Because you are sick to death of trying to be open and honest, sympathetic and patient, loving and mature and understanding and ... adult about this colossally outrageous treatment when you are in pain, goddammit, and nobody gives a shit.

You're glad you broke the phone. The stove iron, too. So there.

Some time later, you are absently studying the map of cracks in the ceiling above your marital bed when the thought comes: I should eat something. You roll onto your hands and knees, lurch to your feet, stagger into the kitchen, yank open various cupboards ... nothing.

No, wait — in one cabinet, pushed toward the back, there is something. A box of uncooked stovetop stuffing. In your effort to snag the box, you knock over your spice rack. Little jars hit the floor and roll in all directions. You grab the box of stuffing, hold it close to your face, and consider its grainy, funny-pages photograph of a fully roasted turkey, lying on a platter and presumably stuffed with the contains of this very box. Or, rather, another box just like this one. Good enough. You carry your provision back to bed with you, haphazardly tearing off the box's cardboard top and using your teeth to rip apart the plastic pouch within. You grab handfuls of the dry, unseasoned contents to fill your mouth. You are short on spit tonight and swallowing is tough.

On one of your semi-conscious trips to the bathroom, you think: I should take a bath. So you plug the drain, run the faucet, stare into the tub as it fills, then peel off your work clothes. You ease your naked self into the hot water. You reach out and pull the shower curtain around the tub to create a humid, makeshift womb. You sit in your quiet, steaming sanctuary and listen to the plunk-plunk-plunk of a diminishing stream of drops into the bath.

On the edge of the tub, alongside the wall, is David's razor — the old-fashioned kind that unscrews open to receive a double-sided blade. You recall David prefers to shave while standing in the shower. You suppose, by now, he must have another razor that stays at Barbra's house. So, then, this one … must be yours.

You pick up the razor, play with it, turn the nut on the handle to expose the blade. You dump the blade into the palm of your hand and close your fingers around its sharpness. Just tight enough to hurt a little. You consider how easy it would be to end all your troubles right here, right now, with the tools you have on hand. This tub filled with nice warm water would be the perfect place to do it, because you are relaxed and comfortable, and the mess you will leave will be easy to clean up later — nothing for you to feel guilty about.

You can't remember exactly how long it takes for a person to bleed out, but you think it happens pretty fast. You remember, in order to do it right, you are supposed to cut along the veins, not across them. You take up the razor in the prune-tipped fingers of one hand and make a tiny experimental nick in the pale skin of your wrist. Blood comes. A tiny amount hardly enough to be called drops. You press your wrist to your mouth and lick the wound. The blood tastes metallic. Like sucking on the edge of a cast iron skillet.

You are surprised by how quickly idle musing can gather itself into an impulse, then be transformed into … planning. Startled by this sudden self-knowledge, you drop the razor, see it sink to the bottom of the tub.

While fumbling after the submerged razor, which scoots away from your pawing, you imagine your building manager entering your apartment with the police and discovering your naked body, pallid and drained in dark water. You realize your corpse might not look (or smell) too good after a couple weeks with no one checking on you. You imagine the reactions of your friends, your parents. You wince to think how angry and disappointed in you they will be. Maybe they won't even give you a decent send-off.

David, on the other hand, will finally see how badly he has hurt you. Then he'll be the one to feel guilty and sorry. Besides, you'll be dead and gone, past caring what anyone else thinks.

Having retrieved the razor, you examine your wrist where you nicked it. The bleeding has stopped, so you take a deep breath and hold it, preparing to reopen and enlarge the cut. Practice makes perfect. Just a little pain for now and never again.

A sudden hammering at your front door startles you. The wet razor slips a second time from your wet fingers. Dammit! Now what? You think: can't even kill myself in peace.

16.

Bill Saves the Day

Y ou stand in the dim and musty hallway of David and Juli's ancient apartment building, knocking, lightly but persistently, on their door. It seems like a good ten minutes pass before you hear anything on the other side that might be a sign of life. Every so often, you call her name. But you do so as softly as you can manage, because though it's Friday evening, it's also almost midnight.

"Juli! Juli!" you whisper-shout into the crack where door meets frame. You are close enough to kiss the wood. You press your ear against the door and listen hard. The muffled crash you hear within the apartment suggests something large and heavy must have just gone over, confirming the presence of an occupant.

"Who's there?!" Juli shouts back at you. She sounds choked, hoarse.

"It's Bill — open up!"

"Dave's not here!"

"I know: he sent me."

Several moments pass in silence before you hear the door chain unhooked, the automatic deadbolt disengaged, the Victorian-era oval door knob turn. When the door opens, Juli is so backlit by all the lights blazing away in the apartment that you see her only as a dark silhouette, looking ninja-like. She backs away, opening the door as she retreats, wide enough to allow you to pass inside.

Standing in the hall of your old friend's studio apartment, a stench of fishy-smoke hits you like a fart from a garbage truck. You survey the wreckage: coat rack toppled over with clothing splayed out across the hall floor, mattress on the living room floor with sheets and blankets scraped into a tangled heap, scraps of cardboard and handfuls of croutons confettied about, the telephone lying in pieces.

"Good party?" you comment.

"You so funny," she replies. But she's not laughing.

"You know, Juli, I've been calling and calling for several hours, but I always get a busy signal. I guess your phone's not working?"

You both glance toward the broken, silent phone. "That's right," she says, "it's not."

Now that your old friend's wife is out of the shadows, you see you were right to come over here in person. Because she looks just as awful as David said she sounded on the phone. Her hair is wet in strips around her face and stuck to her forehead. Her face looks puffy, and there are greenish circles under her eyes. You suspect she is drunk. She is wearing David's rotting old military coat as a bathrobe, and it's soaked in places. She is bare-legged and barefoot. You realize you must have gotten her out of the tub.

You notice she is pressing a washcloth to her left wrist.

"Something the matter with your hand?" you ask.

"Hurt myself a little," she tells you.

"Let me see."

She whips away the washcloth with a magician's ta-da! flourish and holds out her forearm and hand to be examined. You note the tiny cut along the vein on her wrist. It's not very big, and if there was any bleeding, it has stopped. But still. You've worked in Social Services long enough to know a deranged person when you see one.

"Mistake?" you ask.

"I think so."

"Planning any more mistakes?"

She shrugs and changes the subject. "You said David sent you."

"That's right."

"How does that work?"

"He called me, said he talked to you on the phone this evening, said you were in some kind of trouble, that you were very upset. He said he wasn't able to make it home to check on you, so he asked me to do it."

She tosses you a look like you are a pile of excrement extruded by the lowest possible defecating lifeform on the planet, and she has just stepped in you. But when she speaks, you realize her look is not intended for you, the messenger — it's for David. "Did he tell you why he isn't able to come home and check on me himself?"

"No. He asked me, and I said I would."

"Aren't you a prince," she says. But she does not sound particularly grateful. "It's a guy-thing, I guess — no questions asked?"

"I suppose. Lissen, I've kept my promise: I checked on you, and here you are. Now, if you'd rather go back to whatever you were doing before I got here, I can just... ." You make the universal, thumb-over-shoulder gesture for "I'll be going now."

She stands staring blankly at you, so you try again. "Or, if you'd rather, I can stay awhile, and we can talk about it."

She nods and says, "C'mon in — pull up a chair." You understand the invitation, as stated, is intended to be humorous, because (a) you are already inside and (b) there are no chairs in this apartment and never have been. And so it is that you receive, from your old friend's wife, a firsthand view of your old friend's re-arrangement of his marriage.

The dirty rat. You can see how Juli might be hard to live with at times, but that's no excuse. She slurringly outlines what's been going on between them, including their recent experimentation with "Open Marriage."

"I assumed that'd always been your agreement," you say.

"So I'm told," she replies cryptically.

"But that wasn't the case?" you venture.

She shakes her head and bites her lower lip. You can tell she wants to cry, but is unwilling to let you see her.

You realize you have come to a point in this discussion where only two choices are left: either go in deeper or back out and start over. Your Social Services-honed instincts tell you to opt for the latter.

"What did you have for dinner?" you ask.

"Dunno. Nothing, I think. Dinner got wrecked."

You get up from your seat on the floor and make the very short trip into the kitchen to see what might be there that you could work with. The pattern of destruction first evident in the hallway and living room continues into the kitchen. The refrigerator door is hanging open; you shut it. The cabinet doors are all open as well; you shut them. Your toe connects with something that rolls away from you; you look down and note spice jars scattered at angles around the floor.

To your left in the sink is a smelly pot of burned goo, topped off with water from the tap. To your right on the tiny, three-burner stove, one of the burner pans is filled with more blackened goo, and the stove iron is missing. Looking up and over to the narrow space between stove and fridge, you see a large gouge in the wall. When your eye travels down from the gouged wall to the floor, you spot the missing stove iron lying there, broken in two, sprinkled with plaster chips and dust. Your thirty-second survey of the room is more than long enough to determine that nothing here can be even remotely considered food.

"Well," you call back to Juli in the living room, "I see you haven't lost your sense of humor."

You wander back to the living room, where Juli sits on the floor, enveloped in David's Army coat. Her hair is dry now and looks worse than ever. "I believe we'll be dining out tonight," you tell her. "Why don't you get dressed? Clown Alley awaits."

Good ol' Clown Alley — open 24 hours and located roughly a dozen blocks away from David and Juli's apartment, in the borderlands between the Financial District and North Beach. If right now were daytime, it would be in the shadow of the TransAmerican Pyramid. You decide the two of you can walk there. The hike will sober her up. On the street, you take Juli by the arm and help her to practice her walking. You steer her down Bush Street, past Chinatown's Dragon Gate, hang a left on Kearney, stagger past Portsmouth Square, all the while keeping a good grip on your ragdoll-wobbly charge.

"Whoa-oh!" she exclaims as you pull her through a sharp right turn at Columbus.

"Are you gonna puke?" you ask, stopping and pushing her away to arm's length, just in case.

"No, I'm good, I'm good," she replies, then starts panting like a dog going for a ride on the freeway with its head hung out the window.

And suddenly you are arrived.

Better take a cab back, you think. Gravity helped you get her down here, but it won't help to get her home again.

Good ol' Clown Alley — there on the pie-wedge corner of Columbus Avenue and Jackson Street, with its old-timey lettered sign atop a hokey barbershop pole and its stripy awning announcing B-U-R-G-E-R-S and C-H-I-L-I. You've been dining in this dive since you arrived in San Francisco in the late '60s and began searching for a way to satisfy the 3 a.m. munchies. Over the years, you've seen at least half your welfare regulars in here. One night, you couldn't get in at all, because they were filming that TV series, *The Streets of San Francisco*. You spotted the actor Karl Malden, playing detective Mike Stone, waiting in the walled-off al fresco dining area to be called for his scene.

Safely inside, at long long last, you steer Juli around a red pole and plunk her down at a table near the wall, then slide into a seat across from her to watch her. She is propping up her face with her hands, while sinking slowly toward the speckled Formica tabletop.

"Did you polish off that whole bottle of vodka I saw on the counter?" you ask.

"Yep."

"And the jug wine, too?"

"Not all of it."

You watch her eyeballs roll in their sockets, as if she is following an invisible Indy 500 taking place somewhere behind you. You hope the coffee you ordered does some good. You hope the whirlies don't get the best of her in the meantime.

Over grease-ball burgers, you prod Juli with questions till she drunkenly blurts out the rest of her story: the mugging at the start of the week, which David had not bothered to mention to you; her inability to concentrate at work; the overdue rent and extra charges for changed locks and new-made keys.

"Perhaps it's time for you to bag it," you suggest.

"You mean ... move out?"

"Exactly."

"But ... I can't."

"Why not?"

"Lotsa reasons. Where'd I go? Can't pay rent now, first and last, cleaning deposit — can't afford anything. Anywhere. Lotta stuff. To move. David, what about him? I move, that's it for sure for us. Bye-bye. Like, forever."

"Sounds as though you've already come to the end and just haven't noticed."

"No. Not true. Next week ... that's my week." She flat-hands the table for emphasis.

"Juli, listen to what you're saying. He is living with someone else."

She looks up at you with the expression she would give

someone who told her she just ate a dead-kitten burger. Then her face crumples, she buries her head in crossed arms on the table, and sobs loudly. You feel as guilty as if you'd ground up those kittens yourself.

"Jeez, I'm sorry, Juli, but it's simply the truth. You can't keep the worst from happening after it's already happened. And there's no point pretending it didn't happen."

"I know!" she wails and goes back to her sobbing. Other customers in the place glance up — first at her, then at you. You shift uneasily on your hard plastic chair. What if they think you are the one who's making her cry? Across the room sit two dyke punks with prison-chic shaved heads and makeup designed to simulate post-apocalyptic chemical burns and bruises. They are holding hands and glaring at you for what you're doing to Juli. Huge clowns, laughing luridly, sneer down at you from the walls.

You remember that a "clown alley" is circus slang for a real thing — the big-top backstage area where clowns change their costumes, put on their makeup, keep their props. You remember this area is traditionally set up near the animal pens.

You want desperately to be helpful, to be constructive, to be positive. So you try a different tack:

"Alright then, don't you think it's time to make a plan? Then you'll know where you're going, and things won't just keep happening to you."

You feel certain now you are on solid ground, because you are in full-out counseling mode, and you are great at planning ... for others. Too bad you can't manage to do it for yourself. No matter: on this night, you aren't the one in need of a plan.

Under the fluorescent lights, she squints at you like you're a road sign whose words she can't quite make out. "Yeah, okay, well ... where do I start, Mr. Smarty-Pants-Know-It-All?"

As a professional, you have been trained to ignore client sarcasm. "You start with yourself, Juli. Try to think about what you really want."

17.

Juli Makes a Plan

You will find, in later years, you'll have to work hard to remember your last few days here on Bush Street. You will find your most persistent memory will be of watching pallid, shifting downtown light fading to murky darkness tempered by street lamps, which you observe while lying on your back on the floor, fully awake and with every intention of turning on your own lights inside the apartment, yet somehow unable to make yourself do so. You lie there passively, watching smoky half-light pouring through dusty blinds, wondering whether an old day is departing or a new day is starting up.

Church bells reach you from afar. The renewed rush of traffic down Bush Street past your building confirms what you have been suspecting since you returned to consciousness: it must be morning. Sunday, perhaps?

You roll onto your hands and knees, then push yourself up to standing. You pause to steady yourself, noticing you are fully dressed, except for shoes. You urge yourself in the direction of the bathroom to relieve your painfully full bladder.

Christ, what a mess! you think as you journey through the apartment. In the bathroom, the tub is full of water, the shower curtain half-yanked from its pole. You stick your fingers in to test the water, judge the elapsed time — stone cold.

Now that you have achieved auto-pilot mode, you stagger toward the kitchen (coffee-seeking behavior), where you find more ruins: an unsettling mess on the stove, more mess in the sink, jars of spices on the floor, rolled into every corner.

A big hole in the wall behind the stove surprises you. You have a vague memory of having made it. You spot the broken stove iron on the floor. You wrangle a fresh pot from out of a lower cabinet, blast water into it, set it on one of two remaining useable burners, fire it up. Instant coffee will do.

In the hallway leading to the front door, you see that the coat rack, heavy-laden with every possible type of outer garment, has toppled over. As you are setting it upright, it dumps its load of pants, shirts, sweaters, umbrellas, and a camera bag onto the floor. Later for that, you think, kicking separate items into a communal heap.

You pass the front door and notice an envelope has been shoved through the crack at the base of the door. You snatch up the envelope, hold it close to your face, shred it open, using your finger as a letter opener. It contains a note scribbled on a lined page torn from a pocket-sized spiral notepad and a personal check for $15. Both are from the old woman who lives in the apartment next door. You remember she works as a hospice nurse. The note reads: "Baby, don't cry, I love you."

You've met this woman face to face exactly once during the two years you and David have lived here, but suddenly you receive an impression of how many nights she must have sat in her own apartment on the other side of your shared wall and overheard you fighting with your husband. And, later, sobbing all alone. The tidal wave of guilt and shame that follows this realization washes in recent memories you have been evading since you awakened this morning: your horrible week without David, your failures at work, all that bad news about the rent, the humiliation of having to call David at his mistress's home, followed by the even greater humiliation of being dismissed by him.

Like you were nobody. Like you weren't the person he was fucking married to.

And now you also recall a somewhat blurry sequence: how you destroyed the phone, how you wrecked the apartment, how you got into the tub, how you mentally rehearsed ending it all. It had seemed like such an easy out. Now time has passed in your Universe of One, and it all feels like a bad dream. You remember how you came home Friday with such a nice dinner for yourself, that wonderful deli bouillabaisse, but through inattention and sheer stupidity, you wrecked your fish stew and never got to eat it. The boozy memory of your ruined repast feels like a solid punch in the gut. You start to cry, inconsolable over your loss.

You are still sniveling as you return-shuffle back into the kitchen to stir two giant teaspoons of stale instant coffee into tepid water. Then what happened Friday night? You had company. Someone came to see you, one of David's friends — his scruffy friend, Bill. In fact, he said, David had sent him. This small sympathetic gesture by the man you married seems to suggest the possibility of better times ahead for your relationship. But as you mentally reach for this fragile hopeful sign, it wafts away from you and is gone.

Bill was here. He made you get dressed. He made you walk to Clown Alley. That nasty, freaky place. He bought you dinner. Then somehow he managed to get you back home without your barfing your burger into the gutter. He made you lie down on your bed. He took off your shoes and spread a comforter over you. He switched off the lights in the apartment. Then he ... left, letting the door lock behind him.

Jeez, you think, if today is Sunday — those church bells! — all you are efforting to recall happened a day and a half ago. Now what? Where did Saturday go?

You remember Bill tried to tell you something important. You struggle to remember what he said: make a plan. You are supposed to make a plan. Then you'll know where you're going and things won't just keep happening to you.

Great in theory, something else in practice. On the other hand, what else do you have to do today? You rummage through the bookshelves till you find a ballpoint pen and a lined yellow pad. Then you lie on the floor on your stomach and contemplate the empty page, clicking and releasing the pen's tip over and over in order to build up to some words.

What else did Bill say?

He said: start with yourself.

He said: ask yourself, what do you want?

"I want to —

(1) Get David back, save marriage.

(2) Pay rent, other bills.

(3) Clean up apt.

(4) Buy new phone."

You chug a mouthful of room-temperature instant coffee

and ponder your list. When you write it out like that, it looks dead simple.

Or maybe, just plain dead. Because how do you *plan* to make someone love you again and want to be with you, only you? How do you *plan* to make your husband give up his lover? How do you *plan* to pay the rent and bills when you have no money? How do you *plan* the wonderful, fulfilling life that everyone else seems to expect of you when all *you* can see ahead for yourself is the same bleak and blasted landscape that lies behind you?

That therapist David found — that Marsha! — *she* said wanting to save your marriage was not a realistic goal. But, you reason, she doesn't know David as well as you do, and she certainly doesn't know you. Tomorrow is Monday — *your* day to have David back again. Besides, you and David have been together for years. You are married. How can he throw away all this for someone he's known only a few months?

This realization infuses you with an optimism that seems to support your decision — your *plan* — to save your marriage. Only in later years will you wonder why, when you asked yourself, "What do I really want?" — the answer never came back as simply: I want to be happy. All I want is just to be happy.

18.
Juli's Plan B

How strange it feels, after your lost weekend, to be back at work: the darkened reception area furnished with faux-ebony, the new carpet off-gassing poisons, the long, fluorescent-lit hallways, the glass-fronted cubicle offices — all those zoo terrariums housing various human subspecies evolved to survive in the modern world's publishing environments, including your own *Homo editorus servos* var. *productivae*. The two days you were away seem like two years. So much you cannot recall!

Everything is as you left it, including the still-not-completely-proofread galleys of Dr. B's social history of U.S. imperialism in the Pacific. As you review the galley proofs up to the place where you left off last week, you have to admit your painful experiences this weekend do pale in comparison to the daily terrors of those unfortunates living under martial law in a dictatorship characterized by corruption and brutality. But the upwelling of sympathy you feel for this author and his countrymen fades as you recall how demeaning, how arrogantly dismissive he was of the life difficulties faced by you and your peers in college. It wasn't your fault you were born where you were born, then "coddled in American suburbs for twenty years." Were his experiences more valid than yours just because he'd suffered more?

One of the two production editors you support stops outside your cubicle, taps on the glass, then slides the door aside to insert her head. "How you feeling this morning?" she asks. You understand at once she is checking on your degree of recovery from being mugged last week. She has no idea whatsoever that the domestic abuse you suffered since then has quite eclipsed the aftereffects of a mere banal street crime.

"Just fine," you answer, forcing a smily-face. "Thanks for checking."

"I hate to ask it of you, under the circumstances," your production editor goes on, "but I really need to send out the Agonoy-Bugas galley corrections by this day's end. So, I'd appreciate it if you'd get everything to me as soon as you finish proofing."

"Gotcha," you respond, your heart sinking as she slides shut your enclosure and you mentally calculate the time you will need to proof the final 118 pages of this manuscript against the galleys. Even if today were a day when you were able to focus, the odds in your favor are not good.

The thing is, you have other business to take care of, other personal business that cannot wait. You need to make a few phone calls — a thing you cannot do at home right now — and see if you can track down some rent. And you have no intention of working late, because tonight David will be coming home, and you have got to be there when he walks through the door. Thankfully, you spent most of yesterday cleaning up the mess you'd made of the place. No one needs to know how bad it got for you.

You call your mother in Oregon first. You wonder, once again, whether your stepfather moved her up there in part to curb her obsessive pursuit of retail therapy. Nice try, you think, remembering the last time they drove down to the City and he dropped her off at your apartment, supposedly to have lunch with you, but instead she showed up at your place two hours late, toting armloads of shopping bags. She asked you to hide her Macy's and Neiman-Marcus booty and to send her purchases to her, one by one, in the weeks to come. "I don't want to upset Louie," she explained in girl-to-girl conspiratorial tones. As usual, you kept her secret and did as she asked. Your lunch together that day was brief.

She is glad to hear from you this morning. "Oh, honey, it's wonderful to hear your voice," she says with such warmth that you feel immediately guilty for what you had been thinking about her before you phoned. But it will turn out she is not so very happy to hear from you that she is willing to send you the couple thousand dollars you need to make this month's rent and pay off the back rent you also owe. You realize she probably needs every cent she can lay her hands on to cover all her mail order purchases. Which you know she conceals from your stepfather by having them delivered to their rural post office box instead of their home.

"It's okay, Mom," you tell her. "I'll think of something. I always do."

Next, you call your dad. He can loan you most of what you need, but not all. You gratefully accept the help he can give. Then he makes a further offer:

"Juliette, baby, you know, if that apartment is getting to be too much for you kids," your father says, "you and David can move in here for a while, just till you get your bearings."

You are touched by the generosity of his offer, well aware that he has never liked David and cannot understand why, since you are a married woman, you still have to work. In his cosmology, men have jobs, while women stay home and take care of their husbands, their children, and lovingly tend houses in which they all live together in domestic harmony. Years ago, you tried to explain to your father how David is an actor, an artist trying to make a career in the theater, so those old-fashioned rules don't apply. Your dad didn't buy it.

"Family comes first," he said. "Any man who lets his wife work isn't a real man."

So you thank him, but explain how your job is in the City, so it would be too hard to commute from the East Bay where he lives. No need to go into all the recent trouble you and David have been having. You know he would be furious to hear it.

After you ring off with your father, you congratulate yourself on mission accomplished. Okay, his loan won't cover all your current and back rent, but it will be enough to satisfy your building manager, Daddy Ray, and keep his boss, the landlady Mrs. Chin, off your back and his. All you need is some time to work out this situation.

It is 10:30 before you turn your attention to Dr. B's project, setting up the copyedited manuscript side by side with the book galleys in preparation for ping-ponging between the two to make sure the typographer picked up all of the copyediting changes. Tedious business, but someone's got to do it. You work through a good twenty pages of the manuscript, when your phone buzzes. You pick up the receiver, punch the intercom button, connect with reception. You have a visitor up front — David's friend Bill.

"Send him down," you instruct, wondering why your husband's buddy should appear at your workplace.

He arrives carrying a grocery bag from Cala Foods, looking quite pleased with himself. You wave him in. He slides open the glass door, enters your terrarium, stands before you.

"You're looking ... more conscious since the last time I saw you," he says.

"To what do I owe the honor?" you ask.

"Got a present for you."

"Yeah?"

"Yeah," he says, handing you his grocery bag rolled at the top. You accept the offering. The bag is heavy. You set it on your desk, unroll the top, open the bag, and look within.

"Oh, for god's sake," you exclaim. It's a new phone. Or, rather, it's a very old phone — an ancient, black, rotary-dial phone. But, at least, it's a *whole* phone, you think, remembering that your own Touch-Tone is resting in pieces in the garbage. "This looks just like my dad's phone. Will it ... work?"

"Oh, don't worry about that. It's practically an antique, I know. But it's built like a mini-tank, and one of my roommates already changed out the old cord for new wiring with a plug that'll fit your touch-tone's wall jack."

"Thank you," you tell him, sincerely touched by the gesture. Bill shrugs modestly.

"If you can't communicate, you can't make changes," he says.

You nod in agreement.

"So," he says, "what have you decided?"

"Whaddya mean?"

He looks surprised at your question. "About your situation at home? You're moving, right?"

"No, I don't think so," you tell him. "My dad's loaning me some money, so I'll be able to stay where I am. For a while, anyway."

"Sounds to me like you're just putting off the inevitable," he says.

You glare at him. You do not want to hear this. You are not ready to hear this, so you argue your position: "I just need to buy a bit of time while we work this out."

Bill understands that when you say "we," you mean yourself and David. He shakes his head.

"What if no amount of time is enough to work it out?"

"Then, I suppose, I'll be moving. Eventually. But it's Monday. I expect him home tonight." You mean to sound exasperated, but instead you come off as uncertain and anxious.

"Look," he says, "if you're worried about where you can go, I can tell you: Nature abhors a vacuum, so all you have to do is make space and a solution will rush in."

"What's that supposed to mean?"

"What I mean is," he says, "if you were to go back to your apartment tonight, give notice, and start boxing up your stuff, by the time you finish packing, a new home will present itself. That's the law of the Universe."

"There's a concept. Very Zen of you," you reply noncommittally, thinking: Fuckin' easy for you to say. You hadn't noticed before how free with his hippie-dippie advice

186 (*Susan Gee Rumsey*

this man could be. Rather irritating, actually. You are reminded he is a social worker, so no doubt he's used to ladling out all that New Age positive-thinking, manifest-your-dreams sop for all those sad losers who come to him for help.

"Lissen, Bill. I really, really appreciate this phone. You are a life-saver. I mean it. But I have got to get down to business here. See, I'm on deadline with this project, and if I don't finish it by five, this office will be my new home."

He understands, no problem, gets up to go. "Anything you need," he says, "you let me know, okay?"

"Okay," you reply, "thanks so much." You wonder again that he would go to the trouble of coming across town to bring you this old phone and that he even knew where to find you. But you have work to do, and you better do it, if you are going to have any hope of leaving the office on time tonight.

Speeding through the galleys, you finish the project, making your deadline before the FedEx final pickup. Then you rush home with two grocery bags, one containing your new old phone and another containing actual groceries. It's been a hard week since you last saw David, but you survived, and now you feel buoyed up in anticipation of his return. You set your groceries in the kitchen, then go plug in the phone. You crawl around searching for the jack and find it in the baseboard behind the hefty double volumes of the *Oxford English Dictionary* in their dark blue slipcase with the drawer containing a rectangular, handheld magnifying glass.

As soon as the phone is connected, it starts ringing — that same old-timey ring tone you remember from childhood when your family's party line allowed you to eavesdrop on your neighbors' conversations. You feel spooked by the sound, as if the call were coming in from thirty years ago. You pick up the receiver and say hello.

"Hey there!" exclaims the stranger at the other end.

"Um, hello, who's this?" you ask.

"Is this Juli St. James? This is Sasha Lowell. We've met."

Oh dear, you think. It's that street-performing friend of David's, the one he gets his drugs from.

"Uh, David ... he's not here right now," you say. "But I'll tell him you called."

"Never mind that," he says. "I know he's not there. I've been calling you for days, you never pick up."

"The phone hasn't been working."

"Guess not. Anyway, I'm not calling for David — I'm calling for you."

"Me?"

"Yeah — you. I was thinking if you need a place to live, I have an attic available."

"Thanks for the offer, but I'm okay for now."

"Well, think about it. If you change your mind, the offer stands."

At this man's insistence, you take down his phone number. After you hang up, you think this is the strangest conversation you've had in a long time. You check the time: 6:45 p.m. You head for the kitchen to chop veggies for stir-fry.

By seven o'clock, no David. You cast about for whatever else you might do to get ready for him, but nothing presents itself.

By eight o'clock, no David. So you think the unthinkable: you are going to have to call her house again.

"Hello, this is David's wife — would you please put David on the phone?"

When David comes on the line, you cannot fucking believe it. Here it is, Monday night — *your* Monday night — and you are speaking with him at the home of his mistress. You choose your words with care and restraint.

"So, um, what time are you planning to come home tonight?" you ask.

His silence is deafening in its eloquence. Then he says: "I, I've … decided to stay on here awhile longer."

"Really?" You sit back to watch the universe implode. You realize Bill was right: now is the time for you to make some decisions. The dumbbell-shaped receiver of this old black phone feels heavy in your hand. You take a deep breath before continuing:

"Well, I'm thinking … there really isn't much point to this, is there? So … why don't you just not bother to come home at all? Ever again. Okay?"

Before he can reply, you hang up. You don't want to hear his answer.

Oh my god, you think, what *did* I just do?

19.

Dr. Bug-Ass Confronts the Limits of Genius and Assimilation

Living in the milieu of post-colonialism and neocolonial societies, we forget that imperialism dies hard. Moreover, the avalanche of information, the skills to be learned, and the accommodations necessary for survival under the imposed order of colonialism demand an expenditure of energy that diminishes both our public and our private powers of creativity and renewal. The writer, as prophet of the tribe and bard of the nation, may be supposed to be sufficiently well equipped to stay on top of it, but he too becomes caught up and a victim like everyone else. Fortunately, imperialism, though without conscience, cannot silence genius.

You have spent half of this century writing in the master's language. It was your parents' wish that you should "succeed," which meant English, and their wish became yours, in turn, because you wanted nothing more than to be the source of their pride — you, their first-born and only son.

From the start, then, it was English, always English, with never so much as a glance back at your homeland's true language or, God forbid, ever a thought to expressing your literary reminiscences in your local tongue, dismissed as "dialect" by Western European linguists, although this "dialect" had structured the childhood events you would later recreate in fiction. The irony was not lost upon you: the individuals who peopled your novels and short stories would never themselves be able to read what you wrote of them. This was, in some cases, a blessing for all concerned.

However, to choose one language over another is not without its consequences for the writer, and when that writer embraces, as his own, the language of his conquerer, he is not simply finishing the job he started when he voluntarily, even eagerly, surrendered his mind, as well as his life's physical circumstances and, ultimately, the culture that ought to have been his natural birthright.

For nearly forty years, you have lived in this country — this spoiled, greedy, self-satisfied, self-congratulatory nation. Here you have worked and studied, written and been published, and received all the condescending acclaim ever awarded to a well-behaved house pet from an alien culture. Here you have married and raised sons, and, for half your years in this place, you have attempted to "teach" the sons and daughters of the spoiled, greedy, self-satisfied, self-congratulatory men who built and maintain this nation reputed for its "greatness." Nowadays you take up the mask of "Professorship" from long force of habit. Most of your students fear you, and you accept their fear in lieu of respect.

Once you were as young as they are and could hardly wait to use your talent as currency to buy your place in the larger world beyond your remote homeland. So much you wanted to be recognized, even to belong! A lifetime later, you cease to flush with pride when praised in some East Coast literary quarterly for your "near-native mastery" of their language. (Imagine: you — writing so fluently in the language of the oppressor!) Now you know you cannot ever truly belong to this country where you have overstayed your soul.

Nor can you ever truly return to the land of your birth. Your grandparents and parents are dead. Your sisters have forgotten all but the legend of you. Loss of family is the price you have paid for your so-called success.

Moreover, this loss threatens to starve to death any future "success" you may have hoped to enjoy, because your people — parents, sisters, neighbors, all the characters in your village where you grew up — they were the contents of the cooking pot from which you first fed yourself to nourish the literary life for which you knew always you were destined. You love them. However, if you are strictly honest with yourself in the maturity of your life and your art, you must admit that you … look down upon them and pity them at times.

Even your own mother! As much as you are shamed by your memories of how willing you were to trade your own culture for another that never wanted or needed you, you are grieved more to recall her sincere, naïve rural love and hopes for the small-boy you. How could you have known that the distance between you would become so much more than just thousands of miles and could never be bridged?

American society, having received all you once had to offer in exchange for its table scraps of recognition, thereafter failed to replenish your cumulative life experience in any way that could be meaningful for the kind of writer you are. Or were.

Having fully exploited your accumulated store of firsthand experiences, you turned (warily) to literary criticism, then (guiltily) to the slush pile of student fiction scribblings that had gathered behind your office door at the university over ten years' time. You told yourself this renewed interest in the derivative efforts of ill-educated, immature amateurs was an academic search for universal themes, but you hoped (secretly) that winnowing a decade's worth of scanty classroom harvests would provide sufficient nourishment to delay the demise of your own starving creativity.

Four months ago, however, you were granted a life-experience you wish with all your heart you might have been spared: you traveled home to attend the dying of your mother. The call came from the youngest of your three sisters, the one who, having arrived a full generation after you, had never known you except as the visitor from America introduced to her as her "brother" every few years. Now she has been married, a mother five times over, a grandmother even, and already widowed. You arranged a month-long leave of absence from the university to set out immediately, taking the long flight and, by turns, the taxi, the bus, the ferry, and the cart, all in fear you would not arrive in time to bid your mother farewell.

Your mother still lived and breathed at the moment when you re-entered the home of your childhood to find her on a pallet in the main room. You stood in the doorway, suddenly afraid to come in, and listening to vividly colored birds screaming outside, only meters away.

The village doula, who attends departures as well as arrivals, was sitting at your mother's side, and she leaned over to speak to your mother of your coming, the return of the only son. Then she waved you over. You helped the doula to rise as she surrendered to you the place closest to your mother.

Your mother — how small and shrunken she appeared! Only three years ago, on your last visit, she had been strong and vigorous, continuing her lifelong routines with quiet, remarkable determination, despite your father's recent passing. You had offered then to stay with her and try to be of some help, but she laughed and touched your hair in a fond gesture you recalled from childhood, the gentlest refusal you could have imagined. That afternoon on her death pallet, she had seemed to be sleeping, before she opened her clouded eyes to meet your own anxious gaze, smiled with the few remaining teeth she possessed, then spoke in a language you suddenly discovered you no longer understood. Panic rising, you looked to the doula for translation.

The old woman nodded with understanding and responded with simple English: "She say she glad you come. She say she love you. She proud of American son."

"Remind me, please, how I say, 'Thank you, I love you, too.'"

You repeated the words told to you, now become familiar again, and you burned with shame that others should witness your lapse and know that you had forgotten, albeit momentarily, the language your mother first gave to you. You are angry, too, with yourself for having abandoned it. And her.

Then, as you touched her brow, she passed away. "Mama!" you exclaimed as she released her last breath.

"*Nanay*," you repeated.

Weeks later, having returned to your American home, you

tried to distract yourself from grief over all you have lost by turning to concentrate on a review of the page galleys of your most recent book of literary criticism, published by Raker & Ho.

At this West Coast publishing house in San Francisco, you are held to be a "prestige author." Consequently, it rankles you that the handling of your editorial changes is given to some ignorant young fool of an editorial assistant, who has made so many mistakes that you think she (for they are always "she") should pay her employer to allow her to work there. By the time you have reunited a fourth copyediting inquiry on a Post-It note with its proper manuscript page, you have already begun to compose in your head your letter of complaint to their head of production.

Of course, the letter must be in English.

20.

Sasha the Clown
at Home in His War Room

Oh yes, ma'am, you know all about actors and would-be actors. For nearly a decade, you've sold them their drugs (better living through chemistry!) and listened to their tiresome, whiny declamations about how "the thea-tah" is their great and true love, a demanding mistress who insists on claiming all their time and attention. Bullshit. As a street performer, the whole world is your stage.

From Venice (Florida) to Venice (California), you followed the pitches — Nashville, New Orleans, Boston, Denver, L.A., rolling to a hard stop at last in Frisco, that great paradisiacal year-round pitch. Emerald City, USA. It was like a cross-country Connect-the-Dots puzzle, which, in the end, drew a picture of a classic-clown performer, your father's worst nightmare starring his only begotten son. Or, from your perspective, the busker equivalent of a giant Whac-A-Mole game, with you killing at every hole.

Those cry-baby actors have no idea how easy they have

it. All they do is pace around backstage, nervously rehearsing lines someone else wrote for them until the theater doors open, and — voila! instant audience, which arrives obediently at the appointed time and politely takes its seats. Then the curtain rises, and the actors don't have to work hard to convince the audience to like them. A theater audience is already invested in their enjoyment of the show, having spent their hard-earned moolah to purchase the tickets that paid the salaries of the entire company. The actors don't even have to be good — they just have to be not terrible. Either way, they get paid.

You, on the other hand, are on your own, self-employed, and must round up your audience daily. Sometimes it seems to happen by magic, because you've lost track of all the steps you have to take in the process. First, you divert their attention, then their paths. You cause them to forget, for the moment, wherever they were going, whatever they were intending to do right before you caught their eye. You have a hundred different ways to capture them, one by one.

Then, as they stand there, your spontaneously captive audience, you perform bits you've cobbled together throughout the years, a number of them cleverly heisted from various sources that shall go forever unnamed. If you are especially good for that gig (and if the weather is dank and freezing, as City summers tend to be), your captives will remain huddled together (for warmth) all the way through to the end of your show. And then, if you have pleased sufficiently, your wages will be paid in tips. These daily twenty-minute battles for the hearts, if not the minds, of the tourists who come to Fisherman's Wharf is the open warfare and secret romance you carry on with as many civilians as possible every afternoon and every evening of your life. Their approval is your drug of choice.

In the never-ending worldwide battles of performers competing for attention, stage actors are a standing army, while street performers are its anarchists and rebel guerrillas. Good thing there is no universal draft — the casualties would be astronomical.

Now you are making both love and war at home as well. You perform flirtatiously for your foxy new roommate, Juli, who, though she doesn't know it yet, is an appointee to your war cabinet, there to aid you in your quest for world domination.

You feel confident, with her impressive organizational skills, she will be the one to find and secure for you the many legitimate college and corporate gigs that will finally get you off the street and out of the fog. So you perform for her in your living room, with its twelve-foot Victorian ceilings, wall-to-wall mirrors, and decor comprised of every possible type of juggling prop: balls, clubs, rings, fire sticks, chainsaws, and, on one crazy, late-night occasion, a litter of month-old kittens dropped off in a box on your front porch. But you were careful with them: no animals have ever been harmed during the making of any of your shows. Or, at least, the injuries weren't serious. Certainly not intentional.

You present yourself as a juggling clown, complete with the standard-issue fright fringe and traditional red nose. But you are coming around to the understanding that people are less fascinated by your modest juggling skills, which you practice to improve with daily diligence, than they are by your smart-mouth onstage persona, who defends himself against hecklers by saying terrible, shocking things most people only think in their heads. If indeed they even dare to think them.

Until recently, you've relied exclusively on your quick wits and a talent for instant insult you discovered during your academy year. Of late, however, you've been contemplating that you may need to acquire more and better words to throw up, along with your balls, clubs, and knives — and that this may possibly be something your new roommate could help you with. Because not only does she have her own smart-mouth way with words to rival your own, but her comic timing is pretty damn good as well. For a civilian.

When you walk through the front door at midnight, you invite her to help you roll change and sort bills from your hat-passings, a pleasantly relaxing chore for any halfway successful street performer. Banks don't want to deal with all that loose change. Women, on the other hand, invariably love the process. You watch Juli carefully sorting and smoothing out the paper money — usually ones and fives, but sometimes tens, even twenties get dropped in there. You both take special delight in the bills that visitors from Japan have origamied into little, green-and-white frogs and butterflies, beetles and cranes. You watch her separating quarters from dimes from nickels from pennies, stacking them in preparation to be dropped into their little paper sleeves. You observe: her stacks are very neat.

"Well stacked!" you compliment her, then laugh when she blushes.

To be honest, when her ex-old man, David — who you nicknamed "Hoover," due to his impressive ability to power-vacuum up lines of coke — first called to suggest you offer her your empty attic space, because they were finally splitting up and she had nowhere to go, you were hesitant. You figured if Hoover was boinking everything in sight, which he certainly was (including a couple of the tarts you yourself thought you were "dating"), then his lovely castoff probably had similar inclinations and would prove to be a noisy, disruptive roommate. After all, they did have one of those "Open Marriages."

So, while tempted by the opportunity to seize upon her PR skills (which had evidently carried her sleaze-ball spouse further than he'd had any right to expect, based on his wooden stage presence), you do consider your home to be your sanctuary. And you certainly don't want some free-loving, hippie-slut type bringing home the entire 49ers team for a little R&R. Consequently, your offer of space came with a condition: no overnighters. No problem, she agreed at once. She was off guys, she claimed, maybe forever. Never say never, you thought.

But already it's been three months, and the whole arrangement has worked out far better than you ever imagined. At first, she was clearly avoiding you. She'd leave your flat first thing in the morning, hours before you were conscious, to go to her soul-killing little job in publishing, where her talents were most likely being wasted. Then, in the evening, she'd come home and politely chat with you until you indicated you had to make ready for a night of "throwing up" at Pier 39 or wherever. At which time, she would disappear into the hall coat closet and up the twelve-foot ladder that gives access to the enormous attic of your Haight-Ashbury flat. You guess she must have waited till you left for work to use the kitchen, because you never saw her cook, much less eat. And, of course, by the time you got home, she'd crashed for the p.m., all the better to get up for her shitty 8-to-5 in the a.m.

Thus went your household routine in those first weeks. And, early on, you let her be, supposing she needed time to get used to you. You certainly didn't want her to be fearful you'll suddenly go all John Wayne Gacy on her. But then you set about drawing her out, pleading with her for favors, giving her little jobs, praising her lavishly when she completed her tasks successfully. As she always did. If there was an evening when you both were home, you'd beg her to come down from the attic so you could show her "something." Having lived for years among actors, she's clearly learned how to be a great audience and to give back, energetically, as much or even more than she gets from whoever performs for her. Her applause at the end of a set feels like a warm, luxurious shower. The kind with a Euro-style, rainfall shower head.

But the place where the two of you really got acquainted was over money. Lately you'd been ruminating to yourself on how you got your start, hoping for a clue on where to go from here. You'd wanted to perform since you were a teenager, but didn't know what to do or where to go do it. Until one day.

There you were: a dorky cadet at the academy in Boston, on orders of "The General" (a.k.a. your father). There he was: some juggler-mime-clown-guy performing in the Square on a Friday afternoon.

Due to some bullshit fascist ritual you'd been forced to attend that morning, you were even in uniform at the time, a pimply faced, complete creep. But you hung out all afternoon to watch, mesmerized by this busker. By the time he called it a day, you had fallen in love with the beauty made by the touch of his hands. While he was packing up, you went over to talk to him.

Back then, you didn't know anything. You told the guy you really liked his act. Thanks, he said. You asked him how he learned how to do that. Nascent performer, eh kid? he asked. Then he said, well, you could pick it up on the fly or you could go to Clown College. Clown College? you said. There's such a thing? Of course, the guy said.

Back then, all you knew about learning how to do anything new was to go to school to do it. Besides, Clown College was bound to piss off your father more than anything in the world. That alone would be worth the price of admission. In an instant, you decided to do it. Even though it took you a while, including four years of father-financed education at Vanderbilt in Nashville — your place of refuge from the draft — before you were able to put your plan into action.

"So, how'd you get started doing this, Sasha?" Juli asked, startling you as she often did with her freaky telepathic sense.

"Clown College."

"That's a real thing? Like an acting school, like the American Conservatory Theater, except it's for circus performers?"

"Exactly."

"But you never worked for Barnum & Bailey or anything like that?"

"Like other arcane professions, there's room for only so many. And clowning, it turns out, is a dying art. Just my luck. So I work the street."

"How do you stand the insecurity?"

"Hey, no 8 to 5, no neckties, no bosses."

"Hey, no steady income, no credit, no retirement plan."

Though your roommate doesn't know it, you still have most of the trust fund your dad set up for you, available to you since you turned 25. However, acknowledging that fact at this moment would seem to belie your very real and fierce need for freedom and independence.

You and your new roommate had been getting on nicely, when crisis struck for her: she got laid off her job. You wondered what the matter was when she came home one early evening, went straight to her attic, and started bawling. You opened the closet door, mounted the first rung of the ladder to her top-level sanctuary, and called up to her.

"Jujube, you alright?!"

"Not now!"

You thought a moment before deciding to crash her party. "I'm coming up there."

At the top of the ladder and having popped up through her floor, like a giant prairie dog, you find your flatmate curled into a fetal position in the tent-shaped alcove where her mattress on the floor lives, a large window overlooking the garden below behind this three-story Victorian home. Nice view, you think. Then you crawl in next to her and tentatively reach out to give her a little back rub.

"Whatever it is, Juju, it can't be that bad," you say soothingly. "Tell me what happened."

She sits up suddenly, and you retract your hand. Her face is blimpy with crying, and she has snot running out of her nose. You reach into your pocket, bring forth a huge, polka-dotted clown-hankie, and hand it to her. She snickers as she takes it, wipes her nose, offers you a grateful look. When she

tries to hand it back to you, you tell her, "No, it's okay, keep it."
Then she tells you:

"Lost my job today. Laid off."

"Maybe just temporary?"

"I don't think so. My production editors said they thought
I needed to take a break for a while. I guess I've just been too
distracted with personal problems and making too many
mistakes."

"How heartless of them!" you exclaim indignantly,
inwardly gleeful at the golden opportunity you realize is being
handed to you.

"You know what this means, don't you?" she says. "I have
no way right now to pay my share of the rent."

Which was, of course, your cue to reply magnanimously:
"Oh, don't worry about that. I need a press kit, anyway. And so
much more. You can work off the rent."

Thus formally began your roommate's new career as
your assistant — writing a bit of PR, sharpening your resumé,
researching possible gigs for you, making calls, anything else
you can think to sic her onto.

Just one thing: this woman is a human chimney. Always
smoking. You didn't realize quite how much till she got laid
off. Aside from making you afraid she'll set the house on fire,
smoking in bed in the attic, she is just plain driving you crazy,
because, as it happens, you yourself have been trying to quit.
If you're going to devote your life to making a living with your
physical self — your "instrument," as the actors coyly put it
— then you've got to take good care of your body. You can't
abuse yourself 24/7 and expect to be able to depend on that
body, come what may. So you told her: no smoking in the attic

— in fact, no smoking in the flat at all. She has to go outside and either smoke in the garden or on the stoop. Thus far, she's been good about it.

"Excuse me," she tells you twice an hour on those evenings you spend together, "I need to step out for a few minutes."

"Be my guest," you reply brightly, adding under your breath, "since you are, anyway."

You watch her trudging down the stairs to the front door to go out on the porch to poison herself.

21.

Juli Gets a New Home

One big fat surprise that came after you and David separated and you had resettled at Sasha's: everything about your life became suddenly ... so ... much ... easier.

You'd never realized the extent to which you'd twisted yourself into a pretzel in order to stay married to his rotten ass. As it turned out, you were married — but he wasn't. Now, for the first time in years, you don't have to wonder what time he'll be coming home. Or whether he intends to come home at all. You don't have to worry the reason he didn't come home as promised is because you're such a crappy cook and/or lousy lay. Best of all, you'll never again have to grit your teeth and force yourself to endure whatever he wants in bed, out of fear that, if you don't submit, he'll go elsewhere — to someone prettier, more open-minded, more relaxed, and much, much kinkier. Someone who doesn't insist on having a safeword.

All that effort for nothing. Because, you finally realized, that's exactly what he was doing: always going elsewhere, no matter how good in bed you tried to be. Now, you realize, you shoulda told him straight out at the start: if that's what you want — go find yourself someone else to do it to. What a relief to have your body returned to you! No more hurting. No more getting emotionally blackmailed into doing scary, disgusting things. Alone and in peace, you lie in your own bed at night; alone and in peace, you yield to sleep without fear of being awakened in pain.

Yet, even after several months at Sasha's, you sometimes feel depressed around sunset time. As day dims into night, you catch yourself sitting and staring blankly, paused in whatever you were doing. You wonder where David is at this moment, what he's doing.

Then you remind yourself: this is *not* your problem — David is not your problem. Not anymore. But still you catch yourself thinking about him. All those years, all that history — gone like it never happened. Here you are, thirty years old, and you have nothing. You think you must have been in some kind of twilight coma since you graduated from college, and only now are you waking up.

Moving out of the apartment was, as you had feared, one of the harder things in life you've ever had to manage. After you talked to David on the phone and he told you he wasn't coming home that night, you called his junkie-friend, Sasha, to make sure his offer of a place to stay was still open. You told him you'd changed your mind. He seemed surprised, but pleased. You started packing that very night, with only KGO Radio's all-night, call-in talk shows to keep you company. You don't remember crashing, but first thing the next morning, you called in sick at work. Then you went downstairs to give notice to your building manager. You were afraid if you didn't act on impulse to commit yourself, you would lose your nerve entirely. Suddenly, all you could think was: you have to get out.

You hiked up and over the hill to collect boxes from Cala Foods. You made several trips. You briefly considered sticking out your thumb and hitching home with more boxes than you could carry while walking. But you decided against the idea in light of recent news reports about some perv in the area who picks up women hitchhikers and relieves them of their socks. As much as you love the City, you have to acknowledge: it's home to some pretty strange people with some pretty idiosyncratic hobbies.

That afternoon, as you filled those boxes, it occurred to you what a great opportunity this was for you to not only to get rid of David's junk, but also to shed every "ours" object connected with him and your time together. Which turned out to be quite a lot: every piece of clothing he'd ever given to you or had complimented you on, those "super-sexy" thigh-high boots he brought home unexpectedly for you (he said), the framed art prints you bought because you knew he liked them, a vaguely psychedelic flower vase he'd given you early in your relationship, the oversized Royal Marriage Souvenir Plate that you bought because Charles and Diana had gotten married that same summer as you and David. You could see already their marriage wasn't working out, either. All this could go to Goodwill or into the trash or wherever, it made no difference to you.

In the process of sorting and discarding, you couldn't help but marvel at how much, in terms of simple mass and weight, books beat out every other category of material thing you possessed. No surprise a professional editor/wannabe author would be overwhelmed with books.

And you were struck as well by at how little, in contrast, there was of Just David in the apartment. You'd lived together for years in a series of tiny, rundown studio apartments in the City. Yet he'd accumulated — and contributed — almost nothing. And it wasn't as though he'd taken everything he owned to that bitch's place. All he'd carried away was a new attaché case filled with old underpants. If it hadn't been for the evidence that lay before you of David's leftover crap, it would have seemed as though he'd never existed. Then even you would have to wonder if you'd made him up, your invisible husband, just as your friends at work used to tease you.

Worst of all was when you discovered his secret stash. At the back of the hall closet stood his beat-up, old Samsonite attaché case from college — locked, but no match for a steak knife jammed into the key hole beneath the latch and given a good twist. The latch sprang up and the case's top popped open, emitting a leathery fart, a scent you had always particularly liked.

At first, all you saw were a few striped covers of Dramatists Play Service scripts from shows he'd been cast in over the past ten years, including his curled and worn copy of *Dark at the Top of the Stairs*, by William Inge, the same guy who wrote *Picnic* and *Bus Stop*. In an A.C.T. student production of *Dark*, David had played the lead, the philandering salesman Rubin Flood. You remembered how challenged he'd been by the part. As always, he'd had to struggle to memorize his lines. But also, you realize now, he must have been in despair at being instructed at A.C.T. to apply Method acting techniques to a part that could only serve to humiliate him onstage. You wondered in passing whether publicly exposing such vulnerability also takes a similar toll on writers as well as actors. You remembered the playwright, Inge, had killed himself only a few years ago.

You fingered through the accordion files in the lid and found only old tax forms that he'd lied on and party invitations from people whose names you didn't recognize. Not until you dug down and removed the divider to the case's bottom section did you run across his porno stash and sex memorabilia: commercial photos of strippers with phone numbers and scrawled notes promising "TLC"; a couple matchbooks for seedy Tenderloin joints; several personal letters in onion-skin envelopes lined with parchment; a lacy lime-green thong with a crusty crotch. You felt faint as you handled these things.

You stuffed everything back into the attaché. Except for the personal letters. These you put to your nose and found them scented. You gingerly inserted your fingers into one envelope and drew forth the contents. You peeled open the single sheet and read. You carefully refolded the note and replaced it in the envelope, then went on to read the other three — all written on pale pink, onion-skin paper in the same feminine hand and signed with lipstick kisses. Did those lips belong to Barbra? You checked the postmark and saw it was from Cupertino, on the peninsula. Nowhere near where Barbra lived in San Francisco's Outer Sunset District. Maybe Barbra worked down there, but it seemed more likely these letters were from some other random slut.

You replaced everything just as you found it, then pushed aside the attaché. You were constructing a separate little heap of David's things. He still had nearly a month in which to come and get them. You went on to pack your own things, which your father had offered to store for you. The phone rang regularly, its old-fashioned sound of Long-Long-Ago, but you pointedly ignored it, refusing to answer. Finally, you unplugged the phone, so you couldn't hear the ring, be annoyed and possibly tempted to dispose of it the way you'd disposed of your other phone. You had nothing to say to anyone. You called in sick to work another three days. You considered calling in dead.

Packing complete, the Delancey Street movers came for your stuff, and you got to ride up front in the cab of the huge moving van between the two burly ex-cons assigned to be your guardian angels for the day. They drove down Bush Street and turned into Chinatown to access an approach to the bridge near the Embarcadero. On the Bay Bridge, you asked one of the movers what he was in for; he told you: armed robbery. Then he asked you why you were getting out of the City; you told him your husband cheated on you. He laughed heartily, showing a couple of gold bling teeth, and said, "Yeah, we all think we bad!"

When you got to Oakland, your father was happy to see you. After your personal felons emptied the contents of their truck into your father's living room, you and your dad spent the next hour or so carrying boxes to one of two areas he had carefully, lovingly prepared for you — either in his partially finished basement, on plastic tarps covering a dirt floor, or in the large, sunny, back bedroom that had once been your grandmother's. You noted, even though you'd turned down your father's offer of a place to live, he'd still prepared the bedroom for you and David. You'd told him you and David were going to stay with friends, and only your stuff needed a temporary home. You realized that, despite your reassuring lies, your father was looking ahead for you, in case your make-believe situation didn't work out.

As soon as the job was done and your dad sat down to rest in his usual spot in the living room, he became so depressed you found it impossible to be around him for longer than another hour before you felt a headache coming on. You told him you had to get back to the City. You walked the mile or so to the Broadway and 19th Street BART station, caught a train going into downtown San Francisco. Then you hiked up from Powell to go stay in your apartment, empty of all artifacts of your past life, except for what little David still had to collect.

You invited Kitty over for a two-person "House-Cooling" party, sitting on the floor with a giant box of pepperoni pizza between you in the hollow, echoing apartment. And now even David's things were out of sight — stored in one of the lockers in the basement for him to collect from the building manager whenever he got around to it in the next couple of months. You had no intention of calling him again to come get his stuff.

The evening before you were to go to Sasha's with just one suitcase and your new canvas knapsack from Banana Republic, replacing the backpack stolen from you, you went downstairs to the lobby and knocked on the door of your building manager's apartment. Everyone knew this elderly man as "Daddy Ray," his D.J. handle on the tiny, community-access FM radio station with its noise-absorbing egg cartons stapled to the walls of the sound studio, all spray-painted black and splashed in places with silver glitter, which you guessed was intended to represent constellations of stars in a nighttime sky. When he opened the door and saw who it was, he had a big smile for you. He was wearing his long, maroon-colored, heavy silk smoking jacket, his oxblood loafers, and his hat, a natty soft fedora from another era.

"C'mon in, mama. You lookin' mighty fine tonight," he said.

He had invited you to dinner, offering to blow off the last bit of back rent you and David still owed if you would accept his invitation. You suspected he had more in mind than ham hocks in beans with greens, but you were past caring. All you wanted was to clear the debt and have some dinner. The two of you ate on a card table set up in the living room of his tiny ground-floor apartment and covered with an old-timey-looking tablecloth printed with cherries. He told you stories about his adventures as a Pullman porter in the 1930s. He had two pensions, one from twenty years in the Army and another from the railroad, before the war and after his military service. Retired now, he got free rent for managing this building. In addition to his weekly radio show, he was studying to be a travel agent. A real go-getter.

"I know you sad cuz he gone," he said, "but you can do a whole lot better than that two-timing, no-good rascal."

Up until now, it hadn't occurred to you how much your building manager might know about the "two-timing" of your "no-good rascal." You wondered if he'd observed a parade of women going in and out of the apartment while you were at work. Tentatively, you tried to broach the subject.

"Ray, did you ever see … I mean, you're here a lot, and David would have had to walk right past your door, so did you ever notice him coming in with — ?"

But Daddy Ray stopped you in mid-sentence by reaching out to put his big, perfectly manicured hand over yours and give it a warm squeeze. "Oh, baby," he said, "just let it go.

Don't hurt yourself. That's all water under the bridge now."

After dinner, Daddy Ray said he had a favor to ask of you. He turned two big brown eyes and a piteous, pleading-dog expression on you as he indicated the bedroom with an incline of his head. Resigned to the fate of your gender, you rose from the rickety table and went into the bedroom.

Boxes and packing materials and stereo components and cables were strewn all over. The schematics for connecting up all this equipment lay spread out on his bed. He picked up an owner's manual that was an inch thick, printed in six languages. He thumbed through it at zip-speed, like a card shark sorting cards, then tossed it casually back on the bed.

"I'm too old to figure all this out. I need someone with a bright young head on her shoulders — can you do it?" he asked. You guessed you could.

Two hours later, you finished the job. Daddy Ray picked up a vinyl recording of Sarah Vaughan, slipped it gently from its album cover, placed it ceremonially on the turntable, and set it to spin. When the needle connected with the record, a voice as smooth and rich as liquid gold poured from the two-foot-tall speaker towers set up at either end of his dresser. In silence, you both sat on the end of his bed, side by side, between the speakers, and listened through the entire first side of the album. Then you watched as the arm that held the needle reached the middle of the turntable, lifted itself up and off, and swung back onto its hook beside the record.

"That was great," you said, whispering as if in church.

"You don't have to go back upstairs tonight to an empty apartment, you know," he said. "You can sleep here."

Turned out he meant you could sleep on his sofa. He

pulled the satin comforter from his bed and walked out to the living room with it. He arranged the comforter to resemble a turned-down bed and slipped a throw pillow into a fresh cotton pillowcase drawn from a drawer in his tiny kitchenette.

"I spent twenty-two years doing that. Got pretty good," he commented.

Then he walked through the apartment, flipping off lights, and went into his bedroom, shutting the door behind him. You yanked off your boots, peeled off your jeans, crawled into the improvised bed, and drifted off to Sarah Vaughn's liquid voice pouring under Daddy Ray's closed door.

>⛬<

All that happened only months ago, but it feels like years. And now you live here, in the attic of a man you didn't even recognize at first when you arrived because it had been years since you'd seen him out of costume and without his stupid wig and red rubber nose (his lucky nose, you would later learn). When he opened the door to let you in, he was freshly showered, still damp, and wearing an ordinary gray tracksuit. Until he spoke, you weren't certain you'd gotten the address right. Offstage and out of costume, he seemed smaller, somehow, and more nearly ... human.

At first, you hid out, trying to keep to your own space and not bother your strange benefactor. Bad enough you were hardly better than a stray cat, showing up on his doorstep with nowhere else to go. You had no idea how to be a roommate to a man. You'd never been anyone's roommate, not even in college. You'd always commuted to class.

But you love your attic refuge. The huge space runs the

entire length of this Victorian flat, complete with thick, spongy, heavy, red carpeting that Sasha somehow managed to haul up here and roll out on your behalf. The roof of this three-story painted lady is seriously pitched, so your attic ceiling is ten feet high in the middle and about a foot and a half high on either side. A series of skylights makes the place light and airy. You hang your few clothes in the cupola at the front; you sleep on a mattress on the floor in a cozy alcove at the back, overlooking the garden tended by the landlady, who lives in the downstairs flat. You see her occasionally when you are sitting out on the front porch steps, smoking a cigarette. She assumes you are Sasha's girlfriend.

During the first few weeks after you moved in, you loved taking off early from work, riding home on the 7 Haight Muni streetcar line, strolling through the green of Golden Gate Park's Panhandle, the late-afternoon sun already beginning its descent towards the ocean, climbing the steep Victorian front steps, letting yourself in through the vintage glass-paned door, climbing more, even steeper stairs, pulling open the door of the hall closet, stepping inside, and hoisting yourself up the twelve-foot ladder to your new home. Your nest. You expected to reach the top of the ladder and find Narnia. Or maybe meet a time-traveling Dr. Who.

You were scared when you got laid off at work. Fired, really, in a genteel, academic way. Being "let go" — this had never happened to you before, yet you'd felt it coming for a while. You knew you'd called in sick too much, made too many mistakes, worked too slow, were generally distracted since your situation with David went down the crapper. You'd hoped to be stabilized by now — now that your living situation has stabilized. You suppose your editors must have hoped for that as well.

But it never happened; you never regained your footing. More importantly, you'd lost interest. You couldn't get yourself to care anymore. You needed the work, you desperately needed the money, you regretted you'd probably never in your life have another job that other people found so desirable and "glamorous." But you — you simply didn't care.

Fortunately, Sasha appears not at all disturbed by your sudden descent into middle-class poverty. He's fine with your working off the rent by working on his publicity materials. Clearly, he really does want you here.

In fact, you and your new roommate seem to have a special connection. He tells you, over and over, how much he admires and respects you. He tells you he's pleased as anything you accepted his offer to move in. You consider how much trouble he went to in order to install you here in the first place — painting and finishing off the attic (in a rental, for gosh sakes!), dragging all that heavy carpeting up a twelve-foot ladder. And his kindness, his thoughtfulness, his generosity all seem to contradict the impression you'd held of him before you moved in.

You are confused and don't understand the boundaries of your relationship. Even though your stated arrangement with him is all-business and straightforward enough, you feel unsettled by the ever-present undertones of your interactions: the adoring way he looks at you; his references to a shared future in which he compares the two of you to various great artist couples of history; the way he jumps whenever you accidentally brush by him in the kitchen, as if he'd received a mild electric shock; the way he leaves his bedroom door open after he turns in for the night, placing lit candles on his dresser where you cannot fail to see them as you pass by on your way to the bathroom off the hall. An invitation, if ever there was.

And after you got canned from Raker & Ho and had all that free time on your hands, he began insisting you come along with him everywhere he went — at least a couple times a week to his gigs at the wharf, occasionally to parties where out-of-work Shakespearean actors mixed freely with fly-by-night puppeteers and tap-dancing nuns, more and more to the City's many comedy clubs, improv stages, and bars with open mic nights. He said the two of you needed to do research.

In comedy venues, he would hand you the notebook and pen he always carries, ask you to write down every topic touched upon by each comedian in his or her routine. On the way home, he'd ask you to read your list aloud, so you'd have to shout over the roar of the mighty four-cylinder engine of his VW Bug. He wanted to know what you found funny, and he wanted to know why. He really seemed to care what you thought. You realized, with amazement, that anything — literally, any topic — could be shaped into humor. You began to look differently at all the things you'd always simply assumed were irreversibly tragic, and you mentally played with them to see if you could turn them inside out for a laugh.

One special night, it was past ten when Sasha insisted on driving across town to Clement Street in order to hang out at Holy City Zoo. Somehow he'd heard Robin Williams might show up that evening. You were thrilled when, suddenly, there he was — Robin Williams performing a manic set of seemingly spontaneous, new material that he must have been hard at work on, while you watched from a bar stool only ten feet away. Sasha, standing alongside you, was thrilled, too. As Williams sprinted from the club half an hour later to universal cheers, Sasha leaned into you and kissed you on the cheek. No wonder people in these clubs treated you like you were his steady.

Driving home that night, he wanted to talk about what had happened in the Holy City Zoo. But not about the two of you — he wanted to talk about himself and how he compared to Robin Williams.

"So, tell me, Jujube: what's Robin got that I ain't got?"

"Ummm, he's a movie star and you're not?" you venture a lame quip.

"Right," he said, giving you a ha-ha-very-funny side eye as he roared along Masonic Avenue in his VW clown-car. "No, I mean, what's he got onstage that I haven't got? How is he different as a performer?"

A serious question, then, you realize. You try for a serious answer: "Well, he's really good-looking, whereas no one can even tell about you."

"Hmmm, maybe that's just as well. But the point is, people are crazy for him — how come?"

"Uh, he's nice? I mean, he seems nice."

"And I'm not?"

"Not especially."

"Well, what's 'nice,' anyway? 'Nice' doesn't seem like much to shoot for."

"Not 'nice,' exactly." You struggle to say what you mean. "He seems like he actually *likes* the people in his audience. Even when he makes fun of them, he's gentle about it. He doesn't rip them up and stomp on the pieces—."

"The way I do?"

"—the way you do."

"Ouch. But I *do* like my audience. What makes you think I don't?"

"I guess it just doesn't show."

"And I guess it probably helps that Robin Williams doesn't have to worry some cretinous heckler will be waiting till after his gig to kick his ass? Go on — what else?"

You feel yourself to be on a roll: "He's playful. He's like a little kid, meeting other little kids for the first time in nursery school. Right away he goes up to them, makes a game out of nothing, and gets everyone to play. And each time his game is a little different, because the audience is different, and the setting is different, and what's going on in the grownup world is different. And he doesn't need to drag around a heavy trunk with a bunch of props, because anything within reach becomes a prop. The more bizarre and unlikely, the better. And—."

"Okay, okay, I get it: he's an amazing human-otter hybrid. Thanks for taking me seriously and trying to answer the question." At which point he reached over, across the stick shift, grabbed your hand and brought its back to his lips to plant a kiss there. At which point, you feel your neck and face flush hot, and you are glad the street lamps and traffic lights don't give you away.

When you were married, you never noticed other men. Now that you're almost not-married, now that you're living in this man's attic and sleeping right above his bedroom, this particular man's flirty ways take you by surprise, suggesting possibilities you find both exciting and unnerving.

You remember clearly the first time you met Sasha. You'd gone with David on his regular drug run to a rambling, remodeled house in the Sunset District being rented by a couple of second-year A.C.T. students. Several seasoned buskers lived there as well, like caged hamsters in a basement in-law apartment, and Sasha, recently emigrated from Back East, was crashing with them. That was six years ago, before he'd fully settled on his creepy-clown character and gotten his own place. He'd come to San Francisco from Nashville, where he'd been practicing his newly acquired professional skills.

You remember thinking he looked so baby-faced and vulnerable. Almost unattractive, as performers went. He was clearly trying to impress these more-experienced street performers, while sponging up their street smarts, which had certainly not been part of his prep-school education as the son of some important government official or some such thing. You watched him as he chopped coke with the edge of a credit card for the congregated, drug-dependent degenerates, then stuck a rolled-up hundred-dollar-bill straw into his nose. You thought to yourself: he'll be eaten alive out there.

But you made that assessment before you'd met his street-act persona of a wise-ass clown in a harlequin tailcoat, packing juggling knives, fire sticks, and a bullwhip, ready to deliver a good tongue-lashing even to gangbangers and boyz from da hood. Onstage he seemed half a foot taller and frankly a bit scary. But his audiences at the wharf seemed to accept every abuse he dished out. You wondered if it's because he's so full of surprises, always managing to put hecklers in their place without ever presenting any real threat. You thought he was like a pet cat on the bed, beating up the blankets when you waggle your feet. People will laugh at twelve pounds of toughness; 125 pounds of serious puma gets shot on the spot.

Later on, you dismissed Sasha because David so often gave him your rent money in exchange for weed and blow. At that point, you considered him simply David's connection, just another substance-swilling show business lowlife. Now that you live here and have had a chance to watch how the man actually operates in his native environment, you realize David probably grossly exaggerated the amount of time and money he'd spent with Sasha. You don't want to think about where David may actually have spent that time and money.

Ironic to reflect upon how so much of your time and money, past and present, is tied up with this man. Currently, the deal is, you are supposed to promote him and find performance opportunities for him that will get him off the street. But, frankly, he isn't the easiest act in the world to push. You can't do for him what you once did for David — what you *tried* to do for David, which was mostly just revise his acting resume, keep your ears and eyes open for upcoming auditions, and help him learn his lines. For Sasha, though, the college performing circuit seems a likely venue. Anywhere the audience is made up of iconoclasts who enjoy being on the receiving end of some personalized abuse. Certainly not the corporate scene.

If only Sasha would quit giving you mixed signals. Sometimes, usually on those evenings when he lets you help him sort the cash from his nightly hats at Fisherman's Wharf, he gives you worshipful looks and plies you with teasing anecdotes from *W. C. Fields and Me*, a biographical memoir about that great, early 20th-century comic-juggler-turned-comic-actor by his long-time mistress, Carlotta Monti. But other times at home, he seems determined to avoid you throughout the flat, slipping into his bedroom and quietly shutting the door just as you emerge from the hall closet.

A couple times a month after an evening of gigs, he'll bring home some girl. Then he disappears into his bedroom with her, re-emerging hours later, taking her home before you are awake, looking disheveled and shame-faced when you next run into him. You don't know whether to interpret these liaisons and his attitude afterwards as entirely unrelated to you or as deliberate messages of non-interest in you or as attempts to incite jealousy. Too bad if it's the latter, because you never do feel jealous of any of these women. After all, you are used to sharing. And, frankly, it doesn't matter so much to you whether your relationship is strictly business or whether he's game and in the game for more. Either way, you'll be doing his publicity, because, after all, you gotta live somewhere.

22.

Bill Has Reason to Wonder

Only days ago, you spent another three hours with David at his new "office" in the House of Shields, and never once that evening did he mention he and Juli had broken up for good. In fact, the last time you'd heard from him about his home situation was soon after he'd delegated his wife to you, when he first began splitting his time and attention between Juli and this new one, Barbra, in a failed, most likely bogus-from-the-get-go, attempt at "Open Marriage."

Juli, on the other hand, called you at work yesterday to make sure you have her new phone number. And when you called her back at that number, you found out it belonged to that creepy clown-guy who sells blow to your degenerate old friend.

You wished then *you* coulda been the one to offer space to Juli. But everyone living in the house you share seems to be staying put, no vacancies. And the house rules don't permit long-term couch-surfing or even extended room-sharing. It puts a strain on the utilities.

You visit Juli to make sure she's alright. You drive over to the Haight-Ashbury, park alongside the Panhandle, and find your way to the nearby three-story Victorian house she now occupies with that strange man. You press the doorbell, hear its strident ring sounding in the upstairs flat. Through the filmy curtain covering the leaded glass window in the door, you can make out a long flight of stairs running to the upper landing and, seconds later, here comes Juli, running down. The glass prisms of the window refract and deconstruct her image so she looks like Marcel Duchamp's "Nude Descending a Staircase" (No. 2!), rejected by the Cubists in 1912 as too Futurist. In this present moment, the past seems to have caught up with the future, if only for a second or two.

Juli draws aside the curtain to double-check it's you, showing appropriate urban caution, before she opens the door and gives you a big smile. Followed by a big bear hug that takes you by surprise and causes you to briefly calculate when you last showered. On the way over, you had worried she might not want to be your friend anymore, since you are still her ex's old high school friend. Clearly, your fear was unfounded.

Juli shows you around the flat, which is not at all how you'd imagined it would be. True, the living room is odd, with floor-to-nearly-ceiling mirrors, racks of juggling props, and no furniture except a couple of chairs. But the rest of the place seems ordinary to the point of banality. Well, except for the two unicycles in the hallway, a short one and a second one so tall you suppose he needs a ladder to get up there.

You also cannot help but notice: the entire flat is unnaturally clean and neat. A large, pink, cut-glass bowl containing scores of keys sits atop an antique, roll-top desk in the alcove next to the stairs. Next to the bowl is a row of porcelain, circus-clown figurines arranged just so. The bright-white, unblemished juggling clubs in the living room are evenly spaced in their rack, all set to lean at precisely the same angle. You see no accumulated dust on any of the bookshelves, no dust bunnies sticking to the edge of the Victorian-style, patterned rug.

Passing the half-open door of a hall bathroom, you catch a strong whiff of Pine-Sol. In the kitchen, you are momentarily blinded by a flash of sunlight off the side of the stainless steel toaster. The stovetop is spotless, and three identical pot holders hang from the fume hood above it, all facing the same direction on their magnetic hooks. Familiar as you are with Juli's home-maintenance strategy of benign neglect, you feel certain she had nothing whatsoever to do with getting this place stamped with the Good Housekeeping Seal of Approval.

"Wanna see where I'm sleeping?" Juli asks you with a mischievous smirk. You feel glad she looks happier than she has in months. And you feel your face grow hot, as you acknowledge that, yes, you *would* like to see her new sleeping quarters.

You follow her out of the kitchen and back into the hallway, where she steps up to the door of what is apparently a coat closet, grabs its knob, and flings it open with flourish. "Ta-dah!" she exclaims. You see a ladder inside the "closet," leading up to — what? Juli swings herself up onto the ladder, as if she were an ape, and ascends. You do the same.

Twelve feet later, you emerge head-first into an attic — Juli's space — which extends in all directions the entire length and width of the flat, including the cupola at the front of the house. No furniture here, either, but wall-to-wall carpeting on the floor, and the walls themselves are freshly painted. A mattress on the floor fills the alcove created by a large dormer window. A row of three skylights in the sloped ceiling of the roof lets in sun and air. A large skylight over the interior stairway you first climbed to the flat permits an overhead view of anyone entering the front door. Nice setup.

"So," she asks, "whaddya think?"

"Nice setup."

Later, back down in the kitchen, across two fragrantly steaming cups of Earl Grey tea, she tells you the whole appalling story — everything that's happened since the day you stopped by her office to gift her with a new old telephone. How could David have just thrown away this woman, giving the matter so little thought? He must be an even bigger idiot than you ever realized. You'd met Barbra on a couple of occasions, and though it was clear she was well off and generous with her assets, she was also kinda snooty. Not to mention, frankly phony and conniving. And lacquered. Not the sort of person you would have pictured going after David. Even in his current Hugh Hefner imitator phase.

When you first arrived, Juli's new roommate, Sasha, had been out somewhere, performing his circus tricks. But now, with a slamming of the front door and a lot of huff-puffing up the stairs, he has returned.

"Lucy, I'm home!" he brays from the alcove at the top of the stairwell, followed by the audible clink of keys against heavy glass.

He joins Juli in the kitchen and is clearly not at all pleased to find you there as well. Juli, however, seems happy to see him and doesn't look the least bit annoyed that he should intrude on a private conversation between two old friends. You watch as Sasha, still wearing his red clown nose and fright wig, clatters and bangs around the kitchen, opening and closing drawers, setting down the kettle on the stove with more force than strictly necessary, jumping around in his two-tone tights, making wisecracks.

Then it occurs to you: is something going on between these two?

As soon as Sasha leaves the room, you lean across the table and ask: "Is something going on between you and ___?" Rather than risk having the subject himself overhear you saying his name, you incline your head slightly and roll your eyes meaningfully in the direction of the kitchen door, through which Mr. Creepy Clown-Guy passed on his way to infect some other part of the flat.

Juli looks startled at the question. "No!" she whispers urgently, "Of course not." But when Sasha returns to the kitchen and resumes his conversation-destroying routine, you assume she is lying. Why else would he behave that way, if not out of jealousy? So, when he leaves the kitchen a second time, and you hear him slam the bathroom door and start the shower, you turn to Juli and say:

"Lissen, can we please get out of here for a while? Go get some dinner? Maybe catch a show?"

She lights up at the suggestion of going to the movies. "The Strand is showing a John Waters quadruple bill: *Pink Flamingos, Female Trouble, Desperate Living,* and *Polyester.*"

"*Polyester* — is that old or new?"

"Old and new. It's a few years old, but it's his most recent. He hasn't made anything for several years."

"Ran out of bad taste?"

"Maybe so. Though I find that hard to believe."

"Can't say I've ever really been a big John Waters fan. But sure, I'm up for that. We better have something to eat first, though, 'cause I'm guessing I won't feel like it afterwards."

Eight hours later, you and Juli are walking down Market Street to the Chronicle garage on the corner of 5th, where you have stashed your car. The cast of characters on the street resembles what you have been watching on the screen, and you wrap your arm protectively around Juli, making up for the fact that you were too chicken to try to hold her hand in the theater. As you walk along, the soles of your shoes still feel slightly sticky from whatever liquid had been flowing underfoot on the Strand's wooden floor. You attempt conversation:

"So, how about that naked guy in the next balcony down?"

"The one who kept jumping up, shouting, silhouetted against the screen, and then his friends would reach up and grab him to pull him back down — that one? Yeah, he was having a good time, alright."

"I think I got a contact high from all the marijuana smoke."

"You must be a pretty cheap stoner."

"One of my many most-endearing attributes."

She laughs. You hug her in tighter and are gratified she doesn't pull away from you. In fact, when she responds by throwing her arms around you, meeting you breast to chest, and you decide in that moment to take the chance of a lifetime to lean in and kiss her — and she *lets* you! — you have a sudden premonition of events to come. Which leaves you light-headed, heart pounding. You look around, perplexed, because you cannot recall where it was you parked your van.

Three hours later and back in the house you've shared with four other people these past five years, you lie upon your lumpy, sagging, single-occupancy bed, feeling utterly relaxed and content, considering what it is you want in a relationship with a significant other.

First, you want someone who won't screw around, then leave you.

Second, you want someone who'll be glad to see you when you come home, someone you enjoy talking to for hours on end.

She doesn't have to be a great cook or homemaker. She just has to be nice to you, for crying out loud, to be a good friend. She just has to be someone like ... Juli.

You think: if only I could meet someone nice, like Juli.

Then you realize: you already know someone nice like Juli. You know ... Juli. And now Juli is available. Assuming she was telling the truth about that roommate of hers.

23.

Juli Returns to the 8-to-5

E ver since Raker & Ho laid you off and you became aide-de-camp to your wacky roommate, your daily routine has included Sasha's evening ritual of sorting his tribute. Except, of course, on those occasions when he brings home some comely trainee sorter to spend the night. Then you get to lie on your mattress right above his bedroom and listen for hours to them giggling right below you. You wait patiently until they grow quiet before you lower yourself down your twelve-foot ladder to tiptoe into the bathroom and brush your teeth.

But you love it when Sasha returns home alone and wants your company, because these are the only times of comfortable domesticity that the two of you share, when you seem able to chat like actual friends, when he isn't either subtly avoiding you or actively using you as his captive audience to work out some new juggling or club-swinging bit. Sometimes, sitting on this man's bed, separating out — and separated by — heaps of coins by denomination, stacking them on the cafeteria tray he swiped from one of the girls' dorms at S.F. State, and slipping them into paper sleeves, you feel as though you've known him forever.

On such convivial nights, you forget that, until a few months ago, this man was mostly just David's friend and connection, a sleaze-ball street clown who routinely extracted a portion of your rent money from your husband by swapping your cash for his cocaine in tiny origami envelopes folded from dollar bills. Though you'd held it against him, how he played to the weaknesses of your soon-to-be-ex, you did always admire his creative collateral — the clever DIY straw built into each packet.

One Sunday night around eleven, Sasha dumps the contents of his evening's hat onto his bed and waves his hand to invite you to leave off leaning against his bedroom doorframe and take a seat on his plushy coverlet. You watch as he spreads out the coins and bills with graceful fingers to commence the sorting process. You notice a couple non-monetary tips mixed in among the coins and bills.

"Oh, lookie, how did *that* get in there?" he says, pulling a lacy lime-green thong from a drift of paper money.

"Hmmm," he muses, first holding the familiar-looking, itty-bitty garment near one eye, in the practiced manner of a jeweler examining a diamond, before turning sommelier and bringing the feminine bit to his nose to give it a brief sniff. Then he slides open his nightstand drawer, tosses in the tiny web of lace and elastic, and carefully presses the drawer closed.

"One more for the archives," he declares.

"Eww," you reply, making a disgusted face and thinking the bare-assed owner of all these lime-green thongs sure does get around.

But your disgust does not extend to your roommate. In fact, you must acknowledge that, quite apart from Sasha's clowning skills, he possesses a certain charisma. Which must be the reason he gets away with saying such terrible things to people during his act, somehow escaping a beating every night. As jugglers go, he's good, but no juggler is *that* good. And it's not as though he were ... well, all that physically attractive. You pity your ex, who is decidedly handsome, yet sadly deficient in star quality. On the other hand, if David possessed Sasha's perverse animal magnetism, he wouldn't have been content to simply add yet-another thong to his collection. Dog that he is, he would've followed its scent straight to its owner.

"Sasha, how many years now have you worked the street?"

"Seven-ish. I don't count the better part of a year I spent at that Midwestern theme park."

"And in all that time, have you ever had any trouble making enough to live on?"

"Slept in my car upon occasion, but no, not really."

"Not even when you first started out?"

"Nope."

"And in your experience of working alongside other buskers, seasoned pros and complete virgins, how common is it for a street performer to be able to live on just his hat alone?"

"Dunno. Never thought much about it. Besides, it's bad manners to compare hats."

"Well, if you *did* compare hats, how do you suspect you're doing?"

"I suspect I'm doing quite well."

"Then tell me, please: why, since you clearly love doing what you do and since you make such a good living at it, why do you want me to try to find places for you to perform indoors?"

Sasha looks at you thoughtfully, obviously weighing his reply before delivering it. You watch him set aside his habitual sarcasm in order to answer you in a way that you, a non-performer, can understand.

"Jujube, you've been out with me and watched my act often enough to be able to figure out that one." He raises one hand curled into a loose fist and, starting with his thumb, extends a digit for each of his reasons for wanting to get off the street.

"One (thumb): the weather at night in the City sucks. It's cold and wet and windy. Try balancing anything on your forehead in a high wind.

"Two (index finger): traffic along the wharf likewise sucks and is so loud at times that no one can hear me unless I am shouting. This puts undue strain on my instrument.

"Three (significant middle finger): most passersby are in a big hurry and do not give a shit. They glance at me and just think I am weird and creepy.

"Four (ring finger): the merchants love me because I attract crowds, but they resent me, too, because the same people they think are supposed to be their customers give me the money they imagine should come to them instead.

"Five (pinky): kids steal my props, unless I hire some local hoodlum — or you — to watch them."

Having used up the thumb and all four fingers of his left hand, he ticks off a final reason on the thumb of his right hand: "And six: every so often, the cops come and bust my ass. Then I get free rent for the night."

You feel abashed, hearing him lay it out that way. "Guess I

hadn't really put it all together. But, yeah, now that you mention it, I see what terrible working conditions you're exposed to."

"Like I said, Juju: I'm dying of exposure. What's more, I'm on the verge of OT — that's Old and Tired — and I do not want to hit forty and find myself making balloon dogs at kiddie parties."

"You're not really suitable for children."

"So I'm told. One more reason I prefer working the late-night shifts."

"Sasha, but then why clowning, with all the ... getup?" You waggle your fingers at your head to indicate an invisible fright wig, then pinch your nose a couple times to suggest honking an invisible red nose.

He shrugs and replies, "Clowning was where I came in." Then he says you'd understand if, like him, you'd grown up with "The General" for a father and been sent off to Boston to complete your secondary education at a military school during the so-called Vietnam Conflict.

"Your father is a general?"

"My grandfather was the actual general. My father is merely a former lieutenant colonel who acts like a general and now sells pharmaceuticals to his old Army buddies at various government agencies. I was supposed to enlist in the American Way and march in his footsteps."

"Sorry."

"Not a problem."

"So, uh, is Sasha your real name?"

"It's a nickname for Alexander. That's my 'real' name. My father agreed to let me blow off getting a law degree from Georgetown (his dream for me) and go to Clown College instead (my dream for myself), on the condition I never use my real name onstage. See, I'm a junior — a third, actually — so it's fully within my power to humiliate three generations of my family, if I include myself. Besides, 'Sasha' sounds vaguely Russian, and that pisses him off even more."

You want to help this man, but you know you're going to need to do more than just create resumés and organize press photos — you'll have to produce results in the form of actual gigs. Except you really don't know what to do with him. All your experience has been with actors, not novelty acts.

"Maybe you could go into professional theater. That's mostly an indoor thing."

"No thanks. I'd hate it."

"You'd hate acting? How do you know? You could learn."

"I don't hate acting. Just actors. Besides, I'm not sure I could memorize pages and pages of lines that someone else wrote. All my lines are my own."

"Aside from those you've stolen."

"Hey, Juju, gimme some credit for originality. In my time, I've only purloined a line or two in moments of genuine desperation. If you hear someone else doing the same bit as me, they probably stole it from me. But, rather than embrace certain career death as an actor, I'd stay right where I am right now and face a future filled with balloon dogs. Never fear, though: I have my sights set on a different goal."

"Which is?"

"Stand-up. Stand-up's inside. And stand-up's huge. Why do you suppose I keep dragging you to comedy clubs and making you take notes for me?"

"So, instead of being a vulgar juggling clown, you want to

be a vulgar comedian who juggles?"

"Something like that. Perhaps, eventually, simply a stand-up comedian — the purest of all professionally staged lifeforms."

"What: no props, no costume, no makeup, not even your lucky red nose?"

"No, I'm not quite ready to go onstage naked without my character. And it's not as though anyone is exclaiming over 'this face you got!' But yeah, eventually, I hope, it'll be just me up there. Whoever that is."

"At least then I'd know where to send you to audition. I mean, thus far, I haven't known how to help you, you're basically a novelty act."

"And I suppose, thus far, that's why you've been such a crappy booking agent?"

"Thanks a lot. I plan to get better at what I'm supposed to be doing right about the same time you get better at what you do. How long would you need to be onstage during your next incarnation?"

"Twenty minutes at first."

"Twenty minutes is a long time. How much talking do you do now, would you say?"

"Maybe a third of that. More if I get hecklers. That's why I love me some hecklers."

"Three times what you're doing now? Big step."

"I'm writing it all down, Juju, every precious funny thought, pondering how to shift the talk-tricks ratio. I've been doing mostly set bits with patter and expletives for transition; but I can flip that. Just one thing."

"What's that?"

"I can't work out this transition in a vacuum. You've been great, Jujube. A real pal — helping me with my research, keeping me company, keeping me on track. More than ever, I'll need someone to bounce ideas off and try new material on. I'll need someone who can spot my weaknesses. Who better to do that than you? I need you, Jujube. All the way."

As he says this, he offers you what you have come to recognize as his medium-intensity, soulful-eyes gaze, several degrees higher than his soft-focus, sad-dog look of longing. At which point, it occurs to you that possibly, quite possibly, you are being played for your weaknesses. Nevertheless, although you feel your face starting to heat up, you bravely meet his look and solemnly declare:

"Sasha, I promise I'll do everything in my power to support you."

"I believe you, Juju. That's why I'm so confident that, with a helpmate like you on my side, my success is assured." He flashes you his trademark, blindingly brilliant smile. You blink back an afterimage of his teeth.

After this Sunday night's optimistic high, Sasha returns home a week later, in the late afternoon of the following Saturday, with a broken finger. Which shakes you. Because you know perfectly well no one juggles with their fingers taped together. You recall what Sasha said about evolving to standup. You wish he'd already made more progress toward that ambition.

The morning after his accident, you two talk about this. He seems cheerful, keeps showing off the finger he broke. Of course, it would *have* to be his middle finger, now a super-finger taped to his ring finger as a splint. You express concern for how it will be possible to keep your living situation together when he can't perform for a couple of months, maybe longer, depending on the course of his rehabilitation. He makes an effort to reassure you. "We [we!] will be alright," he says. You assume it's the drugs talking.

You want to believe him. But you don't — because you can't. Because, at the moment, he is just another man who said he would look after you, but then couldn't or wouldn't. Until now, you hadn't realized how baseless was the sense of security you had relaxed into. All it took to trash your future was one lousy busted finger.

Once again, you are reminded: your only real security in life is your own ability to take care of yourself and your willingness to do so. You feel the old 8-to-5 creeping up on you again. You don't want to go back to a job in the straight world, but you resolve to call a few of the downtown temporary employment agencies first thing Monday morning. Because you also don't want to have no place to live. You don't even own a car you could sleep in.

When Monday arrives, you contact the same temp agency you started out with when you and David first moved to the City. Fortunately, despite the passage of time, they still have records on you. Which right away puts you back on the list for job assignments. And this time around, temping seems not so bad. You wonder if perhaps this is the effect of lowered career expectations.

In the days to follow, your various temporary bosses are delighted to learn you have actual skills — abilities you take for granted, but which they value: the ability to answer multiple phone lines, sound pleasant, and legibly write down coherent messages; the ability to type and even transcribe tape-recordings from a dictaphone; the ability to use your deep knowledge of the alphabet to file documents; the ability to show up on time at a specified place and remain there, appearing productive, until you are told you can leave.

Having given up resisting the destiny your gender and social class determined for you at the time of your birth, along with any hope you still had for self-actualization, you now go where you are told, do as you are told. And you are surprised to find this cycle is ... a huge relief. Because you know what you are: just another cog in yet-another machine. And that's alright for now.

Meanwhile, your damaged roommate seems hard at work rehabbing himself. When you leave in the morning, usually around 7 a.m., to get to your assignment somewhere in the City, he is still in his bedroom. You assume he is asleep, but you don't really know, because he has taken to closing his bedroom door at night. And when you return in the evening, usually around 6 p.m., he is getting ready to go out somewhere to do something, he doesn't say what. Much less invite you to go along. Even on Saturday afternoons, he is off to Peacock Meadow in Golden Gate Park, where a lot of the local street performers gather. Or to the Panhandle a couple blocks away. He doesn't ask you to join him there, either.

Some late nights, you lie in bed in your attic and listen to the ploppings of dropped juggling balls hitting Sasha's bed. You know what he's doing, because you've watched him practice: he stands next to his bed, so when he misses a catch, the balls land on the mattress, instead of the floor, and don't roll out of reach. From your attic sanctuary, you count the sounds of his drops to know how many balls he's trying for: one, two, three, four, five … six, seven. Pretty good, you think. Not to mention, better than sheep for drifting off.

After six weeks, you notice the tape is off his fingers. It's a Saturday morning, and he stands in the kitchen at the stove, waiting for the kettle to boil water for tea. And while he stands there, he squeezes a tennis ball, over and over, with his left hand.

"What's that for?" you ask, giving the tennis ball a nod.

He offers you a brilliant grin before explaining, "Just working up my grip in this busted hand."

"How's it going?"

"Not bad. Good thing I'm not older or I might really be screwed. Can I ask a favor of you?"

"Sure. What?"

"The clinic gave me a special cream — it's got Arnica and some other homeopathic healing shit in it. I'm supposed to massage it into my hand to speed up the rehab. But it's hard to do on my own. Think you could help me out?" He reaches into the pocket of his bathrobe, extracts a blue-and-white tube, and hands it to you. You take it, uncap it, and sit at the tiny, two-person kitchen table, watching as he brings his tea over to sit opposite you.

He presents his hand palm down, in the manner of a pope waiting to have his ring kissed. You take the proffered hand and gently turn it palm up. Then you observe him observing you as you one-handedly apply a blobby line of white cream to his newly mended middle finger and massage it into his skin. His fingers seem too delicate to belong to a man's hand. You think: this is the closest in weeks that he's allowed you to get to him.

"Back to juggling again?"

"Working on it."

"Any progress on the comedy front?"

"Working on that as well."

"It's been a while since you tried out anything on me. I thought maybe you'd changed your mind."

"Jujube, you ought to know me better than that. But you just reminded me of something I need to tell you: I'm going to be gone most of next week. I've got an important trip to make."

"Yeah, where you going?"

"I'm off to see a lady friend in New Orleans."

You're still rubbing cream into his hand, and you focus intently on this simple task to conceal the sudden small stab of jealousy you feel.

"New Orleans? Like, Way Down South? That's nice."

"So, I have a favor to ask of you: could you reanimate your efforts to connect me with some standup gigs?"

You look up in surprise from your hand-rubbing. "You're ready for this?"

"If all goes well on this trip, I should be."

24.

Sasha's Big Break

The day you broke your finger, everything changed. Just one finger, and you broke it in the most ordinary of ways — for a street clown: stopping yourself atop your six-foot unicycle by grabbing onto a post supporting the upper level of Pier 39, down near Fisherman's Wharf. You knew the second it happened, but too late. In that moment, your only other option would have been to let yourself go flying off their shitty little stage and possibly land in the bay.

The bit got a good solid laugh, though, so you think you may try it again someday, if you get desperate enough. After all, you have nine more digits to go. Anyway, there's nothing quite like an audience laughing when you are in really a lot of fuckin' pain to show you the ultimate bitter/sweet side of being a clown.

Happily, it was your critical middle finger you snapped, so at least you knew you could anticipate some future fun-making during recovery.

At the Haight-Ashbury Free Clinic, they tape your fingers and tell you how lucky you are it's not worse. Soberly, you reflect upon the fragile nature of a busker's existence — how little it takes to put you out of business completely for a while. Possibly forever, if you heal badly. You continue along in this morose line of thinking until they send you on your way with a little paper envelope rattling with Darvons.

You drive home with your busted digit buddy-taped to your ring finger. Thank god, it was your left hand you screwed up, not your right — you can still manage your car's manual shift, while sissy-steering with your thumb and index finger. Flying high on pain-killers by the time you pull into the driveway, you are in a jolly mood. You call Juli down from the attic. The two of you sit on prop trunks in the living room, the practice space you won't need for at least a month. She looks at you quizzically. You answer her unvoiced question by giving her the finger.

She laughs, but follows up with appropriate sympathy, immediately grokking the full implications of your situation: without ten fully functional fingers to manage the mainstay of your act, all your juggling bits that took months to learn and years to perfect mean nothing. Clearly, juggling will not be featured in your near future. Home Sweet Home is where you'll be hanging and healing. Meanwhile, you know all those freaks at the Pier will fall vulturelike on your time slots. You'll have to challenge them to duels later to get your pitch back.

And this is assuming you heal well and can work your way up to where you were before you busted your finger. That first night you take two more Darvons, in addition to the two you took earlier that afternoon, and you crash. You realize you will be severely constipated for the next couple weeks, but you don't care. You are already plotting how to get a refill.

The next morning, after a restless night of pain and anxiety, contemplation and planning, you hold a business meeting with your assistant. Right away, she pops the $64,000 question:

"If you can't juggle for the next couple of months and you're giving up the unicycle for good, what will you do for an act?"

"Most of me still works," you tell Juli, defensively.

"Yeah, you still got your mouth, and words are still coming out of it," she shoots back.

You glare at one another for several beats.

"What're you gonna do for income till your finger heals?" she blurts out. Taken by surprise, you fail to disguise your look of dismay.

"Sorry," she says, "that was pretty insensitive of me."

"No, it's alright. How could you possibly know I am secretly very rich?"

"Oh, right. I've always suspected you of being a criminal mastermind."

You're not rich, of course. But your ultra-conservative upbringing did inculcate you with the basic money-management skills that most of the scabby-kneed adherents of your profession obviously lack. Consequently, you have sequestered the requisite six months' worth of emergency living expenses, though you carefully conceal this fact from everyone — most especially from any woman who might possibly be interested in you. And should your stash prove insufficient, it may be time to tap out that trust fund. Or you could grit your teeth and put in a filial call to The General.

But you see that Jujube seems a little frightened. At which point, it occurs to you: in contrast with your nervous roommate here, your future is so bright you gotta wear shades. At least insofar as life's basic necessities are concerned — whatever money can buy. Never mind the sad, current state of your fingers.

Through no special virtue of your own or any special effort on your part, you were blessed with an upper middle-class existence — essentially, just another ordinary lazy jerk born with a silver spoon up his ass. And though the expectations that accompany such a life of privilege proved stultifying to you, you still must acknowledge: you got a good solid start. Fear of actual poverty has never intruded upon you. Even your disasters (the nights you spent in jail, the car breakdowns in the middle of nowhere, the equipment stolen from your car while you were eating a greasy breakfast in some dumpy pancake house surrounded by dumpy people, etc., etc.) were adventures you opened yourself up to and knew would be temporary. As the gymnasts say, you've always worked with a net.

Your performing career is the sole aspect of your life for which you have never developed any sort of contingency plan. In fact, you have always refused to consider a fallback, because to do so seemed preliminary to selling out at the first sign of anything less than total world domination, and you are adamant in your rejection of even the possibility that you will be anything less than hugely, wildly successful in your chosen field.

"Lissen, Jujube, don't look so scared. We'll handle this

together. We are going to be just fine, I promise you."

Intent on reassuring your roommate/personal assistant/ booking agent/private audience, you reach out awkwardly with your good hand to pat her shoulder, then shift in closer for a tight, one-armed buddy-hug. She relaxes against you for a three-beat count, before pulling away and telling you:

"Thanks. That's very reassuring, but I think it's time I considered some temp work."

"If it makes you feel better ... but you know you don't have to do that. I can support us both. Even with this... ." You raise your bum hand and give her the finger again.

"Great, great. That's just great." She gets to her feet. "Are we done here?"

"No, really I think we're just getting started. But you go on back up to your nest, Jujube. I've got my work cut out for me. I need to do some serious thinking, and you know that's not my strong suit. I'll let you know when I've got anything."

Having projected a nonchalant front to calm your anxious roommate, you repair to your bedroom and quietly but firmly shut the door behind you. Time to do some honest self-analysis — not your favorite leisure-time activity.

Though you consider yourself a good planner, smart and pragmatic, your planning efforts have always tended to express themselves as lavishly colorful, extremely detailed daydreams, which you enjoy immensely. You have an entire mental library of fantasy performance tapes you can call up on demand in order to watch yourself performing at various glamorous pitches, always spectacularly flawless, always with a large, adoring, generous crowd of out-of-towners who've coincidentally just come from their ATM machines and who, having inadvertently withdrawn too much money, prefer to leave it in your hat, rather than walk around the City and risk getting held up at knifepoint.

"Yes!" you watch yourself telling these kindly, naïve souls in your mind-movie, "Let me help you. Don't become a mark — leave your money with me. Better yet, I'm entirely willing to hold your wallet for safe-keeping, while you wander off to explore our beautiful city. Yes, of *course* I'll be here later."

Your imaginary ploy makes you snicker, so you scribble the lines down in your notebook. Who knows? Maybe you can do something with them later.

Now is not the time. Your busted finger aches, reminding you that: (a) your future performances may well not resemble your past performances, and (b) your pain pills are wearing off. You extract two Darvons from your starter stash, gather some spit, and dry-swallow your meds. You did learn a few useful things from being around all those military brats.

The thing that keeps coming back to you is how many *assumptions* you'd been making about your future self based on your past self. Your former self had ten fully functional digits that you'd been training daily. Most of what you presented onstage required a body that worked normally and optimally. Now that particular reality belonged to your used-to-be self. It may also belong to your future self, but in the present moment there's no way to predict this with any certainty.

Sitting there with your taped-together fingers, stiff all over from a rotten night's sleep, dry-mouthed (and constipated) from pain meds, you reflect, yet again, upon how really, truly, deeply tired you are of working the street, always out in the open, freezing your ass off on cold, foggy nights, elbowing past other buskers for the best spots and best times, dragging your gear from place to place. You feel like the Ghost of Marley, Scrooge's business partner: "These are the chains I forged in life!" Plus, you'd let yourself get so prop-heavy, you hardly knew what to do without all your gear. You knew you really ought to do something about this life you'd created, but creature of habit that you are, you'd felt scant motivation to change. What's that old saying? If it ain't broke, then don't fix it. Now, of course, it *is* broke.

So now you look, once again, to your future in your mind's eye, and this time you watch yourself from the back row of your own audience — dropping juggling clubs with loud clunks, covering flubs with ill-conceived patter, losing spectators out of their embarrassment for you. Suddenly, the idea of going back onstage as a shittier version of yourself is even more terrifying than the idea of recreating and offering yourself in a new guise to the world.

Up to this point in your life, you'd always preferred looking to a brilliantly imagined future of your own choosing, rather than a continuation of the unhappy past originally thrust upon you. Now, however, you steel yourself and review your actual memories, the honest, accurate, and therefore painful version, all the way to the beginning of your career, in order to check for where you might have missed the turnoff to an alternate route leading to your destination of stardom.

What a baby you were at the start! Just a chubby-faced boy-man fresh out of Clown College, working your first gig as a clown on weekends at an amusement park in Nashville, Tennessee, y'all. You could juggle a little, mime a little, ride a unicycle, all those basic circus skills. But you knew nothing about working an audience, nothing about interacting with … other people.

You'd never been all that great at people. Too often, men didn't much like you. Or rather, they seemed to like you well enough onstage, not so much offstage. When you were little, your late mother used to say you seemed arrogant to the other boys, always acting like you were so much better than them. You shrugged. What were you supposed to do about *that*? You *were* so much better than they were. Okay, not your looks, but you were certainly about ten times smarter than your classmates. Were you supposed to pretend you didn't notice they were all idiots?

Women, on the other hand, had always appeared to like you just fine, onstage and off. To your perpetual amazement, even your short-on-looks face that clown makeup only improved didn't seem to put them off. Too often, though, their liking turned into wanting a piece of you.

Even your stepmother demonstrated very questionable behavior towards you. For a bride. Though you blame your father for what happened. He shoulda known better than to remarry so soon after mum died — or to go after someone so young. You were just a junior in high school; she was closer to your age than she was to your father's. None of which improved your relationship with your father. No wonder you got sent off to the Academy for your final year of high school.

All of which still makes you wish at times you'd be born gay. Except, of course, you're much too ugly to be any good at gay. Besides, you really like women. You've tried to have girlfriends, but they always ended up interfering in your Life.

Plus, nowadays they're all "liberated" — at least, until they want something from you.

Your last real girlfriend, Tiffany, a live-in relationship that ended three years ago, was just the worst. The ultimate female parasite, she deliberately let herself get pregnant in order to net you. When you offered to finance her abortion, she refused, moved out of the flat you'd shared, and in with a couple girlfriends to form a little triad of welfare harpies. Then she told Social Services you'd knocked her up and abandoned her. These days, she's officially a single mom on public assistance and you are officially a dead-beat dad. Her little trick paid off. Fortunately, though, the state cannot garnish your wages from a job you don't have. Another reason why street performing remained a good fit for you for so long.

But after Tiff had played out her sucker's game on you, you started to seriously consider taking a bend in your career path. You particularly recall, at the end of one especially remunerative evening, the aging, big-haired fox who tottered over to you on six-inch platform shoes. Studded with cubic zirconia, she looked as if she'd just escaped from a mafia casino in Vegas. When you held out your top hat well stuffed with tips, she leaned into it with her pert, surgically altered nose close enough to smell the money, then looked up and gave you a broad, ceramic grin.

"Working out here must be good exposure," she exclaimed in a raspy, smoke-marinaded voice that reminded you of a much older version of the stepmother you hadn't seen for the better part of a decade.

And you — freezing in your sweat-soaked, court jester costume, eyes stinging from the clown white you were still applying back then, balls still aching from this afternoon's lousy dismount from your six-foot unicycle, you replied (imitating her raspy voice), "Lady, I'm dying of exposure out here." Now, you fear, this may literally be true.

You cannot ignore the fact that you are receiving a clear karmic lesson: your "tricks" have taken you as far as they're going to. You must stop trying to become the best you can be at what you were and, instead, you will have to concentrate on evolving.

Having achieved a certain level of prominence in your career field, you find it hard to re-embrace the near-certainty of future onstage bombings. But you know you must accept "dying," so you can return to "killing." Time to get down to business, while you still have enough pain-killers to see you through. You only wish you'd done it sooner.

25.
Sasha Courts the Voodoo Queen

Two months later, you find yourself once again strolling the streets of New Orleans, getting chickenskin chills in the 80-degree heat and 80-percent humidity. More than seven years have passed since your last visit — which, incidentally, had been your first-ever visit to "N'awlins" — and you've changed a lot since then. 'Course, that was before Reagan became president.

It's been even longer since you got your B.A. from Vanderbilt (major in chemistry), your C.A. from Clown College (major in juggling with a minor in prankstering), then moved back to Nashville to work weekends as a fool-in-training. And, for two long semesters, you also held a day job during the week as a lab assistant in the university's clinical pharmacology division, setting up lab stations, washing glassware, cleaning animal cages, and carrying out whatever other menial tasks came your way.

But while you approved of the lab's *raison d'être* and needed the money, you resented the hours you spent there, impinging as they did on your practice sessions for your real life on the weekends. Not to mention, on your nap times. How ironic to think, in retrospect, this very job would provide the catalyst for your next professional step forward.

For several months in Nashville, you threw "Full Moon Parties." This was years before those copycats in Thailand started doing their beach parties on the island of Ko Phangan. Back then, you were living at a hippie house you shared with a collection of post-doc science types who resembled the sort of people your father had once hoped would constitute your cohort. Instead, your invited guests consisted of an eclectic mix of jugglers, musicians, singers, dancers, self-appointed poets, and other performance types whose acts eluded ready-made definition and even description. All were fascinating to you.

One party drew an ancient lab tech who worked in the same building as you and who occupied a category all his own: in his much-younger years, he'd been a stage magician. Nevertheless, sitting in that art-charged chaos among the other guests nearly half a century his juniors, the old guy looked out of place. You wanted to make sure he was comfortable, so you sat next to him to keep him company. You will always be glad you did, because the story he told you that night forever changed the course of your life.

He asked if you'd ever heard of Marie Laveau, a witchy woman who lived in 19th-century Louisiana. When you said no, you hadn't, he went on to tell you more: she was the Voodoo Queen of New Orleans, a talented hairdresser to upper-class women and a healer well known for her magical powers. Reputedly and by virtue of her second husband, she was buried in plot 347, the Glapion family crypt in Saint Louis Cemetery No. 1 near the French Quarter. And what was relevant to you, your geriatric advisor continued, the gypsies believe that, even from the Other Side, she still retains the power to grant the most deeply held wishes of those who visit her grave and pay homage. But to petition her, you must draw an X on her tomb with charcoal or chalk, turn yourself around three times, knock on the tomb, and yell out your wish. If your wish is granted, you must return to Madame Laveau's tomb, circle the X you drew there when you first visited, and demonstrate your gratitude by leaving her an offering.

Of course, seven or so years ago, your most deeply held wish had been to be good enough to claim the freedom of the street and make your living as a busker. But the aspiration had seemed impossible. You weren't much of a juggler then and, despite being a "graduate" of Clown College, you hadn't made the cut for Ringling Brothers.

Now, showing up in costume and makeup for your amusement park shifts, wandering around performing minor tricks, serving as a colorful element in an environment of surreal entertainment was getting you nowhere. No knowledge or mastery of the performing life was required. You'd come to a dead end. So, your wish to become a professional busker was only a wish, but it was a wish you wanted more than anything to come true. In your mind's eye, you were juggling not three, not five, but *seven* balls with no misses. The crowd stood in silence before you, mesmerized, then broke into screaming applause each time you cleanly caught them all... .

"Just be careful what you ask for," the elderly chemist was saying.

"Huh?" you replied, yanked back to attention out of your florid dream of street-performing glory.

"I said: be careful what you ask for. In case Madame Laveau grants your wish. Remember the saying: the solution to your problem becomes your next problem."

But, of course, back then you couldn't *wait* to invite that next big problem into your life. Consequently, right after work on Halloween night (because rumor had it that Madame Laveau was most receptive to requests delivered on All Saints' Day), you left Nashville in your VW Bug to drive all night to New Orleans. You were determined to find the lady and petition her. It was the late 1970s, and you were determined to be ready for the '80s. *Before* the '80s, if possible.

Three roadside naps, two greasy-spoon meals, and one payphone sick call into work later, you arrived midday in le Vieux Carré, the French Quarter, where Bourbon Street was still littered with plastic cups and glittery trash left by last night's ghoulish revelers.

The cast-off tourist map you extracted from the gutter (shaking off drops of some sort of liquid) led you straight to Saint Louis Cemetery No. 1, where the scene that greeted you was not at all the Arlington-style view you'd expected to see. No graves with tidy headstones. No military-style white crosses lined up in neat rows. Instead, before you lay a vast and shambling array of old, dilapidated mausoleums of all shapes and sizes, some of them nearly as high as the wall that surrounded the cemetery. Apparently, death was a lot sloppier here in New Orleans.

But, with the help of that tourist map, you found your lady's resting place, you drew your X on her tomb with a

Magic Marker pen (swiped from the lab), you turned yourself around three times (hoping no one saw you), you knocked on the tomb, and you yelled out your wish:

"Madame Laveau! Miz Marie, I'm begging you, please! Make me the richest street performer ever!"

Then, judging that you'd done what you'd come to do, you left to go to your car, where you'd parked it a few blocks away. Which is how you discovered that Madame Laveau had indeed granted your petition.

You found your car siphoned empty of gasoline. And you, in yesterday's ambitious haste to hit the highway and drive on down, had neglected to bring along a gas card or even enough cash to refill your tank. Dammit, anyway! But the gas thief hadn't stolen your pillowcase of juggling balls you left on the floor of the backseat. So you grabbed your balls (metaphorically speaking), along with the beat-up, old, glitter-and-rhinestones-seasoned hat given to you for luck by your friend, the over-the-hill magician-turned-lab-tech, and you headed for Jackson Square, a pitch you'd noticed on your march to the cemetery.

You'd never before tried doing your thing outside the sanctioned environment of the amusement park, but today it was either busk or die trying. You needed that gas money. And, after two hours and two busloads of tourists, you had enough money to get home and then some. You'd also managed, albeit briefly, to juggle seven balls without a drop. You headed north that evening feeling pretty smug. All the same, it was good, you considered, that gas prices had stayed under 65 cents a gallon and your Bug was still getting 20+ miles to the gallon. Twenty bucks was enough to take you home and get breakfast.

It took a hard walk down Memory Lane for you to realize, instead of heading straight home on that long-ago, fateful day, you ought to have driven back at once to the cemetery to revisit the dusty old broad so you could thank her. For, sure enough, she had granted your wish: after seven-plus years, you'd become a street performer with a bank balance and an excellent credit score. Now, however, you see clearly you never bothered to give credit where credit was due. Like every other egocentric idiot on the planet, you'd taken all the credit for your every success, while fobbing off all the blame onto someone else any time things went down the crapper. Your ingratitude has led you into a blind alley, so shame on you. You will need to change that, if you are going to get out.

Fortunately, your second trip to New Orleans has so far proven far less challenging than your first. This time, you simply drove to the San Francisco Airport, parked in the long-term parking area, boarded your plane, rented a car, checked into a cheap motel, slept in till noon, and then, after a good breakfast at lunchtime, set out directly for the cemetery.

You hadn't figured out in advance what sort of offering you ought to leave for Miz Marie in order to make up for the favor she did you years ago. Walking toward the cemetery, you feel open to suggestions. When you spot a French bakery along the way, you go inside to consider the possibilities. You decide on a chocolate cake — your favorite. And since they have only one, you consider this a definite sign in your favor. Also, the cake is pretty big, requiring two Cajun chicks in French bakery outfits to levitate and lower its mass into a pink cardboard box and tie the package with string so you can carry it. Frankly, the cake seems like a pretty expensive gift for a dead person. But you're in a mood to go all out for the old gal. After all, you owe her. You know this now.

A few blocks later, you figure you better bring along something stronger than chocolate cake to back up your thank-you. From a tiny corner liquor store, you purchase a bottle of the best Napoleon brandy they carry and stuff it in your coat pocket, along with two shot glasses that proclaim: *"Laissez les bons temps rouler!"*

By the time you finally reach Saint Louis Cemetery #1, the afternoon is late. You notice people filing out of a small entrance with an open gate in the stone wall that surrounds the entire cemetery, easily twice your height. This is where you entered and exited before, so you confidently walk up to the gate, carrying your cake box. Right away, a man stops you. Though not dressed as a guard, he obviously thinks he has some kind of authority, because he says simply: "We're closed now."

You panic.

"But the sign says you're open till four!" you plead in a whiny voice you immediately understand is a pathetic invitation to rejection. The man never responds, just keeps ushering people out past you through the gate and onto the sidewalk.

A tour bus pulls up and sits idling, with doors open to let the cemetery visitors board. Minutes later, the doors close with a wheeze and the bus drives away. You stand alone, dejected. At four o'clock precisely, you watch from ten feet away as the not-a-guard draws a chain around the ancient iron gate and fastens it with a hefty padlock. After he turns and steps away from the gate, you go up to the bars and try to look inside the cemetery to see where he's gone. Already he has disappeared.

Why close a graveyard? you wonder, dumbfounded. They don't stop being dead at 4 o'clock.

With no particular plan in mind, you adjust your grip on the heavy cake box, pat your coat pocket with its brandy bottle and shot glasses, and start to walk around the block, eyeing the cemetery's formidable stone wall. The sun is going down. You think: I'm gonna get in there. Who am I going to bother? And what can that guy do to me, anyway?

You round the corner and find yourself on a quiet side street with a large tree about halfway down the block. It occurs to you that you just might be able to climb the tree and hop over the wall.

The tree turns out to be way too tall to climb. But, right across from it and about halfway up the wall, you notice that a stone is missing. Then it seems the niche created by that missing stone could make a great foothold. If only you can get your leg that high. You reach up the wall; the niche is above your head, just out of reach.

The access looks impossible. You think: I'm going for it.

First, you fling the pink box containing the expensive cake over the wall. You think: she's dead, she's not gonna care. Then you begin your ascent to join the cake.

Somehow you manage to inch your way up, digging your fingertips into cracks and crevices. Painfully you pass the foothold, first using it as a handhold, then climbing high enough to be able to bend your knee and work the toe-tip of your shoe into the niche. You test the foothold to make sure you are secure before you thrust upwards quickly, knowing you have only one shot.

Luckily, you manage to seize and cling to the top of the wall with the fingertips of both hands. The middle finger you broke only two months ago sends a sharp pain shooting up your wrist. You wince and lift the finger a couple of hairbreadths, leaving it to your other digits to share the burden. You pray you don't encounter any shards of glass embedded in the top of the wall to deter trespassers. Miraculously, you don't fall. You strain with everything you have (except for one finger), struggling to pull yourself up until you are able to lock elbows and belly your way over the ledge.

From the top of the wall, the familiar chaotic graveyard stretches out before you. You huff and puff and swing one leg, then the other, over the wall. Slowly you lower yourself down along the inside wall until your arms are fully extended. Then you let go to drop the last five or six feet. You land butt-first, careful to hold aloft your still-healing hand. But aside from scraped palms and injured dignity, you aren't hurt. And this isn't the first time you've taken a hard landing on your ass. At least, no one is here to impress. Or to tip you.

Standing up, you remember the bottle of Napoleon brandy and the two shot glasses in your coat pocket. You pat around your coat — nothing broken. You retrieve the pink cake box, now seriously dented on one corner, and you try to pinch it out. You don't open the box. You think: maybe it's not too bad.

All around you are different kinds of above-ground graves — tombs and crypts designed to accommodate a cemetery built atop a swamp. Most of the monuments are constructed of broken bricks and sloppy concrete, nearly all in terrible shape. The first time you were here, on All Saints' Day, the fresh flowers and decorations, pretty as they were, only served to emphasize the ruined condition of the tombs, like poorly applied makeup on an old lady's wrinkled face. This afternoon, they all just seemed sad and abandoned, making this a spooky place. You hope Madame Laveau will be glad you've come back. You hope you don't see any body parts sticking out of the ground.

You glance back at the wall you've just hoisted yourself over. It occurs to you that getting out of here is going to be just as hard as it was getting in, but now is not the time to think about that. You have a grave to locate and no sodden tourist map to help you out on this occasion.

Then you see him, right ahead of you, about thirty feet away down the aisle. The not-a-guard man is staring straight at you. But you don't stop. You keep walking. In fact, you go straight for him, though slowly.

The setting sun is just over his head, and you are walking straight into it. The guy looks like a silhouette, a shadow. You have to squint to see him at all. As you approach, he doesn't move an inch, doesn't yell, just stares at you with his mouth wide open. He seems in a trance. You walk up to him, dented pink cake box in hand, like you've done nothing wrong.

You ask him simply: "Could you please tell me where to find the grave of Marie Laveau?"

He says nothing, just turns his head to look to his left. You follow his glance to the grave next to you, an old crypt whose peeling pink and orange paint you recognize. Paying no further attention to the man, you go directly to Madame Laveau and place the cake you brought for her at the foot of her mausoleum. You greet her with a big smile and a friendly pat, like the old friend you feel her to be. Her tomb is still covered with Xs, some fresh, others barely visible. A few have been circled by grateful successful petitioners; most remain uncircled. Your Magic Marker X from years ago is worn and faded, but you recognize it, so you dig a bit of charcoal out of the hole created by other petitioners, and you circle your X. Then, giving the opportunity a second thought, you draw a new X near your old X.

"Well, Miz Marie, you old darling," you speak out loud to the voodoo queen, "I know it's been a long time coming, but I do truly thank you for all you've done for me. I've had a great run, many fine adventures, and I appreciate every bit of it. Now, much as I am grateful for your support after our first meeting, I know I must move along. And, once again, I find myself in need of your help."

As you talk, you set out the shot glasses you've brought along, work open the bottle of Napoleon brandy, and pour two shots, one for Miz Marie and one for yourself. You raise your glass in a silent toast and down your shot.

"Drink up," you urge her. And after a moment of no response, you say, "No? Too early in the day to get started? Well, let me help you" — then you down her shot as well and refill both your glasses.

After a couple more rounds, which you feel certain were appreciated by the old broad (though she has so far declined to indulge), you are moved to make a more persuasive case for yourself. You begin to speak extempore, telling Miz Marie your life story, how you got here, not bothering to censor yourself, not bothering to keep track of or commit to memory what you are saying for future use. You tell her all you've gone through since the two of you first met: that first solo gig in the square, leaving Nashville to strike out on your own, all the pitches you've worked across the country, ending up in Frisco, becoming a deadbeat dad, the drugs you've done, your efforts to get yourself off the street, your smart, funny roommate who's been helping you.

In that moment, it comes to you that Madame Laveau and your roommate, Jujube, have something in common: both helped you, seemingly, simply because you asked, and neither has tried to acquire you. And there was, once upon a time, another such woman in your life — your late mother. Which reminds you of your otherwise shitty childhood. So, sad tale though it is, you tell Miz Marie about that as well: about your father, "the General"; his drinking and how he punished you by slamming you into walls; your mother's efforts to protect you; the long, painful death you watched her endure; the strangeness of living alone with just your father; the greater strangeness of getting a "stepmom" so young she could have been your sister; how she helped you lose your virginity; your subsequent year at the military academy; your transition away from your father's ambitions for you and toward your ambitions for yourself.

You hear the sharp edges of applause right behind you and, startled, you turn to see who's clapping. It's that weird little man again, who barred you from the cemetery earlier this afternoon, only later to direct you to Madame Laveau's tomb. Whereas before he seemed like a zombie or a ghost; now he is applauding and laughing, a big smile distorting his face.

"Hey, you — funny guy!" he says in an accent tinged with diverse ethnic influences. "How you get funny like that?"

You bow in response, then with a flourish of your hand,

you indicate Ms. Laveau as your accompanist. Once again, you marvel at how other people manage to find so much humor in the fuckin' pain that is the sad-ass story of your life.

"So, you after Marie grant you little wish? Well, watch your step, boy, don't make her work too hard: she give what's asked of her, but she's a business woman, she take her cut. Ya'll talk sweet now."

"Wouldn't dream of doing anything less. But don't you worry, granddad. Ms. Laveau and I, we old friends. I was here seven, eight years ago. Maybe you remember me?"

The guy sidles up to look you over, making a scrunched-up face as he draws close. He seems smaller now than what you remember.

"Naw. Been here more'n twenty years, six days a week, holidays included, nobody gets past me. I'da remember you. Either I wasn't here — or you weren't."

You laugh at that. For a while, you'd thought he wasn't real. Turns out you're the one who isn't real.

"Okay, my friend, guess that wasn't me, guess I'm not real."

But insofar as this moment is concerned, you've never felt so real in all your entire life.

26.

Juli Forces the Issue

T hat clown you live with — he did it! He actually did it: pulled off his entire gig with minimal props, no silly outfit, just a simple black T-shirt and black Levis, and best of all, no makeup, except, of course, for that damn red rubber nose.

He just got up there and mostly talked. And cursed. A few too many fucks, it seemed for an audience with children present, but you've seen — heard! a lot worse. After all, what terrified standup comic hasn't gone for the occasional cheap laugh in a desperate moment?

He juggled some, too, starting up his show that way, playing it safe with only three balls, and repeating a few cascades every so often. But each time was like a weird kind of transition, a way of concluding a story and keeping the audience in a trance state for a few beats in which to think it over before giving them another story. And, you have to admit, it was a damn clever between-stories bit to bounce a single ball and catch it on or in some random body part — neck, mouth, knee, foot, elbow.

You were surprised at how much they loved what he did. You hadn't wanted to say anything to him, but you'd been afraid, if he changed, he would lose his following. How many performers get stuck doing the same thing over and over till they wear out and/or die, because their public continues to demand from them what they became best known for? Like Woody Allen, when he tried to make a serious art film, something other than a screwball comedy.

But clearly, judging by the size of the night's audience, which grew steadily for twenty minutes, and the heft of his hat, the contents of which covered his entire bed in a nice even layer, you'd been right all along: it *was* him they were after, not just his clubs and torches.

He drove you home from the pier in an ecstatic mood, parked his Bug in the driveway, and ran up the stairs to the front door, the two of you holding hands like children at a playground.

"Follow the Yellow Brick Road!" he shouted.

Then, in his bedroom, he held up the pillowcase that served as his money bag to contain the contents of his hats from two shows that Sunday night. You stood next to him as he raised the bag with both hands above his head in a priestly gesture.

"Let's see what's in the collection plate!" he exclaimed, as he turned over the pillowcase and spilled its contents out onto his bed. The Niagara of flashing coins and fluttering bills left you open-mouthed. Then, as if it were a scene in a movie, he turned his back to the bed, spun you around as well, took your hand again, and squeezed it.

"Ready?" he asked. "One! Two! Three — jump!"

Still holding hands, you both fell backwards into a sea of money. There you dropped hands and individually rolled in the waves, giggling like little kids. He scooped up handfuls of coins and let them shower down onto himself. Then he splashed you with dimes and quarters and half-dollars.

"Ouch!" you responded. "Those big ones hurt!"

He gave you his film-star grin and brought his face close to yours. You stared a moment at one another. He reached up and picked off a quarter that had stuck to your cheek. You laughed. Then he hooked his fingers into the neck of your T-shirt, yanked it open, and with his other hand stuffed a handful of change down the front. When you made to fight him off, he jumped on top of you to pin you down and started dumping fistfuls more of change down your shirt front.

"Stop! Stop!" you cried, laughing, getting breathless. And he was laughing, too, as he leaned down and kissed you on the mouth.

Which shut you both up. His handsome-homely face sagged in surprise at what he'd done, and he rolled away to release you. You sat up and shook out the front of your shirt. Coins fell into your crotch. You scooped them up and tossed them aside.

"Guess so much funny-money just goes straight to my head," he said weakly.

"Yeah, it's okay," you replied as if it didn't matter. "But, you know, it's getting late, and I have to be at work in the morning."

With these words, you excused yourself and climbed the ladder to your own bed, where you lay, not sleeping, for long afterward. In the dark, you touched your fingertips to your lips, recreating the sense of pressure there. You skipped brushing your teeth, because you couldn't face going downstairs and possibly running into him again that evening.

The next morning, you left as early as you could manage and spent the day performing, in a distracted state, whatever menial tasks your new temp job required. You touched your lips again. Did that happen? Or did you imagine it? You replayed last night's scene over and over in your mind. You set the incident in context of everything you'd encountered since you moved in with Sasha nearly a year ago.

On the Muni streetcar home, you came to a decision: if he's up for more, then so are you. Your attic is a lonely place. Some nights you ache with loneliness. And on nights when your roommate/friend/employer/whatever-he-is is also alone, right below you downstairs, it's hard to ignore those votives burning on his dresser at night — so inviting when viewed through his wide-open bedroom door.

You realize: after his quick trip to New Orleans and back, he once again started leaving his door open after he turns in for the evening.

You wonder: did he go to New Orleans to break up with an old girlfriend or what? You dread making any lengthy, wee-hour treks to the bathroom.

Unabletobearthepressureofyourambiguousrelationship, you decide to force the issue. You'd been providing end-of-month summaries of what you've accomplished for him in terms of hours spent writing and distributing press releases, researching potential performing opportunities, typing up gig applications on the IBM Selectric you leased when you moved in, organizing files, sorting head shots. The hours you spend productively engaged on behalf of this man's career translate into "wages due," which in turn get deducted from "rent due." For this latest month of your indentured servitude here, you write up your usual, formal accounting summary. Then, in a separate cover letter, you formally invite him, when he returns home tonight, to come upstairs to the attic and ... get laid.

Still home alone, you deposit your note in the designated spot for such things: his bedroom dresser, right next to his damn votives. What a tease, you think.

Early in the evening, from up in your attic refuge, you hear him down below, returning home from, you assume, another gig at Pier 39. You listen as he trudges up the entryway stairs and tosses his prop bag on the bed. A moment later, you *feel* him reading your note.

C'mon, c'mon, you think — c'mon on up. You have your own candles here, already burning.

The great vacuum of silence downstairs ends with a rush of footsteps, fleeing the flat, and the slamming shut of the heavy, glass-laden front door. Oh, hell, you think, *there's* your answer.

So humiliating, his rejection! You wonder, when he will come back? You wonder, when he does, how you will ever again be able to look him in the eye? How could you have been so stupid?! You were so sure you felt something coming from his side. How could you have been so mistaken?! Never before have you made such a terrible relationship faux-pas, mistaking physics for chemistry.

You don't know how you can ever face him again, but you do know you don't want to do it tonight. You blow out your candles. You change your clothes from sexy "comfortable" to strictly utilitarian, pull on knee socks and slip into shoes, grab your purse. You descend the ladder in ape fashion, nearly falling as you make the fastest possible escape, then power-walk your way out the front door.

Dammit! you think. Damn, damn, double-damn! How could you have been so stupid?! you think over and over — tonight's personal mantra. You feel like punching yourself in the face. Idiot! You feel like crying, but you are too angry with yourself to work up any tears. No wonder you never get what you want.

Out on the street, you realize you have no idea where to go. Across the Panhandle to Haight Street, to some bar where you can kill time and a few brain cells? Across the bay to your dad's house, where, in his paranoia about local street crime, he might be too afraid to undo his eight front-door locks and let you in? Once upon a time, you had co-workers you could call in a pinch — not anymore. Most of the friends you and David once had together were more his friends than yours, people from the theater. Even Bill. He's not in theater, but you can hardly take this particular problem to him. You can think of only one person to go to for sanctuary tonight, and that would be Kitty.

You wish you'd thought to call her first before you left the flat. But in all the years you've known Kitty, she's nearly always home and she's nearly always up late and working. Writing with her two televisions blaring movies. She won't mind if you drop in — she used to drop in on you all the time. Once upon a time. Back when you were best friends. Besides, no way are you going back upstairs to use the phone and take the chance of meeting Sasha on your way out a second time.

Already headed north on Clayton, walking with your back to the Panhandle, you turn right onto Hayes and keep going till you reach Masonic. There you cross the street and position yourself on the curb, then stick out your thumb for a ride north on Masonic. In this city, buses and streetcars run east-west often and north-south only occasionally. Kitty lives in the Marina, near the Presidio's Lombard Gate — directly north of you, off the regular bus lines, and maybe as much as an hour away, if you walk up the hill to Geary, then over a couple blocks and down to the Presidio. You suppose hitching's not your safest option, but it's the fastest, assuming you get picked up right away, and it's certainly the cheapest. Besides, how many rapist-murderers are likely to be working on a Monday night?

You're lucky: almost at once, a big, black Camaro pulls over. You bend down to stick your head through the open, passenger-side window and peer in across an empty passenger seat. The car's interior looks pretty clean. As does its driver: a nondescript old white guy, maybe in his fifties, wearing shorts and sandals with white tube socks. Aside from his failed fashion sense, he seems alright and doesn't feel especially creepy, so you open the car door and climb in.

As he pulls away from the curb, he says in a jolly, fake-Irish way, "Well now, young lady, and where might you be going this fine night?"

"Meeting a friend over on Lyon Street, near the Presidio."

"What a coincidence! That just happens to be right on my way."

However, as soon as he stops at the big intersection at Geary, he says:

"But I'll be needing some payment for this lift, you know."

"If I had any money, I wouldn't be hitching."

"It's not cash I'm looking for."

His words stop your heart for a moment and give you a full-body case of goosebumps. Now what? You realize, in this perverse, little one-act play, you are supposed to ask what form of payment he would accept instead of cash. But you are afraid to hear his answer. So you say nothing. He can't rape you while he's driving. You sit and watch and listen to the car's engine as he arrives at the Geary intersection. You feel more and more pissed off as he continues on Masonic, turns right on Euclid, which becomes your old street of Bush (the nice end, you reflect ruefully), then left on Divisidero. What a creep! As if you didn't already have enough problems tonight! You stubbornly refuse to break the silence, until he blurts out:

"I want your socks! Give them to me."

Holy crap! you realize: it's the Sock Pervert. You think you should still feel afraid of this creep, of being trapped in this car with him, but you are so angry about the entire evening, about your entire stupid life, that you are feeling more than a little perverse yourself.

"No."

"Give me your socks."

"No. I need them. Besides, they're my best socks."

"I'll pay you."

"What?"

"I said: I'll pay you for them. How much do you want? I'll give you five dollars."

Five dollars is a lot for used socks that cost you only $1.59 brand-new. But you're angry tonight, finally angry enough to fight back, and you feel perversely stubborn. You are done with always having everything taken away from you. You are done with selling yourself short every time.

"No. Not enough."

"Ten dollars. I'll give you ten."

"Oh, alright," you agree, "take them, then." You pry off one shoe, pull up a pant leg, peel off your sock. You repeat the process on the other side. Moments later, sitting with socks in hand, bare feet in shoes, you ask:

"Where's the money?"

Still driving and with one hand on the wheel, the Sock Pervert digs around in his pants pocket till he comes up with a fuzzy wad of folded bills, fingers them down flat onto the console between you, and peels up the top bill to check its denomination. Without looking in your direction, he chucks it at you. It lands in your lap. With your free hand, you snag it, noting that it is faintly moist; with your other hand, you toss your socks onto the dashboard.

"There you go," you say.

Immediately he pulls over to the curb. "Get out," he says.

"But we're only at California and Clay. The Presidio's another mile from here."

"Get. Out. Now."

"Oh, alright," you say, putting your shoulder to the door and giving it a shove.

><><><

It's past two before you return home. You'd hoped you wouldn't run into your roommate, but as you climb out of the cab that brought you home from Kitty's apartment, you spot his car parked across the street. Guess it's time to face the music. You let yourself in through the front door. As you enter and even before you ascend the long stairway to the second floor, you hear Sasha above, talking with some guy. And the guy is saying: "You need to tell her the truth, man." To warn them of your approach, you slam the heavy glass door behind you.

This shuts them up. You stomp to the top of the stairway and veer toward the "closet" door that conceals the twelve-foot ladder to your "bedroom."

You pretend you didn't hear them talking, that you don't even realize anyone else is home. You have your hand on the closet doorknob when Sasha yells from the living room:

"Hey, Jujube! Where'dja go? I was gonna take you to the movies, but you went out." You think he sounds drunk, his bravado forced. Which means he is truly upset. But damn him, that is not your problem.

"Thanks, anyway," you call back, your tone as casual and neutral as your queasy stomach and despair will allow. "That's very nice of you, but it's been a long evening, and I'm going up."

Crisis averted, you decide. And the next day, sure enough, you both pretend nothing happened. It's business as usual — so much so that you start to wonder if anything *did* happen. Did you actually even write a note? Did he read it? Could you get it back? Would you dare to wait till he leaves for an evening of performance at the wharf, then sneak into his room and paw through his stuff, looking for your ridiculous note? Answer to that last one: no — you'll just have to eat your own stupidity and endure the bellyache of humiliation. You pray the truth never comes out.

What amazes you, though, is that, after a couple weeks of withdrawal and hiding out, he resumes his flirty ways. Is he crazy? Is he cruel? Does he somehow not know what he's doing? You decide, whatever game he's playing, you're not interested. No, you've already had enough of smoke and mirrors. Now you want something real that you can count on, a relationship acknowledged on both sides. Because, as you have discovered, having no relationship whatsoever is a whole lot better than having a bad one.

Now, whenever he flatters you, seems to be flirting with you, even subtly trying to seduce you, you watch him from a distance — like he was a made-for-TV movie, but with the sound turned off — and you remind yourself: this has nothing to do with you. Nothing at all. And because you have become untouchable, you have also become invincible. Nothing and no one will ever again be able to hurt you.

27.

Kitty Speaks Out

When someone is best friends with someone else for as long as you have been (or were) best friends with Juli St. James, nothing she does can surprise you. Nevertheless, after months, even years, of drifting apart, your relationship having dwindled to the occasional newsy phone call, you did not expect to hear Juli's voice on your apartment intercom on a late Sunday evening, sounding like it's reaching you via the first trans-Atlantic cable.

You buzz her in, then leave your front door ajar to go back to your writing. No point in standing and waiting while she climbs the six flights of stairs to your third-floor flat. A few minutes later, she stands before you, huffing, puffing, and looking like hell.

"You look like hell," you tell her, raising your voice over the two TVs you have blaring, playing separate movies from VHS tape decks.

"Thanks for the compliment. Do you mind if we turn down the volume on these sets? I can't hear myself think."

"Oh, sure. I was just writing the Great American Novel. But it can wait."

"I don't know how you can work through all that noise."

"I can't work without it." Then, when she gives you the look that asks, "Are you completely insane?" you explain, "That 'noise' helps me concentrate." At which point, you grasp a remote control in each hand, hold them at hip height, like an Old West gun-slinger, take aim and fire, stopping your two tape players cold. Which leaves your apartment suddenly feeling unnaturally still, all energy gone. "But never mind me and my petty concerns ... what about you? What's up? Why are you here? Don't tell me you were 'just in the neighborhood.' And while you're at it, would you mind taking off your shoes? I'm still trying to keep a no-shoe house."

"Oh, right. Sorry."

"No problem. It's just that, since I never clean, I have to do something to keep down the dirt. Don't you wear socks anymore? Most people wear socks with Earth Shoes."

"Nope. Can't afford them since I lost my job."

Your old friend is exaggerating for effect, you realize this. But still you wince a little and resolve to hold off divulging, until some yet-to-be-determined future date, the big news you've been not-mentioning: which is, you applied for and got the very job at Raker & Ho from which she was laid off. For weeks, you've been meaning to tell her, but tonight is clearly not the right occasion for such an announcement.

"Seriously, what's up?"

"Oh, Kitty, I really blew it this time. I don't think I can go home."

"You mean, tonight — or ever?"

"Ever."

Oh, great, you think, making the intuitive leap from a drop-in visit to an overnight, possibly extended stay.

With a minimum of journalistic prodding from you, she tells you a convoluted, innuendo-laden tale of confused entanglements that would have had Shakespeare gleefully rubbing his hands together, then borrowing the mess to plot his next play. You prod some more:

"If he's been running these head-games, why didn't you confront him?"

"I did. Sorta." Then she tells you how she applied her literary talents to come onto that creepy clown she sublets from. You understand, in the name of friendship, you ought to avoid judgment, but you haven't been feeling all that friendly of late.

"Okay: (a) I don't know why you'd want to get more involved with that man — he doesn't sound like a very nice person, just another user. And (b) you have lousy taste in men."

"Thanks. You're really making me feel better."

"The truth will set you free, honey. I keep telling you: love is not supposed to be so difficult. Haven't you learned that by now?" But you can see she doesn't have a clue. "And, by the way, it's okay to love someone who doesn't love you back. You just have to manage your expectations."

But when your old friend doesn't reply, you take the conversation in another direction:

"Juli, didja ever wonder if maybe you let some of these things happen to you just so you'll have something to write about?"

"That's a helluva thing to say to a friend."

"I wouldn't say it if I *weren't* your friend."

And, in that moment, you are distracted by a fleeting montage of memories from the Santa Barbara Writers Conference you both attended, once upon a time. How excited she was that Maya Angelou would be speaking! You shared a laughably small room with two narrow twin beds, like the cots you suppose nuns slept on in centuries past. You recall wistfully how Juli was so sweetly supportive of your confessed literary ambitions that you forgave her for snoring and grinding her teeth all night.

You and Juli have been friends since your earliest college days. You both knew from day one that you were destined to be writers. Well, at least *you* knew. Looking back now, you can see that, even though Juli wanted it — *said* she wanted it, anyway — she probably never believed she was good enough to have it.

Which is simply not true. She's plenty smart, plenty talented. But she makes these terrible choices. In fact, you have to observe, when she is confronted with a range of options, it's a safe bet she will always pick the one most likely to cause her the most amount of trouble.

For example, the two of you met in the same creative writing class taught by that internationally celebrated asshole. You dropped the class after only two weeks, because it was clear — to *you* — that he was mainly there was to grind down all his future competition before they could even get started. Juli, on the other hand, not only stayed till the bitter end, finishing out that class, but she took the second quarter with him as well. She got her credits, alright, but under those circumstances, you're amazed she ever managed to find the courage to write another word.

In fact, you're not entirely certain she has ever written another word. For years now, you've made it a point to ask her about her work every time the two of you talk, but she is evasive — ever-ready with a "Yes, *but—*." Always says she doesn't have the time, the place, or anything to write about.

And this became especially true after she went to work for Raker & Ho, a job that, you are gradually coming to realize, pays the rent, but in exchange strips a writer of all the left-brain energy she needs to deal with her own literary creativity. In short, other writers had been getting your friend's best hours and best years of her life, while she was holding back exactly *nothing* for her own self.

Exactly what you now fear may happen to you. You can just imagine the perfect editorial epithet chiseled onto your tombstone:

I made everyone else look great.

Then there were the men. When you met Juli in college, she was going with Mr. College Theater, a posturing floor lamp of a man who feigned humility and was anything BUT. Okay, he could be very charming, very erudite, and he could work a room like nobody's business. But, so far as you could tell, he was only into himself. It was as if his life were a Broadway play, he was starring in the title role, and the rest of the world had been cast as walk-ons chosen only to make him look good. Which does *not* work for you. You need to be the star of your own life, not some flunky in someone else's show destined to close after the first weekend.

But there was Juli, swooning over Mr. College Theater, until, honestly, it got so bad that even the rear end of a donkey costume would have run away. At parties, you were simultaneously fascinated and appalled, watching her and noting how her I.Q. plunged at least 30, 40 points every time an attractive man approached.

"Why do you *do* that?" you asked her on one such lobotomized occasion.

"Do what?" she replied.

"Exhibit symptoms of brain damage every time some cute guy talks to you?"

"I don't."

"You do."

After a couple rounds of "do-don't-do-don't," it was clear the discussion wasn't going anywhere. So you dropped it. What business was it of yours if she didn't mind looking retarded while socializing with the opposite sex?

Then, during what would have been your senior year in college, David appeared on the scene with his grown-out jarhead cut in a sea of long-hairs. Within months, you'd moved to the City, and eventually those two followed you over. Back then, with your dead father's estate newly available to you for harvest, you lived in North Beach, near the S.F. Art Institute. Juli and David moved to the Haight. Which made perfect sense. One glance at that man's blood-shot eyes told you everything you needed to know. Big-time stoner. Vietnam vet. Best guess: hadn't spent one single day clean and sober since well before he completed his final tour of duty. All those Nam vets had come back all fucked up. Talk to any one of them for ten minutes, you can tell.

And, no surprise, this guy was an actor, too. Not of the same calibre as her ex, Richard, but coulda been a contender.

Assuming he could keep his mind on the show biz at hand and away from every stray pussy.

You could tell from the start this guy was trouble. You wondered how she couldn't see it. But you had to remind yourself: Juli was born in Northern California, raised to be a Nice Girl in the land of Peace, Love, and Hippies; you, by contrast, came from Southern California, where you were raised by wolves, exposed daily to every type of hustler. Alcoholics? Check. Drug addicts? Check. Snatch-struck boneheads with boners? Double-check. Your friend, in her naïveté, had met David and recognized the hippie, but not the hustler.

You did *try* to help steer Juli away from this good-looking, talented, appealing degenerate, but she kept sticking her fingers in her ears and chanting, "La-la-la-la-la! I can't hear you!" Since you were all living in the same city and trying to remain friends, you continued to visit, sitting up late with her to talk writing, while David was acting in some church basement.

Then one night late, after Juli'd gone to bed on their pathetic floor mattress and was doing her lumberjack impression, sawing wood from a clearcut, in he came. You were still awake on the other side of their curtain room divider, lying on your stomach in your sleeping bag on the floor and reading. Within minutes, he was on your side of the curtain and making a heavy pass at you.

For months afterward, you wondered why you didn't just yell and push him off you. Had you been secretly curious? Horny? Angry with his wife — by that time, they were married — for being so damn dumb and passive? All you remember now is that you seemed to be having an out-of-body experience, your consciousness floating up against the ceiling, watching Juli sleeping on one side of the curtain, while her husband humped you on the other side.

After five minutes of rough handling and by the time he'd gotten off — in every sense of the word — your anger was fully focused on your friend. How could she allow this to happen? How could she not know what he was?

Or was it possible she was actually more perverted than you realized? Would he later confess to her his actions, deliberately manipulating her jealous outrage to achieve new sexual heights? Or, worse, had she maybe been listening all the while, doing god-knows-what to herself on the other side of their Indian print bedspread room-divider?

As soon as daylight appeared, you disappeared, leaving their apartment and going home to shower off his stink and the last crusty traces of dried spunk. No point in sticking around till your friend or the disgusting pig she married woke up. At first, you thought you would wait some days or weeks till the time was right, till you and Juli were alone, so you could fink on him. But, as coincidence would have it, that was to be your last time in their apartment while he was still living there. You couldn't tell how much, if anything, she knew — whether she was a twisted sister or simply totally naïve — but you could never bring yourself to go back and possibly let it happen again.

After that … incident, though you and Juli stayed friends, you met at your place, in cafes, or over the phone. And Juli never questioned the change. She'd call you from home, when David wasn't there, or from her office at Raker & Ho, when she got stuck working late. David you didn't see at all. At least, until Juli's boss sent her to Washington, D.C. to spend a weekend learning about the new "desktop publishing."

She called you in advance to brag about the trip. You congratulated her and tactfully restrained yourself from pointing out that a writer with a day job is better off writing on the weekends, rather than flying cross-country to learn how to push other people's books harder. So, imagine your surprise, when on her very first night away, you answered a knock on your apartment door and found her sleaze-ball spouse standing there.

"How the hell did you get into the building?"

"Hello, Kitty-Kat," he said. "I've missed you, too. I was just about to ring downstairs, when your neighbor was on his way out, so I pushed on in."

"Sounds like you, alright," you said. "Did you lose something? Your wife, maybe? Your mind?"

"My heart, Kitten. Definitely my heart," he replied.

"Don't call me that, I don't like it. You are so fullashit, your eyes have turned brown," you replied.

And yet you let him in.

You didn't need a dinner menu to know what this man planned to order that night. The two of you sat for about twenty minutes on the floor of your apartment, talking about some made-up topic of conversation, while you listened to the electrical charge in the room building up. You heard this charge as an unceasing, high-pitched, buzzing whine, the kind emitted by high-tension power lines. Then the light in your flat seemed to flash, and he was on you: kissing you hard, twisting your breasts under the fabric of your muu-muu, reaching down to part your thighs with his big hand, gasping as he discovered you were wearing no underpants.

Sigh. So, that was episode number-two, and you have to admit the incident fulfilled every single rape fantasy you'd ever had in your life. But after he had retracted his noodle, flipped you onto your belly, and used one hand to hold you down while he used the other to pump himself up again before driving straight for your wazoo, you terminated your contract by kicking out hard in his general direction.

"Owwww, fuck!" you heard behind and above you.

You turned to see how much damage you'd managed to inflict. He was clutching his right eye and cheek.

"Oops, sorry," you responded without remorse.

"The fuck you are," he said flatly.

"No, really. Let me get you something for that."

Moments later, he was a naked man pressing a bag of frozen peas to his face, feeling around on the floor for his briefs.

"Don't worry," you told him, "that big knot will go down by Monday, when Juli gets home. Have you had dinner yet?"

"No."

"Well, then, feel free to take those peas home with you."

And that was that. You had to admit: you felt kinda proud of your work that night.

But you didn't call Juli the following week, when you knew she was home from D.C., and she didn't call you until weeks later. By then, it was clear she had bigger fish to fry in the form of a marriage that even she had to acknowledge was actively falling apart.

The next time you saw her, it was back in her Bush Street apartment to say goodbye to the old place. The apartment was entirely empty, so the two of you reclined on the floor, like ancient Romans whose couches had been repossessed, and ate Hawaiian pizza straight from the box, using toilet paper as napkins. Sitting Shiva for her dead marriage.

A week later, she would move into that clown's attic.

A month later, she would be laid off, putting her at the mercy of one more woman-eating man.

A month after that, you would be awarded the job she formerly held.

And now she appears before you, struggling with the non-problem of having developed a terrible crush on her jailer. Stockholm Syndrome.

It suddenly occurs to you: this could be great material for a novel you will write one day! But if you're ever going to understand the character dynamics of what's going on here, you need to get some answers while you can.

"Listen, Juli, on the subject of head-games, I have to ask: why, *why*, *WHY* did you put up with so much shit from David for so long?"

"Oh, I dunno. Watching our marriage go down the tubes was like living with someone who's terminally ill. I kept thinking there must be something I can do to save him, one more treatment to be tried."

"So you stayed till you were convinced you'd tried everything? And, in retrospect, are you glad you did?"

"Absolutely. If I hadn't, then I'd always wonder if the one thing I didn't try would have cured us."

"But nothing worked?" you press.

"No," she admits, "it didn't. But, at least, I know in my heart I did all I could."

"That's enough for you?"

"It has to be."

You and your friend sit and stare at one another till she breaks the silence: "Look, Kitty, I know you think I'm an idiot and a sucker, but I've got to see my commitments through."

At which point, you lie, telling her, "I don't think you're an idiot or a sucker. But…." You pause before veering back toward the truth, "What about your commitments to yourself?"

"Meaning?"

"Meaning, you give away all your best stuff to others, especially to these unworthy men who seem to have so much appeal for you. Meaning, you never hold back enough time and energy for yourself, so you can do the things you say you want to do."

"I figure there'll be time later for that."

"No guarantees in this life."

"Okay, you're right."

"I know you said that just to shut me up."

She grins. "Kitty, you know me too well." Which makes you both laugh like old friends.

"Then remember this, my friend," you tell her, "just like you are responsible for your own orgasm, you are also responsible for your own creativity. No one else can do it for you."

And, all at once, you realize: you are dead tired. You glance at the clock and see it's nearly one in the morning.

"Listen, Juli, we should wrap this up. I have to get up in the morning."

She looks at you, astonished. "Since when were *you* ever on speaking terms with the morning? What's up with that?"

Oh hell, you think, you can't keep on lying forever to your friend. Not even by withholding the truth. You ease into an explanation: "Well, see, I started a job a few weeks ago."

"A *job*! Since when have *you* ever had a job? I thought your inheritance was enough to cover you."

"Well, sure, it is. The basics, anyway. But it's been years, and I don't have to tell you: living in the City gets more and more expensive all the time."

"Okay. So, where you working?"

"Raker & Ho."

"My old publisher? What are you doing there?"

"Editorial assistant."

"To whom?"

"Sneed and Schmeger."

"Tweedledee and Tweedledum? That's my old job."

"That's right."

"And when did this happen?"

"Two, three months ago."

You watch as she does the math, calculating time elapsed from now back to when she got laid off. Then she says, "So, you must have applied pretty soon after I got canned, that right?"

"I guess."

"But I told you, at the time, my layoff was presented to me as only temporary."

"True."

"But, apparently, you didn't believe me?"

"It seemed worth checking out."

"My job seemed worth 'checking out'?"

"It didn't *seem* to be anyone's job at that point."

"Right."

Clearly, your exchange is not going well. You hadn't wanted to tell her this way — on a late night when you have to be on your feet and fully sentient in a few hours, when she is already upset and you both are exhausted. Now you see your instincts had been right all along: you should have held back.

But the damage is done.

"Look, Juli, I really do have to get some sleep before I go in this morning. You need to crash here tonight?"

"No, that's okay. I think I'll just go home."

"You said earlier you didn't think you could ever go home again."

"Yeah, well, changed my mind."

"Okay, but how you gonna get home? You've already missed the last cross-town bus."

"No problem — I'll call a cab. If you can see fit to allow me to use your phone."

"Better than that, I can lend you cab fare."

"No, I'm good."

Fifteen minutes later, Juli is gone. Maybe forever, it feels like. You push your typewriter off to one side of the bed, flip the alarm on your windup clock, switch off the nearest lamp, and lie back. Still fully dressed, you pull Great-aunt Rachel's hand-crocheted quilt over you and snuggle under, hugging your childhood teddy-bear to your chest, resisting the urge to suck your thumb. The snowstorm of static on your two televisions, still on across the room, lulls you to sleep.

28.

Sasha Resolves to Hit the Road

Well, you've done it again. Once more, you've gone too far. You'd been drawing on Jujube's support so persistently, so focused on your dreams of stardom, you hadn't noticed the extent to which she'd gotten hooked on providing that support to you. Without realizing it, you'd reeled her in; now, you see, you'll have to find a way to cut your line and let her go. Otherwise, she'll pull you under.

Damn her, anyway! But how the hell were you supposed to know? She's so repressed, that one, so distant, you never imagined.... Well, let's just say, her mash note took you completely by surprise.

And so you ran — in sheer panic. You simply got in your car and drove away. Out through the avenues to Ocean Beach, where you parked your VW Bug within sight of the vast Pacific, got out and sat on the seawall, smoked one after another of the cigarettes you'd been trying so hard to quit, stubbing them out on the concrete and chucking your butts over the edge and onto the sand below, thinking, What to do? what to do? what to do?!

Damn her, anyway! The last thing in the world you need nowadays is a come-on from a lovesick roommate. Especially one who's on the rebound.

No way are you going home tonight without a bodyguard. You climb back into your car, drive east toward the wharf, head for the pitch. Luckily, you arrive just as one of your fellow performers (and a customer of long standing) is wrapping up his gig. As soon as he comes off stage and starts packing up, you talk him into making a pitstop at your flat. As enticement, the offer of a half gram of coke, with a couple joints as a chaser, works very nicely.

But, by the time you get home, you find she's not there. You open her hall closet door and call up the ladder — no answer. You climb the ladder to double-check, popping your head up through the floor of her attic loft and scanning around — nope, nobody home. Which is good news ... and bad. Good news because you don't have to face her yet; bad news because there's no telling when she'll come back, so, if she's late, you'll probably have to break out some more marching powder to convince your friend to extend his visit.

Understandably, he is eager to learn the backstory on this mess you've gotten yourself into. And you are so upset, you tell him more than you had intended, forgetting he knows you well enough to fill in any gaps you leave and to interpret your housemate's behavior in context. Which is the problem with friends — they know you well enough to be able to sort out your truth from your bullshit.

As a consequence, he is not as sympathetic to your plight as you might have wished: "You shoulda told her the truth from the start."

"But I never thought she would take it that way."

"Oh, man, try to see it from her side: it's only a few months since she broke up with her hubby — she's sad and lonely. And there you are, being all consoling and sympathetic, muddying the waters of your platonic, business relationship. What's she spozed to think?"

"I never said anything to lead her on," you counter.

"Maybe not, but what did you *do* around her? I've seen you in action — I know how you are: always trying to make every woman love you. I say: show her some respect — tell her the truth. Besides, if a pretty lady is liberated enough to come on to you, please don't queer it for the rest of us."

"Liberated? Yeah, right. All these West Coast hippie chicks are so 'liberated' ... till they want something."

You had just been thinking, Not damn likely, when you realize you just heard your front door open and close, followed by the footsteps of someone trudging up the stairs. Oh god.

Of course, your conversation terminates in that instant, a weighty silence descending upon you and your colleague. In the bell-jar vacuum of your living room, you speculate upon how much, if anything, she may have heard on her way up the stairs. You give your friend the international roll-on hand signal for "Keep talking!" But he is frozen in place. Just as you are. And the Snow Queen continues her ascent. A beat later, you summon your courage and call out to her in what you hope is a casual tone:

"Hey, Juju-bean, where ya been? I was going to take you to the movies, but you split."

You notice your friend giving you a cocked-head, don't-be-a-jerk look, but it was the best you could come up with on the spot. Fortunately, your sorry ass is saved when she calls back:

"Yeah, well, thanks anyway — I made other plans for the evening."

Then you hear the hall closet open and shut, followed by the creaking of the twelve-foot ladder she climbs to her empty loft right above you. You suddenly have a flash of how all this must feel to her, the intensity of her loneliness, and you feel a hot wash of shame for having selfishly added to her already heavy burden of sorrow. You like her, you really do. You never meant for her to end up a broken-hearted casualty in your quest for professional recognition in the Wide World of Entertainment.

"Shoulda told her the truth," your friend repeats, shaking his head.

Over the next few days, you and Juli engage in a complex choreography designed to avoid one another entirely. Fortunately, after months and months of sharing the same flat, you know each other so well that this is fairly easy to pull off. She is up and out of the flat by the time you awaken; by the time you get home from your gigs, she has already fixed herself a solitary dinner, washed up in the kitchen, taken a shower, and retreated to the attic. You wonder where she goes during the day. You think maybe she's still temping, because you've stumbled upon a couple of answering machine messages from an agency downtown. You take care to preserve them, while erasing the calls from her ex.

You count yourself as lucky she hasn't come at you with a knife ... yet. She knows where you sleep. You take pains now to always close your bedroom door at night.

Actually, you realize, you miss your evenings together, her

moral support, the easy camaraderie you shared. In short, you miss *her*.

So you are genuinely chagrined when she leaves you a second note, this one asking simply if you want her to move out. You decide to handle things differently this time. You march straight to her closet door, yank it open, and bawl: "Jujube! Get your ass down here! We need to talk!"

When she comes down and joins you at the kitchen table, sitting stone-faced across from you, you wave her note at her and demand: "And just what does *this* mean?"

"Simply giving you the option of renting to someone else more compatible."

"I don't want to rent to anyone else more compatible."

"What *do* you want?"

"I want us back the way we were."

"I have a problem with that."

You raise your eyebrows, giving her a look you know will read as, "And just *what* is your 'problem with that'?"

She hesitates, apparently searching for the best way to explain herself. "I don't get where you're coming from."

At which point, you can't resist the opportunity to cover your sorry butt and claim, "I don't get what it is you don't get — I thought we were friends."

"We *are* friends, Sasha. But I thought we were starting to be more than friends."

Time for additional butt-covering. "And just what does *that* mean?" you ask, employing a question to shift the burden of self-disclosure onto her. A series of mental images flash through your mind: flirtatious words you delivered with seeming candor, moments of sincere mutual enjoyment, all those lit candles you placed on your bedroom bureau, the bedroom door you left open at night, implying invitation. And that one particular night after that one particular show when, the two of you were home and celebrating your first successful, mostly standup show by rolling around on your bed in the contents of your evening's hat, a field of coins and paper money, and you accidentally kissed her. On your bed, on her mouth.

You ignore the memories and, instead, focus on your sense of disappointment that she actually fell for your bullshit charm. You thought she was impervious. Now that you know she is as gullible as any other female, how can you trust her assessments of what you are trying to do as a performer? If she insists on being "more than friends," she won't be honest with you anymore. You feel so let down, you can barely stand it. You respond by torturing her, just a little:

"'More than friends' — what exactly do you mean?"

"I mean, I thought you liked me."

"I do. But...."

"Not that much?"

"Not that way."

"Gotcha."

"You're just lonely," you hasten to add.

"You're right about that."

"And horny."

"You're right about that, too," she acknowledges and, to your relief, laughs. You laugh as well.

"You know, Juju, in my position, I have to be so careful. You've seen what ends up in my hat. Women are all the time throwing themselves at me, but it always turns out they just want something off me."

She frowns. "Sasha, I'm not like that. I'm your good and true friend."

"My point exactly. I never want to lose that."

"So, it's alright if I care — just not too much?"

"That'd be a good way to put it."

Then you ask a question designed to shift the focus of this discussion further still away from you:

"How long have you felt this way?"

You expect her to reply she'd started having feelings for you only recently. You plan to remind her she's on the rebound, carrying a lot of baggage from her busted-up marriage and simply looking for a place to set it down. Nothing personal, nothing to do with you.

But, unexpectedly, she answers: "I always kinda liked you, Sasha."

"Well, if you felt that way, then why did you move in?"

"I needed a place to live."

Now suddenly you feel very put upon — an innocent, wronged party cornered by yet-another scheming woman out to snare you from the start. You exclaim self-righteously:

"If I'd known *that*, I'd never have invited you to live here."

As soon as you say this, you realize it is true. Because the cost of love, when it is not under your control, is simply too great. You have your career, your *life* to think of. You can't afford to be limited by having a resident girlfriend.

"I know," she says softly, scooting a dead fly across the table with her fingernail. "But I didn't have any expectations. I just thought maybe you felt the same."

And now you don't know what to answer, because you

suddenly realize whatever you say about yourself and your feelings for her — or your lack of them — will hurt her. What's worse, you also realize that, in fact, you actually did miss her during the week or so you spent evading one another. So, once again, you misdirect attention away from yourself and onto her.

"How can you go on living here, feeling as you do?"

She answers with an edge of contempt in her voice. "It wasn't a problem before. It won't be a problem in the future."

Which makes you wonder if maybe you'd underestimated this one. Maybe what you had interpreted as a cool nature that required warming up was in fact a facade of self-control you find surprising in a woman. All you can manage for a response is a nod.

"A couple things, though," she continues.

"Yeah?"

"Why did you invite me to live here in the first place?"

"Your husband —."

"*Ex*-husband," she corrects you.

"Okay, *ex*-husband called me to say you needed a place to stay. Seemed like a good fit."

You watch her consider this idea for a moment before you ask: "What's the other thing?"

"I have to be allowed to bring dates home to stay overnight."

"Okay. Well, just don't bring the entire 49ers team home."

"Oh, please."

"Sorry."

She stands up. "So, are we done here? I have some work upstairs I'm trying to finish."

"Sure, sure." You watch as she turns her back on you to go. Then you call out your plea: "Juli, I'm just not ready to live with anyone yet."

Her back still turned to you, she replies quietly, "You've been living with me for nearly a year now."

Which stuns you with its simple truth. But the deeper truth is you are just not ready to lose a good friend to romance. Because, ultimately, you know, you would lose both.

Next thing you know, a couple weeks later, she has a guest: some grubby, doper guy with the lousy haircut and hippie rags. Actually, you recognize him, you've met him before — an old friend of her ex.

You'd spent the afternoon at the pier, throwing up. After your successful debut as a standup — an evening that culminated in your accidentally coming on to your roommate — you've been allowing your old act to seep back in. At least, as much as your still-recovering left hand will allow. You find you can't work an audience on auto-pilot, you have to stay present the whole time. And yelling out, "Fuck!" every so often doesn't get much of a laugh on a sunny afternoon when your audience is largely composed of young mothers wiping smears of pink cotton candy off their toddlers' faces.

Consequently, you are already feeling mildly discouraged with life by the time you drag your prop case up the long flight of stairs to your flat.

"Lucy, I'm home!" you announce loudly in your best Desi Arnaz impression. Which turns out to be so embarrassing when you find her sitting in the kitchen and *not alone*. Equally bad, *he* is sitting in your seat at the table.

Juli looks up and gives you a big innocent-seeming smile.

You can't read her well enough to tell whether she's just happy to see you or her grin carries a rub-your-nose-in-her-date edge to it. You decide to give her the benefit of your doubt. She offers an introduction:

"Hi, Sasha. How was 'throwing up' today? Have you met Bill before? Long-time friend."

"Hello, Bill, long-time 'friend,'" you curtly address this hippie piece of shit sitting at *your* dining table, in *your* chair. Then you turn to your assistant and offer her a report on your day:

"Two full hats, and they all went home just a little better informed."

"Well-done, thou good and faithful servant of democratic process and the American Way," she replies, then reaches up to her face and pretends to squeak her own nose. When you cock your head, "Huh?" she follows up with the two-handed twisty sign for crazy hair. Oh! your clown nose and fright wig — you forgot.

"Oh, right, heh-heh!" you say. "Silly me."

"I thought you weren't still doing that," she observes.

"Habit before courage," you respond. "Guess I'm just not ready to let go of the gear ... yet."

Juli smirks, shakes her head, and gives you a friendly, exasperated look as you turn on your heel and head for the bathroom to unclown yourself.

Ten minutes later, you are back in the kitchen, wearing a freshly scrubbed face. You haven't been invited to join them, but it's your home — so you invite yourself. Now they are talking about where to go this evening, and somehow you can't restrain yourself from barging into the conversation. Focus,

focus! you tell yourself, then decide to make tea for everyone.

"Tea, anyone?" you announce cheerfully.

Juli shakes her head and gives you a stink-eye glare, which you ignore, feigning innocence as if you had a right and a duty to act as host for anything that occurs in your kitchen. But in setting down the stainless steel tea kettle, which days ago you had polished to a mirror finish, you catch a glimpse of yourself and realize that, out of your clown camo, you just look vulnerable and kind of scared. Immediately, you have an out-of-body experience that allows you to view yourself through the eyes of this scruffy man sitting at your table, and you think: Fuck, what a dick I am!

You excuse yourself, slam down the kettle, hurry to the bathroom, peel off your clothes, and step into the shower. By the time you emerge from the bathroom, freshly scrubbed all over and still slightly damp in your luxurious spa robe, they are gone. Just as you had hoped they would be. You return to the kitchen to put away the extra teacups you'd started to set out, having failed to notice they already *had* their tea.

Late that night, after you have already gone to bed, shutting your bedroom door for privacy, you hear them return, climb the ladder, one after the other, and creak around above your head. It occurs to you, at this point, you could simply put on your headphones and escape all that's going on up there. But your voyeuristic nature won't allow it. So you lie in bed, wondering if sounds generated here by you and various short-term, female companions have been traveling upstairs quite as distinctly as the sounds now drifting down to you from the attic. Which prompts you to recall one of the reasons why you didn't want her bringing guys home in the first place.

The only thing is, you didn't expect to have ... *feelings* about the situation.

No way are you going to be able to stand many nights like this. Too late to reign her back in after you've already given her permission to have a life. You know if you try, she will leave and you will lose her entirely.

Under the circumstances, you can think of only one solution, and that is to take yourself on the road. Getting chosen to perform in the Comedy Competition preliminaries had in fact attracted a trickle of offers to play a few shitty little clubs throughout the state, but you'd been thinking they were too much trouble for too little money, coming right at that time of year when you can anticipate your biggest hats down at the pier. Now, however, you've got a great reason to leave town and to stay away for as long as possible. Or, at least, until your flatmate's little affair blows over.

29.

Bill's Awkward Transition

Y ou've had girlfriends, and you've had friends who were girls. But you've never started out with a friend who was a girl who then became your girlfriend.

You didn't expect the transition to be awkward. But it is.

You winced a little to see how surprised Juli was when you finally asked her out on an actual date. Over the past decade, the two of you have gone to dinner together about a thousand times already. You've even gone together to the movies before.

It was never any big deal when you used to drop by, unannounced, at one of the apartments in the City where she and David lived. If David wasn't home, you hung out together, got stoned, just talked. That sort of non-event had occurred more times than you can recall. And when she tagged along on one of David's visits to you instead, and you two guys sat up till dawn in your bedroom, talking history and playing wargames, Juli even slept in your bed.

But this is different — this is a *date* — and you both *know* it. Fortunately for you, though she was surprised to be asked, she also seemed pleased. Most importantly, she said yes.

When the planet shifts on its axis, everything in the world shifts, too. Stress increases on the tectonic plates that make up the Earth's crust. The effects on climate and sea level are dramatic. Life everywhere is forced to evolve.

The last time you and your friend went to the movies, you'd extended the invitation spontaneously in an effort to get her out of the house, away from her insane, clown roommate. That same night, you'd considered pulling the old yawn-and-stretch, arm-along-the-back-of-her-seat smooth move, something you hadn't tried since you were a teenager. Under the circumstances, though, it seemed unjustifiably sneaky, so you gave up plotting, and the two of you squirmed in separate seats, watching Divine eat dog shit. Happily for you, after sitting through nearly eight hours of truly appalling cinema, walking through a mirror image of parallel social chaos on Market Street gave you full permission to throw a protective arm across your friend's shoulders.

And, at the end of that evening, when you brought her back to her flat, it was *your* turn to be surprised — at her invitation to come in and come up to her attic sanctuary. What followed — a spontaneous and thoroughly satisfying display of mutual affection — was the nicest finish to a non-date that you can remember ever experiencing.

On a *date*, however, you have to *decide* whether or not to *try* to hold her hand or put an arm around her. You wait till well into the second hour of *Out of Africa* before extending your hand, palm up, toward her on the arm rest you share. She takes it. Mission accomplished! You sit sweaty-palmed for the next hour and a half, afraid to move.

Then you go to dinner, and she can't stop talking about David — what an asshole he is! how could he have treated her this way? You realize the movie has set her off. But Juli has always felt free to vent about David to you. After all, they *are* still technically married. So, why should now be any different?

Nevertheless, it is different, because already David is fast becoming her past, while *you*, at least for tonight, are her present. So it seems that, at some point, the two of you — if ever there is to be "the two of you" — ought to find something more ... relevant to talk about. Otherwise, how will it ever be possible for you to have a future together?

You let her get it all off her chest, wishing you had not decided to take her to *Out of Africa*. You wish either *Pee-Wee Herman's Big Adventure* or *Back to the Future* had still been playing. (Not *After Hours*, though — that would only have depressed you.) Then, once she has run down, you and Juli sit silently staring at one another. It is the first time ever that you can remember this happening.

"I guess you'd rather not have to hear all this," she says at last.

"It's been hard on you, I know," you tell her diplomatically.

"And I guess he's still your friend, too," she says.

"Starting tonight, *you're* my friend, first and foremost," you tell her.

"And is that what you want? To be 'just friends'?" she asks.

"Not really."

30.

David Finds His Bliss

Hard to believe you've been living with Barbra in her Ocean Beach condo all these months. And, in all that time, you haven't seen Juli for more than a couple hours total. These days, you feel sorry for your "wife."

The last time you encountered her, it was at her new digs in the attic at the flat of your drug-buddy Sasha. She looked so sad and wan — with her pathetic futon on his attic floor and all her baggy, post-hippie clothes stuffed into cardboard boxes from Cala Foods. Impulsively, you gave her a hug, saying: "It's okay, baby, I've been there, too." You were only trying to comfort her, but — whoa, big mistake! Because suddenly, for no reason, she was mad at you. She pushed you away, shoving you hard in the chest, saying, "I know, you asshole! I was there — *with* you!"

Which surprised you, because just as suddenly as she had turned on you, you realized what she said was technically true. Even though, when you think back on your time together, it seems more like you were living alone. Funny how you can spend years inhabiting the same space as another human being, yet that person makes scarcely an impression on you. You and Juli had lived in the same space, here and there, for so long, but you didn't "live together." You were "married" on paper — now you're getting divorced on paper — but you were never one half of a marriage. You ask yourself: where have I been these past few years?

The answer comes back to you as a montage that starts with your discharge from the service — that peak moment in your life when you balled up your uniform, chucked it in a dumpster in Salinas behind the local 7-11, walked to the I-5 onramp, and stuck out your thumb. Rides were more plentiful in those days, the early '70s, and you made it all the way to the hippie Mecca of San Francisco. Free at last, free at last! Oh, thank god.

In Frisco, you crashed that summer with your hometown buddy Bill, where, you vaguely recall, some kind of unpleasantness occurred with a couple of his roommates. After that, your montage shifts to a series of scenes in the various classes you took at the local state university campus in Hayward, across the bay from the City and within longing distance of it. You remember the college productions you tried out for, the cast parties you viewed through clouds of pot smoke, the braless babes you lusted after.

Then, in the last quarter of what should have been your senior year, you got sick with that mystery blood illness and spent time in the VA hospital. You couldn't finish your classes, you couldn't take your exams. Your college career had ended. By then, Juli had come into your life, but nothing else changed till summer arrived, when you and she moved to the Haight. Another year came and went.

By the following fall, you were back in classes, only now they were at A.C.T., San Francisco's premiere repertory theater. Which also provided you with a steady supply of tryouts, after-parties, drugs, and easy-access twat. You got into the habit of hanging out in a certain local bar in the theater district of Geary Street near Union Square, where tourists went to drink after performances and before last call was announced, followed by the final, assisted stagger up Nob Hill, back to their fancy-ass hotels.

Nowadays, lying in Barbra's California King bed, watching a patch of rare morning sunlight slow-gliding along her bedroom wall, you recall you once had this other life — one in which, most mornings, you dragged yourself downtown to a day job as a telemarketer selling art books from the basement of a crumbling, moldy old building in the Financial District, then went home, most afternoons, to the seedy studio apartment in the Upper Tenderloin that you shared with a woman named Juli. You remember she cried a lot and sometimes yelled at you.

As all those months and years roll by in your memory, the montage of life-scenes accelerates to a blur. You recall, with pride, how your pickup technique got so good that on most nights, at least during the peak of the tourist season, all you had to do was throw your hook in the water and immediately there'd be a bite on your line. You can't even count how many women you've escorted out of the bar and back to their rooms. Thank god for Women's Lib! Now more of them than ever are traveling alone on business. And, separated from their boyfriends, husbands, and kids, they are so grateful for a bit of attention from a handsome local thespian, that oftentimes they insist on paying for everything. They pick up the tab ... you pick up them ... everyone's to the good.

Then you met Barbra at that holiday party thrown by the publisher Juli works for — a Christmas party held in January, ironically — and for the first time in years, the blur that was your life began to slow to a halt. Weeks later, while bartending at an A.C.T. fundraiser (good way to maintain your network), you met this same woman again and were surprised to find yourself fully present in the moment. There she was in her slinky cocktail dress and big hair, looking like a backup singer for a country-western band. But she was obviously rich and important. Casual inquiry revealed she was on the board and had supplied most of the wine for the occasion. Your experience of her in that moment was so complete, you forgot every hippie love goddess you'd ever lusted after in favor of this fabulous, glittering female. Even at the time, you suspected you finally found Ms. Right.

She understood you. She valued you. She could afford you. She didn't yell at you or try to set limits on you — but, of course, you wanted to please her. You think maybe you once felt this way about Juli. After all, she took care of you back when you were so sick and then at the very start of your career. But that was long ago, and you certainly didn't feel that way anymore. So, how could you let your past get in the way of your future? First chance you got, you jumped ship and went to live with Barbra.

Barbra was so happy to have you. Being with her was everything you ever dared to imagine it would be. The two of you spent days on end in bed, fucking, feeding one another, fucking again, sleeping in. All you needed was one another. And pizza home delivery.

After a couple weeks on the desert-island paradise of her triple-wide mattress, she went back to work, leaving you home alone most days. And though you'd been fired ages ago from your telemarketing day job, for a while you still pretended to go in, taking the streetcar downtown, then strolling aimlessly around the Embarcadero or joining the scene in your favorite Fisherman's Wharf bar for a couple hours before heading back to the condo.

And you could get away with this, because Barbra was an independent businesswoman, self-employed, some weeks more than full time, as a retailer and distributor of fine wines. Many days she left home early and came back late. All you had to do to cover your ass was make sure you emptied the contents of your ashtrays into one of the basement garbage cans before evening fell, so she couldn't count cigarette butts. Oh, and get rid of any newly drained wine bottles from her under-the-kitchen-sink stash. No need to leave any indicators in her trash of how many hours of leisure you enjoyed each day.

After a month or so of this, you started to wonder whether you shouldn't at least try to do something else. Maybe get another job so you wouldn't have to keep fabricating your days. But as they had always told you in your acting classes: where's the motivation? Every morning after Barbra left, you would reach down deep to search for some motivation, but all you found when you reached down there was your own cock.

No matter: life was wonderful! You had somehow

achieved a simply glorious existence. You'd been a castaway, nearly drowned in your former life, but then this woman had rescued you and given you a new life. What did she expect in return? Nothing more than a good daily shagging — god knows you'd be doing that anyway. To someone. Somewhere. How convenient that you no longer had to put on your pants in order to take them off.

Your subterfuge ended the day Barbra came home unexpectedly at noon to find you still in bed. Scrambling for a credible explanation, you considered at first telling her you were sick. But she damned well knew you weren't, so instead you went for something closer to the truth: that you'd been laid off. You just omitted telling her the blow had actually come months earlier. She was surprised, then righteously angry on your behalf.

"So unfair!" you remember her exclaiming.

You recall, at one point, you got a little worried, supposing she might expect you to go out and get another job ASAP. Just as Juli would have insisted you do. But Barbra responded as you knew she would: she understood only too well how unsteady "Life in the Theater" was, how most of the time an actor couldn't make enough to live on, but how working a day job sapped all the creative energy one needed to perform.

"Oh, David," she said, "never mind. Don't waste your talent. You should be concentrating all your energies on your acting career."

You could have wept when you heard that. But, of *course*, the pittance you could bring in hawking books would be of no consequence to her. But, of *course*, she would much rather help you become a star. You knew she must be a mover and a shaker — how else could she afford this condo and everything in it?

You didn't tell her (because you don't know how) that, unfortunately, you're really not interested anymore in acting. Voiceovers and commercials are okay, but such gigs are few and far between. The one porn film you did (in secret) while you were still living with Juli — that was fun. But, as it turns out, real, serious acting requiring characterization is just not something you want to pursue. Like your pathetic childhood, the process is excruciating. All that digging around inside, all that turning yourself inside out for the sake of entertaining a bunch of shallow, uncaring, theater-going assholes — no, thank you.

During your second year at A.C.T., you were so proud to be cast as a principal: Rubin Flood, the wannabe philanderer of *Dark at the Top of the Stairs*. Even though it was only a student-director production never destined for the main stage, you brought all you had to your role — attending every single rehearsal without fail, paying actual attention to your blocking instructions, writing out your lines scores of times in order to memorize every word perfectly. By dress rehearsal, you were so much in touch with your character that you cried in the greenroom during intermission. At which point, one of those vile little stagehand cunts spotted you, strolled over, and asked sneeringly, "Identifying, are we?" You looked up, open-mouthed, tears streaming down your face, and felt as if she'd just kicked you in the nuts.

The show's run of two performances, a Saturday evening and a Sunday matinee, went fine. At least, you think they went fine, though afterwards you could hardly remember a thing about that weekend. You got a standing O on Saturday night — this much you do remember. Or maybe it wasn't you that drew the ovation, since in the egalitarian custom of repertory companies, everyone in the cast came out together after the curtain closed. Or maybe the applause was mostly for the student director, whose passing grade would be dependent on this show. Or maybe it was everything about all the rest of the show and the audience didn't even like you. No matter. Afterwards, as you sat at your dressing table scraping off your stage makeup with cold cream and Kleenex, you already knew in your your heart you would most likely never again try out for anything serious. Method acting was simply too painful.

Even the greatest and most moving performances of your life would serve only your audience, never you — a now-empty husk. You remember how quiet and thoughtful Juli was after the Saturday night performance of *Dark at the Top of the Stairs*. You feel grateful all that happened long before Barbra came along, so she never saw it, never had reason to go all quiet and thoughtful about it.

And speaking of empty husks, it suddenly occurs to you to consider all the many ways in which theater and sex resemble one another. For one thing, they both require acting skills. If you want to be successful, you must constantly pursue casting opportunities, and you must audition regularly. With both pickups and tryouts, you must be prepared for rejection. But while being chosen by a woman you just met (even an obvious skank) means your fun is just up ahead, being chosen by your new director means your pain is just about to start. And in either context, dying is always likely — in bed (and in the old meaning of orgasm), it's good; onstage (in the sense of total fuckup and complete public humiliation), it's bad. Comparing theater and sex, side by side, you have to say: you'd take sex over theater every time. And, for the most part, you have.

But, for the foreseeable future, you plan to do ... nothing. Absolutely nothing. And though it bothers you (slightly) that you can foresee the possibility of growing bored eventually with your current life of delicious indolence, truth is: you never allow future concerns to interfere with present pleasures. This is your one real talent — a super-power for self-indulgence. What's so great about deferred gratification, anyway?

Which is why it doesn't worry you in the least to find yourself still in bed at three o'clock in the afternoon. However, you *are* out of cigarettes — and *that* is a crisis — so you force yourself to get up, shower, dress, and pocket Barbra's spare front door key. On your way out, you check your image in the mirror Barbra hung on the wall next to the door so she can check her teeth for lipstick and/or spinach. You give yourself a movie-star smile and are gratified to see you've still got it. You think: those caps on your front teeth were such a good investment, you're glad Juli insisted on buying them for you. Then you saunter off in the direction of the corner store in a quest for more smokes.

It also doesn't worry you when you find yourself stopping right outside the local bar two doors down from the corner store and receiving a pleasant whiff of cigarette smoke, booze, sawdust, and alcoholic sweat. You peer into the darkness just in time to hear a crash of glass — another empty bottle flipped by the bartender into a trash can behind the bar. A cheer rises up from the bar's patrons, their collective attention fastened on a ballgame that's playing on the screen of a big TV that hangs from the ceiling.

At home, you are truly blessed with access to more alcohol under the kitchen sink than you could imbibe in a month of consumption. And it's all good stuff (except for that single curious, ancient bottle of homemade, rotgut red you ran across during one of your daily explorations). But the liquor at home does not come with company — at home, you must drink alone. On the other hand, your under-the-sink liquor center is free, while company here has a price. And you are a little down on your luck these days.

Ah! but then, you remember: you have $20 in your pocket, conveniently borrowed from Barb's wallet this morning while she was in the shower — the price of admission to an afternoon of camaraderie. And you observe: you can buy smokes here, too. So right on in you walk.

You go straight to the bar, then turn to survey the room. Of the eight people inside, six are male, including the bartender. Two are female. Not the odds you are used to downtown, but good enough.

You review the candidates to identify the more attractive of the two women present. One you judge to be in her early-to-mid-forties, with big tits, big hair stripped a few too many times, press-on nails, saggy-baggy upper arms, and a rhinestone tennis bracelet. The other is a black-haired, dark-complexioned, slant-eyed, flat-chested human rodent of a female, in her early to mid-twenties and wearing an oversized white T-shirt and gray sweat pants. You like her exotic air. You are drawn to her youth. The young ones never ask for much — they haven't figured out that they can. You notice the rat-woman is hunched over, nursing a shot of something that looks like scotch. You consult the bartender, and moments later, you approach her with a drink in either hand.

"Mind if I join you?" you ask, using your best trained voice, which you know from long experience will turn her head.

"Please do," she says, smiling coyly and meeting your gaze by rolling a sideways look up at you. You note she has some kind of accent. Sounds like an Eastern Bloc country. Russia, maybe. You set her glass down before her, pull out the adjacent chair, and get comfortable. You hold your glass up to clink with her. When she touches her glass to yours, you are startled by a brief whiff of Pine-Sol that wafts across to you.

31.

Barbra Gets a Heads-Up

Y ou let me down, missy. Big time."

This is what the man who'd always been your best client is telling you as you stand there before him, feeling like a kid in trouble. Mr. D'ombre, wine broker at House of Shields, known to his friends as "Uncle Jack," is a big man, both physically and socially, and he is widely reputed to have been a dangerous criminal in his younger days. But, until now, you'd never seen any signs of his having another side. Until now. Now he looks like a wild boar standing upright, wearing a three-piece suit.

"You made promises to me. And I made promises to others, based on your promises. My collector is waiting for that Lafite."

"Please, Mr. D'ombre ... Uncle Jack—" you start, seeking safety in the personal history of easy familiarity you have with this man.

"Never mind the excuses," he says, holding up his hand like a traffic cop to stop you mid-sentence. "I want to know what happened to that wine. You were only supposed to transport it. A simple pickup and delivery. Did you sell it to someone else at a better price?"

"No! I would never—."

"Break it?"

"Certainly not."

"Stolen?"

"Maybe. I don't know. It … just disappeared, that's all."

"Nothing just disappears, missy. You're lucky I got insurance on that Bordeaux. But if it's breakage, those tight-asses are gonna wanna see some shards and a label that looks legit. Meanwhile, I'm also stuck having to work up a fake for my collector."

"I'm really sorry, Mr. D. How can I make this right?"

"When I know the answer to that question, I'll tell you. Until then, our business is concluded."

And so you are trembling as you leave your former best client's place of business at the venerable House of Shields. What had you done with that wine? In recent months, you've taken to keeping your fancy stock and collectibles in the trunk of your car to protect them from becoming accidental imbibement at home. But this one particular old wine was *so* very costly, you didn't want to take a chance on getting rear-ended or broken into. You'd thought yourself so clever to conceal it for a few days in your condo among the cheap Safeway and Cala wines that people brought to the dinner parties you no longer hold. These never got opened because they weren't good enough to drink, but they were too good to throw away. Eventually, you'll donate them to some art gallery reception or maybe where Loren works, at their Christmas party in January.

As it is, the past couple of weeks are a blur in your mind because your cousin, Dodie, had flown down from her home in Seattle to stay with you. Dodie (or Dodo, as some of her family called her behind her back) was a shy, unhappy girl, a year younger than you, and always the needy type, lacking personal initiative. When you were growing up in Northern California, you remember, you dreaded Uncle Mike and his family coming out from Ohio to visit your mother, his older sister. Dodie, short for Dorothy, was Uncle Mike and Aunt Amelia's only child, and whenever they appeared with their pale, pudgy daughter, you were expected to act like a surrogate big sister and show her the ropes of living on a farm. This you resented, because you, too, were an only child and had no wish to share your bedroom, your things, your friends, or anything else you considered to be yours.

Being forced to be a big sister, even for just a week or two, had spoiled more than one summer vacation for you, that was bad enough. But then she followed you to UC Davis and into your mother's sorority. After she pledged, it was decided she should be your roommate. After all, as the house president pointed out, you and she were blood-related. You remember the day she moved into your room, plonking her fat ass down on the other twin bed that for months had been your dumping spot for books and clothes. She looked up at you with her speckled pig-nose, gave you a big gummy smile, and declared: "Now we really are sisters!" Which made you cringe inside.

On her own, Dodie had no life. Except for going to class and fulfilling her responsibilities to the house, she'd just sit around all day, waiting for you to come home. Now, years later in San Francisco, she was just as helpless and pathetic as ever she'd been in college. So, during her two-week stay with you and David, and since you couldn't weasel out of work, you rented a car for yourself — a business expense, after all — and left your own car with David so he could take up the slack and show your old friend around.

Was it remotely possible they'd opened that wine? The very thought of such a thing happening gave you a moment of vertigo. No, not possible. You would have seen the empty bottle on the table or in the trash, along with all his filthy cigarette butts. Besides, David is much too much of a wine-snob to open anything from the dreck cabinet under the sink. Not that he actually knows anything about fine wine, but he loves to show off for company, pretending everything of yours is really his as well.

Frankly, things are not going well for David. Or with you and David. You can see that, but you don't really understand what's wrong. Your happily-ever-after ending, which had felt like a new beginning for you, was only a short few months ago. Now your relationship is not turning out as expected. Now the skies over your Magic Kingdom romance have grown dark and clouded.

You retrieve your car from the Palace Hotel's parking across the street, your own beautiful BMW again and not some crummy rental Honda. For three days, you've been spraying the interior with Lysol and air freshener, but it still reeks from cigarettes. You *asked* David to please (*please!*) not smoke in your car, but clearly he forgot. Or simply ignored your request. You fume about this, knowing that if the inside of your car stinks, then most likely you stink, too. You are surprised to discover, when you get to the attendant's booth, that you have to write a personal check because you aren't carrying enough cash to get out of the lot. Thank goodness they know you in this place. Nothing is working today.

Driving home along Geary Boulevard through the Richmond district, you try to puzzle out what the hell is going on with David. Okay, at the start, he called in sick for a couple weeks and they let him go. Being out that long is always risky with these little part-time jobs. Limited commitment on both sides. But no matter, hawking books on the phone was a terrible job, sapping all the energy he needs to throw himself back into acting. With your encouragement, he gave up looking for a replacement day job and agreed to concentrate on what really matters for him.

You paid for head shots. You paid for his resume to be redone. You paid for new clothes. You got him privileges at the House of Shields (which, after today, are most likely in the toilet). He seems to have had a few auditions, but no offers. You cannot understand it because you know perfectly well what he is capable of, given the right part. That A.C.T. student show, for example — *Dark at the Top of the Stairs*. He was amazing as the lead. That was at least three years ago, a year or two after you'd been invited to join the board. But you'd remembered him for it.

His last audition was six weeks ago, and nothing since. Of course, these past two weeks while you were working, he was helping you by entertaining your cousin. But, frankly, you can't help wondering if he's really all that interested in having a successful career as a professional actor. You go off to work in the morning, and sometimes when you get home, you find him right where you left him, watching stupid game shows or *The Dukes of Hazzard*. Once in a while, you find him glued to *The Love Boat*. You hope he's planning to audition for the show.

This afternoon in your condo, however, your TV is silent and the screen black, and he is nowhere to be found. But it can't have been all that long since he left. You feel the TV for traces of residual warmth. You switch on the air conditioner to clear the fogbank of low-hanging cigarette smoke. On your way to the bedroom, you count the number of coffee cups scattered around: four. You wonder why he seems unable to use the same cup more than once. You wonder why he cannot manage to transport all his cups to the dishwasher. Like a normal, civilized human being.

The bed is unmade. Of course. So much for your love-nest! His good slacks are still lying on the floor where he dropped them and stepped out of them the day before yesterday. You resist the urge to pick them up, to hang them up. You're not his mother. You walk over to the pants and give them a vicious kick into a corner, out of your way.

The phone on your dressing table rings. This is the same turquoise Princess telephone you had in college, the one your parents bought you for your twenty-first birthday. Reaching for it always makes you smile.

"Barbra Blair. Wine, Women, and Song — and Wine! Barbra speaking."

"Barb! It's Lorie. Are you busy? May I drop by?"

"*Querido*, of course! *Mi casa es tu casa* — siempre!"

"Are you alone?"

"Yep. Just us chickens. Where are you?"

"I'm at the Cliff House. Give me ten minutes to settle up."

You hang up feeling sad at this reminder of how much Loren can't stand David. It used to be that he felt so comfortable here with you that often he wouldn't even call before stopping in. And he certainly never checked to see if you were entertaining. But since David moved in, Lorie never visits spontaneously. If he does come over to find David here, he turns all remote and formal. You miss the predictably easy, chummy relationship you used to have with him. You miss his lapses into campy story-telling, so funny because they seemed so bizarre coming from him. You wish you could revive what you used to have together, but you don't know how.

While you wait for Lorie to show up, you head for your red kitchen to check again under the sink in the dreck section where you are certain you stashed that Jefferson bottle, worth more than you make in a year. There must be at least two cases' worth of assorted wino wines in here, but nothing rare and precious. You slam the cabinet door shut. Are you going insane? You feel grateful Lorie is on his way over. He always makes you feel normal.

You have just finished retrieving a pair of men's balled-up, dirty socks from underneath the living room sofa, when Loren rings you from below, and you buzz him in. Minutes later, you greet him with pleasure, stepping up to give him a big hug. He feels thin and fragile through his jacket, all ribs and shoulder blades. He smells odd, too. When you separate, you observe that he looks pale and sickly. You want to ask if he is alright, to find out what's wrong, but your lifelong fear of germs makes you recoil, afraid to pry.

As soon as Lorie's butt hits the sofa, however, you are surprised to realize all he wants to do is talk about David. A few days ago, he was down at the pier, he says. He'd stopped into a restaurant where he is friends with the owner. He'd spotted David there.

"So?" you say, making the universal hand-rolling gesture for "Get on with it."

"So, Barbie, he was *not* alone. He was there with another woman."

"Okay. So, what did she look like?"

"Very pale. Short and fat. Sprayed with rhinestones."

You nod and shrug. "One of my sorority sisters — a cousin, in fact — she was staying with me for a couple of weeks."

"Yeah, well, your cousin was face-sucking with your boyfriend in the bar."

You stare at your friend and mentally calculate how long it's been since the last time you and David had sex. Weeks, it's been weeks.

In this moment, the subtext of several other little moments between you and Dodie are becoming clear to you, and you feel sick to your stomach. How *could* she?! Family does not steal from family. Except when they do.

But you do not feel like defending yourself this afternoon. Or your relationships. Instead, you go on the offensive.

"You don't like him."

"No, I don't."

"That's fairly ironic, coming from you."

"What's that supposed to mean?"

"Well, you might consider that, really, it's *your* fault I don't have a significant other, a husband, kids, or a real home."

"How do you figure?"

"Obviously, if you hadn't been so … '*experimental*'" — you

toss out the descriptor as if it were an invective — "I would have all those things. And so would you."

"Barbra. You *know* it would never have worked out between us. I can't be what I'm not. And you wouldn't have been happy with the pretense."

"The way it worked out didn't work out either."

"No, I guess not."

You both realize it is time for Loren to take his leave. He stands, preparing to see himself to the door. You don't get up. But before he departs, he stops to tell you:

"Barbie, I know you think a lot of this guy, but he's no good. He'll only hurt you. I'm just trying to be a friend and spare you the pain I know you're in for."

"Thanks for the heads-up," you tell him, "I'll keep that in mind."

"You deserve better, my dear," he says. "Much, much better."

Then he's gone. And, in that moment, you feel it will be a long, long time before you see your childhood friend again.

32.

Loren's Own Road to Hell

Leaving Barbra's condo, your sense of irony kicks in, and you think: my goodness, *that* certainly went well! You decide it'll be a cold day in Homo-Hell before you go to see your bitchy old friend again.

Last week — on "a dark and stormy night" — when you dropped into the bar at the Old Swiss House at Pier 39 and spotted none other than Barbie's David with his giant hand stuck up some fat chick's skirt — in a truly banal display of hetero infidelity — you hoped you'd be able to talk Barbie into dumping her gold-digging playboy. Instead, she wrestled the conversation to the ground and made it about you and about her — and about the two of you together, that impossible future you'd inherited.

You could find nowhere to go with the conversation. So you took your leave. In the past, such an incident would have sent you scurrying for the apparent safety and secure familiarity of the metaphoric closet where you have lived most of your life. But now, with the help of your support group, you are finally fully out (or nearly so), and you refuse to keep secrets. Including the secret of yourself. Including any secrets from yourself.

When you think back on your early years in San Francisco, especially how you treated Barbie during the six months she stayed with you, you feel ashamed. Either you made your rounds using her as a beard, or you snuck out for a few surreptitious libertine hours, during which you dismissed any enquiries regarding your old friend by referring to her as your "own personal fruit fly." You see now your excuses were intended not only for your new best friends *de la nuit* — heaven forbid they should question which team you were playing for! — but for yourself as well.

To be fair, throughout your college years and even afterwards, you and Barbie had tacitly agreed to save face for one another. Which sometimes put you in close, if awkward, physical proximity. You two were childhood friends and sometimes even roommates, but you still needed to keep her at a comfortable emotional distance. Later on, you became disgusted with her approach to finding romance. One married man after another. Mostly arrogant, pompous, playboy theater-types. All those calls she made to their wives, tormenting those women for no reason. It was just plain mean. You questioned whether you could even be friends with someone like that.

After your terminal diagnosis outed you, however, you understood better how Barbie must have felt when she was first introduced to your deviant nature. You were innocent of any ill intent. Yet still, you managed to destroy every hope she'd ever clutched to her bosom for the life she thought she should and would have, if only you had made different choices.

Simply by being yourself, you'd trashed all her plans and left her with no future. Now AIDS is trashing all *your* plans, and you understand only too well what it means to have no future.

It's irrational, but to some extent you share Barbie's view of yourself and can't stop blaming yourself for having ruined her life. You hadn't planned to be what you are, you hadn't wanted it, you hadn't even known at first what "gay" or "bi" was. You would so much rather have been uncomplicatedly straight. Or even uncomplicatedly gay. But, dammit, here you are, this is who you are, and, just as the guys in your support group told you: you can't allow yourself to feel one bit sorry for trying to make the most of who and what you are. You only wish that being yourself and attempting a search for the meaning of *your* particular life hadn't come at the price of disappointing your family and everyone else who gave you a start in that life. Barbie hadn't done anything to lose you. It's just that she could never *have* you. Not in that way.

Fifteen years in the City had brought you into contact with too many other men who, despite their "other nature," had married high school and college girlfriends. Some married out of love and fooled around only on occasion. Others married out of desperation, in the hope that their wives' pussies would magically turn them straight, so they'd never again catch themselves looking with longing at a man who passed them on the street. Either way, the whole charade was sneaky and disrespectful of their matrimonial choices — usually perfectly nice women who tried and tried, but never understood what was wrong. They blamed themselves, poor things.

These days, you no longer have the energy required to keep up a front the way you used to. Since you're dying anyway, you may as well let it all hang out and exit this life a better human being than you lived it. Face to face with mortality, as part of putting your affairs in order, you are determined to set matters straight. So to speak.

You started by resigning from your job. You hadn't been all that effective for months, anyway. One little phone call from the clinic had transformed you into a cucumber queen. Now that the coast-to-coast party circuit was no longer a moral option and chastity had become your chosen lifestyle, you could not ignore how bored you were at Raker & Ho.

They tried to get you to stay. Until you told them why you were leaving — specifically *why*. Then they were relieved to see you go. They threw you a last-minute going-away party at which each person who attended was asked to write his or her name on a disposable red cup with a Magic Marker pen. In the name of industry hygiene, they said. The entire office staff was there, even that Amazon of a new editorial assistant for the two Mrs. S's.

Later that evening, as you stood alone in front of the building, holding your one pathetic banker's box full of personal items and waiting for the cab that had been called on your behalf, you turned your head and deeply inhaled of the sweet sugary wind blowing in from the fortune cookie factory down the block. It was probably the last-ever time you would smell it! Tears came to your eyes. You wondered how you would manage to survive all this? Then you laughed, realizing you wouldn't.

Raker & Ho had given you a nice severance package and even helped you get on disability. You swallowed your pride and applied for food stamps at County Social Services. Your eligibility worker, a scruffy hippie-looking guy, seemed friendly enough, but strangely possessive of his bottle of White-out correction fluid. How ironic you should be sitting there in your best blue blazer, sporting your second-best yellow power-tie, while this man, who was trying to help you to be able to afford to go on eating, was dressed in a well-worn plaid Pendleton over a Fabulous Furry Freak Brothers T-shirt. Not bad looking if he would cut his hair, you reflected, but obviously straight as a highway crossing the Great Plains. You wonder why heteros so seldom have any fashion sense or even inclination. It was this, more than anything else, that made you suspect David was a closet case.

You thought you'd miss your daily sojourns at Raker & Ho, but you never did. What you did miss was the pleasant anticipation of your next Big Apple junket. Not to mention, the aura of glamour that once clung to you whenever you mentioned where you worked and what you did there. But it was fine, just fine, simply being yourself for a change — restful even, with no façade to maintain.

Right after you quit Raker & Ho, you woke one early morning in a panic, heart pounding, soaked in your now-usual night sweats. You thought you were dying. You wondered if you should call 911, but what could they do? Either you'd die before morning came — or you'd going on living awhile longer. You considered what regrets you'd have for this life if you didn't make it through the night. When morning arrived and it was clear you were still alive, you vowed to do things differently in whatever time you had left to you.

Of regrets, you realize you have two. First, aside from Barbie, who now hates you, you have no one you can call a true friend. And, second, though you call yourself a "writer," all you really are is a dabbling, would-be scribbler who's spent most of his life fooling around in the name of "acquiring experience."

Until your diagnosis, you'd supposed writing was where you would spend the rest of your life after you became an auntie, too old to be of any interest to anyone. In fact, by the time you started working in publishing, in a status position that supported the lifestyle to which you aspired to become accustomed, you'd done just enough actual writing of your own to have discovered it was damned hard work.

Worse, you discovered it was not only possible, but even quite likely you could write and write and write and write without ever getting anywhere close to saying anything meaningful. You were afraid you had nothing to say; you were afraid you never would. Maybe it wasn't in the stars for you to be given anything important to say. You were forever preparing and never doing. Maybe, like Dorothy Parker, you hated writing and only loved "having writ."

Until your diagnosis, you imagined everything you were doing or not doing was merely rehearsal. Clearly now, rehearsals have ended and the curtain is going up on opening night. You, the playwright, are having a bad dream in which you find yourself onstage, before an audience, appearing in a play you have yet to write.

A wave of nausea washes over you. Since in this moment when you are standing in the living room, the kitchen is nearer than the bathroom, you dash for the kitchen sink to throw up. Dammit! you think, wishing you hadn't left so many unwashed wine glasses in there. The mess you just deposited will be nasty to clean up later.

Feeling much clearer now, you slog back to the living room, go to your desk, and sit, kicking aside Big Red's cover with one fuzzy-slippered foot. With a sense of grim resolution, you flip on Red and read, once again, the words God left for you: "Gay is more than sex." The time has come to write the memoir begun by that opening statement:

"Gay is more than sex. I always knew that. Even as a little country-boy virgin whose only knowledge of 'sex' came from watching bulls topping cows, I knew myself to be different from other little country boys. But I didn't understand how. Or why. Or anything. Until I went away to college in the big city, where I majored in literature and began reading the books written by others like me:

> *E. M. Forster*
> *William Somerset Maugham*
> *Thomas Mann*
> *Oscar Wilde*
> *Jean Genet*
> *Yukio Mishima*
> *Federico Garcia Lorca*
> *Marcel Proust*
> *James Baldwin*
> *Christopher Isherwood*
> *Truman Capote*
> *Tennessee Williams*
> *John Rechy*

"Which made me realize I was not so very different, after all. I was not alone on this planet, not a mutant. Or the last of my species. Or the first. There were many more creatures like me. In fact, if the card catalog of the university library could be counted on as a witness, our numbers were legion. I just needed to go out into the world and find my people."

If only, having found your people, you can then find the courage as well to claim your true self.

33.

Bill Seeks Permission

It's not like you have some irrepressible urge to confess — you weren't raised Catholic. It's not like you need David's permission to date (and bed!) Juli — he's not her father. And you're not asking him for her hand in marriage. But you prefer to have everything on the up and up. Also, you want to make sure he's really, truly done with her before you allow yourself to get any more involved.

So it is that you finally make a point of driving out the long straight slide down Fulton to Ocean Beach to pay your old friend a visit. The timed traffic signals give you green lights the whole way, which fills you with a sense of optimism about your future. You are slapping your steering wheel and bopping your head along with the Doobie Brothers' classic "One Step Closer" as you pull your van into a curb space across from Safeway, at the end of the long block occupied by the ritzy condo building David has shared with that skinny home-wrecking bitch these past six months or so.

David rings you in and receives you in princely fashion, as if he himself had created and financed this environment of repressed excess. He takes from you your moldy old jean jacket and grimy baseball cap, fingering them gingerly, and hangs them in the hall closet. He escorts you into a living room carpeted in a quarter acre of icy-white shag and populated with ebony leather-clad furniture, like an art installation of Angus cattle grazing after a snowfall. He offers you some kind of pungent mixed drink made with liquor that, in his wildest dreams, he could never have afforded on his own. When he sits opposite you on the couch and crosses his legs, in manly ankle-to-knee fashion, you see he is also dressed better than you can ever recall. His shoes probably cost more than Vermin the Van, the vehicle you drove over in.

Now you get it: your old friend is being "kept." And the realization comes upon you that, had your old friend been a woman, you wouldn't have given a second thought to the circumstances of his current "success." Slutting around in search of a well-heeled, generous new host, then settling down parasitically to allow oneself to be bought and paid for was a traditional gig—for women. Historically, they'd had few options. But when a man chose this same "career path," it somehow doesn't sit right. You are distracted from the pleasantries you are exchanging by the contempt you are feeling.

You are also surprised and annoyed by the pity you sense he feels for you, grubbing along as you do in Social Services. You view yourself through his eyes and see the only thing that functionally distinguishes your do-gooding self from your dead-end clients is which side of the desk you sit on.

While David pontificates at you about some minor point of history connected to the First Balkan War of 1912-13, he fusses with a pipe he can't seem to keep lit. Considering all the dope he's smoked in his lifetime, you'd have thought he'd have the knack by now. At last, having managed a couple good draws, he leans back to release the smoke with an expression of satisfaction. You flash on a mental image of Popeye the Sailor-man and wonder, momentarily, just what *he* smoked in his famous pipe.

You hear a key in the front door. David, by now stretched out on the sofa, hears it, too. At once, he sits up, planting both feet on the floor. He reaches over to give the couch cushion a rub where the heels of his shoes had been, then glances up at you with a sheepish look. "Mustn't mar the furniture," he says.

Barbra appears in the arch of the foyer. She has big hair and is dressed in a dark blue business suit — the straightest woman under the age of fifty you've ever seen up close. You met her only once before, months ago at the House of Shields, and it was dark in there, but she seems harsher now, more brittle than before. Not the way you expect a woman in love to look. You suspect she is not entirely happy with this man whose marriage she broke up in order to get him. However, in this case, her win is proving to be yours as well, so you are grateful to her.

She puts on a big smile for you and comes forward with hand outstretched to shake yours. You stand, take her hand for a moment, then lean in to give her an awkward hug and a pat that is buffered by her shoulder pads.

"So nice to meet one of David's friends for a change," she tells you. You tactfully do not mention your earlier meeting with her. After all, it was months ago and it was dark in there. As you sit back down, you wonder whether David has any friends left to be met.

Greetings complete, she does not stick around. With a quick "You'll have to excuse me," she leaves for the recesses of the condo. You and David watch her go.

As soon as you hear a door shut in the distance, you lean forward and blurt out:

"David, I have to tell you something — I'm dating your ex." Your secret exposed, you feel a wave of relief wash over you.

David stares blankly in your direction for two beats, apparently taking time to digest your statement and its relevance, if any, to him. Then he blinks, nods, and earnestly advises you:

"Be careful, pal. Because you'll never be able to get rid of her."

"I don't plan on getting rid of her."

"Just don't say later I didn't warn you."

All questions of exes and others settled for the time being, you and David return to discussing the antecedents of the War to End All Wars. At some point, while reviewing the order of battle for the French Corps, he tells you a dirty joke:

"Why do women have legs? Answer: So they won't leave snail trails as they move around from place to place."

He sniggers at his own adolescent humor and doesn't seem to notice you don't. This visit goes on for another forty minutes before David stands up and you understand it is time for you to leave. Something between the two of you has shifted again, and you wonder if this is the last you will ever see of your old friend. Again. Your lying, depraved, disgusting old friend.

Then you are walking along the damp sidewalk, headed for your van parked at the end of the long Ocean Beach block.

You can hear the surf rolling in, massively, on the other side of the Great Highway. You take a deep, salty breath and look up to the night sky. No moon, no stars tonight. Heavy fog from off the ocean conceals the rest of the cosmos from view. But you admire how the light from the street lamps turns the fog all silvery, and you wish you were stoned right now. Funny how David, perpetual stoner that he is, never once offered you so much as a toke all night long, only booze. You wonder if Miss Barbra, She-Who-Must-Be-Obeyed, has banned illicit drugs from her dwelling.

You have nearly reached your van and are in fact already digging into your jacket pockets for your car keys, when you hear fast-moving footsteps coming up behind you. You freeze in a startle of fear, then wheel around to face whatever is moving toward you. Someone calls: "Bill! Wait up!" You see Barbra hurrying toward you. She is carrying the baseball cap you forgot to retrieve from the hall closet.

Once again this night, relief washes over you. "Oh, thanks, I forgot," you explain unnecessarily as you take back your favorite Grateful Dead bear cap, circa 1965.

"That's alright," she says, puffing a little. "I wanted to speak with you, anyway."

You stand there, waiting. She catches her breath, but can't seem to get started on whatever she wants to speak about with you. You observe she has changed out of her stiff career clothes into a loose African-style caftan with leopard-paw prints. She is shorter than you realized. She is also barefoot and has brushed out her hair, flattening it. You think she looks better this way. You feel sympathy for her in this new vulnerable state, followed by guilt for Juli's sake, as you remember how, for months, this woman tormented your new girlfriend.

"I want to ask you a question," she says at last.

"Please: ask away."

"I wanted to ask you ... what is the matter with your friend? Why doesn't he work? In the seven months we've been together, he's done pretty much nothing. I thought it was just the difficulty of finding work in theater. But then he told me he doesn't want to do that anymore. So I sent him to a life-coaching program to help him find himself. But I'm not even sure he's going."

Uh-oh, trouble in paradise already, you think. And it surprises you David would quit the theater and actually tell someone the truth about it. But you keep these thoughts to yourself and return her question with a question: "So, what *does* he do?"

"Honestly? So far as I can tell, not a damn thing. He's still in bed when I leave for work in the morning. When I get home, he's stretched out on the sofa, watching TV. He says he's had a hard day in the program, and the ashtrays are empty, so I have to believe him."

"But you don't?"

"No. I don't."

She screws up her face. Clearly, she was hoping for some pointers from you — The Old Friend. "Well," she asks thoughtfully, "Is there something I can do about it?"

You consider whether her question is prompted by concern for David, concern for herself, or concern for a return on her investment. You wonder whether she cares more about David than you gave her credit. But what can you possibly tell her that would be useful or even make her feel better?

You shrug and reply, "No, I don't think so. That's pretty much the way he is. The way he's always been. I've known him twenty years, and I can assure you: he mostly doesn't work. Not willingly, at least."

"I see," she says. "Well, thanks for talking to me about this."

She turns and scampers back to her condo, bare feet slapping wet concrete. You watch her go, wondering if you shouldn't have offered to walk her back to her door, settling on waiting till you see she's reached the outside of her building safely.

Then you climb into your old VW van and start the engine. As Vermin warms up, you pat yourself down, checking your pockets for the ten bucks you remember carrying along just in case you and David decided to go out for drinks tonight. Nothing. Which is strange because you definitely remember stuffing money into one of your pockets. Maybe you lost the bill when you pulled your keys from your pocket and didn't notice because Barbra appeared with your cap a moment later?

You consider getting out and searching around the sidewalk in the dark. But it's cold and wet out there, and you're beat and just want to get home. Tomorrow someone will find your ten bucks and be happy. Besides, what the hell, David gave you at least that much in liquor tonight. Not to mention, a whole lot more. Your karma is still in balance.

34.
Barbra Tries to Help

Look, Barbra, the truth is, I hate acting. I just hate it." This is what David had to tell you one night after you cornered him over dinner, then kept at him for an hour more.

At one point, he tried to escape. Claimed he was out of cigarettes. Oh no, you don't, you thought.

"David, if you walk out of here tonight, don't plan on coming back."

"You're kicking me out?"

"Could be. Your decision."

At which point, he sat himself back down. Hunched over on your sofa, feet flat on the floor, elbows on thighs, big hands dangling between his knees — he reminded you of a man sitting on the toilet. You felt an urge to spray him with Lysol. He reached for his pack of cigarettes on the coffee table, shook it, found it still empty. He glanced up at you with a bitter expression, balled up the pack, and chucked the wad at your potted ficus in the corner. He missed. His empty, balled-up pack then became trash on your carpet.

"Smoke your pipe, if you're so desperate."

You'd supposed you had a man living with you, a grown *man*. Turns out he's a spoiled brat.

How this got started, you were *trying* to talk to him about where he goes on those evenings when he leaves in search of "some air." You were also curious to know what he is thinking about when he says he has "a lot on his mind." You were working up your nerve to ask him the real question: who, exactly, had he been groping in the bar at the Old Swiss House the night Loren spotted him? Was it Dodo, as you suspected?

But then he dropped his bombshell: he doesn't *want* to remain in theater. Acting is too stressful, there's no work, most jobs hardly pay bus fare. Besides, he says, if you really want him to be a star, the two of you will have to move to L.A. Or New York City. He doubts you are ready to up-end your life. He's right on that score.

"Okay. If you don't want to pursue acting, what *do* you want to do with your life?"

He shrugged no comment. Exhausted after another hour of hammering on the psychic wall that he has erected around himself, you retreat to your bedroom and slam the door. That night he slept on the sofa.

You were desperate to fix the situation and get your life back on track. The next day, you signed David up for six weeks of a career-planning workshop downtown, so he could figure out what he wants to do with his life. He didn't want to go, said he couldn't see the point of it. You told him: attending this workshop is a condition for his continuing to live here. He shrugged no comment.

Thereafter, he dutifully left the house every morning,

came home every night, but never mentioned the workshop. Now he seems resentful you would insist he do this thing for himself, so you don't push it. It's enough that he's going.

You cannot help noticing, however, that he often comes home after you do. Even though his workshop days end a couple hours before your work days are over. You hold off making dinner. When he finally drags himself home, you ask him what the delay was, where he's been. Usually he tells you that he and some of his fellow workshop attendees stopped at some local bar to discuss all that they learned during the day. Sometimes when he tells you this, he is cheerful; other times, he seems morose. You have some insight into what his ex might have experienced.

You don't know what to do.

35.

Sasha on the Road

After having spent six weeks OTR (On The Road), you are, as of this day: AOF — Altogether Officially Fucked. For five weeks and four days, your rolling prop case had managed to follow you into one plane after another as a carry-on. But just this morning, you'd been forced to surrender it to a representative for Idiot Airways as checked luggage, your homemade case having been deemed too big and too unwieldy to stash in the minuscule overhead compartments of their bush plane that brought you here to WhatTheFuck, USA.

And now, of course (of *course!*), your case has gone missing. Along with everything inside: costume, juggling props, makeup, even your wig — a security blanket that you *still* feel you must have on hand in order to screw up your courage to stumble onstage and stand before a roomful of drunken strangers, a number of whom would be just as happy to entertain themselves by kicking your sweet ass for you, should you cross paths at night on a dark street in this desert shithole. And so now, you are … AOF.

Thus, you recall your last exchange with your flatmate before you hit the road for the summer. The temperature of your home environment had recently dropped below 32 degrees following your rejection of her. And as her romantic interest shifted from sad clowns to hippie scum, the two of you have not been especially friendly. No more late-night, coin-counting accompanied by intimate chit-chat on your bed. No more, "Hey, Jujube, check this out!" impromptu, wee-hours practice sessions in your living room studio. Long before you left for the summer, she'd been holding herself apart from you, maintaining a cold, distant, 100-percent professional demeanor. Dammit.

But, at the very start of your summer standup adventure, before you can even leave town, she comes home from work to catch you wrestling your prop case — heavy sonovabitch that it is — down the long, steep front steps of your flat to the street, where your VW Bug is double-parked. With one wheel of the prop case stuck on the edge of a front step, you look up, then down to the sidewalk where she stands: hand on hip, in her career-girl drag, wearing a little DiFi suit and blouse with a big floppy collar bow and an exasperated expression that you know only too well is intended for you, only you.

"Oh, you're home!" you exclaim, stating the obvious. "How was your day?"

Without bothering to answer, she mounts the steps to where you stand stuck, grasps the handle at the bottom of your prop case, gives the case a quick yank to free it, and helps you lower it the rest of the way to the sidewalk. Then she says: "Thought you said you don't need all this stuff anymore."

To which you reply irritably: "Fuck you very much, Mrs. DeMille."

In response, she gives you the finger. But you have to admit: she has a point. This tour with its stops in a panoply of podunks was set up by a couple organizers connected with the Comedy Competition, and you are *spozed* to be presenting yourself as a standup act, not a cigar-box juggling clown. You repeat to yourself: intellect, not just attitude ... intellect, not just attitude. But you're anxious, scared even — what if you find yourself onstage with nothing to say? How will you fill in the time till it becomes clear you have died?

Help me, Madame Leveau!

"Jujube," you plead, "gimme a break and wish me luck. Please. I'm already freaked. I need my props as ... you know — props."

At which point, she switches to giving you a hard-luck stare, puts a hand on each of your shoulders, presses down lightly to give herself leverage, and raises herself on her tiptoes in order to deliver a kiss on your cheek.

"You're gonna be great, Sasha," she whispers into your ear. "You. Are. Gonna. Be. *GREAT.*"

Which sends you floating all the rest of the way to your car, levitating your prop case into it, and settling in for the long drive to San Diego, your southernmost intra-state stop. But before you throw the car into gear and pull away, you pat your thigh to check the contents of your pants pocket. You are reassured by the reply squeak of your lucky red nose.

Six weeks later, you think: whoa, crazy! as you investigate your saggy, stained Motel 5-1/2 mattress for bedbugs, your bathroom water glass for fingerprints and lipstick smudges, your toilet seat for specks of dried urine and stray pubic hairs. When you do this at home, Jujube sniggers at you, your OCD-ness. Can you help it you're a textbook Virgo?

Before leaving home, you'd imagined that going on the road would help you escape the awkwardness of your domestic situation. And that much has been accomplished. But, in addition, you've gotten to experience nearly every possible travel mishap short of being on a plane that crashed or a train that derailed. Blown engine? You had that right away, outside Fresno. Which is how you ended up in a rental car. Flat tire? You had that as well — an hour west of Stateline, on your way to Reno. You even had your luggage lost once before — on the flight from Vegas to Austin. You suspect the organizers of this comedy tour used a dart board to set up your itinerary.

You were really scared that first time your prop case went missing in the friendly skies. Fortunately, the airline saved you, with forty minutes to spare, by delivering your prop case backstage to the community college auditorium in Redding. *This* time in Bakersfield, however, you know better than to expect an eleventh-hour reprieve. Since your arrival and check-in midday today, you've gone outside at least half a dozen times to the motel's pay phone, plugged change into the coin slot of that antique device (still a dime for a local call here in the boonies!), dialed the airport on the sticky rotary dial, and begged the luggage handler/janitor to "check again" for your black, wooden, rolling crate embellished with stickers and glitter.

"You can't miss it," you told him for the sixth time. Your last call, at ten minutes past five, went unanswered. Most likely, everyone has gone home for the day. And you were warned already there would be no more flights till tomorrow — *after* your show tonight.

Anxiously, you reach into your pants pocket to fondle your lucky red nose. You give it a gentle squeeze and are gratified to hear its little squeak of reply.

Sometimes, when everything goes to shit, there's nothing to be done about it, except to lie very, very still while Fate backs its truck over you. With three hours to go before you have to navigate the six or so blocks to the oil rigger/cowboy dive-bar where you are scheduled to appear, you realize you'd better try for some shut-eye. You peel back your nasty, repellent bedspread, lie down fully clothed on your bed, with its scratchy blanket and oily mattress that smells of twenty years of cigarette smoke, and clutch your damp pillow.

If only your mind would settle down as well.

You wish you were home in your own nice clean bed with the sheets you yourself have ironed just the way you like them. The Land of On-the-Road is filthy and uncomfortable. Your gigs suck. You'd asked Jujube to get you inside, and she did that. But it turns out, except for the better weather, inside isn't necessarily an improvement over outside.

The worst thing, however, is the loneliness. Week after week. You get off work when the bars close. Each new town is a strange place where you don't know anyone. You barely even know where you are. The people who hired you went home hours ago. The people you perform with on any given night are a bunch of self-absorbed, malcontent losers. You miss the freewheeling camaraderie of the street. There you were a king among paupers. Here you have to carry weed to start a conversation.

Something no one has ever really appreciated about you is you are actually quite domestic. You love your home, even more so now that you can't spend much time there. You want your personal environment to be beautiful and comfortable and perfect. Most guys, if they have any thoughts at all about their surroundings beyond the decrepit recliners they sprawl in while watching TV football, are content to delegate anything having to do with housework and home maintenance to their wives and girlfriends. You, on the other hand, are only too happy to while away the morning standing in your shower enclosure, a cup of bleach in one hand and a toothbrush in the other, scrubbing the grout between backsplash tiles.

You think back on the past year and realize, with some surprise, that despite your busted digit and your roommate's unreasonable expectations, everything in your Baghdad-by-the-Bay had been right and righteous and in its rightful place. You had present gigs and future prospects. You had your home *and* you had someone to look after your interests when you couldn't be there.

And, to your amazement, it was great having someone to come home to — someone to ask: how'd it go today? You never wanted to be married or even have a steady girlfriend. Memories of Tiffany and how she ruined your reputation at Social Services were still painful. When you considered what she'd done to you, you were content to take revenge on her entire sex. On the other hand, to have a friend, a true friend, even if she happened to be female — that was a new experience for you, one you were reluctant to release.

Things had been working so well, until Jujube lost her head. You needed her skills. She exercised them on your behalf.

You repaid her. But then she wanted more. And, frankly, you didn't think you had it in you to give more, the sort of "more" you suspect she wants from you. What if it didn't work out? You'd lose what you had, everything you still need. Now that she's retrenched and is treating you with appropriate professionalism, you can't fault her. But you miss the easy times, the laughter and sympathy, the friendship.

Any other female, you'd have cut her off long before now. God knows you've dealt with this kind of situation often enough in past years. So, the first "I love you" out of their mouths, you sent them packing the very same night. Okay, not *that* very *same* night. You'd wait till morning to put them out. You're not a complete idiot.

The point is, you *never* allow such things to get out of hand. You're a cautious man, especially when it comes to affairs of the heart, and in such matters you always ... take ... it ... slow. But how the hell can you do that, when she is *right there*, in your house, in your face? It's one thing when you're in control — quite another thing if *no one* is in control. You don't want to open a can of worms you can't close back up again. How much simpler life was back in the day when you had zero interest in being in love, when all you wanted from any woman was to be *used* by her for a while. Then you'd break her heart for her and she would leave you. Alone.

You conk out in mid-rumination ... and wake up in a panic a couple hours later when the tinny clock-radio in this dump fires off some AM station Golden Oldie: 7:30 p.m. Shit.

You peel off your sweaty clothes and step into the scabby, plastic shower, where hard water from the tap has laid down stripes of various mineral colors. Water sputters out of the nozzle near your head. You do your best to work up some semblance of lather with the tiny, hard, pink bar of generic bath soap. You smear it around on yourself. This will have to do.

You towel off with the one ratty towel they give you here. Then you dig around in your backpack for a clean pair of underpants, which you started carrying with you on every plane, because you learned your lesson after the lost-luggage incident in Redding. Fresh underwear — at least, you can do that much for your audience tonight.

Out on the sidewalk, you can smell the heat of the day rising from the asphalt of the street and the millions of acres of desert scrub just outside of town. You feel strangely elated, unencumbered, and free as you set out on your six-block stroll to the local dive where you'll be performing. Probably the only spot within a ten-mile radius that's big enough to have a stage and a sound system. You look around for the herd of big trucks at rest; you sight their massive shadows in the distance.

Your spirits lift — no greasy makeup, no too-tight-in-all-the-wrong-places costume, no junk to drag around.

On the other hand, nothing to hide behind or to protect yourself with.

You set aside that last thought — it can't help you.

You stop, close your eyes, throw back your head to mentally direct a prayer heavenward: Madam Leveau, please, *please* remember me tonight! You recall it worked before, it worked before. At the pier in Frisco, it worked. Even if you said fuck a few too many times. Not like that's gonna matter here. You're going to be fine — no, in fact: you. are. gonna. be. *GREAT!*

The bouncer door-checks you and points you to an archway on the other side of the large, open room with a bar along the back wall, an actual proscenium stage (with a curtain, even!) at the front, and half a dozen dinner tables set with votives in between. You must cross this space to get backstage. You glance up at the stage. Some fat guy in black jeans and a black T-shirt is doing a set at the mike. He is soaked in flop sweat.

You scan the row of redneck, red-faced, rural types hunched over their beers at the bar, as well as three or four date-night couples at tables, to see how this obviously urban comic is being received. Not so good, you're guessing, as the room is pretty quiet, with not so much as a guffaw from the entire lot. You think maybe they are all peacefully slumbering in their seats.

Since you will probably be going up next — no drawing straws for position on this billing, they just give you a start time — you consider how your fellow performer may be helping or hurting you for when your turn comes. You decide he's helping you by setting the performance bar so low that, even semi-conscious, you could crawl over it on your hands and knees.

On the other hand, since this loser has put your audience to sleep, it will be your job to wake them up so you can do what you came here to do: entertain them with yourself for half an hour, at least. Somehow you will have to get their attention. Already a plan for how to do that is coming to you.

You remind yourself: you *want* this. Instinctively, you look around for emergency exits.

Backstage you are met by your producer/director of tonight's pathetic production, a tiny gal with a nose ring, a twinkle in her eye, black hair down to her ass, an impressive rack for someone of the Asian persuasion, and the husky voice of a barfly. Her name turns out to be Min. You think, Minnie Mouse. Easy to remember.

"Finally made it, I see," she says. "Heard all your gear lost in transit. Getting so late, I start to wonder if you plan to show up at all."

"Show's gotta go on," you reply lamely, mesmerized by her tits.

"I heard great things about you from your publicist. She says you never fail, you're funny just standing there," she says, leaning in with her sculptural shelf that comes to just about navel-height on you. She reaches up to pet your shoulder in a way that gives you a shiver.

"Uh, thank you very much," you respond with your best Johnny Cash impression.

"Well, better get ready," she says. "You can change in the toilet."

"Change? No thanks, I like myself the way I am," you tell her. You slip off your shoes. You peel off your shirt, baring your chest. You reach into your pants pocket and extract your lucky red nose; you fix it to your own nose and pinch it to make it squeak. Finally, you undo your belt, unzip your zipper, drop your pants, and step out of them.

"All set," you tell her, standing backstage in your nice fresh boxers and socks.

Moments later, as you are carefully folding and stacking your street clothes, you hear a smattering of applause from the house. Fat-Boy-in-Black blows past, spraying you with sweat. "All yours," he says on his way to the toilet.

"I'll go announce you now," Min says. "While you're on, you want me to hold your clothing for you?"

"Much obliged, m'am," you tell her, faking a country twang. Then you ask, "Mind if I borrow three cans of beer for the set?"

She gestures help-yourself toward the case of Miller High Lifes stacked against the wall behind her, then pushes through the heavy, dark curtain. Her announcement of your name, repeated twice for emphasis, reaches you in a muffled way.

You take a deep breath and expel it slowly to center yourself for the next half hour. When Min returns, you press your bundle of pants, shirt, t-shirt, and shoes, sole to sole, into her hands, then fumble around for the break in the curtain.

Catching sight of the light, you push forward and head for the stage, where you stand before the audience, clad in only your underwear, socks, and red rubber nose, holding three cans of warm beer — an image you know damn well cannot be topped for getting the crowd's attention. Maybe you won't even have to resort to expletives tonight.

For four eternal beats, the place is silent. You look around the room, surveying your largely male audience. Then you start to juggle the three cans of beer you picked up backstage. Juggling always relaxes you. It's what you like to do whenever you feel anxious or lonely. But tonight, you realize, you don't feel anxious or lonely, just a little chilly.

"Is there a doctor in the house? Anyone? No doctors? How about an intern? A first-year medical student? Fans of *St. Elsewhere*? Anyone? No? Looks like I'll have to save myself, then.

"My name is Sasha, Sasha from San Francisco, and I thank you for your respectful show of silence. I've been so busy lately, I appreciate having this little bit of quiet time to myself.

And please don't be concerned: I don't need a doctor — I only wanted to see if it would be just like the dream. You know: that one where you suddenly find yourself naked in public. Sure, go ahead and laugh all you like, but when it happens to you...."

What follows — a sudden explosion of raucous laughter, hoots, and cat-calls — is music to your ears, the opening you'd prayed for. You continue, gathering steam:

"Actually, in San Francisco, my hometown, it doesn't matter if you walk into a bar without your pants, because we live in a 'Clothing Optional Zone.' In fact, in a lot of our bars, people tend to like you much better if you come in without your pants.

"Where I live, recreational nudity isn't just for hot tubs and beaches — it's our religion. Besides, my invitation for tonight didn't mention whether your event was formal or casual, so I thought I'd wait till I got here to decide what to wear.

"But as I was saying: my name is Sasha, and I don't need a doctor right now, but if I did, I could always phone my father — because he *is* a doctor. An Army doctor, in fact — the kind who can shoot you, then dig out the bullet. A full-service service man. I call him 'The General.' Actually, he's not a general, I think he's a colonel. But he'd like to be a general, like his boss, the Surgeon General. And if he were a general practitioner, instead of a lab rat in uniform, I'd call him 'The General General.'

"How many of you here have fathers who are doctors? No one? Well, how many of you here have fathers? That's more like it. But I see a few of you don't, and maybe you've been feeling bad about that. You don't realize, though: you could be the lucky ones.

"My father started his career in Korea, in a *M*A*S*H* unit — you know, like the old TV series that ended a few years ago. Later on, my father was stationed in Europe, in France, then Germany — I think his commanding officer was Dr. Mengele. Now he works in Washington, D.C., putting warning labels on things. He got the idea for that from my mother when we lived in France. As a toddler, I was a biter, and she used to sew a label onto the front of my little shirt to warn the au pair. I'm grateful we hadn't been sent to Germany yet or else she might have had me tattooed instead with the words: '*Achtung*! He bites!'

"My father was a stern man — still is. And after I survived my childhood and had demonstrated some potential for having a future, my father intended that I, his only son, should follow in his footsteps and become a doctor, too. Or at least go into the Army and let them finish the job of making a man out of me. For sixteen years, it had been my father's shame to have a mouth-breather for a son. Our relationship improved a lot after I had my tonsils and adenoids out. Up to then, I thought I loved him — after my surgery, I realized: I had Stockholm Syndrome.

"I hated the military school where he and my new stepmother sent me for my last year of high school — all that regimentation. And I wasn't much interested in the practice of medicine. Except for the drugs — that part was good. But, to please the old man, I attended the Ivy League university of his choice and enrolled in a pre-med course of studies. He was paying for it, after all, and when I registered for the draft, my Selective Service Lottery number was, like, 3. I knew I was facing either a paper jungle or the kind with flying disease vectors and sniper fire. So I put on a lab coat and spent four years learning to concoct various potions. My favorite one can make anything smell like dog shit, and you never get the stink out. If any of you here are interested in the recipe, see me after the show — I'm gonna need a few bucks to catch the Greyhound bus back to San Francisco.

"But all that was years ago, and as you can see, I didn't go into medicine. Or the Army. Though if I *had* become a doctor, I woulda gone into psychiatry and spent my vacations analyzing myself. I could even have prescribed my own drugs. Come to think of it, maybe going into comedy instead was a mistake: I still have to do all my own analysis, but I also have to accept a group rate for spending time with you. ... That's right, sir — go right ahead and sneak out in the middle of my set. I'll still get paid the same.

"Ever notice how other people's expectations of you affect the way you see yourself? Especially when those other people are your parents? I'm happy to say the last thing my father ever expected me to do was become a clown — a full-out, professional, juggling clown, complete with this red rubber nose.

"But that's what I did. I figured it was more honest to present myself as a real clown than to do like most people and be a clown who's just pretending to be a doctor or a soldier or whatever. I thought my father would disown me after I completed my post-grad course of study at clown college. But, to his credit, all he asked was that I not perform under the name we share — I'm a junior to his senior. My high-class, debutante girlfriend, though — she dumped me. Turned out she didn't want to marry a clown, she'd rather have the fake doctor.

"But about other people's expectations of you? Either you accept them as your own and try to make them work in your life. Or, if the suit or the lab coat or the uniform doesn't fit, you reject other people's off-the-rack expectations and try to create your own expectations for yourself. We could also call them 'goals.' Or maybe even dreams.

"So, how about you? We're all grownups here tonight — we should be able to discuss this. Just pretend I'm Phil Donahue. How many of you ended up doing what your parents wanted you to do? And how did that work out? You, sir — yes, you, the man 'dressed for success' in the David Byrne oversized jacket: What did your parents want you to grow up to be? And what is it you do now? And is that what you wanted? And if it isn't, then do you have any idea ... why you can't do what you want?"

Thus it came to pass that you did your first forty-five-minute set of your life without costume, makeup, or a single prop. Just your lucky red rubber nose, which you squeaked in approval of your audience as they applauded you at the end of your gig.

36.
Juli Gets Divorced

Yo have discovered you can gauge your readiness to divorce David by your ability to deal with the divorce papers. When first you moved into Sasha's attic, you couldn't bring yourself even to touch them. A couple weeks later, you had advanced to sitting down with the papers, attempting to decipher them, then staggering to your feet and clambering down your twelve-foot ladder to run to the bathroom and throw up. The second time you found yourself with your head in the toilet, you thought: coincidence. The third time you found yourself driving the porcelain bus, you realized: this reaction must be a pattern. The fourth time, you understood the meaning of the pattern.

A month later, you tried again, making sure to approach the problem on an empty stomach. Nothing to lose. But this time, narcolepsy set in: suddenly overcome with irresistible fatigue, you had no choice but to lie on the floor next to your typewriter and nap for an hour and a half. The same thing happened two days later ... a week later ... several days after that.

The final strategy devised by your subconscious to keep you from filling out your divorce papers was a sudden, near-total loss of reading comprehension. You fed each legal-length form under the platen of the IBM Selectric you'd leased and named Betty Blue, you rolled the sheet up to read its text, you positioned your hands to begin typing, filling in the blanks, and you ... could not remember a thing of what you had read only twenty seconds ago. This subconscious subversion remained in force only a couple of days, but, taken all together, your serial neuroses cost you nearly four months of waiting time before you managed to cut yourself free.

How ironic, you thought, that two people can marry in less than an hour, but require a year to divorce.

Then there were the filing fees to be earned, which took weeks more before you could afford to have David sign the papers. Sasha helped you earn that extra money. When you told him the reason you needed actual cash and not just credit toward rent, he seemed eager to help. In the past, you would have interpreted his response as a sign of his interest in you. Now you realize he only wants your professional services. He knows full well, the sooner you are free of your ex, in every sense, the sooner you will be able to devote all your energy and attention to him. Thus, step by step, you have come to understand your role here: to serve.

Each time you phoned your father to see how he was doing, he offered you space, a place to stay till you could "get back on your feet." This most recent time he made the offer, you accepted. On impulse, you told your father, yes, that would be great, you'll move to the East Bay as soon as your flatmate returns from his business trip. You don't want to leave the flat empty.

But you are always a little sketchy about the parameters of your life when talking to your father. You remember how much he disliked and disapproved of David. You remember how awkward it had been to tell him that, though your marriage was failing, you had decided to stay in the City and move into a flat you would share with another man, who was "just a friend." You know your father thinks his soon-to-be-*ex*-son-in-law is a cad (and he's right); you don't want him to think his daughter could be a slut.

When Bill first suggested you ought to move out of Sasha's flat — that was early on, after your third "date" and before Sasha went on the road — you were hoping he'd ask you to come live with him, but he didn't. He just said, yeah, you oughta do that. And the subject hasn't come up since. So maybe, you think, he's not especially into you, after all.

To be fair, you get why Bill's roommate situation allows one-nighters, but not live-ins. With four male roommates and one bathroom, competition for access to plumbing can be fierce. And it's not like *you* can just push aside last night's dirty dishes and pee into the kitchen sink drain like one of the guys. Or step out the back door, unzip your fly, and wee-wee off the back porch into space. Nor is the nightly crush for facilities exactly conducive to romance.

If, in fact, romance is even what you have going on. Because it's hard to tell at times. The transition from platonic friend to fuck buddy or lover or whatever this new relationship is — or will be — seems mainly characterized by Bill's cagey new self-protectiveness. He always seemed so open before; now you are left to guess what he's thinking or feeling most of the time. You are starting to wonder whether, maybe, by getting into bed with this man, you've lost him as a friend, someone you can still confide in. Since what you mostly have to confide at this point is all about him.

More than anything, you've felt so lonely this summer. The man you married in order to save your relationship is gone forever. The man you thought was interested in you personally only wants you professionally. The man who used to be your good friend seems to be growing increasingly distant. The worst thing, you see now, is having lost all sense of what your future *will* be or even what it *could* be. You never before realized how important it is to have someone on whom to fasten your hopes. Even during your terrible years with David, you always had that much, at least — a persistent hope that the next thing you tried would be the miracle cure that would save the marriage. Because you didn't understand your case was terminal, you kept searching, relentlessly searching, for a cure. Ultimately, all you could do was let go and let die.

When the phone rings, some psychic sense informs you: Sasha is calling. Grateful for your early-warning paranormality, you prepare yourself as you reach for the receiver. You intend to greet your roommate or whoever answers the phone with chilly professionalism. After a summer of living alone, you are still hurt, humiliated, and angry to have been rejected. Your hurt and humiliation make you feel weak and worthless; your anger, however, convinces you that you are strong. You hope, when the time comes, your anger will empower you to leave this place. And him.

But, as soon as you hear his voice on the phone line crackling with distant interference, you are thrilled to hear from him. Your friend. Despite everything that's gone on or not gone on between you.

"Jujube, howzit?!"

You imagine him standing in some sticky, chewing-gum-clotted phone booth at some filthy, broken-down gas station in the middle of nowhere, tumbleweeds rolling by.

"Sasha! How's life on the comedy circuit?"

"Clinging by my nails. Last night was weird."

"Yeah? Weird what way?"

"I did two sets in my underwear."

"Yeah?"

"Yeah."

"But you killed, right?"

"Laid them out deader than a family of gophers after a golf course poisoning."

"What? With no costume, no makeup?"

"Just my birthday suit, my Fruit-of-the-Looms (clean, of course), my lucky nose, and six more feet of cord than my mother ever gave me."

"Yeah!" you exclaim and high-five yourself, thrilled by his victory over this gig. Which. You. Got for him.

But as quickly as your euphoria arrived, it departs. Professional update over, only personal matters remain.

"Hey, Sasha," you start out slow, working up to your news. "I was gonna wait till you got home, but since you called, I guess I need to tell you … I'll be moving out pretty soon." You wait for a response. It's a long time coming. You sit and wait and listen to the static crackling on the line, like Muzak for robots.

"I wish you wouldn't go," he says at last.

"It's already set," you tell him.

"No way I can convince you to stay?"

"Sorry, no."

"You're moving in with that guy who was over?"

"Who, Bill? Naw, he's just a friend. I'm going to go live with my dad for a while."

You can tell Sasha is surprised by the news. You catch a glimpse of yourself through his eyes and realize he must have thought you were just another female parasite, living off one man after another. He must have supposed you'd been pursuing him as a likely host and, having failed to pin him down, was moving on to someone else. He wasn't prepared to have you retreat on general principles.

"You don't have to do that," he says.

"No, really, I do."

"Can we still be friends?"

"Of course," you tell him. "We'll always be friends. That's one of the reasons I'm leaving: so we can still be friends."

He accepts your explanation and doesn't ask for clarification.

"But is it worth a buck?" he asks, alluding to the late-night memories you share of solo performances delivered to an audience of one.

And you respond in kind: "Hell, yes, I'd give you a buck."

After you hang up, you feel calm. No anger left in you, only love and gratitude for all you have received from this strange, driven man: a place to live when you had none, a new focus for your affections that made you realize you were actually capable of being interested in someone else once again, support for making the final break. He hadn't been able to give you what you thought you wanted, but he still gave a lot. More than he realized.

You even dare to feel a little sorry for him, because he's missing out on so much. He probably supposes you are still the same girl he fled at the beginning of summer. But you are changed, you are free now. When he gets home next week, you will be on the verge of gone.

Tonight, though, you go down to his bedroom, light the votives he keeps on his dresser, stretch out on his bed, and roll yourself up into his shiny, red-and-black satin bedspread. You bury your face in his pillow, which, despite the clean linen, still smells like him. You inhale deeply.

"Oh, Sasha," you exhale.

Now you understand those baby monkeys you studied in your college psychology class. Taken from their real monkey mothers and caged with surrogates of either wire and cloth or wire and wood (the latter constructed by scientists to hold monkey-size baby bottles), the infants preferred to cling to the soft, cushy cloth-mothers, who offered fake comfort, over the hard, cold wooden-mothers, who delivered actual sustenance.

37.
Why Barbra Can't

Y ou leave the city and drive to your parents' farm six hours
away. Interstate 5, straight as an arrow's course for much of the
way heading north, parts the land. Through one long stretch,
recently harvested fields rush away from you on either side of
the asphalt, as if your vehicle were a ship trailing an expansive
golden wake. Past Sacramento, there's really nothing out here.
The unbroken horizon ahead tricks your eyes and your mind:
you imagine you can see the future. You wish it were true; you
are afraid it is.

A day's drive to see your parents isn't all that far away, yet
it's been several years since you were "home." You don't miss
it. Your life is no longer here. In fact, every time you do come
"home," you feel uncomfortable, a failure. Which is strange,
because in your real life in San Francisco, you have a great job,
a listing with the local Better Business Bureau, a lovely condo
in one of the world's most desirable cities, a big, remodeled
kitchen with every possible appliance and gadget, a closetful
of clothes with labels that count for something at the sports

club where you are a member, an actual garage in which to park your new leased car, a brand-new mobile phone, season tickets to the local repertory theater where you are a board member, and much, much more, as befits your status as a fully realized YUPPIE — a young urban professional, the likes of which your parents never see, except on those rare occasions when they see you.

Most of the people you grew up with have no idea what you do for a living or what you've achieved in your adopted hometown. All they know is you're still single in your mid-thirties and haven't returned with any grandchildren to delight your aging parents. Some remember you from high school, from that time when Lorie and you were king and queen of his senior prom and deemed "Cutest Couple" in your junior yearbook.

A few still remember how, all those years ago, you quietly became un-engaged from him. They didn't blame you. The breakup was clearly his fault, since he was off with "those dirty hippies," and, besides, everyone knows that long-distance relationships are hard to sustain. But they felt sorry for you. Which was worse. And they are still a little surprised, maybe disappointed, you never found a replacement for King Loren. Or Queen Loren. Whatever.

You're glad you arranged to stay with your folks only this one Thursday night en route to Seattle. Your sorority regional isn't until Saturday evening. Tonight you'll have to sleep on your squeaky old twin bed in your shabby old childhood bedroom, which your mother converted ages ago into her sewing room. You don't look forward to that experience.

But, tomorrow night, you'll have a nice room with a big

bed in the same hotel where the event is being held. You can get a good night's sleep, party with your sisters the next evening till dawn, crawl to your room and crash, then hit the road again the following midday. If you're not too hung over and your driving muscles seem up to the challenge, you may even try to make it in one go from Seattle to San Francisco. With any luck, you'll be home a little past midnight.

Part road trip, part overdue family visit, part sorority reunion — it's crazy, because you could have either just flown up or skipped the whole thing. But you really, really want to get away by yourself for a few days, and this seems the perfect excuse. You try to not think of what David may be up to in your absence. You hate that he'll have the run of your place while you're gone. You wish there were boarding kennels for men.

Your nerves don't kick in until, about an hour or so away from your childhood home, you glance over and see Mt. Shasta peeking around the passing hills to your right, as if watching for your arrival. You feel a mixture of reassurance and guilt. Fifteen minutes later, Shasta rises up directly ahead of you, stands there for a moment, with authority, then she withdraws to let you continue. You turn off I- 5 at Yreka, head directly for the mountains, up to 4,000 feet, until you crest the summit and descend into verdant Scott's Valley.

Finally pulling onto the well-graded dirt road that leads to your parents' house, you know your mother, at least, will be waiting to greet you as soon as you shut off the engine. Your dad will probably be in the barn, tinkering with something. He's getting so old — they both are — he could really use some help around the place. If everything had worked out as God intended, you would have been able to give him that help.

Loren would be managing both places, his parents' and yours as well. He'd have been able to afford to hire men to work those lands and the stock they support.

And your mom would have company. Not only you, but your children as well. Her grandkids. You know she gets lonesome out here. You feel a pressing guilt until you remind yourself: none of this was of your choosing.

You didn't ask to be born in the middle of nowhere. Or raised to believe that the boy next door was the love of your life and it was God's will you should be joined with him forever in Holy Matrimony, except he turns out to be gay and only likes you as a friend. Other people made those life-decisions for you. Without regard for the actual human being you are.

Your real life — the life you chose for yourself — started nearly twenty years ago when you returned home after your disastrous Christmas break in Berkeley, then reconciled yourself to attending junior college for two years before transferring to UC Davis. You wouldn't have even pledged your mother's sorority if you hadn't felt so alone at the university. It makes you smile now, to think that both you and Lorie went Greek at UC. These days, with David in your life, you at least have someone you can talk up to your sisters, even if you can't show him off to your folks.

You turn off the circuitous, two-lane country road onto your parents' gravel drive, then around the side of the house and under the big cottonwood that stands in their back yard. That tree was planted there by your father's father on Arbor Day 1919, the spring after World War I ended. Two chunky cattle dogs come racing around the side of the house, barking like a pack of ten, announcing your arrival. You get out of the car expecting to see your dad's old dog Señorita hobbling after to keep up, then remember she's been dead and gone for ages. In fact, she could be buried under this very tree. You wonder if these two are her pups or grandpups or even great-grandpups. They don't know you. As you get out of the car, hesitating at the blast of Indian summer heat, they keep up their hostile barking and block your way to the house.

"Bogey! Bacall! Shut your yaps! Off!"

This command comes from your mother, who, as you had anticipated, has come out onto the wide sleeping porch to greet you. She is wearing a loose-fitting, flower-print housedress tied at one side, a type of garment you accept as natural here on your mom in the country, but would find laughable on anyone in the City. The chastised dogs trot away as if they'd never seen you in the first place. You go to your mother, up the four worn wooden stairs to where she stands holding the screen door with her back, and you give her a big hug. In that moment you have forgotten that neither of you is the touchy-feely type. But it's been so long since your last visit, she has already responded, hugging you back.

"Mama," you say.

"Barbra Anne," she replies, then holds you at arms' length so she can look you up and down before giving her verdict. "Oh my, you are so thin."

From the front door, you follow her inside into the kitchen, letting the wood-frame screen door bang behind you, a sound of childhood. Your mother's kitchen, which she inherited from her mother-in-law, your grandmother, is the largest single room in the house. It still features your mother's "new" stove, which was manufactured in the 1920s and came to her as a wedding present the following decade: an enameled, cast-iron cabinet range, large and heavy as a VW Bug, with five burners, two ovens, and a built-in incinerator. Its special magic is that it is a combination range, which can be fired with wood or coal in winter, with propane gas in summer. Before gas was available in this area, your mother and grandmother used wood for cooking and coal to warm the place.

As you look around the kitchen you know you have stepped back in time: nothing changed. Your mother's clunky countertop accouterments — her giant toaster, her bowl mixer, her breadbox — everything is right where you remember it always was. And, of course, everything is spotless. Not so much as a coffee cup or dirty spoon in the ancient, pitted porcelain sink. At least, you have this mother-daughter shared obsession for cleanliness. You note a pie sitting on her cooling rack on the Formica countertop, which explains the seductively friendly flakey dough smell that pervades the room. You think, if this were your kitchen, that pie would have already found its way out of your reach at the bottom of the trashcan. You like to cook; you just don't like to eat.

The long, heavy wooden table that used to dominate the room dominates it still, standing in the center of the floor, with five chairs placed around it and a sixth chair out of the way against a wall. There is one chair each for your granddad, your grandmama, your dad and mama, and you. Three of these chairs are most likely no longer used, your grandparents having died long ago and you away in the City this past decade. You note your parents' place settings remain exactly where you remember them always: your father at the foot of the table, your mother to his right. She gestures toward the chair to the left of your father's placemat — *your* chair. You sit in it, and she takes her place opposite you.

"Pie?" she asks. "It's fresh. Apple."

You shake your head. "No, thanks, mama," you tell her. "I'm not hungry."

"You're too skinny, Barbra Anne. Boys don't like girls who are too skinny. I'm sure Loren doesn't like you being so thin."

You stare at her, amazed at how twenty years of history could just drop out of her brain like that, and you think: ma, what you don't know, Lorie doesn't like girls at all. But what you say is:

"Remember how, when I was in high school, you were always saying I was too fat? How 'boys don't like girls who are too fat'?"

"Well, seems you've gone overboard. Like you tend to do."

You laugh at this. "Yeah, well, you're right about that."

"Seeing anyone special?"

You think a moment before answering, "No, I guess not."

"That's not what I hear."

"Yeah? What do you hear?"

"I hear you have someone living with you. An actor."

"Really? Who told you that?"

"Your Aunt Amelia called to chat — that was three Sundays ago — and she mentioned that your Cousin Dodie stayed with you in San Francisco right before she surprised everyone in the family by flying home unannounced and getting married out of the blue, despite her weight problem. No ceremony or reception or anything, just a city hall elopement before running off to Mexico. No wonder we didn't hear about it. She's Dodie Rodriguez now, by the way.

"Anyhow, I got a second surprise in that same conversation, because I also didn't know a thing about this fella you never mentioned. So I felt like kind of a fool before your aunt, when she told me that Dodie told her that you were living with some tall, good-looking actor."

"Is that right? Well then, must be true."

"Don't pull my leg, Barbra Anne. Are you or are you not living with someone? I hope you don't imagine this fella has any intention of marrying you. He's already getting the milk for free, so why would he care to own the cow?"

You snigger at your mother's analogy and make a mental note of Dodie's having tattled on you. "Honestly, ma, don't trouble yourself. That guy's not important, and I seriously doubt I'll be getting married any time soon."

"Honey, you can do better than some actor."

You see your mother means well, so you try to reward her charity towards you. "Thanks, mama. Let's hope."

"It reminds me: are you staying over for the weekend? Pastor Break is giving a special talk on Sunday: 'Finding True Love In These Uncertain Times'. Sounds uplifting. Might do you good."

"It does sound uplifting, but no. I'm just here for tonight, then in the morning I have to hit the road in time for the regional reunion in Seattle Saturday night. I'm sorry, mama."

"Oh, I suppose. Well, at least you can go congratulate your cousin on her marriage. I heard she's going to be back in Seattle from Mexico City. And if they've got a program with everyone's names on it, pick me up one. I want to find out how many people I used to know are still alive."

"Sure thing. Or you could come see for yourself if you

packed a weekender and kept me company on the drive up. It'd only be a couple nights away from home. Dad won't mind."

"Maybe not. But I'll mind if he sets the house on fire trying to get his dinner. These days I don't dare leave him on his own for more than a few hours at a time."

"Where is dad, anyway?"

"Most likely he's in the old barn, trying to put something together. He's forever up to something out there. Takes stuff apart, but never gets it back together. But don't you worry: he'll be in for supper. That much you can always count on."

38.

Barbra Is Counseled by Her Sorority Sister

Sisters converge on Seattle from all over the region, up and down the West Coast, different campuses, different graduating years. Most of these women you don't know. You're impressed by the range of ages and types who've already filled the hotel's too-brightly-lit ballroom. The real diversity, however, seems to have been cornered by the younger set. Not something you remember from your college days. And all the older women look pretty much the same. Like your mother, only better dressed, more turned out.

You scan the room for women about your same age — still on the sunrise side of forty. You expect to find them seated near the band. And so they are. As you approach them from across the room, you deliver a broad, overhead, parade-float wave to their table and watch the ripple of faces turning toward you, one after another: Sonja ... Bette ... Monica ... Astrid ... Joan. As well as someone who doesn't turn around and whose broad back you don't recognize.

Of this herd of female competitors in the world, you are most glad to see Sonja, even though it's only been a couple months since you last saw her. She stayed with you over that long weekend on her way to Hong Kong. You remember you were so busy with work, but David showed her around the City, as he had done earlier with Dodie. He even drove Sonja to the airport. You wondered that it took her so long to drop you a line after she got back into the country, to thank you for your hospitality. When her note finally arrived, you were surprised by its formality.

When the one woman at the table who hadn't yet turned your way finally does, you see it is Cousin Dodie. And, oh my god, your mother was right: she's gotten so fat! Way heavier now than when she stayed with you and David. If this is what marriage does to you, you are never getting married. Never, never, never.

Dodie catches sight of you and, unlike your other sisters, she does not light up with a big smile. Instead, she almost looks frightened. You recall you never did hear from her since she visited you. You had supposed it was because, since you and she are family, you didn't need to send those bread-and-butter notes back and forth. Now you're thinking it's guilt.

You mean to talk to her, to find out what really happened during those two weeks she stayed with you. And ... oh yeah, to congratulate her on her marriage as well. Even though she never bothered to invite you to the wedding or the reception. Except, oh yeah, that's right — they eloped after a visit to city hall. But first you need a drink to steady yourself, so you veer off towards the no-host wet bar, pointing and mouthing to mime your intentions to your sisters.

By the time you return to the table near the band where your age-mates are encamped, they are already starting to sprawl in their chairs. You scan the row of bodies for Dodie. She is missing in action.

"She went to the ladies' room to puke!" Sonja yells over the music.

You commandeer the chair still warm from Dodie's triple-wide butt and put in the required twenty minutes of sisterly camaraderie, before catching Sonja's eye across the table. You lift your empty glass full of melting ice cubes and gesture with a tilt and thrust of your head toward the hotel's dark and cavelike bar off its brilliant ballroom. You get up and move in the direction of the bar, cautiously picking your way along the edge of the dance floor, as if it were an ice rink. The three generations of women currently comprising the freeform, stomping mob on the floor are dancing in couples and in clumps, with both a few, mostly older men and any number of a variety of women. When you glance over your shoulder, you see Sonja following a few steps behind you.

From within the dark bar, the reunion hullabaloo recedes in the distance as if the ballroom had suddenly shrunk to the size of a doll's house. Here in the bar it is quiet and cool. You seat yourself in a padded, naugahyde booth as far away as possible from the reunion you'd traveled hundreds and hundreds of miles to attend.

Two beats later, Sonja drops down next to you. She embraces you with her long, graceful arms and kisses you full on the mouth. You are surprised. But flattered. You use your cocktail napkin to wipe off the lipstick smear you're afraid she's left on you.

One more drink, and she is telling you what you need to know.

"Yeah, that's right: so I woke up that morning I left for Hong Kong," she is saying, "and that guy you live with...."

"David."

"... David ...." When she says his name, her upper lip curls in a sneer. "*David* was fondling my breasts, kissing my face, sticking his tongue in my ear."

You literally feel all the blood drain out of your head, leaving your brain high and dry. An explosion of intense heat ignites in your chest, radiating out across your entire body, like waves from an atomic bomb. For a moment, your vision fades, going dark around the edges, so you fear you may faint. Then, despite the fact that you are wearing a sleeveless, backless, seriously décolletage, halter-top formal gown, you start to sweat. Profusely. You use your cocktail napkin to blot beads from your upper lip.

You know you are staring at Sonja, your friend, as if you just watched someone being raised from the dead. You wonder whether the person who died, then came back, was in fact *you*. You feel ... confused. And short on air to breathe. She interprets your expression correctly.

"Yeah, that's right," she says. "But don't worry: nothing happened. Though it sure as hell could have — if I hadn't told him to get his hands off me or he'd lose the use of them."

You haven't eaten for twenty-four hours, and the booze is starting to get to you. You think how much you like this city of Seattle — so much like San Francisco with its waterfront and all these hills — yet with none of the problems facing you in the City. You think you could move here and make a clean start of your life. Your mind immediately races ahead in planning mode, and you wonder how much you could get for your condo in San Francisco. You notice the bar's selection of quality white wines in Washington state is decidedly limited. It's pretty clear they could use your expertise and connections.

You feel slightly dizzy as your mind suddenly reverses course and races back to that day when Sonja left for her purchasing junket in Hong Kong. Another one of your super-busy workdays. You remember getting home that evening and asking David whether Sonja got off okay. Boy, was *that* ever the double entendre of the century! You remember he shrugged and told you, oh sure, not a problem. You didn't press for details — what reason did you have to doubt him?

What reason, except ... Lorie's earlier warning to you about seeing David sucking face with Dodie at the Old Swiss House at Pier 39, the last time you heard from Lorie.... .

Your circulatory tsunami comes roaring in again, and now you feel your face burning with shame. Once more, Sonja calls it:

"Honey, I am *not* making this up. You need to get rid of that guy. He's just using you."

Cornered by truth you don't wish to acknowledge, you counter with the best defense you can manufacture on the spot: a good offense.

"Well, David *did* mention you'd come on to him."

"Oh, he did, did he? Well, if you don't believe me, go check with Dodie. She wasn't nearly as good at putting off that scumbag hoser. He shagged her so hard I'm surprised he didn't break off his thing inside her."

"She told you that?"

"No, not in so many words. But yeah. And you know, nice Christian girl, she doesn't lie. But don't worry, she hasn't spread any rumors. No 'bride' wants a tale like that going around. I don't think she would have told me at all, except I ran into her at the store, when she was up from Meh-hee-co visiting her folks, and I happened to mention I was leaving for Hong Kong to buy more optical crap and planned to spend my weekend layover with you in San Francisco. Hey: 'my layover' — that coulda been a good one, eh?"

You realize, at this juncture in the conversation, you are supposed to say something. *Something.* But just now you are watching a mind-movie of your last visit from Lorie, when he came over to warn you off David. You are hearing his description of the "short, fat," "very pale" woman he claimed he saw kissing David in the Old Swiss House bar. Dammit to hell.

You stare in a trance state at Sonja. Your mind is blank. You go on staring.

"Lissen," she says, "I'm only telling you this for your own good."

You remember Loren saying the exact same thing. It occurs to you: this probably means Sonja and Lorie are actually your real, true friends.

"Okay," you respond. "Thanks. Sorry I didn't believe you at first."

"Oh, honey, it's alright," Sonja says with a shrug, raising her empty glass and yours to the bartender to solicit another round. "I know how you feel. That's why I got rid of Buddy. He was great in the sack, but he was such a bastard."

39.

Barbra Learns about AIDS

Soon after your return from Seattle, you are surprised by a call from Loren's mother, Elaine. You are even more surprised when she tells you she is right here in San Francisco and has been for the past month, staying with her son, sleeping on his sofa. Just last week at your parents', when you asked your own mother about Lorie's folks, how they were doing, she told you Mrs. McMaster had been out of town for a while, but she didn't know where she'd gone. The two didn't keep in touch the way they once had.

Now, for this woman who once upon a time might have been your mother-in-law, you put on your best country-girl-from-a-good-family demeanor, express pleasure at hearing from her, and ask politely what she's been doing during her visit. Right up front, she tells you she's been caring for her son, because he's ill. Her frankness, so West Coast urban of her, startles and comforts you. She was always this way, even when you were little and hanging around the McMasters' place. You ask her what's wrong with Lorie, and she tells you: AIDS — Loren has AIDS.

"I knew you'd want to know how sick he is."

"Did he ask you to call me?"

"No. But when I told him I was going to, he didn't say not to."

AIDS. That means he's going to die. They all die.

AIDS. You've read only guys get it, nearly every one of them gay or a needle junkie. Also, that poor kid, the bleeder who got a bad blood transfusion. You wonder: can women get it?

Who knows how easy it is to pass along germs? Or how long those germs might survive in any particular spot? It's been months since you last saw Loren. You talked on the phone a couple times. So you already knew he was sick, really sick, and that he'd stopped working, even from home. But he never told you exactly what he was sick *with*. And you, with your germ phobia, hadn't asked because you were afraid to know.

Fearful as you were, you did offer to visit. But he blew you off. Don't bother, he'd said, I remember how germs freak you out — let's just stick to phone calls, I know that works for you.

But now his mother is *telling* you: come see her son. In person. Her son who has AIDS.

"He's been so depressed, Barbra. I think seeing you would really do him good."

"I don't know, Mrs. McMaster."

"Barbra, please. As a special favor to me. I have to leave in a few days. I promise I'll hose down the apartment with Lysol before I go."

In the end, you couldn't find a way to say no.

After you hung up, though, you got to thinking: what if you

can still get it from something Lorie'd touched the last time he was here in your apartment? Maybe the special fancy tea cup you'd always put aside just for him?

You glance around the condo. David, of course, had not seen fit to be here to greet you when you returned from Seattle around midnight Sunday. But since he'd had the place to himself over the weekend (and Heaven only knows what he'd been up to), you came home to his usual dirty dishes abandoned in whatever location the food was consumed, ashtrays full of cigarette butts, and clothing items deposited at intervals.

Even before you unpacked from your trip that night, you went to work on the mess, falling into bed around dawn. David never came home that night and didn't call. He was clearly surprised when he wandered in early Monday afternoon and found you already home. Then you remembered: Monday evening had been your original return date, the time when you'd told him you'd be back.

Now, a week later, the place appears to be in order. After your conversation with Lorie's mom, however, every surface seems to be crawling with life-threatening germs. You can practically see them wiggling around. You start in the kitchen, that very evening, spraying and scrubbing every last object and surface — every glass, every dish, every bit of silverware, the countertops, even the insides of drawers, the knobs on the stove, the handles on all the cabinets, everything. Then you boil the oven mitts and mop the floors with Mr. Clean.

Hours later, you have finished the kitchen, and once again David hasn't come home. Which is just as well, because you still have the bathroom to look forward to. Tired as you are, all you need to keep yourself going is to recall Lorie's recounting of his adventures here and in New York City. You cringe at the potential for contagion and powder the bathtub with Bon Ami.

>~\\\//~<

It takes your old friend a long, long time to answer the door. When he does, you hardly recognize him. Gone is the abundant, shining, gold-brown hair he was so proud of and used to wear coyly slipping over one eye. Now he has a buzz-cut right up against his scalp and even that looks patchy. The former athlete is pale and emaciated. Always such a dandy with his custom-cut suits and silk ties fastened in complex knots, he comes to the door wearing baggy sweatpants with holes at the knees, a *Chorus Line* T-shirt, and his ancient bathrobe from high school, which you're guessing his mother brought down with her when she came to visit. It appears several sizes too large for him.

"Lorie?" you ask, hating yourself because you know how uncertain you sound.

"The one and only," he replies and does a little tap dance that ends with an open-handed, palm up, ta-dah! gesture. "Do come in and make yourself at home."

You go sit in the living room on his grand leather furniture and stare out his picture window that looks onto Fillmore Street below. You realize you haven't been here since the house-warming party he threw years ago with all his faggy friends in attendance. Some friend you are.

You notice boxes of his belongings stacked up against the wall near the foyer. You cut a glance in that direction and raise an eyebrow to ask him, What's going on?

"Oh that," he replies with a dismissive wave, "— my stuff. A lot of it, anyway. We had a garage sale last Saturday. Those are the leftovers, everything that didn't sell. We'll be donating it. That's part of the reason my mother came down — to help me with this mess. I just can't do it. But I've got to pay the mortgage. I want to stay here as long as I can."

"But why, Lorie?"

He looks at you, and you see your old friend's eyes staring out of the mask of an old man's face. The old man's expression clearly indicates he knows he is dealing with someone fairly retarded.

"Barbie, I haven't worked, really worked and gotten a paycheck, for six months. My parents are helping me, but they can do only so much. I just got on disability. That's good, but it won't cover everything. Actually, it hardly covers anything. And I'm starting to need nursing care, too. I can't do things anymore. It isn't going to get any better."

You imagine the expression on your face is that of a person who's been punched unexpectedly right between the eyes. Loren shrugs, a gesture indicating he forgives you for your inexcusable naïveté.

"It's not like I'm special or anything," he says. "So many have died already, you know."

You didn't know. You simply didn't know. You resigned from the theater board after David moved in. From that point on and without Loren in your daily life, nothing brought you into direct contact with this new reality of life in the City. You see that Lorie was your liaison with this hip new age, and now all you know is your career of keeping high-level, aging, mostly straight alcoholics comfortable, your perfect apartment that no longer feels like a home to you, and your unfaithful live-in lover who treats your condo as if it were a motel with rooms that he rents by the hour. If only he *did* put that much toward your mortgage!

A kitchen timer goes off on the end table next to Loren. He picks it up, shuts it off, reaches behind himself to a table abutting the back of the sofa. He grabs a handcrafted Guatemalan basket and brings it around to set it in his lap. The basket is overflowing with a rattling collection of amber and green plastic bottles of pharmaceuticals, pills and capsules of many colors, sizes, and shapes. He digs around in the basket, looking for the exact pills he needs at this particular hour. But just as he locates what he's been looking for, he glances up and thrusts the basket toward you, saying:

"Oh, so sorry! Guests first."

He laughs at his own joke till he sputters into a coughing jag, then brings the basket back to his lap and extracts two pills from one container, three pills from another. You notice his hands are a little shaky; he has trouble with the child-guard caps. You ask him how many pills a day he has to take. He tells you he isn't sure, but it's around thirty. He asks you to go into the kitchen and get him a glass of water. When you hesitate, he embarrasses you by reassuring you that you can't get AIDS from handing him a water glass.

"Christ, Barbie, if that were even a remote possibility, do you think I'd bring my own mother in here?"

"Of course not," you respond stoutly, though in fact you are not entirely certain that is true. Which is probably the reason for your shallow breathing. That, and the fact that you are just plain scared.

40.

Bill Leaves Town

After a decade of toiling away in San Francisco County's Social Services, your compassion account for your fellow human creatures living on the edge is flat-busted. No wonder you were so happy to be offered a new job working on an oil exploration crew.

You hadn't formally applied for the job. The work you'd be doing was way off the mark from anything you'd ever done these past ten years. Or ever in your life. But it was just one of those things: you ran into an old Army buddy ... he told you what he'd been up to ... you told him what you'd been up to ... you told him you really wished you were doing something other than what you were doing. A month later, he called to tell you there was an opening with his outfit: one of his crewmen was in the hospital after he got involved in a bar fight in Thermopolis, Wyoming. He said you should apply for that guy's job. If you got the job, you'd have to leave right away for Wyoming and spend a few weeks there, but afterwards you'd be sent back to the Bay Area.

So you applied for the job. And the Universe gave you the nod: you got the job. A sign to you that it's time for your life to change.

Then you realized: in terms of your relationship with Juli, now is not exactly the best moment in the world for you to leave town. After months of awkward dating, the two of you are just beginning to hit your stride together, transitioning from a "me and you" into a "we." You liked that. For years, this was exactly what you'd longed for — to be half of a "we." But this new couplehood was a fragile, sensitive thing. Being in relationship this way was a whole lot different than simply being friends. Suddenly, you both had ... expectations of one another. And as you are coming to realize, wherever there are expectations, there is the possibility, even the likelihood, of falling short and failing.

She's been talking about getting out of Sasha's place. He's still out of town, on the road, but soon enough he'll be home. She says she wants to be gone by the time he returns. You'd prefer it that way, too — for her to *not* be there when he gets back. But despite her tentative, un-subtle hints about the two of you moving in together, there's little you can do about this aspect of your relationship. At least, not yet.

You don't have your own place to offer her. Not yet. You've simply never been able to afford it on your own. Not working in Social Services. And although your new job will soon change that and enable you to get your own place, the Catch-22 is: in order to pursue the job that will provide the money that will pay the rent on your own place, you have to leave town entirely. Potentially for nearly as long as you and Juli have been openly acknowledging yourselves as a "couple." Dammit, anyway!

For the present and foreseeable future, therefore, you need another way to secure your relationship. And the only way you can think of to hold onto your place with a young woman on whom you have designs is ... well, marriage. Drastic, yes. But it's not as though you just met. You've known one another for ages; only your status as a couple is relatively new. And it's not as though you feel you need to brace yourself for any big surprises. The only big surprise you've given one another thus far is how well Friendship-Turned-Significant-Other works.

In the past, this decision would have been one you'd have wanted to discuss with ... well, your friend David. However, in this instance, it is obviously inappropriate. Besides, in a way, you *have* already discussed it with him, when you let him know you were dating his ex. And he's already given you the go-ahead, clearly assuming your objective was simply to gain access to his ex-wife's knickers and that, as soon as you achieve your goal, your main problem will be how to cut her loose.

No doubt your roommates and some of your friends will view your decision as impulsive. But it wouldn't be the first time you'd married on impulse. Then there will be those other friends — the ones aware of what a horn-dog David is — who will tar Juli with the same ugly brush for having married the aforementioned horn-dog in the first place. They'll be the friends who'll try to talk you out of "getting involved with a woman like that." But they don't know Juli.

You wondered if you should have hooked up with someone else over the past decade. But it wasn't as though you'd had a lot of options to choose from. For fifteen years, you hadn't had much going on. Nothing whose end you couldn't predict by the time dessert arrived. Some of your dates needed only one evening to be weeded out forever. For example, that beautician you took to see the film, *My Dinner with André*. She sided with the adventuresome, spoiled André Gregory character, while you sided with the comfort-loving, security-seeking Wallace Shawn character — and that was the end of it. Even Tarzana, the hippie love-goddess you lived with for nearly three years and never once saw clean and sober — you always knew your pairing was mainly for the sex, the one thing in the world she was not too lazy to do.

Over the past decade, you reckon, you never entered either a theater or a woman without first checking for the exit signs.

Now, with Juli, it's different. You have no intention of exiting this relationship. Indeed, it worries you some that, should the two of you break up as a couple, you could lose your friendship as well, if you can't figure out how to transition back to your former state. This possibility crossed your mind early on and nearly stopped you cold just as you were working up the courage to ask her out that first time. Too late to worry any more about that. Now your choice is clear: the only way to go is forward. Otherwise, hey — severe tire damage.

So, the plan you've worked up goes like this: you propose, Juli says yes, and then, whether or not she remains in Sasha's attic, the fact of your engagement secures your relationship, and she'll be waiting for you when you return in a couple months from whatever god-forsaken Heartland shithole the oil crew takes you to. Without further ado, you head across town to Juli, stopping by Safeway to pick up some flowers to accompany your proposal. For all your hippie values and aesthetic, when it comes to romance, you are a conventional man at heart.

When you arrive at Juli's, however, you see right away she is not in the best of moods. She thanks you for the flowers and offers you a kiss on the cheek. You watch as she fills an unwashed pot with water, sets it in an already crowded sink, and plunks your bouquet in the pot so your flowers can wither and die more slowly.

A couple days ago, when you called to tell her about your new job, she seemed happy enough for you. Now, clearly, she's had a chance to reflect upon what your new job will mean for her when you leave town for all those many weeks. She's also had time to fester over her limited options for moving out of Sasha's place. You realize the choice comes down to either remaining at Sasha's or moving into her dad's house on the other side of the bay. That's all she can afford.

"I'll call you every week and send you postcards every time we hit a town," you offer.

"Okay," she counters. "And how will I be able to get in touch with you?"

"Well, you can't. Not really," you admit. "Mostly we'll be in the field, sleeping in tents, nowhere near a pay phone."

She nods, considering this idea, her expression turning sour. And all at once it occurs to you: the circumstances of your new job will make you as unreachable to her as David had been throughout most of their marriage. You lean forward, moving to close the distance between you.

"You know, I'm not like David," you venture. "You won't have anything to worry about while I'm not here."

"That's comforting," she says, sounding unconvinced. "What, exactly, do I *not* have to worry about in your absence? Please be specific."

It strikes you as odd she wants you to say these things out loud, but you comply. "Well, alright," you say. "You certainly don't have to worry about my going out on you and picking up strange women in bars. Strange women frighten me. And you don't have to worry about my running up a tab at the local sex shop. I hate those places, they're always sticky. And you will never, ever have to worry about my exposing myself to underage girls. I'm embarrassed even to be seen by grown women."

You have not finished listing David's perversions, performed at one time or another, that Juli won't have to worry about you performing, when her expression stops you cold. Excuse me, it says, but I was not previously aware of these prior behaviors. At which point, you realize you've been listing David's aberrant behaviors on the basis of his past bragging confessions to you — *not* on the basis of what Juli herself had vented. You also realize all she knows about, most likely, are Barbra and perhaps a handful of passing affairs with other women. She really has no idea of the full length, breadth, and width of how truly twisted her ex is.

Only now, of course, she does know, because of you and your big fat mouth crammed with your own careless, thoughtless foot.

Silenced by new understanding, you and Juli sit and stare at one another. After the longest two minutes of your life tick past, she breaks the silence with a question you know instinctively can have no answer that is right (i.e., safe):

"So: how long have you known about the things David was doing while we were living together?"

"Ummm ... always?"

"You *always* knew what he was up to?"

"Yeah, I guess. I mean, pretty much. There might have been other stuff he never mentioned." You wince after this last divulgence, which you allowed to slip out before you could stop to fully appreciate its implications.

"And you never said a word to me?"

"No, I guess not."

"Why not, Bill? I thought we were friends."

"We were friends. I mean, we *are* friends. We've always been friends. But David — *he* was my friend, too." Suddenly, you feel defensive. And you resent the feeling. "In fact, I knew him for years before you two ever got together."

Her expression is darkly inscrutable. "I see," she says evenly. "So it was a 'guy-thing' conspiracy that you knew about all this stuff he was doing, but you never bothered to tell me — your Other Good Friend?"

Okay, you have to admit she has a point. But *why* is this so important?

"Why is this so important to you?" you press. "If I *had* told you what David was doing, on the side all along, what possible difference could it have made to you? There was nothing you could have done to stop him or make him change."

"No, that's true," she acknowledges. "But at least maybe *then* I wouldn't have *stayed* so long in the relationship. I thought it was just Barbra he was involved with. Maybe a few other women. In passing. I had no idea he also did all those other sick, twisted things. If you were *really* my friend, you would have told me and let me know what I needed to know in order to make an informed decision about my own future."

Then she adds, before you've had a chance to fully digest these thoughts: "Just think how humiliating it is for me to know you knew all this stuff was going on, while I didn't know a thing. Even though I was *living* with him. Tell me: did other people know what David was up to?"

"Yeah. Pretty much."

"So: *everyone* knew? Everyone. Except me, of course?"

Not trusting yourself in this moment to be able to speak, you nod: Yes. Everyone knew. Everyone. Except you, Juli. Of course.

"I guess, then," she concludes, "we were never quite such good friends as I thought we were."

You sit, staring, not knowing what to say. How can you prove the depth of your feelings at this point? You suddenly remember why you came here today, what it was you had originally wanted to ask of her. But the look on her face right now is all wrong and says: whatever you want from me, you aren't going to get it. Not now. Maybe never.

You mentally tuck your undelivered marriage proposal back into your pocket and stand up to leave. "Guess I should go now?" you ask.

"Yeah, that would be good," she says. "I'm kinda tired."

"You know, I'll be leaving for the field on Monday, and I won't be back for a couple months. I thought we could at least have this last weekend together."

"Um, no," she says. "I'll be kinda busy. I've decided to move into my dad's place."

"Well, that's good, that's a good decision. I'll call you there. First chance I get."

"Yeah," she says. "You do that."

You're well on your way home to pack before you realize you don't have her father's phone number. You don't even know his name or exactly which East Bay city he lives in. And though you phone Juli at Sasha's several times throughout the weekend to ask for the number, there is never any answer. And though you leave multiple messages on her roommate's answering machine, she doesn't return your calls.

41.

Juli Gets Another New Home

It feels strange to be in the East Bay again, living with your dad in the wood-frame, Craftsman-style home that once belonged to his parents, your grandparents. You realize, though you grew up in the East Bay, mostly Oakland, your years of living in San Francisco have turned you into a City Snob. Like everyone else living in the City, you never willingly crossed the bridge to go to anywhere in the East Bay unless you absolutely had to and there was no way to avoid it.

Now that time has come when you absolutely have to and there is no way to avoid it. Living with your father — something you hadn't experienced since you were not quite eleven years old — feels like a demotion in life, not only because you are no longer an independent adult, but also because you are on the wrong side of the bay. This is the price you must pay for failure in both your professional life and your personal life.

What's more, stepping into your father's living room feels like stepping back in time. There, on either side of the fireplace, which hasn't worked since the 1950s, are your grandparents' chairs — your grandfather's La-Z-Boy to the left of the hearth, your grandmother's rocker to the right. His massive, gray recliner still carries the burn holes in the right arm where the glowing hot tips of his cigarettes touched and melted the naugahyde when he nodded off during ballgames on TV. Her high-back platform rocker is covered with the same scratchy fabric that covers her little footstool where she rested her gnarled feet like a troll queen holding court. He died in 1966; she went only a few years ago. Both of them seem to haunt this place.

Your father's seat, a straight-backed wooden chair, also stands where it always did, against one wall and next to a tall end table where he always sets his beer and his pack of Camel cigarettes within easy reach. There is no chair here for you, there never was — after all, the last time you spent any appreciable time in your grandparents' home, you were a little kid. Later on, when you visited, you sat in the Guest Chair opposite your dad. You can still see the stain on the carpet next to one leg, the place where your grandmother's tiny ferocious terrier used to pee when no one was looking.

But now it is Day One of your actual residence in the family home, and your dad invites you to sit wherever you like. You bypass the Guest Chair where Petie's territorial mark has stained the carpet and bleached the wood.

You also bypass your grandfather's chair, pushing down a dislodged memory of a long-ago family barbecue when you were five, when the entire family, except you and grandpa, was in the backyard, and grandpa had you on his lap while he sat in his recliner. You remember how the corduroy on your bib overalls was strained as he worked his big, calloused carpenter's hand down into your cotton underpants to touch the soft place between your legs. You remember how you squirmed away, hopped off his lap, and glared hard at him with all your five-year-old ferocity before running outside to join your grandma, your parents, and the new baby in the backyard. You never said a word to anyone about what happened that afternoon a quarter century ago. But you never sat in grandpa's lap again, and you don't sit in his chair now. Instead, you go to your grandmother's chair with its scratchy fabric that raises a rash on the skin of your bare legs.

Your father, a man who's only happy when he has something specific to be happy about, a man whose default setting is despair, is happy now to have you under his roof. He sits in his chair with his cigarettes and beer and rambles on at length about everything wrong with his body, this house, the neighborhood, the world. He even turns down the sound on the TV, which is always on (and pretty loud, because he is partially deaf), in order to have this conversation with his daughter. You sit, watching him and ignoring the pressure that is building up under your temples.

You are remembering the last night you spent under the same roof as this man, your father. That was over twenty years ago; you were nearly eleven. Earlier in the day, your mother had had a "talk" with you. She explained that she and you would be moving the following morning. Your mother, like your father, was an unhappy person. Over the years, you'd become well acquainted with the extent of her unhappiness. As far back as you could remember, she had used you as her confidante and confessor. In fact, you could not remember a time in your short life when you were ever free from worry, when you didn't carry on your narrow child-shoulders the burden of being your mother's Best Friend, overwhelmed with the knowledge of grown-up problems about which you could do nothing.

On that last day of your childhood, she outlined her plan to you: the next morning, as soon as your dad leaves for work, she will call the movers. They will come, pack up everything, and take it all somewhere else. After tonight, you won't live here anymore. You won't see your dad anymore. She made you promise, when your dad comes home from work in a few hours, you won't say anything about tomorrow's big plan. She swore you to secrecy. So you promised, you crossed your heart, you hoped to die.

Your memories of the twenty-four hours following your mom's talk now seem more like a watching a movie than recalling a scrap of your own lived life. In your mind's eye, you seem to be sitting next to or standing just behind your own self. There you are, when your father comes home, carrying his curved-top metal lunch pail in one hand, a clinking six-pack of Budweisers in the other hand, shoulders sagging, cap pulled down low on his brow.

"Hi, Dad," you announce when he comes through the door, as your mother had instructed you to do, even though he doesn't speak to you, doesn't even seem to see you. You are only ten and a half, but you understand this is the final time you will be required to perform this ritual.

Your last supper with both your parents is a silent affair during which you say nothing. You clean your plate, as is expected of you, and you ask to be excused. But after you go to your room and lie on your back on your narrow bed, where you've slept since you started school, you imagine your parents still sitting at the dining table together one more time. The secret you have been keeping from your father all evening feels like it is taking up too much space in your skinny chest, making it hard for you to breathe. You are anxious that this secret your mother is making you keep may suffocate you while you sleep.

Your parents had given you the only bedroom in their one-bedroom apartment; they sleep on a hideaway bed that pulls out from the living room sofa. You lie on your bed in the dark, staring at the blackness of the ceiling. The windup clock in the living room begins to strike, and you count each bong till they stop at eleven. Eleven o'clock is well past your bedtime, and you know you are supposed to stay in bed, no matter what, but you get up and tiptoe down the hall to take one final look at your father.

On the sofa bed, he lies on his back, spread-eagle, snoring like a slow-moving train. Your mother once told you that your father, before he went into the Army, was an amateur boxer and got his nose broken twice; this was why he snored so loudly.

Your mother is sitting and watching *The Twilight Zone* on the same ancient black-and-white TV set before which, only a few years ago, you sat on the floor, watching *The Mickey Mouse Club*, *Howdy Doody*, *Captain Satellite*, and *Captain Kangaroo*. You see that she is repairing socks, a mending basket in her lap. She hears you creep in and looks up. You stand there in your thin, wrinkled, Donald Duck pajamas, memorizing this last view of your father. She smiles at you in a way you would now recognize as conspiratorial. You say nothing, but go back to bed and surrender to childhood fate.

Fate arrives the next morning. The movers show up soon after your mother calls them. Next, your great-aunt, your mother's mother's baby sister, arrives to pick you up and babysit you for the day. Aunt Ruby takes you grocery shopping and lets you put whatever you like in the cart. You chose animal cracker cookies, the kind that come in a box made to look like a circus wagon with animals in cages. Also, Hires root beer. You put two bottles in her grocery cart, and she says nothing.

Then she takes you to her dark, stuffy apartment with the wagon-wheel furniture and fixes lunch for you — a baloney sandwich with mayo on puffy Wonder Bread. She fills a green, dimpled plastic tumbler with half whiskey, half tap water and transports it into the living room, where she sets it on a TV tray next to her big gold recliner. Then she switches on the television and settles in to watch *Rawhide*. You play with her black Persian cat named Boy, a relentless hunter who brings in bats, still living and undamaged. Boy will not suffer teasing; he scratches you so you bleed, but you suck on the back of your hand and say nothing.

A block away, train tracks run through the neighborhood, and whenever a train comes, it shakes Aunt Ruby's apartment as if it were about to crash through the wall. As each train approaches, blowing its horn and pounding through its right-of-way, your great-aunt struggles out of her chair and turns up the sound on the TV. But she does not turn the sound back down after each train passes, so by the end of the afternoon, the television is on really loud. Someone in the next apartment bangs on the wall. Finally, your great-aunt gets up and turns down the TV. The banging stops.

When evening comes and it is time for her to take you home, you are surprised your home is not where you left it. All at once, you understand the meaning of "moving." In the search for your underwear and stuffed animals that night and in the days to come, you forget about your father. Only at dusk, as day fades into night, does an aching panic set in to remind you of what you have lost.

Except for a single incident that occurred soon after you and your mother left your father, nearly a decade would pass before you would get to see him again. In the cheap studio apartment in the crummy East Oakland neighborhood where you went to live with your mother after she ran out on your dad, you were crouched inside the padded fortress you'd constructed of sofa cushions and blankets. Your mother had already taken the bus to work as a salesgirl in downtown Oakland, and you were on your own for the day. But, inside your fort, you felt safe, reading Oz books in the dimness with your flashlight until a hard knock sounded on the front door. You froze and listened. Your mother had told you: when you are home alone, *never* answer the door. No matter who it is.

Nevertheless, you were curious. When you poked your head out between the blankets and cushions, you could see, through the gauze curtains on the picture window next to the front door, the shadow of a big man wearing a cap. It was late afternoon, and the west-facing window received full sun, so the man's shadow was dark and intense. You meant to hide until this stranger gave up and left. But then you realized the TV was on, tuned to Saturday morning cartoons, Bugs Bunny and Casper the Friendly Ghost. And the sound on the TV was turned up much higher than usual, so you would be able to hear it inside your fort. This, you understood at once, was probably a dead giveaway to the fact of your being home. A second knocking on the door sent you dashing for the television to turn it off.

The shadow came to the window and shielded his eyes, trying to see through the gauze curtain. "Juliette, honey! Open the door — it's your father!" Dad! you realized, Dad! But your mother told you: when you are home alone, don't open the door to anyone. "Anyone" includes your father. This you understood. So you sat and you did nothing.

He hammered on the door, calling your name over and over. "Juliette! Juli! I know you're in there!" You slipped back into your fort, grabbed your mom's bed pillow, which you'd been using to reinforce a cushion wall, and covered your ears with it so you couldn't hear him. Your father stood there on the porch — for hours, it felt like — beating on the door and yelling your name. You prayed: please, dear God, make him go away, make him go away, make him go away….

Finally, he went away, and this was the last you would hear of him for years, until after you graduated from high school and called yourself a grownup with the power to decide who you would see and not see.

It's funny, but it took all those teen years before you really thought about your father and the fact that, for much of your growing up, he wasn't in your life at all. Though, in fact, he wasn't there much before your mother left him, taking you away with her. When you were very little, yes, he was your dad, teaching you how to slow dance by letting you stand on his feet, teaching you how to whistle real loud, how to blow huge bubble-gum bubbles, picking you up by one arm and one leg and spinning you around in a circle until, when he set you down, you were so dizzy you fell over in a laughing heap. But a few years later, after your baby brother wandered into the lake, your father was already too tired and too drunk to have much to do with you.

Now, in your thirties, you and your father are strangers to one another, trying to be family. But you can see he doesn't know whether to relate to you as the little child you once were or as the woman you have become. And you — you have no idea what to do with a father.

Worse, you are staying in the room where your grandmother, your father's mother, once slept. And if any room in this house is haunted, it is certainly this one. When you and your mom left your dad with an empty apartment, nothing in it but his clothes, his old Army cot, and $15 of beer money in an envelope containing the brief kiss-off note your mother had penned as explanation, he had little choice but to come here and live with his own parents.

Then they died — your grandfather twenty years ago, your grandmother only a few years ago — and now the house is his. But you still feel your grandmother's presence in this house, a tiny, haughty woman who slept with a pistol under her bed and cash under the carpet. One time, long ago, even before you started school, you wandered into the kitchen of this house, where your grandparents were having an argument, and you watched as your grandmother settled their disagreement by slapping your grandfather full across the face. Now it was her bed you would be sleeping in.

Your first night staying with your father, you are already in bed when you hear a knock on the door.

"Yes?" you answer.

"It's me, honey, your dad."

Who else would it be? you think. But you are touched by his announcement and the diffident way he comes to you.

"Hi, Dad. Come on in."

He opens the door and peers around it before stepping inside. He too is in pajamas, with a plaid flannel bathrobe. He looks smaller than usual. "I just wanted to say good-night, honey."

"Thanks, Dad."

He comes over to your bed, your grandmother's bed, leans over, and awkwardly kisses the top of your head.

"I'm really glad you're here," he adds.

"Me, too, Dad."

"Sleep tight, don't let the bedbugs bite," he tells you as he creeps away.

"You, too, dad."

42.

Juli Tours Her Past

Applause still fills the college theater as the house lights come up. And once again, Katherine, despite her big mind and great heart, has been tamed. Her hand, now and forever after, is ready to do Petruchio ease. You hate this play. You hate the Summer Shakespeare Festival at the college. You still hold a grudge against Shakespeare.

You stand in your row of seats to allow the audience to squeeze past you. Playgoers file up the aisles, like a congregation leaving church, except they are chatting, laughing, sounding happy and well satisfied with tonight's performance. They've had their fill of entertainment for one afternoon. But you haven't had yours. Not yet.

Most will go home now. You have other plans. You make for the nearest exit and, once outside, head 'round the back of the theater. There you join a thin migration of family, friends, and fans, all eager for backstage contact with their beloved ones and summertime stars. Close Encounters of the Third Kind, the way you see it.

Together you will wait for the costumes and the makeup to come off, for the actors to appear from their dressing rooms, playing themselves again. Then comes the flurry of hand-waving, smiles breaking, little squeals of recognition, embraces, tears — the show after the show. You can almost hear the hiss of dressing-room showers, the shouts and hoots. You can almost smell the gathering smoke as everyone lights up in unison, all preparing to wait for the last few players to emerge, an opportunity to give tribute, to commence drinking and partying.

How many times in your life have you been here in this place? Dozens, certainly. A hundred, maybe so. Feels like a thousand. Ten thousand. Your last time here was nearly a decade ago. Long ago, but it's not as though you can't still remember how to get where you are going. You pass a family group — relatives of one of the youngsters in the cast, no doubt — asking an usher for directions on how to get backstage. The woman mouths the words, "green room," like it's a foreign phrase whose pronunciation she's unsure of. But the usher smiles. She has given the password; he points her in the direction you are already headed. You climb a cement stairway to the stage door entrance and stroll on in as though you belonged here.

Inside, the aftershow activity has already crested. As always, you are impressed by all the cables and coils, curtains and flats, along with the matter-of-fact attitude of the stagehands who know what to do with all this gear. But it wouldn't do for you to stop and stare. You must stay in character for your performance. You turn at the prop table and stroll on into the green room.

Here you remind yourself of post-production protocol: secure an inconspicuous corner, whip out your smokes, light one with appropriate flourish, and ... wait. You regard the others who have gathered to wait in this space. For example, that other woman alone like you, a blonde sitting in an overstuffed, well-worn armchair that you recall from many years ago.

No, on closer examination, you see she is still a girl, not yet a woman, perhaps eighteen or nineteen, about the same age you were when you still got a kick out of waiting backstage for your big-star boyfriend. You watch her through your own personal fogbank of cigarette smoke and see she has both elbows propped up awkwardly on the chair's arms.

No, she hasn't quite mastered her technique yet — the ability to loiter for half an hour, an hour, or more, all the while looking perfectly at ease as if nothing in the world could be more natural or even desirable than to spend the best evenings of one's so-called precious youth in some lousy theater green room.

Most of the actors have left by now. So you suppose the dozen or so remaining loiterers are likewise waiting for Him. The blonde girl still sits sunk in her armchair. And now everyone's anxiety is in evidence: could He have left already? Did we miss Him? But you smile to yourself, knowing He is always the last one out — milking each audience for all they're worth. And proof of commitment, to boot.

And now the dressing room door swings wide, and a deep, resonant voice — a *trained* voice, mind you — calls out *"Arrivederci! Ciao!"* to someone in the company. Like a roomful of RCA dogs, all heads turn towards the sound of that voice. His Voice. Armchair Girl looks up expectantly; you take note. Everyone makes ready to greet Him, straightening clothing, brushing back hair, standing at attention.

And here He is — hooray! We break into one big communal grin, which clearly pleases Him. He acknowledges individually The Important People. He gathers The Dear Friends around Himself like fuzzy warm blankets. After all, what are we doing here if not tucking Him in for the night?

As he approaches, you are, once again, impressed by his height. Always a standout onstage with nothing he could do about it. No spears or tea trays in this player's future. Leading roles only. From the first, it was an all-or-nothing genetic destiny.

He greets a shorter, husky man who is wearing an eloquently expensive business suit. "Great show, Richard," the man says as they shake hands in firm masculine fashion, then step forward into a hug. Easy now. You grit your teeth in sympathetic anxiety, holding your breath as you wait to see who starts patting whose back first — that universal social cue signaling the time has come to terminate the embrace.

The two men cease their back-patting simultaneously. Then Richard steps away and replies, "Thank you — glad you enjoyed it!" — thus, nailing the interaction. You are thrilled to watch your old boyfriend offering up just the right combination of professional humility and enthusiasm. An admirable portrayal of sincerity.

Next Richard turns to an elderly couple, shakes the old gentleman's hand, embraces the tiny, shrunken woman. He is so tall, he must bend way over to offer his hug. No back-patting this time.

"You were wonderful!" the old woman says, her voice frail and quavering.

"Thank you, Grams," he responds. "And Gramps — thank you both for coming. I know what a long drive it is."

On down the line he moves, rewarding the rest of his fans with brief doles of attention. All must be recognized for their service. Armchair Girl is on her feet now, eager for her turn. He gives her a big bear hug, burying her face in his chest, smothering her. And as he embraces her, he looks over the top of her head to see ... you, standing alone in your corner. You nod slightly.

"How did you get here?" he asks the girl as he releases her, skipping no beats, betraying not so much as a flicker of surprise at your sola appearance.

"I borrowed my father's car for the day," she tells him, beaming proudly. You wince, reminded that you, too, had to borrow your father's car to get here this afternoon.

"Wonderful," he says as he turns to everyone who's been waiting indulgently. "What do you say? Shall we all go out and have a drink? Let's meet at La Trattoria." Again, you wince, hearing the name of the venerable local restaurant, this town's one classy dining establishment and the very spot where you and Richard broke up right after you graduated from this very institution of higher learning. Serves you right, you think.

"We've got to start back," his grandfather says. "It's late and your grandmother's tired."

"Oh, Daddy," the old woman says, gently slapping his shoulder. Her tone suggests resentment, but a moment later she takes the old man's arm with obvious affection, and you are filled with envy. You stand quietly in your dark corner, hoping they won't notice you. It's been ages since you last met them, and they are more infirm now than you remembered, but still....

Others also beg off for the upcoming evening. With regrets, of course, but they are anxious to start their long drives and get home to relieve their babysitters. They say goodbye as the remaining half dozen people prepare to go have that drink, buttoning coats, feeling for keys, patting wallets and purses. You see most of them don't know one another; they only have Him in common. He leads the group; you trail behind. You don't need attention now. You know your time will come later.

Nevertheless, you feel an inappropriate upsurge of jealousy and pique, watching Armchair Girl walking alongside him, so close on his arm. You have no idea who this young woman is, but the nature of their relationship is clear enough.

"How do you know Richard?" she is asking you an hour or so later from across the table at La Trattoria. You are startled by the question, afraid its answer was all too obvious.

You can't help smiling a little. You have to bite the inside of your cheek. In the darkened bar section of this old restaurant, you can't see well enough to tell whether she is fishing for information or simply making conversation in a casual way. It was not a question you could have asked her with anything remotely resembling innocence. Yet there she is, sitting right across from you, and your instincts tell you she *is* still innocent. Could anyone be so dumb? Were *you* ever that naïve? You can't remember that far back.

But already you can tell you've had too much Chianti and communal pizza, and now some scruffy neohippie-looking guy is softly plucking out a song on his guitar to create atmosphere. You feel a tearful gush of compassion for this little girl — a child, a sweet naïve child — and you want to protect her.

"We were friends in college. Right where we saw his show tonight," you tell her truthfully, but evasively, leaving it at that.

"Oh, yes," she says, "I see." But she sees nothing. "Yes," she says cheerfully, "Richard was a senior there, back when my older sister was a freshman. I used to push my bike all the way up the hill to campus to visit her while she worked in the costume shop. Then I'd coast down the hill at about 100 mph, trying not to get killed. Those were the days."

You stare, struggling to regress her in order to place her. She would have been a little kid then, not even in high school. You run time backwards to when you could possibly have seen her, to a point even before she had started menstruating. You do the math; the equation depresses you.

But right she is about one thing: those were the days, for sure. Days of trouble back then. Already trouble. The awful pressures of what to do with your lives after you graduated. Him knowing perfectly well what he wanted to do, but not knowing how to go about it. You knowing only that you were a good student, but with "no special great talent." The auditions, the resumés, the summer shows in community theaters. Trying to find a way in — or a way out. Other people moving in to take your place, new ones coming along each year. You wanted things to go well for the two of you. Richard had been your boyfriend for five years already, since your senior year in high school, then all through college. You wanted the two of you to be right for one another.

"And, uh, what are you doing now?" you ask her, trying to

demonstrate interest, needing to distract yourself from your memories. She tells you about a professional theater company she has written to — maybe she can work there after she graduates from college next spring.

"Sounds great," you respond, with manufactured encouragement.

Last call from the bar is your cue. It's only a quarter to nine, but tonight is Sunday evening, and this old restaurant, with its dark, smelly bar, closes at nine on the Sabbath. As the barmaid collects glasses and empties ashtrays, you bid goodnight to Armchair Girl. Other people are leaving as well, so you know you won't stand out. Richard waves benignly in your direction; Armchair Girl offers you a big parting smile.

"Nice to have met you," she tells you, clinging to Richard as they walk, arm in arm, toward the front door.

"You, too," you tell her, turning away and heading for the restrooms, knowing he will need a few minutes to get rid of her.

When you return, you find him sitting alone in the darkened bar.

"Like some company tonight?" you ask.

"Love it," he says.

>⇢◦\ᴪ/◦⇠

"How about this Green Hungarian as a night cap?" he suggests, pulling a slender bottle of wine from an upper kitchenette cabinet. He dusts it off with his hands and wipes them on an already filthy dish towel lying crumpled on the counter. This place, what a mess it still is! But you are pleased the bottle is dusty, unopened. Waiting for you.

"That's fine," you tell him. "I like that one."

"Me, too," he says. The two of you eye one another suspiciously, both thinking: we've never had Green Hungarian together. Never. Each of you speculating where the other may have had it. With whom. Under what circumstances. Your relationship with Richard had been a history of firsts. Once upon a time. But since you parted, every new life experience has been given away to someone else. You feel a tidal surge of sadness wash over you for everything you and this man no longer share and never will again.

"You know ... ahem," Richard says, clearing his throat in that peremptory way he does to signal to all present he is about to make a self-important announcement, "I had sup-*posed*, when you left me a phone message requesting a comp for tonight, that you would require *two* tickets, not one." He raises a meaningful eyebrow.

"No, no," you reply, casually ignoring his subtext in a way you understand he will find annoying.

"Well?"

"Well — what?"

"Well, does *he* know you're *here?*" Richard asks. After all these years, he still refuses to speak the name of the man he imagines you left him for.

"Of course, *David* knows I'm *here*," you say, deliberately lying, while simultaneously emphasizing the name of the husband who obsessively cheated on you, then abandoned you long ago. Turning away from this line of conversation, you idly open the refrigerator and note its contents: a cardboard container of what appears to be Chinese takeout (marked "lo mein-beef"), a jar of Grey Poupon mustard, a box of Gallo rosé, and one half of a half gallon of stomach-settling, 2 percent milk. The sight of which brings back old memories:

"Richard, you still barf right before each show?"

"Every time. Just like clockwork. Now in my seventeenth big year of stage-fright regurgitation. When I hit my twenty-year anniversary mark, I figure I'll throw a party for myself and buy all-new china."

He says this while pouring the wine with studied flair into two colorful plastic tumblers. He is serving it "on the rocks," over frost-bitten ice cubes you watched him extract from a battered aluminum ice cube tray by banging the tray sharply on the edge of the kitchen sink after he couldn't budge the lever. Glasses filled, he twists the corkscrew to eject the cork, which he then hands to you.

"Here," he says as he offers you the cork, "you can suck on this." His ancient jest dates back to your first year in college, when you were new to alcohol and prone to passing out during your third drink.

You give him a dirty look. He laughs and hands you your tumbler.

You head toward the living room area with your full glass; Richard follows you with his own glass and the bottle.

"Well ... doesn't it bother him?"

"No, why should it?" you reply, papering over one whole truth with half of another.

Richard nods, but keeps his eye on you. As you settle in on his sofa, you feel him looking straight through the sophisticated pose you are trying to present all the way to the person you truly are. His intrusiveness provokes you; you feel the old fears rising. All those years you waited around for him — just say the word. Now you see: it was stupid of you to come here. Your life with this man is over. Tonight is simply a diversion, a nostalgic tour of the ancient section of a dead city. He accepts you now only because old, worn-out intimacy is better than none at all.

Sitting next to you, politely spaced, he reaches over to top off your glass. And while you are within striking distance, he takes a close look at you, then asks, "Pimple?" He taps his own nose on the side to indicate the location of a disfiguring blemish on you.

Your fingertips fly to the side of your nose to check, and when you find the skin there is smooth, you remember this is in fact the place where, a couple of days ago, you broke a blood vessel from crying too hard. You decide this is a good time to return fire, changing the subject back to him:

"So, how long have you been living in your parents' pool house?"

"A few years. But only when I'm in the Bay Area. I still have my apartment in L.A. for when I'm working down there."

"And how often are you 'working down there'?"

"Of late? Not a whole helluva lot," he admits.

"Roommates down there?" you inquire gently. When he nods, you ask, "How many?"

"Only two at present. There were three, but I think one of them died. Or he may have moved back to Kansas to go live in *his* parents' pool house. Or got a job waiting tables on a cruise ship to Alaska. Something of the kind."

You look around the two-room pool house he inhabits, noting the pictures on the wall, the books and nicknacks on the shelves, the pile of dirty laundry on the floor near the door

— all depressingly familiar sights. Following him in his flashy car from the theater to the suburban ranch house you still remember so well from your high school and college years, you felt as though you'd driven through a black hole straight into a time warp. Now you understand how he is able to afford his flashy car and expensive clothes.

"And your folks, they're...?"

"On a cruise ship in Alaska. Don't worry: they won't suddenly appear."

"Just as well."

The worst is wanting to know all about his other romantic relationships during your years apart so you can torment yourself with the information. You want to pry into his personal life by pretending to be a long-standing, concerned, good friend. But you sense he's wise to you. He won't tell you a thing. And you can't risk pressing.

You are torn. In fact, he is your old friend. You want him to find somebody nice and be happy in his life. But also you are scared he will do just that and forget all about you. You are sorry his personal life is so barren. But also you are pleased it is, so that you still have a place in it.

Serves him right. He should see what a good deal he passed up.

"If only you could have waited a little longer," he tells you, as if reading your thoughts. It gives you a chill.

"Years I waited."

"Was it the money thing? The security?"

"Commitment, that's what I needed. You weren't willing to make it."

"Back then, I had other commitments I needed to keep."

"Right."

"My career, I mean."

"Oh, sure," you respond, offering him a slightly more sympathetic tone. This game the two of you play — "If Only" — it's ridiculous, meaningless. Yet you go right on playing.

"You know," he says, "if only you could've lightened up, been a little less ... possessive. All I needed was some space."

"Well, you certainly got that. How'd it work out for you?"

"Nowhere near as well as I intended it should," he laughed bitterly. "'But 'come, come, you wasp, i'faith you are too angry.'"

"'If I be waspish, best beware my sting.'"

"'My remedy is then to pluck it out.'" He waggles mustache-like eyebrows at you. Despite your irritation, you laugh.

"May I remind you," he continues, "you broke up with me, I didn't break up with you."

"No, you just kept inviting other people into your life until it got so crowded in there, I was squeezed out." Like a turd, you think to yourself. You were squeezed out like a turd.

"Did you ever suppose I might be engaging in a bit of psychologically healthy, age-appropriate experimentation before settling down with just one person?"

"No."

"Did you ever imagine I would be likely to come after you later and try to get you back?"

"No."

"And, if memory serves, after you split, you got yourself re-involved so quickly, I never had a second chance. Guess you were all done with me?"

You stare, suppressing the impulse to defend your past actions, while weighing the truth of his implied accusations.

"Well, we can revisit that issue at some future date," he continues. "But, for now, I must tell you: I had something else important planned for this evening before you turned up so unexpectedly."

"Yeah, and that would be?"

"Turner Classics is running *Carefree* tonight at ten-thirty. You know: Astaire and Rogers, '38, the one with the Irving Berlin song, 'Change Partners'? They don't show it very often. I want to tape it for my collection."

"Can't you program your VCR to record it?"

"No. I haven't been able to figure out how to do that. But don't fret: it's short, not even an hour and a half."

And thus you find yourself sitting alongside your old boyfriend on his ratty sofa in his parents' pool house, watching a grainy, black-and-white RKO film. After a few minutes of story exposition, you attempt to settle in, leaning up against Richard and slipping your arm through his to try to take his hand. He shoulders you away. "Quit pawing me," he says, keeping his eyes on the screen. You sigh and retreat to the far end of the sofa, curling up against its scratchy armrest instead. You'd forgotten how it irked him to be treated like a human petting zoo.

By the time Ralph Bellamy knocks his fiancée Ginger Rogers out cold and her doctor, Fred Astaire, marries her, you hear gentle, rhythmic snoring coming from the other end of the couch. Richard himself is out cold, defeated by theater, alcohol, and cinematic nostalgia. You scoot over next to him and gently extract the remote control from his limp hand in his lap. Then you wait till the closing credits have run to stop the VHS tape and power down the machine.

"Richard," you whisper, touching his shoulder and giving it a light shake. No response. "Richard!" you whisper more urgently, increasing the intensity of your shake. He wakes with a start, his empty hand clenching reflexively on the remote he supposes he's dropped.

"What?" he snorts.

"You crapped out," you tell him. "But don't worry, I got the whole thing."

"Good," he sighs, pushing himself up to standing, swaying slightly from the change in altitude. "This nation is grateful for your service. Well, you got your couch there."

"No way I'm sleeping on any damn couch."

"Oh, alright then, c'mon. I'll give you The Grand Tour. It won't take long." You follow him as he shuffles into the other room. His bedroom.

Now, after a ten-year hiatus, comes the Moment of Truth. He turns his back on you to undress, sitting on the edge of the bed. Shirt off first — the easy part. Shoes drop to the floor, one ... two. Don't they make jokes about that? You realize he's stalling for time. Pants drop to the floor. That characteristic clunk of belt buckle makes you want to burst out laughing. And, in a flash, he's between the sheets, quick so you can't see, can't get a good look. He reaches over to his nightstand and switches out the light.

Okay, you think, if that's the way you want to play ... this is war, and you are armed with a different strategy. Best defense is a good offense, right? If there's one thing David taught you, it's how to be offensive.

So: you stand up, right at the foot of the bed, right in front of him to perform your amateur strip tease, with the light of just one lamp burning in the other room and a streetlight flooding through his window. Peeling off your clothes ... yes, this body's still got a few good miles left in it.

You look up, expecting to see a slightly pained expression that is a mixture of physical wanting, embarrassment, and anxiety, because you know perfectly well, from long association, that your immodesty embarrasses him as much as it pleases him. But when he meets your gaze, you see shadows of other things that unnerve you: enmity, anger, resentment. You see this man doesn't really like you. You think maybe he's not so hard up for intimacy, after all. At least, not for the worn-out, threadbare intimacy you are offering. Maybe he's just too polite to say no to you. Not to mention, the obvious — now that you think about it — *inconvenience* you represented to him tonight, the awkwardness of having to fit you unexpectedly into his schedule.

All this comes to you in a flood of awareness while you are stripping. Now *you* feel guilty and ashamed, knowing only too well how you'd feel in his position. At this point, however, with your blouse already off and your bra fully unhooked for the big reveal, you are committed. But you can at least give him a break. You turn your back to finish undressing.

As you stroll toward "your" side of the bed, you recognize his headboard as the same one he had in high school — the main witness to the official surrender of your virginity during another, long-ago weekend when his parents were away. When you hear snoring, you sigh. Yes, it was definitely a mistake to come here.

Gently, from the foot of Richard's bed, you lift the red-and-yellow striped afghan you know his mother knitted for him, and you return with it to the sofa in his living room. From there, his snoring is muted. But you remember he gets louder as the night wears on, and you never were able to sleep through that racket.

⚜

In the morning, when you wake up on the couch, your mouth is dry and tastes like a vacant lot. So much for a night of smoking and drinking and too much ... remembering. You tiptoe into the bedroom to find Richard still asleep, passed out with his head rolled back on his pillow and his mouth wide open. Once upon a time, when you were nineteen or twenty, you would have thought this was cute, you would have found the sight of the roof of his mouth endearing. Now, however ... clearly, you two are an idea whose time has passed. You leave him mentally to the allurements of the Armchair Girl.

While you are staring at him, you notice, sticking out from under his pillow, the corner of some small publication, dingy yellow-beige with stripes. Curious, you inch forward and stealthily tug on the booklet to expose just enough of the cover to be able to read the title. Turns out he is currently sleeping on a Dramatists Play Service script of *Harvey*, by Mary Chase. You smile, reminded how intensely superstitious this man is, still convinced some mysterious process of psychic osmosis will help him to learn his lines. You think this is maybe the only acting tactic you never saw David try.

You feel awful. You need to brush your teeth. You slip out of the room and wait till you get into the bathroom to start coughing. You shut the door behind you, turn on the shower, and cough into one of his towels. A thick plug of phlegm jumps into your mouth; with effort, you swallow it down. You take a deep breath, and your chest wheezes like a sick kitten. You can smell the air you are exhaling, and you know this feeling of awful doesn't stop at your mouth — it goes all the way down. Oh god, you think: I must be rotting from the inside out. You remember it was Richard himself who taught you how to smoke, back when you two were seniors in high school. As of this morning, you resolve to quit. You don't need it anymore. You don't want it. You are done.

Before you step into the shower, you check yourself in the medicine cabinet mirror over the sink and find your face scrunched up and pocked from being slept on and pressed into coarse, scratchy upholstery fabric. A deep crease runs south from the corner of your mouth to your chin. Your eyes are puffy and gray-green underneath. Ugly face. Fortunately, you know that washing up and brushing your teeth will repair your appearance. Your flesh will firm up, your color will return. Soon as you pull yourself together, everything will be alright.

For a while, at least. But, you also know, it's only a matter of time. Someday you'll wake up looking like this and it'll stick, you'll stay this way. Then what? Who will love you after time has caught up with you?

You shower and wash your hair with Richard's cheap, overly perfumed shampoo. You brush your teeth with the toothbrush you brought along in your purse because you had a feeling he'd let you stay. You get rid of as much of the night before as you can. Then you go into the kitchenette and start the coffee. From the alcove that serves as his kitchen, you can hear

Richard still snoring from his bed. But the coffee is perking, so it won't be long before Lazarus returns from the dead. Not a moment too soon, either. Just before decomposition sets in.

He shuffles out, wearing a tatty old bathrobe you also remember from long ago. He blinks at you, bleary-eyed. You smile kindly at him, knowing you look fine now, all freshly hosed down and smelling sweet. He stretches, and you can see how glad he is you're already up and about and standing six feet away.

"Shit, it's hot in here," he says. His first pronouncement of the day.

"I know. 'God be bless'd, it is the blessed sun'! Also: we left the heat on last night. But I turned it off. Want some coffee?"

Once the two of you are face to face over coffee and cigarettes it is time to make a bit of departure conversation and ease yourself out of here.

"Call me sometime?" you suggest.

"I regret to say there's little chance of that," he replies flatly.

"Why not?"

"Well, among other things, you are a married woman."

You smirk inside, recalling how, on more than one occasion with you and with others, he had not allowed this legal technicality to stand in his way.

"Well," you reply, "what if I weren't 'a married woman'?"

"Then re-assessment might be called for. But perhaps I best mention: when this show closes, I'll be returning to Hollywood, giving up my apartment, and moving into a condo that my parents helped finance for me."

"Congratulations. So how does that relate?"

"Because I won't be … alone. A friend is moving in with me. In fact, she's there now, getting the place fixed up."

"That's nice. What's her name?"

"Tina, short for Christina."

"Oh, how sweet. Have you two been together very long?"

"A couple of years."

"A couple of years," you repeat absently, your mind reaching back to where you were, exactly, with your life and your own relationships a couple of years ago. "That's a long time."

"I suppose."

"And what does … Tina do?"

"Oh, she's an actress, of course," he says with a dismissive wave of his hand, as if shooing away a fly. "Who else would I meet?"

A cocktail waitress, maybe? you think. But you refrain from delivering this slight, and instead you wonder whether any room in his new condo will be large enough to contain all the oxygen he and his "friend" Tina will demand for themselves.

"At least, you'll have so much in common."

"Yes, I am fairly optimistic."

Good luck, you think, remembering this is the same man who never in his life broke up with anyone. His strategy is to drive away each girlfriend past her expiration date by making her so miserable and unhappy that she leaves him. It'll be a lot harder to get rid of her when she's living there in his own place with him.

You realize: you are all out of sympathy for this man. You realize: for years you've been running on the fumes of nostalgia, but now you are completely out of gas. You remember his expression last night right before he passed out — his disapproval, his disgust, even — and you realize: it is quite likely you dislike him just as much as he dislikes you.

Half an hour later, you are back behind the wheel of your father's big Buick, with your window rolled down and the engine running. Richard is trying to give you directions for how to find your way out of this suburban neighborhood of cul-de-sacs and get back on the freeway.

"That's okay," you cut him off impatiently, "I remember how to get out of here."

He laughs, sounding relieved at your imminent departure. "I suppose you do."

"Well, thanks for ... everything. You'll forward me your new address in Hollywood, yes?"

"Of course. Just as soon as I'm settled."

Yeah, you think as you pull away from the curb, taking one final glance backward in the rearview mirror. Like *that* will ever happen. Besides, you realize: he doesn't have *your* new address, either.

43.

David Out of Control

O n a new moon night, the jungle is darker than any place you've ever been in your life or could ever have imagined. You shut your eyes, you open them again — no difference. All around you is black, wet void. But quiet it is not. One lesson you've learned since you came to Nam is that the jungle is a living, feeding entity. Even now in the dark, you can hear creatures scrabbling, crawling, hopping, flopping, slithering, buzzing around in search of other creatures to devour. Which may include you.

This very moment, you feel a mosquito or some bug-thing boring into your brow, right between your eyes. But you dare not reach for it or slap it for fear of attracting the attention of the Viet Cong snipper you know is surely out there, waiting for you to reveal yourself. Just as you are waiting for him to reveal himself.

In bootcamp, when you demonstrated your expert marksmanship, you were so proud. You never supposed it would take you here to a primitive camp-out in a steamy, stinking, black jungle, where you would spend the night listening for sounds suggesting footsteps, resisting the urge to slap the bugs that are sucking your life-blood. Every minute you are here, you are afraid.

When you finally *do* hear an oncoming rustle in the foliage that can only be a human being, you hold your breath, not even daring to exhale. Footsteps approach, but you know you must wait until you can be certain your shot will kill. Whoever fires first reveals his position; the flash of a shot that does not kill gives the advantage to the Enemy.

You feel him getting closer and closer. Now you can almost smell this gook. You feel the heat of his body in the dark. You know it's time to take your shot. It will never get better than this. Slowly, steathily, you go to position your weapon, and ... you cannot move. To your horror, you realize your body no longer obeys your commands. You are frozen in place. You know you are clutching your weapon, but your arms and hands are numb, unable to feel it.

Then comes the flash, and in that blast of light you see a monster, mouth open wide, revealing a gap as black as the jungle all around, teeth dripping blood. No bullet tears through you, but the creature crazy-laughs and brings his rifle butt down hard on your forehead, crushing your skull at the temple. Still paralyzed, you are done for.

You shout and wake, heart hammering your chest. At once, you realize: (a) you are *not* in the jungle, *and* (b) you have wet the bed. Hot urine bathes your thighs; shame washes over you. But whose bed have you fouled? You look around. Afternoon spills through the big industrial windows. Dust motes whirl in the sunbeams. You sit up amid scabby, scratchy blankets on a filthy, damp mattress on the floor. Next to you is a young woman — very young and very naked with a tattoo on her back of a giant octopus writhing up from the sea. She lies on her stomach, out cold and chuffing away. You strain to recall how you got here.

You lie back down on the giant wet spot you made and try to reconstruct. It is afternoon. You are lying here naked with this young woman. You must have had sex. Of course, you had sex. Then you both must be stoned as well. But she is passed out — so whatever you did must have been downers. And you don't see any paraphernalia. Uppers require paraphernalia.

Fuck. Where *are* you? Try again: afternoon … lying here naked … young woman passed out … you fucked her. The inside of your head feels like slow liquid. The light is too bright — afternoon. You close your eyes.… .

Shaking you awake, she is. Hard. Fallen asleep, you must've. Space around you, all dark now.

"Davie! Davie! Wake up! Don't check out on me!" she yells, gripping your bare shoulders, slamming your body against the rough surface you are lying against. You will yourself to open your eyes, then grin stupidly at the naked girl sitting on your chest, staring at her double-Ds bouncing up and down, up and down. Fuck it, you're still alive.

"Hey, hey," you say, reaching up to grip her skinny upper arms with your big hands. "Easy now."

"Didn't you *feel* that?!" she exclaims, breathlessly.

"What?"

"An earthquake, you ass-wipe!"

"No. What are you talking about?"

"We just had a major fucking earthquake, you douche! Seismic 1000 or whatever!"

"Yeah. So? What am I supposed to do?"

"If we're going to Hell, you could at least be awake for that."

Which gets you to sitting up. You must concede: she has a point.

She leaves the bed and pads, barefoot and bare-assed, across the huge dusty space. "Back in a sec," she calls over her shoulder, "gonna pee." You watch her go, shuffling toward a dark doorway at the opposite end of the expanse. As she goes, you admire the colorful yakusa-style tattoo covering her back. You wonder how long she spent getting inked.

You also wonder: who is this woman? this girl? While she is off peeing and cannot object, you get up and go to her bag, which sits on a nearby ratty armchair, open and spilling its contents onto the seat. You rummage briefly through her junk to find her wallet, pink vinyl with a Hello Kitty! logo. Ticking through her frequent-this and frequent-that cards, you come across her student body I.D. card for Mercy High, the local Catholic school where you enjoy hanging out: Mary McGowan, birthdate April 5, 1970 — age sixteen. Fuck it all, jail-bait!

It's coming back to you now. How you borrowed Barbra's car for the day. How you drove to Mercy and parked around the corner in that dignified residential neighborhood between 19th and Junipero. How you started whacking off underneath your leather bomber jacket as the girls in their black and white uniform skirts (concealing pure white cotton underwear!) left school for the day and trailed past Barbra's car. You were horrified, at first, when three of them stopped at the car and peered in to see what you were up to. They laughed, as young girls are wont to do when they first sense the worldly power they will soon possess.

Thank goodness you always have a bit of dope on hand. You released yourself, still under cover of jacket, reached into the breast pocket of your shirt with two scissor fingers, and pulled out a couple of tightly rolled joints. "Party, ladies?" you suggested. Two of them drew back, but one leaned in — that was Mary. She was quite obviously the most, um ... developed of the three girls (most likely a senior, already eighteen, you guessed), and, it turned out, she was a bad girl, delightfully forward with some dope of her own to offer.

The live-work co-op loft South of Market was her idea, and you weren't about to argue. Clearly, she had older, more advanced friends willing to share their dirty, paint-splattered space. It's good you need so little to keep you satisfied.

You scramble back to the exposed mattress on the floor, toss aside the nasty blanket, grab and flip the mattress to hide your cold, wet piss-puddle soaked into the filthy, blue-and-white mattress ticking. When you grab for the blanket you'd tossed aside, a used condom full of your own splooge shakes out. You dimly recall your resentment when she insisted you wear it.

"Hey, I am *not* dying for sex," she told you frankly. "Haven't you ever heard of AIDS?"

But, all the same, you were excited, interpreting the fact that she carried her own condoms as a sign she really wanted it, too. And by the time she'd outfitted you deftly using her mouth — something not one of your several hundred other women had ever done — you had totally forgiven her for demanding you wear a raincoat.

When Mary pads back into the studio and glances up at a screened clock face on the wall, she goes frantic. "Davie, you gotta get me home! It's nearly nine. I'll be grounded for the rest of the school year."

"Okay, yeah, don't worry, I'll take care of it," you say, stumbling to standing. When your bare feet touch wetness on the floor at the edge of the mattress, you remember your accident. But there is nothing more to do about it, so you get dressed, walk away with your leather jacket slung over your shoulder, pretend nothing happened.

Out on the street again with Mary, you remove the parking ticket pinned under one of the windshield wipers of Barbra's car. You unlock the car, get in behind the wheel, and reach over to stuff tonight's ticket into the glove box along with all the other tickets you've accumulated. Mary climbs in on her own.

"Drop me at school, okay?" she says. "Cyndi will cover for me. Especially after I tell her I won the bet we made about you."

You turn towards this child, bewildered. "You made ... a bet about me?"

"Yeah," she said. "I bet I could get you to fuck me without your ever checking whether I was underage. Like, would you be more concerned about getting laid or getting busted? You never asked, so I win."

44.

Barbra Gets Her Lorie Back

Y ou and Lorie haven't been this close since he came out to you at Christmastime 1969. Even throughout your many years in the City, you were not so close as this. You still resented his rejection of you. On some level, you found it unintelligible that you should lose him to another man. And not just one man — but, really, *all* men.

Besides, it hurt you that he should always have so many men, while you had none. At least, no man who didn't already belong to someone else. And even though you could see how you did this to yourself by only going after married men, it still hurt.

"You know, don't you?" asked Loren, "that lots of married guys swing both ways." He noted your raised eyebrows. "Oh yes, dear, indeedy, they do."

He went on to explain that there was no way to estimate how many homos use wives and kids as cover in a straight world. Some, it seems, found themselves after they got married — that could easily have happened to him and to you. Others thought it wouldn't matter if they enjoyed boys on the side; Lorie said he could never have done that to you, it would have been so dishonorable. And the rest, he said, are trying desperately to go straight, but will never make it, because "once you find out what you really want in life, you can't ever go back."

You saw his point. If he had married you after he realized where his true tastes lay (so to speak), it could only have hurt you both. Just think if you'd caught him in bed after you became Mr. and Mrs.! You'd be divorced now, and how would you have explained *that* to your parents and everyone else in town? Or to your children?

No, you had to agree: everything had worked out for the best, and it was only *you* who'd wasted your own time by going after inappropriate guys. Loren had never wasted his time. Good thing, too, because who knew he would have so little of it? Even so, what little he'd had (but didn't know he would have), he didn't waste that, either. He enjoyed his life and even accomplished a few things. You only wish you could say the same about yourself and your own life. You never enjoyed much of any of it. You certainly never accomplished anything of value.

At least, not until these past few months when you have come over here to Lorie's apartment nearly every day to look after your old friend. As liberated as you consider yourself to be, you always liked cleaning and cooking for someone else; now, finally, someone else really appreciates it.

Loren can't eat much or else his guts go into an uproar — all those parasitic infections, the fungus in his mouth that can't be treated because the treatment would probably kill him along with the thrush. And with all those antibiotics he's taken, is still taking, he probably doesn't have any intestinal flora left. After all he's been through, all he's fought his way past, it would be so degrading to have to lose him to diarrhea. So you work hard to find and cook the things he likes, can maybe still taste a little, can still tolerate.

But mostly, when he is awake and in his right mind (i.e., not on the morphine drip), you just sit at his bedside and chat like the two old friends you are. You pick through the photo albums his mother brought down to him. You gossip about "Whatever Became Of...?" the people you both knew in high school. You have sock-monkey fights.

You realize that, by now, David thinks you are seeing someone else. But you no longer care what he thinks. You don't worry about where he might be. If he is there and not passed out on the couch when you leave your condo, you tell him the truth: you are going over to see Loren. When he gives you that smirking "Sure, you are" look, you don't argue the point. You haven't told him how sick Loren is or how worried you are. David hasn't earned the right to know what's going on with you. He never will. One day you'll change the locks and put his stuff out on the curb. Right now, however, you're too busy looking after your friend.

Months ago, you confessed to Loren you'd discovered he was right about that short, fat, pale woman he saw in the bar with David. You apologized for not believing him. You apologized for being so nasty to him, instead of thanking him for being a friend, a true friend, and for wanting you to have all the information you need to make your own best-possible life decisions. Maybe, just maybe, if you'd believed him back then, you wouldn't still have this problem to deal with now.

One night, thanks to Lorie's mom, who'd carried half the contents of his old bedroom at home down to San Francisco, you and he were paging through his high school yearbook for his senior year. You were laughing about the various girls who'd tried to get between the two of you, never imagining, at this early stage of your lives, that no person of the female persuasion ever would or ever could really have him. Then you stopped laughing and you asked:

"Do you remember that old cattle dog, Señorita, we had on dad's farm?"

"You mean the one who was so in love with one of your goats?"

"The same. Her whole life, she only had eyes for that goat, that one old goat, Pixie. And she was always that way from the start. She would follow those goats out into the side yard, then lie on her belly in the dirt and stare at Pixie for hours. It was as though they'd known one another in some past life, been madly in love, and now were separated by having been reincarnated as two different species."

"Yeah, I can see that."

"That's the way I think of us."

"Yeah, I can see that, too."

"So ... maybe next lifetime around? Whaddya say?"

"I'll see what can be arranged upstairs."

You were happy with his answer. You sat pretending to read, while he pretended to sleep. But, stubborn as always, you waited till his steady, deep, and regular breathing let you know he really was asleep. Then you quietly set aside your book, crept over to your lifelong friend, the dearest human being you had ever known, and watched him as he peacefully slept.

45.

Why Loren Can't

B ut I really think I'm more the dog," is what you tell Barb after a moment's reflection.

"Yeah? How's that?"

"Easy. I've totally lived a dog's life: existing in the moment with no conception of real time, ready to try anything once, free of self-awareness, forever begging for treats, will eat anything."

"Like, say, your own vomit?"

"Only if it's still fresh and warm. Please, I do have standards."

"You're awful hard on yourself. What about: loyal, dependable, forgiving, unconditionally loving?"

"And always drinking lots of water!" you respond, reaching for some humor along with your sippy cup from the hospice people.

You both laugh at that. Then, with a serious face, Barb adds, "Also, you accept yourself, and you enjoy the journey."

"Well, I *did* do that," you admit. "I just wish I'd

accomplished more. All that education and experience — what the hell was it for? Nearly forty years on this planet, and I feel like I understand nothing. It's only now, with the End in sight, I feel I may actually be catching up to the Meaning of It All."

"You're in a mood tonight."

"Sorry, Barb. Guess I'm just crabby and in need of my evening nap."

You don't want to admit to Barbra — or even to yourself — how much you ache with regret over never having written that Great American Novel. Or how the reason for this oversight has suddenly come to you: as writers go, you're no damn good.

Unable to talk about this, you pretend to nod off, so you can think about it instead.

After ten years of failure to produce a cohesive novel, you scaled down your expectations and decided instead to produce a series of stand-alone short stories — picaresque and innocently erotic — that, taken together, would constitute a somewhat fictive memoir or autobiographical novel reminiscent of Giacomo Casanova's classic oeuvre, *Histoire de ma vie*, only much shorter, much kinder, and with an all-male cast. In your travels, you'd met so many fabulous men, and you wanted to enjoy them all over again.

But you'd set your intentions during what you have come to realize was the Homo Golden Age, before AIDS arrived to spoil the playful celebrations of self-discovery and exploration. Instead of simply trying for a literary facsimile of partying along with them into Eternity — an implied open house invitation to all — you ought to have been memorializing them and exulting *their* courage to live life to the fullest as their own true selves. Especially since, now you see, some were destined to have even less lifetime than you.

Alas! as you mentally turn page after page of your book-length manuscript (working title: *I Regret Nothing*), you see that what you have actually created is a passable one-handed reader, light-weight whacking material to serve and service America's Most Closeted. Who now will be too afraid to ever come out. Your inner writer gave it his best shot; your inner editor sees, all too clearly, how vapid and DOA the writing is. Pretty sad because, though it embarrasses you to admit it even to yourself, you really *wanted* your own share of literary immortality. You mentally return the manuscript to its hiding place at the bottom of your underwear drawer.

No fair.

You imagine what you would have said at the office to a writer who brought you such a manuscript. You would have been kind, of course. In a world ruled by style manuals and intellectually haughty critics, most of whom sincerely believe they could do better than the clients they serve, Loren McMaster has a reputation for kindness and compassion. So you certainly would have been kind, would have spent a couple of evenings of personal time giving the work a thorough reading, attaching notes written on yellow Post-Its to the margins, folding them over before neatly stacking each page. You always took a keen personal interest in your writers, even those who were clearly incapable of submitting a manuscript that your house would accept and publish.

Such as yourself, for example.

You would have returned the manuscript to its author with respect, as clean and unsullied as it had come to you and with all its pages in proper order. You understand what a pain it is to retype pages stained with a reader's coffee mug rings or smudged with cigarette ash. You know each manuscript you see is most likely the only extant original in the world — the author having retained merely a copy for himself and each publisher having jealously insisted on holding that original for ransom, a tacit guarantee that no other publisher had received a simultaneous submission.

And though you would have "rejected" the manuscript, you would have done it gently, so as not to damage the writer, knowing he might later blossom and flourish. Indeed, you would have encouraged him, congratulating him on having gotten this first load of dreck out of his system. Now he would be free to go on and produce something truly fine.

But that strategy assumes, of course, the writer is young and has time enough to go on and produce more, better books. Indeed, how many times have you read — and even declared — that novelists do not begin to hit their stride until their forties? Unfortunately, in your case, despite your relative youth, you will not have time to go on and produce more and better. And even if you did have the time, you no longer have the ability to concentrate for more than a few minutes at a stretch. What's more, you no longer have the strength to speak your truth.

Which is just one of the many reasons AIDS is such a bitch: it wears you down to nothing with all the accompanying opportunistic infections and hostings, like some horrible roommate who throws a party while you're out of town and invites in all these street derelicts who wreck your place. You might have coexisted peaceably with this guy, but not with the dozen or more creeps he allowed into the apartment.

What can you expect, now that you have almost no immune system left?

For example, at present, it turns out you have a fungus. Your doctor hadn't a clue. It took your mom, here on her visit, to figure out what that white junk in your mouth was. Apparently, mostly only babies get thrush. You'd been wondering how you could have gotten cottage cheese stuck to the roof of your mouth. Now you know. And now your doctor is trying to decide how aggressively to treat you without making you sicker. But, of course, this latest fungus took hold right after you'd been treated with those super-antibiotics for the stubborn kidney infection that developed soon after you were catheterized in the hospital during a recent bout with pneumonia. Those antibiotics seem to be very good at killing the bad bugs, but they work like Roundup, killing everything else as well. Who knew you would need to hang onto your good bugs just as much as you would need to get rid of the bad bugs?

Once you understood that what had seemed at first like a never-ending case of the flu was in fact your own private death sentence, you called your folks and asked them to please, please come visit you. You were suddenly possessed of a powerful need to confess yourself and everything about you to the two people who'd brought you into this world. Your mother agreed at once. But she must have had some presentiment of what you intended to tell them, because, though you'd wanted your dad here as well, your mom came alone. Later on, she explained to you: he isn't ready, he may never be ready, he's too scared, he cannot bear to hear it.

Anyway, she didn't seem all *that* surprised when you came out to her, then told her how ill you were. If anything, she seemed relieved to hear your confession. At least now she had an explanation for all your mysterious comings and goings over the years, your persistent evasions since you left home long, long ago.

Your mother planned to stay a week. She ended up staying a month. And soon after she left — you watched from your big picture window as the taxi-driver crammed his trunk full of her luggage — Barbra arrived in her place. It was her first visit since your house-warming for the flat, four years earlier. Out of nowhere, she called to say she was on her way over. As soon as you opened the door and saw her stricken expression, you knew for certain she'd been talking to your mom.

That was six months ago. Since then, Barbra — former fiancé, forever friend — has come over to spend time with you nearly every day. At first, she took a two-week "vacation" and spent her days cleaning and cooking for you. After she went back to work, she always stopped by on her way home. Some days you don't know what you'd do if it weren't for her.

You've been tempted, on more than one occasion, to ask about that dick-wad living with her, what he thinks she's up to with all her disappearances. But you don't want to hurt her or anyone else at this late stage. Besides, you already know the answer to your question. Men like him always attribute their own depraved motives to others. He probably thinks she's having an affair with the 49ers.

One depressing truth you discovered, as your illness became too obvious to hide, is that most people don't want to be around someone who's sick. Especially someone who isn't ever going to get well. Even if the illness isn't contagious in any of the ordinary, G-rated ways, superstitions still attend, and close friends will retreat because they cannot bear the thought of losing you. Only the truest friend will find the courage to consciously face this fear and step forward, instead of sidestepping and abandoning you. But once that friend *does* appear, he or she can be a magnet to draw others to you.

Barbra, it turned out, was your magnet. Actually, more like a tow truck. You admitted to her that, soon after your diagnosis, you'd started to attend a gay men's support group organized through Pacific Medical Center, but you'd dropped out after your first couple meetings. When she asked you why you hadn't stayed on, you told her you'd been too busy — back then, you were still working.

But the truth was, back then, you were still too embarrassed to be seen openly as one of "them," to be known as belonging to *that* group. Those men were so unapologetically ... queer. The guy who painted himself gold and walked naked in the gay pride parade pretending to be Montezuma, one of the Aztec emperors (probably Moc II, conquered by the Spanish) — *he* was in the group, for Christ's sake. And when you actually met Marvin, as a person, you hadn't even recognized at first he'd also been your ... waitress on any number of late-night occasions at Hamburger Mary's.

But Barb, when she heard how you'd quietly withdrawn from the group, visited Pacific Medical Center with the intention of tracking down the guys. And when she was told the membership was confidential, she went directly to the Alta Plaza, where the group sometimes met, and chatted up the bartender till he produced the group leader's name and number.

Fortunately, Cal, your group leader, has an excellent memory for names and anecdotes, so he didn't put her off. Instead, he helped her parlay her contact with him into a network of five more guys (two of the group's original members having passed in the intervening months). Every remaining guy in the group responded to Cal's invitation to contact your "sister," and she, in turn, scheduled visitations and made sure you had company for at least a short time every day. You refer to these visits as shifts of "babysitters," but you are grateful for the human contact.

Then, after Barb began caring for you — scheduling the guys to look after you, keeping your apartment spotless, filling your kitchen with food — other friends, men you'd partied with for years, semi-anonymously, started dropping by, bringing gifts of cassette tapes (and a boombox!) and more food, entertaining you. Distracting you from your pain and disintegration. You didn't try to explain Barbie. They all just thought she was your actual sister or your fag-hag high school friend. You let it go at that. The truth was — and always will be — too complicated for you to understand, much less explain.

At first, she seemed a little stunned by the incoming campy tide she'd set in motion. But you noticed she warmed up over time. In fact, these days, your brittle old friend seems mostly content. She seems to enjoy looking after you and not only cooking for you, but for your friends as well. She clearly likes the banter and stories of happier, more hopeful past times. It's been weeks since you noticed her spraying anything with Lysol.

Occasionally, you still feel guilty for having ruined her life. But more and more you accept that your lives simply went the way they went and all judgment after the fact is irrelevant. After your friends finish dinner and head for the clubs to dance off the calories, you and Barbie have after-dinner conversations, and she stays till you fall asleep. You suspect she likes watching you sleep until the night attendant from hospice arrives to keep you safe for the rest of the night.

"Lorie, wake up! You're having a bad dream." Barbie is shaking you gently by your thin, bony shoulder.

"Huh? What?" you choke out. Then backing up into consciousness, "What was I doing?"

"You were moaning and laughing at the same time. It was kinda creepy. What were you dreaming about?"

"I was a soul being tortured in Hell, and I was playing all the parts, including the Devil."

"Seriously?"

"Naw, just kidding. I don't remember a thing."

But in fact you *do* remember. On this night, you dreamed you only pretended to fall asleep. You waited till you heard Barbie leave, then — gently, gently — you got up, crept to your dresser, and opened your underwear drawer. And though it was the hardest thing you'd done in weeks — or maybe ever in your life — you carried your manuscript to the bathroom, dropped it in the tub, and set fire to it, crunching up the pages you'd laboriously typed on Big Red, one by one, encouraging the conflagration.

"Now I am burning your child, Nerol!" you whispered fiercely. "Burning it, curly-locks!"

You worked quickly, knowing Ernie from hospice would arrive shortly. Ashes were accumulating, covering your feet, building up around your ankles and shins as you squatted there awkwardly in the narrow tub. It was getting harder and harder to clear a space to set fire to the pages. It seemed as though each page you burned took up more space, instead of less. The bathtub was nearly full, you were waist-deep in black, feathery ashes. Desperate to make space, you reached for the faucet and turned on the tub tap full-blast, intending to sluice away all remnants of the charred pages. But they were plugging the drain. The tide of ashes rose higher, threatening to spill over the tub's edge and onto the floor. Then you heard Barbie calling your name.

Funny, because in fact, in your waking life, you had been contemplating how you might destroy your manuscript in order to ease your own passage out of this world. After all, there are worse things than dying — even worse things than being a young man grown old before your time. Leaving behind a stack of hurt and regret for those who had cared about you in this life — that's worse. You would rather go to your grave having people think of you as a never-was than a never-could-have-been.

But as long as your manuscript still exists in this world, down there in your underwear drawer, it keeps calling out for attention, demanding an audience. It is, after all, the one significant piece of your own writing that you'd ever managed to finish. And even if it's the worst dreck anyone ever produced, at least you know you did what you could, you did your best. That will have to do. The night you completed your draft, you were frankly proud of your accomplishment — for one entire evening. The next morning, as you paged through it again, you could hardly believe this was yours, that you had actually written this tome. Post-partum, it seemed impossible you could have created the work.

"Barbie?"

"Yes, Lorie."

"Do me a favor?"

"Anything."

"In my bureau, the bottom drawer with the underwear, there's the manuscript of a book I wrote."

"You wrote a book? I thought you'd given up trying to write."

"I almost wish I had. But sometimes a book refuses to give up on you."

"Fiction?"

"Let's call it a 'sentimental memoir with fictive elements.'"

"Alright. Why are you telling me this?"

"Because ... I want you to read it. I want one other human being to read it — someone who really knows me and who cares about me too much to judge me by it. But I want you to read the whole thing here in this apartment and not take it away with you. That manuscript is my original, the only copy in existence. Then, when you've finished reading, I want you to replace the manuscript in the drawer it came from, sprinkle some underpants over it, and forget about the whole thing until after I'm gone. At which point, I want you to burn every last page in the bathtub and wash the ashes down the drain. Okay? You might consider washing *my* ashes down the drain, too, at the same time."

"I'll pretend I didn't hear that last bit. You want me to destroy your only copy of your book?"

"Yes, that's it exactly."

"But why?"

"Because it's a piece of shit."

"What if it's not? Would that negate your stipulation?"

"Not in the least. And in regards to the quality of the writing, you'll just have to trust me on this. Who's the editor in the room, anyhow?"

"Okay, chief."

"Not that kind of editor, dear. You'll do as I ask?"

"Of course. But, after I've read it, do you want to talk about it? Do you want my opinion?"

"Not especially. For one thing, as I was saying, it's shit. For another, it's not your taste in shit. I know that, and you'll know that, too, as soon as you read it. But I don't want to hear about it."

"What if I like it?"

"You won't. But all I care about is that, after you read it, you still like me."

"I will. Nothing could ever change that."

"Good. Thank you." And, with that, you close your eyes and drift off.

46.

Loren's Last Day of True Joy

Don't forget, Lorie: it's your birthday."

Barb tells you this as she cleans you up after your dinner and changes you into a fresh set of baggy sweat clothes. A sudden memory comes to you — of being a kid and hosing down your 4-H heifer to get the mud and manure off. Then you recall that "a down cow is a dead cow" and how she's got to be made to get up, even if she doesn't want to. You try a little harder to help Barbie dress you.

"My birthday?" you ask as Barbie unhooks the morphine PICC line taped at the crook of your left arm and feeds your arm through the cut-off sleeve of your sweat shirt. She pulls the shirt down over your head and holds out the right sleeve so you can work your own arm through. Dressing complete, she reattaches your PICC line. You glance down at the new red tracksuit-style sweats and entertain yourself by mentally selecting a silk tie to accompany the outfit.

Which makes you laugh out loud, a brief expletive of a guffaw, like something that might have started as a burp and ended as if you'd sat down hard on the ground, having missed your chair. Which makes Barbra pause in her tidying you up and look at you strangely.

"Did I hurt you?" she asks.

"Never," you tell her.

"Well, just remember," she continues, "the whole group is coming over this evening to help you celebrate."

"My birthday. January 22nd, right? How old am I going to be?"

"Thirty-nine. One year older than me. Like always."

"Oh, that's good, isn't it?"

"Sure it is."

You are vaguely aware that in the past you would have dreaded the occasion: thirty-nine — so *old*! A Youngman no longer, that's certain. But today you feel only a vague sense of triumph. These past two years, when you feared you'd never make it this far and your work on the planet was still undone, you'd wake in the night, panicked, sweat-soaked, heart hammering to get out of your chest. But you used your fear as motivation: it's now or never!

Nowadays, with the aid of your morphine drip, you sleep more or less soundly through each night. Of course, your personal version of the Great (Gay) American Novel is merely a complete first draft you managed to review only once, and Barb will be the only person ever to have read it. Nevertheless, you are ... if not exactly happy, then at least content with what you did.

During your life, you were a reader and you were an editor, and you dealt with final results, however imperfect they might be. As a reader, you had a choice: you could either put aside a book or force yourself to plod through it. As an editor, you were more proactive, finding good and worthy manuscripts that deserved to be published. You worked hard to help each writer say whatever he was really trying to say and in the best possible way.

But as a writer ... as *the* writer of your own book, you finally came to grips with the true process of writing. You learned about the high anxiety of confronting that first blank page rolled into the typewriter platen as you began your journey of exploration. Now you know the struggle of making yourself return daily to your personal literary expedition. So many mornings, you realized you'd rather scrub out the toilet than sit down and write.

Back when you still had energy, you'd rattle around your flat, neatly lining up books, records, ties. You'd spend an hour rearranging throw pillows. You'd stretch out on your big leather couch to read yet-another trashy genre novel — a gift from Barbie, who hoped to keep you entertained — to be abandoned halfway through the third chapter and tossed on the pile of dreck stacked in the hallway near the front door. You remember wandering into the kitchen, opening the refrigerator, looking inside at nothing in particular before shutting the door and shuffling away.

It turned out there are ten thousand ways for a writer to procrastinate, and you found them all, including a few you invented on your own — anything to avoid driving deep into the unknown interior of your own mind, that hidden world of beauty and pain concealed within you. Any day you managed, before sunset, to convince yourself to sit and type just one full page of text — that day you counted as a victory.

However, after you made Writing My Book the number-one priority of however much life you have left, the process became easier and easier. You stopped wandering around your flat, ghostlike and distracted, hoping inspiration would strike you on your way to the bathroom. Instead, you brewed your morning coffee, sat down at your desk, and turned on your typewriter, determined that Inspiration should find you already typing at the moment she chose to drop her load of museness on you.

Then, after a morning of honest work and even modest results, you found everything else in your life organized itself around you. Your day became bullet-proof ... golden. And at bedtime, whatever had been going on in your book that morning shaped your last conscious thoughts for the day. You lay in the dark, relaxing into the oblivion of sleep, confident your subconscious mind would be hard at work on your behalf all night long, so that, when you awoke the next morning (assuming you did), you would find your muse standing at your bedside, arms outstretched to you, holding a package with your name on it.

God, all those years you wasted working in publishing! Wasted as a writer, anyway. As an editor, you were better than simply good; you were maybe even great. Though it's hard now for you to imagine how you could have managed to remain behind a desk, concentrating on any one thing for so many hours every day, day after day, after week, after month, after year.

You see now you didn't really know as much as you thought you did back then. You just didn't get it. If only you hadn't gotten sick, if only you still gave a shit about other people's books, you suppose you'd be an even better editor than before. Too bad you'll soon be dead and never find out.

It occurs to you: every editorial type in a publishing house, from lowly copy editor to exalted acquisitions editor, should be required to write his or her own book, start to finish, simply to have first-hand experience of what it takes to do that. Then writers would garner more respect from the very professionals who are supposed to be helping them. For that matter, all book critics as well — those smug bastards! — should be made to earn their credentials the same way. You roll onto your side and feel around inside your nightstand drawer for a pad and pen to scribble a note to yourself. Maybe you can work up an opinion piece about the differences between writing and editing. You could title it, "From Creation to Critique."

Moments later, you exit the drawer empty-handed. You think of asking Barbie to quit bagging dirty laundry from your bedroom hamper and bring you a pen and pad. But your brief search has already exhausted you, and the brilliant idea you had a moment ago is already fading away. You lie back to rest in the hospital bed that they brought in a couple weeks ago.

Since you no longer have your book-in-progress to think about, you close your eyes and count your blessings, a meditation suggested by your hospice attendant, Ernie. You have so much to be grateful for!

Gratitude Item #1: Your book is done.

Gratitude Item #2: You still have your flat, and somehow the bills are getting paid.

Gratitude Item #3: Your parents still love you. You suddenly remember your dad phoned you this morning to wish you happy birthday.

"I love you, Son" — that's what he said.

"I love you, Dad" — that's what you said.

Gratitude Item #4: Your relationship with Barbie is healed. She has become a real sister to you.

Gratitude Item #5: You have more real friends now than you ever had in your whole life. They are friends of the heart who truly know you, who know the full extent of who and what you are, but who love you just the same.

You feel ... free and forever excused from any need to impress anyone.

You hear your doorbell ring, that strident, old-fashioned buzzer and, moments later, a commotion at the front door. Sounds like Barbie is letting in a bunch of people. The boys? You remember: your support group is coming over to help you celebrate your birthday.

Gratitude Item #6: You are having another birthday! That proves you are still alive.

Barbie comes into the room, carrying a red Macy's bag.

"What's in the bag?" you ask, taking some wild guesses.

"Oh, you'll see," she says, coyly. "This is *my* birthday present to you. The guys will help you figure it out. I'm going to take off now. See you tomorrow."

She sets the bag on your nightstand, pushing aside your basket of pills, and takes both your hands in hers to give them a squeeze. Then she turns her attention to your morphine drip.

"Would you like me to disconnect that for you? Just for the party? Cal can hook you up again at any point. Or Ernie will be here in a couple of hours, he can do it."

You nod and watch as she undoes you, admiring her steadiness. You feel a twinge of anxiety, nervousness over the possibility that pain will assert itself and have its way with you.

But you let that thought go, along with everything else. One thing you have learned, this past year or so, is how to enter fully into the present and push aside all past regrets, all future fears.

Besides, the boys are here, and collectively they always know what to do. You close your eyes to let her work. You hear subdued conversation, punctuated with giggles and shushings, coming from the living room.

Barbie is kissing you on the cheek. "Happy birthday, Lorie. Be good now."

She leaves your bedroom, and moments later you hear a smart rap-tap-tapping on your bedroom door, accompanied by the words: "Knock-knock!"

"Who's there?" you answer dutifully.

"Doris."

"Doris Who?"

"Doris open, so I thought I'd drop by!"

"Well, c'mon in, Doris!"

"Well, so I shall, Mary! So I shall."

It's Cal, with his handsome, smiling face. His startlingly white teeth are a reminder that he is the only son of a Mormon dentist. Even though he is African American. "Let's get you up and onto the runway. Your public awaits."

Smirking, you bat your lashes at Cal and flutter a pretend fan after the fashion of an imaginary antebellum Southern belle. "Alright, Mr. DeMille, I'm ready for my close-up."

Cal helps you out of bed, down the hallway, and into the living room with such efficiency and grace, you are reminded he is a nurse by training. Of course, since he tested HIV-positive, he no longer works hands-on with patients. But this men's support group is still his baby. Who better to lead it than a man who can fully appreciate the situation from the perspectives of both medical professional and patient? It amazes you that, in well over a year of meetings with this guy, you have never once seen him down or depressed. You wonder what his secret is for maintaining emotional equilibrium.

Though Cal seems clearly gay, you heard somewhere he didn't get HIV in the usual ways, through unprotected sex with another man or IV drug-use or contaminated blood transfusions. It was more like an on-the-job injury, or so the rumor went. But, of course, the group never discusses *how* anyone got sick, the problem being the illness itself and the limitations it imposes on you, not how you got it. Too often, outside of an HIV support group, that particular discussion topic of how you got sick opens the door for the highly vocal self-righteous to preach that "AIDS is God's way of punishing you for your perversion." This is the last thing you need to hear as you are already hurrying to catch up with your Maker.

Speaking of which, your living room looks like the waiting room to get into Heaven. There's Marvin sitting on the sofa. He's Chicano and came to this country illegally. He started as a farm worker in California's Central Valley, but soon gravitated to the city to live out his true nature at Hamburger Mary's, everyone's favorite South-of-Market, after-hours refueling station. You remember seeing him there in the wee hours of any number of late nights, even before that afternoon when you met him in your support group. He was the first drag-queen you'd ever had for a waitress.

"Oh, man, my feet, they are *killing* me!" he'd told you one night as he got ready to take your order. You looked down to see that he was wearing unusually high platform shoes with plastic goldfish swimming around inside the heels.

"Why don't you switch to something lower?" you suggested in your usual, innocently practical way.

"I can't wear flats with this outfit," he declared.

Later, you didn't recognize him at first, out of makeup and out of context as he was. But he recognized you. And he was pretty excited to hear you were an editor, because he'd written a memoir telling what it was like to grow up where a kid who was different, in the way he was, would certainly be tormented and might even be killed by people he knew. You listened to him tell how it was to be sixteen and cross the desert alone, then find his way into a society he knew nothing at all about, except for what he had seen on American TV programs. You thought, as you listened to his tale, he was the bravest man you'd ever met.

Kevin, parked next to Marvin on the long section of your L-shaped leather sofa, is by far the most fey of your group. He's a temp secretary and sometime personal assistant who still works long hours and occasionally amuses himself, at the eleventh hour in whatever office he's been temping in, by mooning the copier, which he says is "nice and warm." You will always remember Kevin telling you how, once upon a time, he was just leaving work, already on his way to a big date, when his boss asked him to stay after hours to prepare some bullshit report of several hundred pages. Supposedly, the report was needed first thing in the morning for a meeting with the organization's president. So Kevin blew off his date, stayed at the office till nearly dawn, then left the finished report on his boss's desk with a Post-It note that said: "I quit! Please note: I have inserted, five times at random intervals, the words, 'Fuck you, Mr. President.'"

You found such guerrilla tactics absolutely shocking. And terribly thrilling.

"Do you think your boss found all five fuck-you's?" you had asked Kevin after he finished his story.

"I'm certain he didn't," Kevin replied.

"How can you be so certain?"

"Because I inserted only *four* fuck-you's. I just love imagining him clutching his little bottle of Liquid Paper in his trembling hand, searching frantically, right up to the start of his big important meeting, for that final fuck-you."

Sitting at your massive roll-top desk with the chair swiveled around to face the room is Brandon, the man with whom, under circumstances other than mutual terminal illness, you might have hoped to spend the rest of your life. Though, ironically, that is exactly how things are turning out. In a very much abbreviated form.

Tall and slim, patrician-looking, pipe-smoking, and straight-acting, Brandon was a college professor from God's Central Casting. And because he taught Literature, he was the only one of your support group who actually understood what you did for a living. Or knew the never-ending pain of having an unborn book stuck inside you.

He was also one of the few men you knew well, though not intimately in the technical sense, who'd lived his life as closeted as you, only to be outed by illness. And he'd taken his early subterfuge even farther than you, because he was married with children. Children who were just now old enough and worldly wise enough to be embarrassed by having a gay dad. He lives apart from them and talks to them on the phone a couple times a month, but never sees them. His wife, the woman who will sooner rather than later be his widow, tells these children their father is in Greece on sabbatical. And he, sensitive to her feelings of personal failure and revulsion, maintains the illusion.

Meanwhile, he worries about his youngest son, Owen, whom he suspects is just like him. But he doesn't know how to broach the subject with his wife. The time for a sensible sit-down talk between parents united on behalf of their kids has passed.

You wish so much you and Brandon had met earlier in your lives. Perhaps if you'd decided to attend S.F. State, where he taught, instead of UC Berkeley.... But, no, he was a few years older than you, and even as you were receiving your undergraduate degree, he was already standing barefoot on the beach at Stinson next to a girl with flowers in her hair, wearing a wedding dress made out of an old lace tablecloth. Only in a kinder, gentler alternative universe could you have gotten together with this man of your dreams.

Rounding out the group, sitting on the shorter, loveseat-size section of your sofa are Tod and Leonard, a couple who've been together for nearly twenty years. Tod is a musician — classical violin; Leonard works backstage in the dressing rooms at the opera house. Tod is HIV-positive; Leonard is HIV-negative. Nevertheless, Leonard insists on accompanying Tod to nearly every meeting of his support group. You suspect this is because he blames himself for Tod's illness. He was, after all, the one who suggested bringing in a third party to "spice things up."

But it was Tod, with his romantic nature, who made the fatal mistake (literally) of falling in love with the boy. And the boy in question, a singer in the opera chorus who was content to be kept for a time, died months ago — of complications from AIDS. As have so many, you thought, mentally reciting the mantra of your era. Until the boy's death, Tod had been doing alright, maintaining pretty fair health despite an immense viral load and dwindling immune resources. Now, however, he was clearly on a slippery slope to his grave. Every time you saw him, usually medicated into sleep with his head on Leonard's lap, you reflected on how much less gay being gay had become in just a few years' time. You wondered if Leonard would still attend this group after Tod passed. You wondered who would go first — Tod or you.

You look around your living room, taking in these men at one continuous glance, and think: *I love you.* You love them as a group, and you love them as individuals. You are glad you wrote about them, and you are glad one other human being in the world, your soul-sistah Barbie, has read or will read what you wrote, because you know she has also come to love them. You remember that Native American saying about how those we love never really die until everyone who was touched by them and who loved them is gone from this earth. You send up a brief, silent prayer for Barb to live to be 100, at least. And for her to find someone to love and be loved by in the way she had once wished from you.

Cal settles you in your La-Z-Boy recliner, the guest of honor in your own home, and disappears into your kitchen.

Kevin jumps up and follows after him. Moments later, you hear Kevin exclaim:

"Ouch! Dammit, that *hurt!*"

And Cal responds: "Well, Mary, try lighting the candles from back to front instead of randomly."

When Cal reappears, he is carrying a sheet cake at arms' length, blazing with so many lit candles that you seem to feel the heat as he approaches. He sets the cake on the coffee table before you.

"We're really sorry about where we burnt the veneer, just a little, on your kitchen cabinet. I don't think it'll show much after I scrub off the soot," Cal apologizes.

"My god!" you say, leaning back from the intense heat, "How many candles are there?"

"Seventy-nine," Kevin answers, coming up behind Cal. "That's for your thirty-ninth *and* fortieth birthdays. All things considered, we thought it best to—."

"To give you a leg up on that novel you've been meaning to write," interrupted Brandon. "It's common knowledge that most of the world's truly great writers have produced their finest work after the age of forty. So we wanted to give you a running start."

You let this idea sink in, feeling your heart rise in your chest. For a moment, you can almost believe the collective solicitude of your friends is capable of bending time in your favor.

"Alright, alright!" Kevin interrupts. "Now, let's sing 'Happy Birthday!' and put those candles out before the tabletop melts."

So, they sing, and they watch as you lean toward the

conflagration and make feeble efforts to blow out the candles for your birthdays. "Can I get a little help here, d'ya think?" you wheeze.

Kevin says: "Well, c'mon now, girls. It's not as though we don't have enough collective experience blowing."

"Speak for yourself, Kevin," says Brandon.

But still it takes the entire group to extinguish the blaze.

"There!" Cal exclaims. "Quick, Lorie, make a wish!"

"I already have," you reply. "And it has already been granted."

After your cake, which no one really touches, except for Marvin, who loves sweets, Cal presents the red Macy's shopping bag that Barbie left for you.

"This birthday present is the culmination of a conspiracy on your behalf," he explains. "Your sister went shopping for you, and now your friends are going to show you how to use what she bought."

You watch as he extracts gold, silver, and pastel boxes from the bag and hands them to each of the guys to be unwrapped, one by one, then set on the coffee table that's been wiped clean of warm frosting.

Makeup. It's all makeup. Oh, and a gold lamé turban. And a fur stole. Just rabbit, but after all how many wearings is it going to get? You are astonished. And lightly afraid. Here is territory you've never dared to trespass on your own. Now suddenly the door to your closet has swung wide open. You look up at your friends with trepidation smeared across your face.

"Now, don't give us that look, honey," says Kevin. "You don't have to do anything but just sit back and relax. All shall be done for you."

Marvin stands up, knits his fingers together, and stretches his arms out before him, like a pianist warming up to play. "I have the very most experience here."

"Oh, sit down, Mary!" Kevin says. "Your 'experience' would be perfect if he was answering a casting call for a John Waters film. But I thought we agreed we're going for something more subdued and natural, yet still glamorous. Isn't that right, Leonard?"

"Indeed," says Leonard. He stands up, carefully rearranging Tod, who had fallen asleep against his shoulder. "My years backstage have taught me something."

"Spackling opera divas," Marvin replies bitterly. "Did you bring your best trowel?"

"Excuse me, but I'm also a consulting aesthetician for the cosmetics department at Nordstrom," Leonard adds.

"That's right," Kevin says, "so he knows about colors and seasons, like whether someone is a Spring or Summer or Fall or Winter."

"Oh, yeah," says Marvin, "then what season am I?"

"Same as me," says Kevin." "Season of the Bitch."

"That's enough," Cal says. "We're wearing out this man on his birthday. He doesn't need to listen to your bickering all night long."

"Let's drape you, so I don't get powder and goop all over your nice furniture," Leonard says, as he breaks the seal on a bottle of liquid foundation and vigorously shakes the bottle to mix its contents.

Fifteen minutes later, you can see on the faces of your friends that Leonard's efforts are beginning to bring results.

Marvin is standing at Leonard's shoulder, watching

intently. He picks up a tiny tray of eye shadows and rubs a fingertip in one of the mini-troughs.

"Put that down!" Leonard orders. "Don't stick your finger in someone else's makeup. You'll contaminate it."

"*Lo siento!* Say, this is really good stuff."

"Yes, it is," says Leonard, who answers over his shoulder as he keeps working on you.

You take pity on Marvin. "Marvin," you say, "after tonight, it's all yours. My gift to you."

"Hey, thanks!" says Marvin. "Every time I dress up, I will think of you."

"Lorie," says Leonard. "Don't move, please. I'd rather not put out your eye with this mascara brush."

After Leonard applies your lipstick ("Go like this with your mouth.") and has you blot your lips on a tissue, he removes the sheet he'd tucked around you, carefully folding it to contain escaped face powder and other stray cosmetics. Then he steps aside to face the group and gestures to you presentationally.

"Ta-dah!" he says.

You hold your breath, watching your friends' faces for their response to your enhanced appearance. Like a theater audience sitting in stunned silence at the final curtain of a play that no one had wanted to end, they seem momentarily frozen in place.

Then Tod says: "Lovely. You look lovely." Everyone glances over at Leonard's partner, still lying on his side on the couch, but no longer asleep.

"You look like Carol Channing, but with broader shoulders," says Kevin.

"You look like your sister," says Cal.

"He can be his own sister," says Marvin.

"That doesn't make any sense," says Kevin.

"Sure, it does," says Brandon. "Loren, I think what Marvin means is now we can see you in your true nature."

"Let me see, too!" you demand.

"Of course," says Leonard. "But let's add the turban and stole first, so you can enjoy the full effect."

At this, you smirk. "Had I but known," you say as he adjusts the turban to cover your bald head, "I would have had my hair done today ... had I but hair."

"Oh, shut up about that," says Leonard. "You look fine."

"'I always look well when I'm near death,'" you tell him, quoting a line from the 1936 film version of *Camille*.

Leonard stands you up and turns you to face your living room mirror mounted over the fireplace. You look in wonder at a woman who could be Barbie's sister staring back at you, her red, red lips slightly parted. How thin you've become! And yet, in this guise, it suits you. Great cheekbones. And your eyes look huge and full of soul. Makeup notwithstanding, it's pretty obvious you've been terribly ill. But while, as a man, you were merely pathetic and disposable, as a woman you seem elevated to ... tragic. Like Marguerite in *Camille*. You turn toward your friends to address them as Marguerite:

"'It's not a dream.'"

And Brandon, English professor and film buff that he is, takes up Armand's part: "No, it's not a dream. I am here with you, at last."

"At last."

"You're weak."

"No, no. Strong. It's my heart. It's not used to being happy."

"I'll love you all my life. I know that now. All my life," he says. And you reply: "It's hard to believe that there's such happiness in this world." Then you bow deeply, feeling your strength nearly spent. You receive a smattering of applause.

"Leonard," Cal says, "please sit Our Lady of the Camellias down before she collapses onstage."

And somehow you understand that the evening of your thirty-ninth and fortieth birthdays is drawing to a close. This is the point at which on any normal night with any normal group of friends, you might have expected everyone to describe what they have planned for the upcoming weeks and months — and to ask you what your plans are. But, of course, in a group where nearly everyone is officially terminal, conversations regarding future intentions tend to lack conviction. And you've noticed that, since you formally entered hospice, your friends tactfully avoid asking what you have planned even for tomorrow.

It's early still, only a bit past eight-thirty, and it occurs to you that, with your friends still here and the conversation petering out, you could hold a little sing-along till Ernie from hospice arrives. After all, your *Cabaret* album is still on the stereo turntable. But, when it comes right down to it, you are already exhausted from the evening's festivities. And besides having pretty much no voice left, even croaking along with Liza seems just too ... faggoty.

At nine o'clock, your front door buzzer sounds. It's your caretaker, Ernie, and Cal goes to the door to let him in. Ernie has his own key, but he always forewarns you of his arrival, not wishing to frighten you by showing up unexpectedly.

Ernie knows everyone, and they know him as well, so there's another few minutes of hello-goodbyes among everyone, accompanied by some brief explanation of your makeover and what transpired here tonight.

"Very good," Ernie says, nodding vigorously. "Very good."

The boys leave as a group, with only Cal and Brandon hanging back. Cal — you owe him so much. For bringing the group together, for bringing you into the group, for mobilizing them in support of you.

"I love you," you tell him simply. "Thank you. For everything. Forever."

"I love you back, man. It is my privilege to know you," he replies solemnly.

Brandon waits until it's just you and him in your living room, with Ernie gone to the kitchen for something.

"Words fail me," he says, then leans down and kisses you on your foundation- and powder-coated forehead, right below the line of your gold lamé turban.

"'Oh, don't let's ask for the moon. We have the stars,'" you tell him, quoting from *Now, Voyager*, letting Bette Davis's character in the 1942 film speak for you. Simultaneously, you wonder how you might possibly be able to work tonight's drama into your manuscript, which you had imagined was finished.

Ernie escorts Brandon to the door, then returns to you in the living room. You have pressed a cassette tape into the boombox the boys brought in for you and are advancing the tape nearly to the end of the first side of the 1964 original Broadway cast recording of *Hello, Dolly!* Just one for the road, you think.

"Getting late, buddy," Ernie says. "You must be tired after all your celebrating."

"I am," you agree. "But I just need to try something before I turn in."

Ernie sits down to watch you as you perform for yourself in the mirror, lip-synching to Carol Channing's first-act finale solo, "Before the Parade Passes By." Kevin was right: you *do* look like Carol Channing! How very satisfying!

Near the end of your number, you turn toward Ernie, who is grinning broadly at your pantomime. As the tape clicks to a stop, you bow and he claps.

"There now!" you exclaim, overheated and sweating heavily. "I'm ready for my *bed*, Mr. DeMille!"

But moments later, Ernie is guiding you down the hall to your bathroom instead. "Didn't your mama ever teach you anything?" he asks. "A real lady always removes her makeup at the end of the day."

47.

Barbra at Loose Ends

Since Loren died, you hardly know what to do with yourself.

At first, you had tons to do. You arranged for his cremation and a memorial service, which you held in San Francisco, where most of his friends are. As the executor of his estate, you settled all his bank and credit accounts. His former employer, Raker & Ho, always generous with their golden boy, had sent him home to die with a life insurance policy; you visited the R&H office to let them know he'd passed away. Then you drove "home" to present a beneficiary check and his ashes to his folks. And to spend some time with your own parents, who hadn't seen you since your drive-by en route to Seattle, so long ago it seems like it happened in another lifetime.

Which is when you realized you like Loren's parents a lot better than you like your own. Back when you and Loren were in grammar school and junior high and high school, you never really saw it, but his folks were always a big part of the attraction. His mother especially, with her open mind and easy-going way — the exact opposite of your judgmental, disapproving mother. Meanwhile, his cheerful, friendly dad was nothing like your silent, remote father who seemed to have no idea what to do about a daughter. You wondered how those two men could have been friends all these years.

But, you have noticed, men in general seem to have an ability to set aside their differences in a way women never can. During the time you were caring for Loren, coming in daily to cook and clean for him, you met tons of his male friends, most of them gay and some of them former lovers, a private history they made flamboyantly public. You suppose it helped they mostly believed you were his sister, not a past rival. But the point was, they all shared a real love and brotherly concern for Loren, which took precedence over anything and everything that had occurred in the past. And now these men are your friends as well. You realize Loren gave you an extended family.

After you delivered his ashes to his parents, his mother rode back with you to San Francisco. The two of you worked together to clean out her son's condo. But there was no hurry. He'd left the apartment to you on the conditions that you (1) eventually pay back the money he'd borrowed from his parents to buy the place, and (2) never allow David to set foot in it — a condition you were only too ready to keep. You realize that, in addition to a family, Lorie gave you a home as well. Which was good, because you have come to hate your own place. You can't wait to sell all that modernistic chrome, with its violent red kitchen, and put your equity into Loren's cozy Victorian flat. You'll miss having the ocean right across the street, but you look forward to getting sunshine on most days. You are sick of cold, gray fog.

As Loren's mother carefully emptied his bureau and filled the boxes she'd set on his bed, she reminded you, if Loren had been drafted into the service twenty years ago, instead of going to college, and he'd been killed in Vietnam, you and she might have been working together just as you are now. Except that you'd both had him all these many years, instead of losing him after only a few. She had a point, but you weren't quite ready to accept it or use it to assuage your grief. Or your guilt and shame. You still have regrets. You realize Loren was right: you *are* the goat, stubborn to the last, while he was the dog, forgiving everyone. Everyone except himself.

"Oh my, look at this," his mother said as she pulled one sweater out of the pile she was working on and held it up for you to see. It was his letterman sweater from your high school days. She pressed her face into the bright red and gold yarn and inhaled. "Go, Miners. I'm keeping this one," she said. "It still smells like him."

You never imagined your very best time with the love of your life would be his final few months, when he was too ill and too weak to do much more than allow you to feed him by hand like a baby bird. Actually, with his bald head, prominent eyes, and wide-open mouth, he looked a lot like a baby bird toward the end. Or a little old man. And you thought then: this is how it might have been, decades from now, if things had worked out like they were supposed to. Or like you'd once fantasized they were supposed to.

Because you no longer believe in "supposed to." Now you know things work out however they work out. Once upon a time, you believed Loren could change himself, if only he had wanted it badly enough. Now you are convinced he was born the way he was and he would only have been fooling himself to pretend to be any other way. Despite the grief and disappointment you still sometimes feel, you came to admire his determination to insist on living as his own true self.

His mother pulls open another drawer and finds it full of brand-new cosmetics, barely touched. She rolls her eyes and says, "I won't even ask. Unless you want any of this stuff, I'm dumping it."

You glance at the packages. "No, thanks, Elaine. I'm a Summer; Lorie was always the Spring." When she looks at you, puzzled, you explain: "Seasonal color analysis. So you can pick the right clothes and makeup for your seasonal type. Lorie was a Warm Spring. I'm a Cool Summer."

Mother Elaine receives this explanation with a nod. "I see I still have a lot to learn," she says.

"Elaine?"

"What?"

"Don't toss that makeup. I just remembered who it's supposed to go to."

"Barbra?"

"What?"

She has turned to face you. "You knew about him for a long time, didn't you?"

It is your turn to nod.

"Since moving down here to San Francisco?"

"Before that."

"Since college?" When you nod again, she concludes, "That must have been hard on you. You two were always so close growing up, we felt sure you'd end up together."

"We sort of did," you say and shrug.

"No, dear. You know what I mean. But I guess it wasn't in the cards, was it? At least, no other woman got him, eh?" You both smile at this.

Then she goes on. "You know, dear, until a few months ago, his father and I had no idea. We simply didn't understand he was ... that way."

You shrug sympathetically. "How could you possibly know?"

"The thing is, I didn't learn there was such a thing as homosexuality until maybe ten years ago. Even then, I guess I imagined homosexuals were some sort of mythical creature. Like unicorns and centaurs." You both laugh at this. "It wasn't until that one character on the TV show *SOAP* —."

"Jodie Dallas? The Billy Crystal character?"

"That's it. Anyway, it wasn't till him that I could even conceive of how it might be that someone could be ... gay. I guess we're kinda behind the times in the boonies. And the fact that my own son was still unmarried after all these years, well — his father and I just thought he was real picky about who he wanted to settle down with. We should have known: if *you* weren't good enough for him, then no woman could be."

You realize you are blushing at the compliment. But she isn't done yet. "I like it that he left you this apartment — it feels like we still have a bit of him around. Even though I lost a son, perhaps I still have a daughter?"

She reaches out and embraces you the way your own mother never does, which at once pleases you and makes you profoundly uncomfortable. But you allow her to hold you till she is finished. When she releases you, she goes immediately to the closet and opens the door to reveal multiple tie racks affixed to the back of the door. A gorgeous rainbow garden of ties, perhaps a couple hundred, hangs there.

"Any thoughts on what to do about these? Goodwill?" she asks.

"You still sew?"

"Of course."

"Well, maybe you could take the collection home with you and work them into a memorial panel for Loren to go into that new AIDS quilt — the NAMES Project? Some of his ties are so wide, you might not even need to piece together all that many."

"I like that idea. You get the specs. I'll handle the production."

While Mother Elaine is visiting the bathroom, you quietly open the underwear drawer, extract his manuscript in its stationery box, and slip the box into your tote bag. His mother doesn't need to see its contents.

>~~\\\//~~<

A month after Loren died, you picked up at work right where you'd left off. You were lucky: despite the cutthroat nature of this business of distributing fine wines and spirits, your fellow reps, being aware of why you'd taken time off, had taken pity on you and split your distribution to keep you going.

Loren had been worried that spending so much time with him would damage your career. But that was something of a joke. Though you made great money and had definite enthusiasm for your product, what you did wasn't any sort of profession or calling or dream you had for your future self — it was just a job, an obnoxious job with great incentives. In passing, you wondered whether part of the appeal you'd held for David at the start had been the endless stream of "office supplies" you brought home.

And, now, you *are* "home." Or, at least, you are in the place you picked out, bought, and paid for. And you are alone. Right now, there is no sign of David, the man you picked out and *thought* you'd bought and paid for. Once again, though you've been out all day and most of the evening, nothing in the house has been disturbed. Which means it is impossible David has been here — David the Human Tornado.

You wander from room to room, considering what is yours and what is his. Then it hits you: except for the garbage and disorder he typically leaves around, he's just never had much presence in this place. Everything here is yours, except for his clothing — which, technically, is also yours because you picked out, bought, and paid for that as well. And, for the moment, everything here is exactly where you'd want it to be, exactly where you thought it should go. A thought occurs to you: can it be you never made space in your life for him? You thought you had, but maybe you didn't. Why did he never claim space for himself? Why did he never claim *you* for himself?

You are tired of his living here, yet never being here. You are tired of trying to figure out your relationship. Only a couple years ago, you thought it was all so simple: a man is unhappily married to the wrong woman; he meets and falls in love with the right woman; he comes to live with Ms. Right, and they live happily ever after — right? Wrong. He never even married you. Even that little bitch he was with before — at least, he *married* her.

And now you have to admit: if he *had* proposed marriage to you, you might not have accepted. In fact, you most likely would have turned him down. After all, marriage would have given him immediate ready access to half your assets. Clearly, not a wise idea. No, you'll never trust any man ever to have so much power over you as that.

When Loren died and you took that month's leave, you cut back on David's allowance, supposing the message would be clear: no more free lunch, buddy. Yet he persisted. Seems he didn't get the memo. You wish he would simply move out and take away what little of him still remains in this place.

Standing in your blood-red kitchen, idly wiping down an already sterile countertop, you feel a fever come over you, followed by a chill that shakes you head to foot. You go into the bedroom, slip out of your shoes, and, otherwise fully dressed, you crawl into bed. Within minutes, while you are wrapped in blankets against the chill, another fever strikes you. Followed by another chill. You think how exhausted you have been of late. Every bit of you feels fatigued and ancient. At night, you cannot sleep. When you do fall asleep at last, you awake only a few hours later, heart racing, bedclothes soaked with sweat.

You had supposed your symptoms were simply a letdown after months of care-taking, followed by months of grief and carrying out the onerous responsibilities of estate executor. But now, oh my god, you remember everything Loren experienced during his long, slow, undignified demise. And you wonder: is it possible, even remotely possible that you, too, have AIDS?

You and Loren were ever so careful with his syringes and bedpans and all that other medical paraphernalia. His doctor assured you that you can't get AIDS through nonsexual contact. But what do doctors know? When that first case turned up at

S.F. General, they put the patient in quarantine in an oxygen tent and were afraid to enter his room, fearing the contagion was airborne. No, they don't know everything.

The next day you call your physician and tell him you want to be tested for AIDS. When you go in and he verifies your request, he looks surprised. "Women don't get AIDS," he says. Nevertheless, you tell him flatly, you *will* be tested here — or else you will be tested at the Free Clinic. Either way.

He asks you what makes you think you have AIDS. You tell him about the fevers and chills, the heart palpitations and night sweats, the terrible fatigue and sense of weakness that never go away. He shrugs with an ill-disguised lack of concern.

"When did you have your last period?" he asks.

"I don't know," you respond. It's not something you've been tracking of late. "Three months ago? Four? It's been a while. But I've never been very regular."

"Well, you're probably either pregnant or having an early menopause."

"Menopause?" you echo as a wave of shock washes over you. "But I'm not even forty." You already know for certain you can't be pregnant.

"It's nothing, you'll see," he says. "We'll give you some pills and you won't know the difference." Then he keeps on talking, and you watch as he tears a couple of sheets off his prescription pad and hands them to you. You've missed the whole thing, all his instructions.

"What?" you say blankly.

He looks at you with professional contempt.

"I *said*: go right downstairs to Lab C in Basement A and get your blood drawn, then walk over to Building 62, take the second bank of elevators to the third-floor annex, and leave a urine sample at Lab F. Weren't you listening?"

You apologize for not understanding, as you always do when men in positions of authority fail to make themselves clear. Then you go round to the various laboratories in the medical center, depositing appropriate body fluids at the assigned drop points.

The following week, a nurse practitioner calls you with the results: you do *not* have AIDS, but you *are* in menopause. "Pretty far along," the nurse emphasizes. "So come in and get your pills, and we'll take care of all those unpleasant symptoms of your illness."

Until then, you had not been aware that menopause was considered an illness or even a medical condition that required treatment. On the other hand, you didn't know you could become a crone at the age of thirty-eight. So much for the children it is now confirmed you will never have. Turns out David ruined your last chance to have a regular life.

The next day finds you down with a sick headache that woke you in the middle of the night. You didn't even realize you were having a migraine until you found yourself on your knees in the bathroom, holding onto the toilet and vigorously emptying the contents of your stomach into it. You vomited till nothing was left inside you. Then you vomited some more. Apparently, your stomach was slow to realize its job was done.

Afterwards, you lay down upon the bathmat and realized, with dismay, you had another killer headache coming on. Third one this year. You took a handful of Advils, already knowing they would do no good, then staggered down the hallway, crawled back into bed, and stuffed your head between your pillows to kill any light or sound that might possibly reach you.

Twelve or so hours later, it still feels as if you'd been harpooned in the head. You've read it is impossible to remember pain, but that's a load of crap because, even though your migraine has mostly dissipated, you can still definitely feel where it was. You push aside the pillows, uncovering your head. You regard the quality of light playing upon the ceiling of your bedroom, where you have spent so much time alone the past few years. As you look toward the window, you are unsure whether the day is beginning or ending. Time seems to have quietly drawn to a standstill.

Sometime later, the doorbell rings: FedEx delivering a package to you. Signing for the delivery, you learn it is already nearly five o'clock. You think David came home sometime during the night, but you're not certain — maybe you dreamed it or hallucinated it — and anyway, at this point he's nowhere to be seen. You open the package, one of those heavy brown paper envelopes padded with nasty gray dust balls, and extract a videotape. You turn it over. No label, but a ragged page torn from a spiral notebook is taped to the top. You peel off the note and read:

"You bitch, he's mine now. If this doesn't kill you, I will. I know where you live."

Oh god, you think, oh god. But the death threat acts like a shot of B-12 and a call to action. You walk straight to the VHS player, press on the power, turn on your TV, feed the videotape into the slot, give it a shove. As the tape begins to play, a grainy moving image appears of a naked woman sitting on the edge of an unmade bed. Then a naked man steps into the frame, grasps her shoulders, and pushes her onto her back. She sticks out her tongue and gives him a lascivious come-on. He throws himself on top of her, grabs her wrists, pins her down. Her nipples dance as he rides her. Rides her hard. All this takes place in silence, like homemade porn from the 1920s, before talkies.

You don't need to watch any more of this — you already know who the man is. If you hadn't recognized his ass and general contours, as grainy and scarred as the tape is, you certainly know that sado-move with the pinned wrists. Oh god. So, you don't need to watch any more, yet you do, because, like any terrible, hideous accident you might suddenly find yourself driving past on the freeway, you cannot take your eyes away.

The tape is not long, not more than ten minutes. The more riveting part comes nearly at the end, after the man leaves the frame and the woman, naked, gets up to switch off the camera. As she fumbles for the off-switch, she jostles the camera, so it briefly pans another part of the room. When, for a moment, the image settles on a familiar dressing table with an oval-shaped mirror sporting angel's wings and, on the wall next to it, a large, framed photo of ... your parents, you suddenly recognize the location as ... your own bedroom.

Then the tape runs out, the machine is thrown into reverse and begins speedily rewinding. You roll onto your back on the sofa and shut your eyes, listening as the rewind finishes, pauses, then begins to play again.

Lying there with your eyes closed, you realize every dog in the neighborhood is barking. You can hear them up and down the block, and across the street as well. For several minutes, they keep it up, barking and barking. Then you hear a sound that could be a freight train barreling toward you at top speed, heavy boxcars roaring on the track, except you are next to the ocean with no trains anywhere around for miles.

Suddenly, your building is shuddering, creaking, and swaying as if it were made of cardboard and someone had grabbed and was yanking two opposite, diagonal corners. The power goes out; the tape player grinds to a stop. Earthquake — it's an earthquake you're having. A pretty big one.

You remember there are things you are supposed to do in this moment to save yourself: get under something, a table maybe, or into the door frame. You are supposed to want to protect yourself, to save yourself, to not die. But instead you go on lying there, thinking how this must be the way the ants living in your little kids' ant farm felt whenever you shook their home to ruins and how amazing it is you can remain so calm, watching your world collapsing around you, because, really, you just don't care, anymore.

48.

Juli's Father Comes Undone

It's after Labor Day before you start to notice something is wrong with your father. You come home from work, from whatever front desk, padded cubicle, or dense-storage file room the temp agency sent you to that day, and you find him sitting right there in the living room, like always, watching the six o'clock news, like always. But it takes him forever to acknowledge you. He just keeps staring at the TV and feeling his right hand and arm below the elbow with his left hand.

"Something the matter with your arm, Dad?"

"Don't know. Guess not."

"Then how come you're rubbing it like that?"

"Been kinda numb lately."

"Hurt?"

"No. Just numb. Swollen, too."

You look and see this is true. His fingers and the back of his hand are puffy and pale. "How long has this been going on?" you ask.

"Month. Six weeks, maybe."

It gives you chills to realize you have been here for longer than that, but you hadn't noticed anything wrong.

"How'd you first notice it?"

"Just woke up this way. Thought I'd slept funny on it."

"And what does your doctor say?"

"Don't know. Haven't gone."

This is not the response you expect from your life-long hypochondriac of a father. He's always made an avocation of going to see the doctor. He's accumulated a modest, but reliable collection of dysfunctions — incipient glaucoma, intermittent tachycardia, pre-hypertension, mild arthritis, a hernia, and a handful of rectal polyps. He's always seemed to enjoy discussing his ailments in detail. Before you moved in, many of your phone conversations began like this:

"Hi, Dad. How you doing?"

"Oh, not so good."

"No? Sorry to hear it. What's the matter?"

"Haven't been feeling too well lately."

"How so?"

That question — "How so?" — has generally been all the invitation he has ever needed to begin reciting his litany of illnesses. Over the years, you've grown familiar with the multiple malfunctionings of your father's body. He has so many pills in his house, he's arranged them all on a lazy Susan on the kitchen table, a pharmaceutical carousel. It takes him half an hour to dose himself each morning. Now the revelation that he hasn't called the doctor about his hand and arm — or even complained to you — arouses your suspicions: he must have finally come up against something so serious it has frightened even him into silence.

"So, your arm's numb and swollen. Anything else?"

"Keep forgetting things."

"Like what?"

"My military I.D. number, my Social Security number... ."

"Dad, you haven't needed your military I.D. number in over forty years, and you can look up your Social Security number any time. What else?"

"My leg's bothering me. Those damned stairs in back... ."

"Which leg?"

"The right one."

Oh god, you think, same side as his numb arm — he must have had a stroke. He doesn't know it, but he had a stroke.

"Dad, you have to go see the doctor. What if you had a stroke or something?"

Oh god, you think, but *when* could he have had a stroke? You've been here for weeks. Shouldn't you have noticed a thing like that?

So, after your conversation, you put a lot of energy into trying to get your father to go see his doctor. But he is stubborn. One morning, he calls your temp agency with a message for you that says, okay, he'll go to the doctor. You think he probably got tired of your nagging at him. By the time you rush home, however, you find him still in his pajamas, the same ones, you suddenly realize, he's been wearing for weeks. He tells you he's changed his mind, he wants to hold off awhile longer. You are furious.

"Don't do this to me!" you yell at him. "Dad, please! Please go see the doctor. You've got the appointment. Your car's in the driveway. I'm right here. All you have to do is get in, and I'll take you."

He gets up from his usual place in the living room and walks out like you aren't there. That's your dad. If he doesn't want to listen to something you have to say, he simply pretends he doesn't hear it. You follow him, shouting, pleading. He shuffles off, trailing his bathrobe ties. You corner him in the kitchen. Trapped between the sink and the stove, he turns at last to confront you.

"No," he says, "I won't go. That's final."

"But, Dad, *please*. What if you have another stroke? How will I take care of you?"

"If I don't get better soon, I'll go get a bottle of booze, finish off all these pills. God knows, I've got enough medication in this house to kill half a dozen people. I'd like to die. That's all I really want — just to die and get it over with."

This is not the first time you've heard your father say such a thing. He's been saying it for years and years. But now, under the circumstances, you have to take him seriously. You call his doctor for advice.

"It certainly sounds like a stroke," the doctor agrees. "And depression is very common in such cases. It is depressing, after all, to wake up one morning and find your parts not working properly. However, a patient has the right to refuse treatment. If your father doesn't want to come in and be seen, there's nothing we can do, no matter how ill-advised we may think he is. All you can do is use persuasion."

As the weeks go by, however, you watch your father deteriorate. He gets so he can't write, not even to sign his name to a check to pay his utility bill. Never much of a talker to begin with, beyond his endless litany of illnesses, he speaks less and less. And when he does, you have a hard time understanding him. You watch as he drags himself from room to room, wandering ghostlike. He's already taken a couple of bad falls while you were at work, and his right side from his waist to his shoulder is black and blue. He certainly can't drive anymore. You keep plying him with persuasion.

"Dad, this is getting worse. Please go see the doctor."

He says nothing.

"Well, at least, Dad, why don't you move into Grandpa's old bedroom upstairs? I don't want you going up and down those back stairs."

The house has two perfectly good bedrooms upstairs, where your grandparents once slept — separately, like the good Victorians they were. But dad still insists on staying in his basement room, the one he came back to after he got out of the Army, then again, after your mother left him. You want an answer. You wait. He doesn't say a word.

"Dad?"

He says nothing.

"Dad, I'm talking about your moving upstairs. Are you listening to me?"

"No."

"Well, if you won't go see the doctor and you won't move upstairs, then at least use your cane so you won't fall head first down those goddam stairs, and I come home after work to find you lying at the bottom with a broken neck!"

To think it has come to this: now you can hardly talk to your father for any length of time without losing your temper completely. Every time you leave the house, you want to get in his car and drive and drive till there's no more road left. You go into your grandmother's bedroom, now your bedroom, and slam the door behind you. A nervous tick has started up in your left eye, twitching uncontrollably every few seconds. You lie down on your grandmother's bed, now your bed, and your bones feel watery. You realize, with everything that's gone on in your life these past couple years, you are soul-tired.

You listen to your father foot-dragging his way through the kitchen, then the step-by-step muffled thuds as he descends that perilous back stairway. You think about how long all this has been coming on.

Before your father retired, he spent his days driving his paneled truck around the university campus all week. On Friday nights, he'd go have a beer with the guys. But those relationships must have been a limited thing, because they didn't survive his retirement. What did survive were his routines. Your father was regular to a fault: always shined his shoes on Sunday, always rolled his socks military style, always hung the coffee cups on their hooks all facing the same direction. Even in retirement, he rose at the same hour every morning, weekday or weekend, and, just as a man in prison might do, he marked off each day on his kitchen wall calendar with a big X, noting if there'd been rain the night before. Dad had no particular interests insofar as you could tell, but the regularity of his habits gave him the appearance of momentum.

By the time your grandmother died and left him the house, he'd been living in it for a couple of decades. Looking back, you realize he'd been slowing down and narrowing his frame of reference for years, day by day, until at last he'd come to an uneasy rest in front of his TV set, with a diet soft drink in one hand and a low-tar cigarette in the other. He still did his wash on Monday, his grocery shopping on Tuesday, his housework on Wednesday, his yardwork on Thursday. However, through years of practice, he'd gotten the whole routine down pat, which left him plenty of time for sitting in the living room with the drapes drawn and the blue-white fluorescence of the TV screen making his bald head look like it glowed in the dark.

You realize: even though your father's malady has been quietly developing for many weeks, only recently has it reached a point beyond anything you can bear to shoulder alone. You need perspective. You need to talk to someone, someone who knows you well, but likes you anyway. You need a friend.

You tiptoe into the dining room, where your Dad's phone sits on his desk in the corner, and you call Bill. Even though it's been a couple months, and you haven't talked to him since that last day at Sasha's. At the time, you felt justified in sending him away to his new job for not being a good enough friend. Now you know, at this juncture in your life, he is the only friend in your world who will do. Besides, you miss him.

49.

Bill Forgives Juli

When Juli sent you away with your tail tucked between your hind legs, you were confused. How could a relationship that had seemed so promising end just like that? Were you really such an asshole? Was *she* really such an asshole? You resent her characterization of you. How can she *not* understand you were David's friend all those years? Even before you met her. You didn't do anything wrong. It's not your responsibility to fink on your friend to his wife. It already sucked hard enough that you were supposed to be his friend, yet you considered him a turd.

This is what you get for getting involved with someone who's crazier than you are.

Besides, you remind yourself, before he and Juli split up, you *had* tried to talk to David about his behavior. On several occasions, you tried to talk some sense into him. And this was ages before you had any kind of vested interest in the situation. Why didn't you tell her about *that*? You didn't, because you forgot, taken aback by her outpouring of venom.

Also, maybe, you still felt guilty about making a move on your friend's wife. Even though it was clear his matrimonial ship had sunk. At first, you were delighted to realize the two of them would never, ever get back together. But then shame set in — the discomfort that comes from knowing you stand to benefit from another man's misfortune. Even if he himself didn't see it as misfortune.

Which is why you went to the trouble of visiting David in his fancy new digs, with his wealthy new mistress — to tell him you were, um, seeing his wife. Or, rather, his ex-wife. And you were glad, afterwards, you did this, because seeing your old friend so happy about the split seemed to free you from the burden of guilt you'd been packing around. He actually imagined he was better off now!

But you also saw, clearly for the first time, he wasn't really your friend at all. Because he lied to you. And he looked down on you. Friendship, you remind yourself, is a relationship between equals, requiring mutual respect. Now you understand this man you've known since high school, a parasite and a pervert, considers himself so much better than you. You hadn't realized it, but you weren't even playing in the same league.

So, Juli's charges against you feel unfair. You're not the bad guy here. You *are* on her side; you *are* her friend. Hurt and angry, you think: how dare she judge you for your past actions using the current standards of your present friendship? Maybe you're better off without her, too!

Except that ... without her, you have ... nothing — no lover, no wife-to-be, no long-time friend, no future hopes, no nothing. And, in the wake of your present misunderstanding, this stupid miscommunication, you feel more alone than ever. You remember the happy, contented six months before your falling-out, and deep grief washes over you for what you *almost* had. But lost.

These are the night-thoughts that come to you during your eight weeks of working your new job, your new profession, on an oil exploration field crew. You play and replay images of your now-past relationship, over and over in your head. You sit outside your tent on the Great Plains. You watch stars swirling overhead, while still keeping an eye out for wandering cows that could trip on and break the lines of your company's magnetometer.

Just the awesome sight of these stars — more than you've ever seen in your entire life up to that point — comforts you. Their vast cosmic patterns seem to put all your tiny troubles in perspective. There they are, minding their own business, unaware of you and the rest of humankind, so far away. They have other, more important priorities. And it occurs to you: so do you. Or perhaps you should. With the example of the galaxy above you, you manage to set aside your thoughts about Juli for a while and ponder the Meaning of Existence.

What surprise it is, then, to come home after your field summer and find a phone message scrawled, while you were gone, by one of your semiliterate, semiconscious roommates, on the back of an advertisement for Chinese take-out: "Judy called. Says she *needs a friend*! Go get her, Mr. Natural!"

Notwithstanding the messed-up name, the note includes a phone number with an Oakland prefix. Which you suppose must be her father's number. Your hand holding the note begins to shake. You turn over the flyer to check the expiration date on the takeout special and get an idea of when Juli might have called you. Relief floods over you when you see the coupon is still good for another week.

But, whoa! you think: what's *this* all about? That she would try to reach you, saying she "needs a friend" — maybe she's decided you *are* a friend, after all. Which is good. But when you recall the pain she caused you, her grossly unfair accusations, you consider not returning her call.

Except, really, you *are* her friend, even if she no longer wants you as a lover. And friends forgive friends their trespasses. You sense she must have been pressed to the limit to have reached out to you like this, after sending you away without so much as a forwarding address or phone number. Besides, what the stars over the Great Plains taught you is: you are nothing if you are alone without your relationships.

So, you call. And she answers. And as soon as she hears your voice on the phone, she starts blubbering. Then, right away, you know you are back in her life. On what basis, you don't know yet. But, definitely, you're back.

Something to do with her father. You offer to come over, wherever "over" is. She sounds frightened, says no, she'll come to you. She needs to talk about what's going on with her father, but she can't do it right there, right in his house. You remind her of the limitations of public transportation in the San Francisco Bay Area, even during the day. She says, no big deal, she can borrow her father's car.

Okay then, you tell her, come on over. She knows where you live. She also knows you have four or five roommates who may be listening in at any point, so forget about privacy. She says it doesn't matter, she'll come. Then, together, the two of you can go someplace else and talk.

An hour later and just as the late-afternoon sun is bouncing Maxfield Parrish pink-and-gold flecks off the windows of your neighborhood, she stands at your front door, looking tired and hollow-eyed. You notice her left eyelid twitching every few seconds. You grab your jean jacket from its hook by the door as you step out onto the tiny porch, take her hand, and walk her down to the driveway where your brand-new car is parked, a used Chevy that's a lot flashier than the stripped-down VWs you usually drive.

But she shakes her head: I'm in a yellow zone. At the end of the block, in front of the corner panadería, with its window full of big pink cookies, sponge cake, and loaves of bread shaped like alligators, she hands you the keys to her father's car, a giant Buick of the kind favored by the low-riders of this section of the City. You make a mental note to be careful where you park it when you return — and then you head for Ocean Beach. You recall there's something comforting about the rhythmic beat of the surf, especially at sunset.

Parked off the Great Highway, below the Cliff House and the ruins of the old Sutro Baths, she spills her guts in the front seat of her father's car. Moving to his place from that crazy clown's flat in the Haight was supposed to have been a better situation, but it isn't turning out that way. Her father is sick. Had a stroke, she thinks. Won't go see his doctor. Seems to be getting worse. And worse.

You don't know much about medicine, but after years of working in Social Services, something about this situation doesn't jibe. People who have strokes are supposed to get better, not worse. They have their stroke, which wrecks them for a while, and then gradually they get better, though usually not entirely better. You propose to drive her home and come in to see him yourself. You suggest maybe you can convince him to get himself checked out. But she doesn't want that. Today ... tonight she only wants a sympathetic ear and a few hours of escape.

It's dark by the time you leave the beach and drive back downtown so you can take her to a nostalgic dinner at Clown Alley. Over greaseball burgers and beneath the gaze of the lurid wall-clowns, the two of you laugh together like it was old times before your falling out. Then you drive her home to your flat in the Mission, parking in a well-lit public lot a couple blocks away. You know it'll cost you, but you don't care. It's a small price to pay to get your friend back. You ask her to spend the night. She says yes, but first she needs to call her dad, so he won't worry about her.

After she makes her call, she joins you in your squalid bedroom that's not even as well-appointed as some of the third-rate motels you've lately stayed in. You've spent all evening comforting her. Now, with a sigh, she holds you, comforts you. And you are only too willing receive the solace she offers.

50.
Juli Gets Her Bearings

For weeks now, the center of your life has been your father's ever-deepening incapacity, a black hole into which all light is drawn and extinguished. You awake each weekday morning, throw on a bathrobe, and descend the treacherous flight of stairs into the basement room where your father sleeps. Down here in the basement, it is dark, damp, and smells of mold. You knock on his door. Then you call to him to make sure he is still alive.

"Dad! Dad! It's morning. Are you okay?"

You wait until you hear a groan and a mumbled, "Okay." Then you tell him you are coming in.

His actual bedroom is not so bad, if you can appreciate its spare, army barracks aesthetic: bare floor, narrow single-person mattress on an iron frame, ancient foot locker. But at least the inside of this room is clean and drier than the rest of the basement. And he has his own half-bath with a toilet and sink, which he has thus far been able to manage on his own. Hanging on the wall across from his bed is an old, broken, pendulum clock. Now, as always, you cannot help yourself from glancing at it to check the time, even though you *know* it stopped working years ago and was set by your father to 7:22 a.m. — the exact time Abraham Lincoln died on April 15, 1865, after having been shot the night before by the actor John Wilkes Booth in Ford's Theater in Washington, D.C. You wonder if this is why April 15 was chosen as the day tax returns are due, an annual national day of mourning and tribute.

At dawn, you bring him coffee and toast. Then, if you have a temp job that day, you pull yourself together, make sure his water carafe is filled, and leave for the City, walking along Lake Merritt to the BART station at 19th and Broadway. It is the same route you used to walk with your mother, except that was years before mass rapid transit. Back then, she would walk you to the big main library downtown, built around the same time you were born, as if it had been made just for you. There you learned to read, even before you started school.

In the evening, you come home and make dinner for yourself and your father. As ill and worn-down as he is, he retains the old-fashioned, Midwestern manners his parents insisted upon, and so he appears at the dining room table fully dressed. You marvel at this and the fact that, though he can barely walk, he still manages to pull himself up the basement stairs, one step at a time, pausing to rest every third stair. You notice his shirt is buttoned askew and his socks are two different colors. You smile and set his dinner before him.

A meal nowadays is typically a quiet affair. You tell him about your day. He nods and grins. You ask him about his day. He shrugs and shakes his head. You notice he isn't smoking.

After more than half a century of inhaling Camels, first non-filtered and later filtered, he isn't smoking. Not at all. You can't recall the last time you heard the characteristic sound of a Zippo lighter clicked open, then snapped shut. The teasing smell of lighter fluid. Now you are the only one in this house contributing to the poisonous atmosphere. You offer him one of your Marlboro Golds. He shakes his head and grins. You wonder what's going on inside him to make him reject this habit of a lifetime.

After dinner, you help him down the back stairs, clear the table, wash the dishes. Then, Sunday through Thursday nights, you go to bed in your grandmother's bedroom, the nice one at the back of the house. Right above where your father sleeps on his narrow cot. On Friday and Saturday nights, you hang the damp dish towel on the stove handle, get in your father's car, which he ceased driving months ago, and go to bed at Bill's place in the City.

Before you took a chance and called Bill, you were letting yourself be consumed entirely by your father's health crisis — every day a new challenge to try to get him to visit his doctor, to try to get him to do something about himself. You felt it was your responsibility to make him do what he clearly had no wish to do. Your focus was so tight that your world had shrunk down to mainly following your poor broken father around his house, berating him.

But Bill said the same thing, more or less, that your father's doctor told you weeks earlier: you can do only so much. And Bill, being a former social worker, added that you need to take care of yourself as well. He said your satisfaction and happiness count, too. In the month that you and Bill have been back together as a couple, it feels like your life has begun to settle and your world has ceased to shrink.

You had forgotten what a good friend Bill is. Not the romance of the ages. Not the all-consuming, swept-away, sand-in-your-panties love affair you used to think you wanted. But an honest, reliable partnership, the idea of which would have held little interest for you in your younger days. He is strangely free of any exalted dreams of personal achievement and glory. Which, for the first time ever, makes you the interesting (i.e., screwed-up) one in the relationship. Too bad you have "no special talent" to exercise.

But Bill takes issue with this early assessment. "Complete and total crap!" he exclaims, after you once described how your creative writing instructor dismissed you. "I know you wrote all of David's resumés and bios and promotional stuff, because he certainly never could have done any of that on his own. And you managed to get gigs for that weird clown you were living with — I'm sure that took some creative writing. You just never write for yourself. Is that why you went into editing? Someone else puts all the words together, but they're not quite right, so you come along and fix them?"

"Something like that," you acknowledge.

And, you suppose, he does have a point. Not that wordsmithing for others gives you anything to write about. Besides, with your father in the shape he's in, you are so anxious and exhausted that sitting down to put words on paper is the last thing in the world you feel like doing.

"Let's go visit the stars next weekend," Bill suggests. And when you give him the universal "Uh?" look, cocking your head like Nipper the RCA dog, he clarifies: "Let's go camping."

You point out, with your father an invalid in his house, you barely feel comfortable being gone for the night here in the City, where you are reachable by phone and only half an hour's drive away — much less out in the middle of nowhere, where you would be several hours away and entirely unreachable.

"It's just one night we'll be gone. Maybe you can get that neighbor of your dad's to come over, give him dinner in the evening, then check on him in the morning."

"Mrs. Mitkin, you mean? Maybe," you agree, silently dreading the thought of Mrs. M on her own inside your home.

But you call her anyway and ask her to come over, because you really want to run away with Bill, even if it's only for one night, and you don't know how else to go about it.

Over years of visiting your father, you've seen plenty of Mrs. Mitkin, because she was perpetually running out of sugar or eggs or flour or coffee, and your father, with his Midwestern manners, would always invite her in while he went to the kitchen to find whatever it was she claimed she needed. From the start, she made you nervous.

Now here she sits in your grandmother's big, overstuffed chair with the doilies pinned to its upholstered arms, rocking vigorously and chattering on and on about the folks across the street, that couple in the green house there, and how many times each day they change their clothes ... about the woman two doors down on the other side of her, those three bratty kids of hers, each of them by a different father, none of which ever married her, shameful ... about the young couple who live on the other side of her, how they let their dog wander over the neighborhood, shitting on everyone's front yard but their own. You stare at her with wonder that anyone could talk on as steadily as Mrs. Mitkin can, with scarcely a pause for breath.

Once again, you think, here's trouble. Mrs. M seems to know everything about everyone, and you dread to speculate what she tells your father's neighbors about him. About you. She's a tiny woman, barely five feet tall, but like most condensed goods, she has a strong flavor. You remember your father telling you she was a widow. You never met the poor man while he was alive, but you figure she must have power-mouthed him to death.

She's just lonely, your father suggested. That was years before you came to live here, and you had politely agreed. But now that this is your home as well, you always peek through the blinds of the living room window before going out the front door, trying to avoid leaving the house if she is on the street, knowing any chance encounter will surely cost you at least half an hour. No matter how hard you try to break into her monologue to excuse yourself, she never shuts up long enough for you to get a word in sideways. With Mrs. Mitkin, rudeness is your only means of escape. You use it now.

"Mrs. Mitkin! Please listen to me!" you shout at her, startling her into silence. "I'm worried about my dad. I think he had a stroke, but he won't see his doctor. I need to go out of town overnight next weekend, and I want to ask a favor of you: could I give you a key to the house and ask you to give him dinner that evening, then check on him the next morning? I'll be home by late afternoon. Would that be alright with you?"

You are not surprised when, at your mention of giving her a house key, she lights up like the annual Christmas tree on the White House lawn. "You betcha!" she agrees eagerly. "What are neighbors for?"

So it was settled. A stunned look, possibly of alarm, passes over your father's face when you tell him Mrs. Mitkin will give him dinner next Saturday night and check on him Sunday morning. But when you tell him the reason — that you are going camping — he grins and reaches out with his good arm to pat your hand.

You had forgotten: your father loved to go camping. He hasn't been anywhere in years. Certainly not since he retired to look after your grandmother. Maybe not since before your mother walked out on him. But you remember how it was when you were little and he got his annual two weeks of vacation: he would tie his heavy canvas, army surplus tent onto the roof of his car and hang a wet canvas water cooler on its front grill. Then, with your mother on the passenger side of the wide front seat and you in the back seat, squeezed between the ice chest and the thick sleeping bags in smelly canvas bags, he would drive for hours on the highway till he could turn off onto a dusty gravel two-lane road that ended at a wide, shimmering lake in Northern California.

Your mother dreaded these trips, probably because she was left in charge of the backwoods cooking, cleaning, and childcare. Never a strong planner or organizer, her approach to packing consisted of bringing everything she owned, in case it might be needed. With no museums to visit, no theaters to attend, and no department stores to shop, your mother had little entertainment between meals aside from sitting in a camp chair, reading biographical novels by Irving Stone and slapping mosquitos.

The summer of your fourth year was your Golden Age — two weeks spent wading in the warm shallows of an alpine lake, smooth pebbles underfoot, searching for tadpoles and frogs. You still have a tiny black-and-white photo of yourself from that trip in which you are standing on a big flat rock next to the lake, a child-size fishing pole in one hand and a toy pail in the other. On your face is a confident, satisfied, beatific look. And though the photo with its deckled edges is black and white, you can see that your eyes must be the same color as the clear sky above. Camping holds good memories for you.

You feel guilty, but resolved. Guilty because you can see there will be no more camping trips for your father. Resolved because you really want to do this. It takes your father to absolve your guilt.

The Thursday before the weekend you and Bill intend to camp, you come home to a surprise: a brand-new camp light is sitting on the dining room table. You switch it on — battery-powered. With two fluorescent tubes to provide strong illumination in an upright position and one end to serve as a flashlight end. Sweet.

Your father left the consumer half of the warranty card tucked under a corner of the lamp. When you pick it up to examine it, the date from early this year and your father's legible handwriting on the card tell you he purchased the lamp six months ago. Before he got sick. Your father, who hadn't been camping in decades, must have planned, or at least hoped, to go again someday. With you, perhaps. A wave of pity sweeps over you, drawing hot tears.

But the warranty card makes you smile. Your dad was always the only person you ever knew to actually fill out and send in those product warranty cards. He even did this with products he gave as gifts. And if the gift ran on batteries, he installed those as well. But he wouldn't have put batteries into this lamp six months ago, because batteries can leak. So the warranty card is six months old, but the batteries must be new. You wonder how the hell he managed to insert the batteries himself, with just his one good arm and hand.

His message to you is clear: take this lamp and enjoy it. You remember how your mother insisted on having a good lamp to read by in the evening, and you are touched by how much your father wants you to be happy.

51.
Juli Goes Camping

Bill picks you up at your father's house early Saturday morning. The back seat of his new Honda, clean and dry compared with his old VW van, is piled high with gear. You get in the car with your urban-style suitcase and your new camp light. He glances at the lamp and says you don't need that, he has a couple of lights packed already. You tell him you are bringing it along just the same.

"Where we going?" you ask.

"Lake Bowman."

"Where's that?"

"Nowhere, more or less — that's the best part."

But it turns out the lake is somewhere, about four hours away — two short hours of easy driving for more than a hundred miles on the freeway, followed by two long hours of hard picking your way along the final fifty miles, at the pace of a motorized snail, on backcountry roads. During which time he sang, a cappella, every single hit Hank Williams ever had in his short life of twenty-nine years. Now you remember how it felt when your dad had been behind the wheel nearly thirty years ago, watching walls of dust thrown up by his old black Pontiac on the dirt roads or bumping along on stony tracks hardly wider than a service road. You hoped you wouldn't meet anyone coming the other way, and you didn't.

Finding a campsite is hard. Of the few actual sites marked out, all appear to be filled, occupied with tents and laundry lines stretched from tree to tree or marked as taken by a lawn chair in the parking space. But as Bill circles the campgrounds a second time, you spot one last site: a pleasant-looking area with its own small grove of trees within walking distance of the lake. He pulls into the "driveway" to survey the site before making a commitment. He turns off the car engine, and you both open your doors simultaneously to step out, stretch, and consider where to pitch the tent he brought. The pine needles underfoot feel soft and springy. You inhale sun-warmed air spiced with evergreen and childhood memories.

While exploring the site, you spot a red baseball cap hanging on a tree branch about six feet beyond the end of the site's parking space.

"Look at this," you say, pointing at the cap. "You think this space is already chosen?"

Bill measures the distance with his eye. "Naw, probably the last occupant just hung it there while he struck camp, then drove off and forgot it."

By mid-afternoon, the car is unloaded and the two of you are setting up camp. You see camping has evolved a lot since your father's day. No more grungy, Spanish moss-colored, army-surplus canvas tent, stinking of mold from the previous summer's dampness and so heavy that erecting it was a two-person job, even if one of the people just stood in place and held the other ends of things.

Now you watch as Bill zips open a long stuff bag and extracts a dainty, deep blue, nylon bag, along with the thin, flexible shock-poles that will be bent into a series of arches to support the structure. But first Bill spreads out a new, fake grass-colored painting tarp to protect the bottom of his delicate tent, then unfurls the Gore-Tex igloo. You watch as he fits the sections of poles together, end to end, and arranges them like giant pick-up sticks on top of the collapsed tent.

"This is the part where I need some help," he says.

"What do you want me to do?"

"I'll thread the poles through these little sleeves along the seams of this side of the tent, and you thread your sleeves on your side. Then I fit my end of each pole into a corner tab near me, and you fit the ends of each of your poles into your corner tabs."

"Sounds like a plan." But you find the process is more easily described than accomplished as you grasp and strain to pull each of your tent corners toward you while simultaneously struggling to direct one of three pole tips into its corner tab.

"Wrong pole!" Bill shouts, curtained behind the tent.

"Okay!" you shout back, breathing hard and grabbing the next pole over, which has been menacing at you with its waving tip.

But that was the worst of the tent-raising, and the process was complete in minutes. Bill empties another stuff bag. More nylon and shock-poles fall out.

"What's that?" you ask.

"Rain cover," he replies.

"It's not going to rain," you say.

"You never know," he says. "Besides, this is a brand-new tent, and I need the practice."

"Aren't you supposed to nail down the corners or something?" you ask, remembering how your father struggled with various ropes and stakes hammered into the ground.

"No pegs or guylines required," Bill states. "Besides, once we throw all our junk inside, this tent isn't going anywhere."

Camp established, you and Bill amble down to the lake. When you reach the water, you pull off your shoes and socks and wade on in. The chill of lake water, followed by spreading warmth, and the feel of smooth round pebbles underfoot, are sensations you have not enjoyed since you were little, and they stir deep cell memories.

You gaze across the bank to where huge boulders are gathered at the water's edge, and you squeeze your imagination to conjure up a Norman Rockwell-style image of your dad, sitting and fishing from one of the flat-top boulders. You notice his imaginary silhouette is smoking a pipe, and you are surprised to remember he used to smoke a pipe. You wonder idly when it was he went back to cigarettes.

You wonder if this is the same lake you used to come to when you were a kid. Or if it was some other lake in the Sierras? You realize you may now never know, since you can't ask your dad. Or, rather, you can ask, but he can't answer. Maybe your mother remembers.

You look out across the lake, where late afternoon is casting sparks on the water. Somewhere nearby, two little children are shrieking and squabbling. You can't see them, and their piercing, sinus-clearing little voices do not reveal their genders. You can tell, though, one is older than the other. The disagreement goes on for a while, then ceases. In the sudden quiet, you feel uneasy. You look toward Bill, but see he is simply happy, wading around aimlessly with his pant legs rolled up to his knees. No conflicts in that man. As long as he is enjoying his life, he has no complaints and asks no questions.

He comes up behind you, wraps his arms around you, kisses your ear. "I want to talk to you about something," he says.

"Let's go back to camp," you suggest.

"Can't we stay here awhile?" he says.

"No. I'm going back now."

"Something wrong?"

"No, no, nothing wrong. But my feet are freezing, I'm hungry, and I want a cigarette," you tell him, already heading for shore. He shrugs and mutely follows you back.

At dusk, at dinnertime, Bill starts rummaging in the boxes he packed for the trip. He pulls out a two-burner camp stove and screws on a hose. Then he digs through other boxes. "Uh-oh," he says.

"Something the matter?" you ask.

"Forgot the propane."

"And so?"

"So, no hot dinner tonight."

"Worse: no hot coffee in the morning."

"True. But that doesn't mean we have to go hungry. Looky here," he says, up to his elbows in the large cooler, "— a loaf of French bread, a block of cheese, a bag of cookies, and two bottles of wine. I'd say we have our four basic food groups all covered."

"Absolutely," you agree as you light up your second cigarette since you arrived at the lake. You have been trying hard to cut back, and the six you smoked since you woke up this morning is a new record in abstinence for you. You quietly pat yourself on the back.

In darkness silvered by a full moon, Bill is opening the second bottle of wine when a monster truck drives in, country western music blaring from its speakers, loud even though contained within rolled-up windows. In the moonlight, you can just barely make out that the cab is occupied by two people. As soon as the driver shuts off his engine, the music cuts off, and as he climbs out, you know trouble is coming.

"Hey," says the guy. In the dark, he seems seven feet tall and three feet wide. In the dark, he sounds menacing. And drunk. And maybe stoned. "This is our spot you're in."

"Good-evening to you, too," Bill replies evenly. "When we arrived this afternoon, we didn't see that the site was marked in any way."

"Didn't see my cap hanging on that tree back there?"

"We did, but we thought someone had left it behind by accident. It's still there, if you want it."

"What about this spot?"

"What about it?"

"This is our spot."

"Not anymore. I'm sorry we didn't understand how you marked the site, but we're all set up now, and we're staying the night."

"And just what're me and my girl supposed to do?"

"I don't know. You could check the ranger station. Maybe they can help you out."

You listen to Bill being very polite, very clear, very adamant. You are reminded that for years he has worked with deeply upset people who are living perpetually on the edge.

"Well, if that don't beat it," the stranger says. Then he advances, and in that moment you think maybe he will attack both you and Bill.

But, as he stalks to the back of your parking space and continues on into the trees, you understand he is hunting for his cap. You listen to him crashing around in the bushes. Then he hulks back to his truck without saying goodbye. He climbs into the truck, slams the door shut, starts the engine, pumps it to a roar.

You expect him to peel out at once, tires screeching. Instead, he sits there, engine chugging, for several minutes while the woman sitting next to him chews him out. Even with the truck windows closed and her exact words unintelligible, her furious, hysterical tone is unmistakable. You wonder what they've been smoking.

You never hear exactly when they leave, because you have already retreated to Bill's brand-new pavilion of a tent and cast yourself onto the brand-new inflatable mattress to sob deeply into the brand-new double sleeping bag you and he will share tonight. You keep thinking: why don't I get to spend even one beautiful night under the stars without everything turning to shit? Why don't I ever get to have what I want?

But what you are remembering is another camping trip, long-ago, with your parents and ... your brother. You were ... six? Going on seven? And, for a couple years, you'd had a baby brother. He needed a lot of attention, and you understood your mother had a lot less time for you.

It wasn't bad the first year, when he mostly lay on his back in his crib, either sleeping or screaming. But as soon as he was able to get up and crawl, then walk, nothing was the same at home.

As much interest as your parents took in your brother, that much interest he took in you. He followed you everywhere, like a grubby, drooling dog. If you told him to leave you alone, he wouldn't. If you ignored him, he doubled, then redoubled, his efforts to get your attention. If, at your insistence, your mother removed him, he cried, then hollered, then banged his head on the wall or the floor, over and over, the way he did every evening after your mother put him down to sleep. He only wanted to be with you and to do whatever you were doing. But he broke your crayons, tore your books, ripped the limbs off your stuffed animals. You hated him.

One bright, chill morning during what you now realize must have been the last time you went camping as a child, your father had come back to camp for breakfast. He'd gone out fishing early, before anyone else was up, and he planned to go out again to finish off the morning. As usual, you would accompany him on this second trip to the lake, helping by carrying his tackle box, and returning with him at midday for lunch. You had no special interest in fishing, but you liked to wade in the shallows, turning over rocks to reveal big green frogs, which you sometimes managed to catch and tote about in your pail for the afternoon.

This summer of your seventh year, your brother, who'd slept through most of the trip the year before, was all over the place, trying to dig in the fire pit, chew on pine cones, climb onto the rude wooden picnic table and jump off. Now that you and dad were heading for the lake, he wanted to go with you and do that, too.

Your mother objected at first, but she must have been tired and stressed from trying to keep up with housekeeping and cooking in the rough. Also, you remember, around then, she was sick a lot, throwing up — could she have been pregnant again? So, that morning, when your father told her, good-naturedly, not to worry — that he and you would keep an eye on your brother, so she could take a nap — she gave in.

You weren't happy about it. First, your baby brother took up all your mother's attention; now he would be taking up all your father's as well. When you reached the lake and your Dad set to his fishing again, you went back to frog-hunting and, sure enough, your brother was right at your heels. He was no good at frogging, too little to turn over the stones, too slow and awkward to catch the frogs as they emerged. All he could do was scare them away.

So you told him to go sit with dad. But he didn't want to sit with dad; he only wanted to spoil your game. You told him — and suddenly you remember this clearly — to either go bother dad or find his own damn frog place. Then you turned your back on him and went on with your little-kid play, trying to ignore him as you would have done at home.

You were supposed to help your parents, but you didn't. You were supposed to watch him, but you didn't. For a while, you heard him shrieking with glee nearby. Later, you didn't hear him, but you didn't think anything of it. Then your father was crouched in the water next to you, shaking you by your shoulders and asking you where your brother was, only you didn't know. And then he was rushing back to camp, with your limp, wet brother dripping in his arms, leaving behind all his fishing gear. And you.

You made your way back to camp alone. You were six, going on seven, after all. When you arrived, your parents were already in the car, about to drive away, your father behind the wheel with a look of desperation on his face. Your mother, her head bent so you could not see her face, must have been holding your brother in her arms on her lap. As you watched them leave, you heard your name spoken by a lady standing right above you. Then she was telling you everything was going to be alright, that she would look after you till your folks got back from the doctor in town.

And so you had dinner with these strangers, the Boltons, whose campsite was across the way from the pit toilet outhouse full of spiders. And then it got dark, and you watched the couple play cards by lantern light, while their four boys, ages nine to fourteen, roasted marshmallows and shouted stupid jokes at one another around the campfire. Eric, the eldest, showed you how to make knots with string.

The lady, Mrs. Bolton, had just finished suggesting there was room for you in their tent that night when in the dark your parents' car pulled up, and your mother came for you. You watched the two women as they exchanged a look, and your mother shook her head. Mrs. Bolton dropped to her knees to hug you and kiss you on the top of your head.

So, it was just the three of you in the tent that night — your mom on one side, your dad on the other, and you in the middle. Just as it used to be. Only, on this night, your mom was crying, while your dad lay silent, not sleeping, not snoring. And when it became light in the morning, they struck camp silently. Your mother gave you cold cereal and milk, then went to talk with the Boltons, while your father loaded the car. Your father drove you and your mother back the way you'd come in, but before he got on the highway, they stopped in a small town, where you waited in the car alone while they went into a small building with a cross on the sign out front.

More silence on the long drive home. Your mother explained they had to leave your brother at the hospital, because he "didn't make it." And then she said — and this part you now remember clearly —

"Don't blame yourself, it's nobody's fault."

By which you understood, even at the time and at your tender age, it was entirely your fault. Your brother was dead and only because you were supposed to watch him, but you didn't. All you had cared about was what you wanted.

So now, nearly a quarter of a century later, you observe yourself grieving for, if not your brother, then a time before everything went wrong and it was all your fault. Bill unzips the tent fly and joins you.

"What's the matter?" he asks.

"Why does every good thing in my life get wrecked? Why don't I ever get to have what I want?" you respond between choking tears.

"Hey, hey, that idiot is gone, so forget him. Don't be silly. Nothing went on here that holds some greater meaning in your life. You know that, don't you?" Bill says, switching on the battery-powered lamp your father provided.

"I guess," you say, shuddering as you repress a sob.

"Well then, what's wrong?"

You look up to stare into Bill's face and briefly consider how you might go about explaining how tonight you experienced the sudden and unexpected alignment of two timeframes of your life — the Now of your thirty-second year, in which you are a recently divorced woman out camping with her new boyfriend to take a break from living with her sick father, and the long-ago Then of your seventh year in which you had a brother, but he drowned and destroyed your parents' marriage. How could you have forgotten a thing like that?

"Well?" he presses.

"Nothing," you say at last. "Everything's fine." One day, probably, you'll tell him, but tonight it's too big and too confusing to go into.

"Good," he says, looking relieved. "Let's call it a night, then. I'm beat, and I see you are, too."

That night, you lie awake, pretending to sleep, with your back to Bill and his arm around you. Over and over you replay the memory of how your last camping trip ended, trying to see and feel more with each replay — what you were doing moments before your father grabbed your shoulders and shook you, how abandoned you felt as you watched your parents drive out of the campground, the snot dripping from your mother's nose as she told you they had to leave your brother at the hospital, how scared (and pleased) you were to realize you were rid of him, likely forever.

"You're safe here, I hope you know that," was the last thing Bill said to you before he fell asleep. You listened to him puffing softly and regularly on the back of your neck until you, too, fell asleep.

Sometime later in the night, you awake to Bill's gently shaking you and whispering, "Juli, Juli. Wake up. Wake up."

"What?" you croak, staggering toward consciousness, struggling to throw off the troubled dream you'd been in the middle of.

"I need to ask you something."

"What?"

"You wouldn't want to get married, would you?"

"What?"

"Married. Do. You. Want. To get. Married?"

"Hadn't thought about it."

"Well, think about it. Okay?"

"Okay."

"And let me know."

"Okay."

Bill lies back down and reaches for you in the dark. You snuggle deep into the double sleeping bag with his warmth at your back.

Outside the bag, it is freezing. Outside the tent, you hear crackling in the bushes, followed by snarling and hissing sounds, like small dinosaurs fighting nearby.

"What the hell is that?" you whisper.

"Raccoons. Don't worry."

Awhile later, all is still outside. You listen as a pattering on the fabric of the tent begins. One tap, then two, then a steady tippity-tap: it's raining. Turns out Bill was right. You drift off.

With the approach of dawn, your eyes open and you watch the walls of the tent grow more and more visible. You listen to Bill's regular breathing that tells you he is still asleep. You pull an arm out of your warm sleeping bag and touch the nylon wall. Condensation from your breathing all night pools at your fingertip and forms a large drip that heads toward your tennis shoes set side by side next to the cloth wall. You drag the shoes a few inches away from the wall, then bury yourself in the bag and go back to sleep.

When you wake again, it is to the sound of Bill singing you a coffee-delivery song he is making up as he goes: "Here's your coffee! Your very favorite coffee! Very special coffee! For you!" The tent fly unzips, and as the door falls away, he thrusts into the opening a fist holding a speckled blue, enameled tin camp mug from which steam arises. Morning light silhouettes him with its brilliance. He crouches over you and carefully sets the cup into one of your nearby shoes.

"Cup holder," he explains.

You sit up and remember you have no propane and so, theoretically, no way to heat water for coffee. "Where did the coffee come from?" you ask.

"Wandered around and met some of our neighbors. A nice young family on the other side of the campground — a guy with his wife and two little kids, the Boltons — he filled your cup."

"Thanks."

"You're welcome."

He sits and watches you sip coffee (the enameled tin so hot against your lower lip!) and struggle to wake up. "Do you remember what I asked you last night?"

"Sure."

"What do you think?"

"I think I have to think about it."

"Okay," he says, "but you've probably noticed by now that patience is not exactly one of my strong points."

52.
Bill Finds Himself
Back in Social Services

Such a great inspiration, you thought at the time: to take Juli out camping to see the stars. She's been so depressed about her dad. You remembered how it had comforted you to see all those stars when you were out in the field this summer, shooing away cows all night long. You wanted that same Zen experience for her — that sense of cosmic Eternity and of everything being Perfect and Complete in the moment.

Who knew that an overnight camping trip would turn out to be the most expensive date you'd ever proposed in your entire life? It was one thing to go star-gazing on the company's dime, quite another to arrange a whole trip yourself when you were starting out with virtually no gear and, prior to this summer, hadn't been out of the City in years.

You tried borrowing the company's tent that you'd used in the field, but apparently they'd had trouble in the past getting their gear back from their field droids, so no more loaners. You'd have to go elsewhere and get your own. Besides, you still needed a couple of air mattresses and two sleeping bags that could be zipped together, a camp stove, cookware, and camp lights. All of it to be stashed in your new car, which, to be fair, you bought when you were first starting this new job and felt unusually flush. You cringed when the cashier at REI rang you up and you saw the total. Gore-Tex is so expensive! But if all were to go as planned, the expense would be well worth it, because you and Juli would be using this same gear for years to come. Cheaper than an engagement ring.

You've already decided you want to marry this woman. As difficult as she is at times, no one better has come along in more than fifteen years of sporadic dating. Or, rather, lots of women have come along, but there's always something wrong with each one. There's lots wrong with Juli, too, but somehow it doesn't matter much. You suppose this is because the two of you started out as friends and have stayed friends for years. And the bonds of friendship being what they are, it's a lot harder to force a comparison of Juli with your mental profile of the Ideal Woman than it is with someone you've dated for only a few weeks. Juli is already her complete self, lovable warts and all.

And although David warned you that you'll never be able to get rid of her, you can hardly imagine a better recommendation than that for someone you think you want to spend the rest of your life with.

You didn't know how the situation with her father would wash out, but you knew it was bound to, one way or another. The way Juli described it, he was probably headed for nursing care. You couldn't say for yourself, because you'd never met the man, had never even been inside his house. Juli always came to you in the City. Even on the morning you were going out of town on your camping trip — which you planned as the perfect occasion to finally deliver your marriage proposal — when you picked her up at her dad's place, she came out to meet you, suitcase (suitcase!) in one hand, fancy new camp light in the other.

The drive up to Bowman Lake was beautiful and soothing, the way only a drive in the country with your own true love can be. And seeing the lake for the first time was like seeing paradise laid out before you. You imagined raising a glass of wine to Juli at sundown, then popping the question. Something like that. You didn't know yet how you would do it, but you were sure inspiration would come when you needed it. The thing was to stay Zen, to remain in the moment and to trust all would be well.

By mid-afternoon when you arrived at the lake, only one campsite was left. You took three turns around the camping area to be sure. As you pulled up to the only unoccupied site, you did spot a red baseball cap hanging on a tree branch, partially out of view at the very back of the site. But seeing no confirming signs of occupancy — an open waiting lawn chair, a beach towel spread like a tablecloth on the camp table, a plastic bag tied over the numbered campsite post, a cooler in the drive — you decided to ignore the cap. That was your first mistake.

Your second mistake was in not having taken the time to practice setting up your gear at home before you dragged it all out here. Who knew these new nylon tents had three different sizes of shock poles? Or an attachable rain cover that was impossible to figure out? The instructions must have been translated from Chinese or Korean, and in any case, you were embarrassed to disclose to Juli that you needed them. Juli, on the other hand, revealed to you a heretofore-unknown aptitude for spatial relationships and basic mechanical engineering. She got the rain fly on the tent in about 30 seconds.

After the fiasco with the tent — which turned out alright, but was still a fiasco in your mind, because your masculine dignity had been compromised — your manliness score evened out to a win-some/lose-some draw. You had remembered the air pump for the mattress, but forgotten the propane for the stove.

Camp established, you and Juli wandered down to the lake, where at once she took off her shoes and socks and waded in. You followed her, sensing that the big moment had arrived. Sunlight glistened on the lake, spraying the surface of the water with sparks. The water was chill, the stones underfoot smooth and soft. At first, she seemed carefree and simply delighted to be here, surrounded by lake and sky. You waded around, working up the nerve to ask her this most important question of your life.

But in the few minutes it took you to screw up your courage and come to her, you realized something in her had shifted. You approached her from behind and wrapped your arms around her, but she felt stiff and unyielding.

"I want to ask you something," you told her. But she showed no interest in whatever it might be you wanted to ask, just insisted on going back to camp. You asked her what's wrong; she went off about her cold feet, empty stomach, need to smoke. Strike one.

So, you resolved to try again after dinner, such as dinner was likely to be, with no propane and just cold fare. Fortunately, you brought plenty of wine.

But just as you were opening your second bottle of vintage to accompany the cookie course of the meal, this jerk drove up in his big-ass truck, stereo thudding away, and — wouldn't you know it? — demanded your campsite. *His* campsite, he insisted, indicating the red baseball cap that you noticed when you arrived, but which was now invisible in the dark.

Generally you are someone who avoids conflict and confrontations at all costs. And, under different circumstances, you might have yielded to this low-life sonovabitch who was twice your size and clearly stoned. But it was a long day that thus far hadn't gone the way you intended it should, so you refused to give in. You hadn't worked in Social Services all those years for nothing. Instinctively, you knew how to stonewall this guy without enraging him further. And he seemed to know when he was beat. He stalked to the back of the campsite, rooted around till he found his cap, then climbed back in his truck and sat for several minutes, getting his ass chewed by his old lady. Smelling the dope smoke drifting from the truck cab, you thought, had circumstances been different, you might have invited this fella to join you.

By the time he roared off and you looked around for Juli, she had already retired to the interior of your new tent, where she was sitting on your new air mattress with your new sleeping bag drawn up around her and bawling into one of the little plaid camp pillows. When you asked what's wrong, she exclaimed:

"*Why* does every good thing in my life turn to shit? Why don't I *ever* get to have what I want?"

You reassured her the redneck asshole in the truck was gone and wouldn't be coming back, that everything was fine. But she was not mollified. She claimed, "Well then, everything's just fine" — and went right on weeping. Briefly you wondered if you'd been working yourself up all day to propose marriage to a crazy person. But, no, this is Juli, your friend, you remind yourself. You remembered everything she's been through these past few years and that now her father is sick and probably dying. She's just upset, you told yourself, it will pass. As for you, you need to get Zen and stay Zen. You need to trust.

"Let's call it a night," you told her. "I'm beat, and so are you." And a moment later, just before you fell asleep, you added: "You're safe here. You know that, don't you?"

That night, though, you found yourself awake, fully conscious and convinced that if you didn't ask her right now, right this minute, this night before your courage failed you, you might not ever do it. You sat up and shook her gently by the shoulder.

"Juli. Juli. Wake up. Wake up, okay?"

She's a heavy sleeper, and it took her a while to come around. "Huh?" she responded.

"I need to ask you something. You wouldn't want to get married, would you?" In the moonlight silvering the inside of the tent, you could just barely make her out, staring at you like she was hypnotized. So you try again:

"I said: Married. Do. You. Want. To get. Married?

This time she heard you. "Dunno. Never thought about it."

"Well, think about it. Okay?"

"Okay."

"And let me know."

"Okay."

Mission accomplished, you both settled down. Somewhere nearby, raccoons were fighting, and then it began to rain. But you were a happy man, a man with a future. It occurred to you that, with all the moonlight and upset tonight, you hadn't shown her any stars, but hopefully you'd have years ahead of you for that.

The rest of the trip seemed to fly by. You woke up early and went to cadge a cup of hot coffee for Juli from one of the other campers — that family with the kids on the other side of the grounds near the pit toilet. They understood and were only too happy to oblige.

By mid-morning, you and Juli were breaking camp, badly, throwing all your wet gear randomly into the rear end of your hatchback. What the hell, you could sort it all out later, after you got home. You wondered whether, instead of having to set up the tent again so it can dry, you could simply take it to the corner laundromat and run it through the dryer. Back on the road with Juli curled up in her bucket seat, you kept hoping she would mention your proposal, give you an answer. But she stayed quiet the whole way, and you supposed she was thinking about her father, worrying about him. You always enjoyed driving, but until this past summer, you hadn't been out of the City in years and hadn't had much open road.

Returning to the San Francisco Bay Area, you can feel it — noise level suddenly rising, pace picking up, energy intensified — even before you see the metropolis rolled out before you. And the bay, that magnificent bay! You know which freeway exit to take, but Juli has to guide you through several Oakland neighborhoods to the far side of Lake Merritt and the

Craftsman-style house where she's been living with her father these past few months. You expected to be simply dropping her off, just as you had picked her up early yesterday morning. But in a moment of gallantry, you decide to carry her suitcase and camp light for her to the front door. And then you hear it.

From her father's front porch, you hear him far away, moaning over and over, steady and regular as ocean waves breaking on the shore. Juli turns and gives you a frightened look. You know you will have to follow her inside.

As you come through the front door, right behind Juli, the house is filled with his moans. You glance around the living room, then look to the dining room beyond, where the floor is strewn with newspapers, and the air is close and fetid, stinking of urine. He seems to be somewhere in the back part of the house. You ask Juli if she wants you to come with her.

"No, stay here," she says. "Dad's really private." Then she heads toward the sounds of his distress, while you sit on a coffee table, alternating between chewing on your nails and knitting your fingers together. You need to jump up and *do* something. At the same time, you wish yourself a million miles away. For Juli's sake, you had come in; for her sake, you restrain yourself now. What next? Why did you sign up for this?

Juli shrieks from far away in the back of the house: "Bill, get down here quick, please! I need help!" You sprint toward her cry — through the house, out a back door, onto a steep, narrow, rickety wooden stairway with a landing and an acute turn halfway down.

Juli's father is an old man sprawled at the bottom of the stairs on the concrete floor of his own basement. Even with years of social service home visits under your belt, you are shocked for the moment. Wearing only a bathrobe with nothing under it, her father is exposed and in obvious pain, clutching at his robe, twisting the fabric, grimacing, moaning.

"Help me," she says. "I've got to get him upstairs. I can't do it by myself."

"Maybe he shouldn't be moved," you venture. "What if his back is broken? Or his neck?"

"It's not!" she says. "Are you going to help me or what?"

"Okay, okay," you say and get ready to assist her, thinking this is a helluva way to meet the father of the woman you intend to marry. Though you don't really want to touch this old guy in his pee-soaked robe, there's no avoiding it now. Ten years in Social Services, you've seen worse, but every drama was always someone else's life, never yours.

Tentatively, you try to adjust his arms and legs, and consider the steepness and sharp turn of the staircase. This isn't going to work, and you know it. You aren't a big man; you have no medical training. What if you drop him on the way up? What if he *does* have a broken neck, and you kill him trying to save him?

You look up at his daughter with an expression you hope communicates a plea of helplessness. "Juli, please, I can't."

She stands there, white-faced and shaking. "This is terrible," she says. "Whether he wants to or not, he is going to the hospital. Right now."

"He's clearly in no condition to refuse."

"That's right," she says, snapping her fingers like you just reminded her of the magic words she'd been trying to remember. "He's in no condition to refuse. I'm calling 9-1-1."

53.

Juli Takes Care of Her Father

Frightened as you are, this is the opening you had prayed for. You take one last look at your father lying on the hard, cold cement of the basement floor, bellowing and thrashing like a buffalo caught in a pit trap, before you march up the basement stairs he'd plummeted down, go straight to his ancient rotary phone, pick up the receiver, and dial 9-1-1.

Fifteen minutes later, you open the front door to two paramedics and six big firemen. You hadn't known you must specify "medical emergency only" when calling 911, or else they automatically send the fire department as well. The firemen, always gallant, tip their fire hats and leave as soon as you finish issuing directions to the paramedics: "Straight back and down the stairs to the basement. My dad fell. My friend is with him."

By the time you have shut the front door and turned to walk shakily back to the basement, the paramedics are there with your father, already checking his vital signs.

"Blood pressure 180 over 90, stable. Pulse 72, strong and regular," one paramedic announces. He glances up at you for further explanation. You, in turn, glance over at Bill, standing next to the old workbench where, decades ago, your dad built your little red barn with its hinged roof. Bill shrugs his helplessness. You look back to the paramedics.

"I think my father had a stroke a couple of months ago. For a while, he was doing pretty well, but lately he's been a lot worse. Now he's taken a fall."

You are light-headed with guilt. You think maybe you didn't try hard enough to get your father to the hospital. It seems crazy to you, having to tell these guys that your father had a stroke weeks ago, yet nothing has been done for him. What kind of daughter ignores a parent's desperate medical situation?

"I couldn't get him to go to the hospital. Please, please take him in."

You can feel your face burning with shame, but the paramedics just nod noncommittally and go about their business, asking your father questions, getting no responses, stabilizing his neck with a collar, rolling him onto their carry-out stretcher, fastening him down. You and Bill follow them up the stairs. You cannot help noticing, as weak and disoriented as your father is, he still fights being strapped down and carried away.

When the medical palanquin reaches the kitchen, the paramedics adjust their burden for the final dash to the ambulance, idling out front. The man at the foot-end of the stretcher says: "Don't worry. We'll get him there. One of you, go collect whatever medications he's been taking; the other, please run ahead and open the front door for us."

While Bill escorts the paramedics and your dad out of the

house, you grab a shopping bag and fill it with bottles of pills, capsules, drops, clearing both the Lazy Susan and the window sill in the breakfast nook. By the time you are standing out in front of your father's house, the ambulance is gone as if it'd had never been there. For a moment, you wonder if you just hallucinated the events of the past hour.

"C'mon," says Bill. "They've gone to Oakland Kaiser."

During your long afternoon and evening in the emergency room, you become your father's spokesperson, answering the questions he cannot answer for himself. You are relieved to find the doctor attending your father is a woman about your own age. She asks about his condition leading up to this point; you tell her everything. She frowns as she listens.

"Yes," she says, "it does sound like your father has had a stroke. But, normally, we expect a good deal of recovery over the first three months, then further recovery over the next nine. Has he been seen by a neurologist?"

"No."

"Has he had a CT scan?"

"No. He refused to be seen at all."

"I see. Well, I'm going to order some tests. You may as well go home. Your father's not going anywhere tonight. Someone will call you later."

She herself calls you eight hours later. It is well past midnight. Bill returned to the City ages earlier.

"I have the results back from the CT scan on your father. I need a radiologist to confirm, but I think we've found a tumor in the left hemisphere of your father's brain. Quite a large one, too, about the size of a baseball."

In the days that follow, your father gets to see more people and do more traveling than he has in years. He is taken by ambulance across the bay to be seen by a team of specialists at the Kaiser in Redwood City, on the peninsula south of San Francisco. Then he is transported back to Oakland Kaiser. You have already talked with a dozen different doctors, all of them kind and careful not to make promises. A neurologist on the peninsula calls you.

"We've put him on cortisone to reduce the inflammation surrounding the tumor. He's also being rehydrated. We've discussed some aggressive measures, but he's in such poor condition, and, at his age, he probably wouldn't make it through the surgery. Sometimes we try radiation on brain tumors, but your father's tumor is so large, I don't think the treatment would have much effect. Perhaps if he'd come in a month ago... ."

Yes, a month ago, you think. A month ago, your father had still been able to walk, to answer questions with a nod or shake of his head. But that time is past. You steel yourself and ask the one question you already know is useless, because no doctor can answer it with certainty:

"How long has he got?"

The neurologist is silent on the phone for a long minute. "We can't be very definite," he says at last. "A few months at the outside, perhaps only a few weeks. Patients with tumors like these usually don't last long."

"What should I do now?"

"I'd say you'd better start looking around for a skilled nursing facility."

A social worker at the hospital gives you a list of nursing homes, and you pay some visits around town. You are determined to search till you find one that smells right and is willing to accept a patient who has no hope of getting any better. You consider yourself fortunate to find what you were looking for in just two days' time. Only a couple months after you called Bill because you so desperately needed his friendship, you sign the papers and arrange to have your father brought to his dying place.

The hospital stay has done him good. He is alert and glad to see you the first time you visit him at the nursing home. Nothing coming out of his mouth makes any sense, but at least he is clean and free from pain. His doctor promised you: no pain.

As time passes, however, you watch him slip back down. You understand, of course, the tumor is still growing. Everyone knows this. But you also suspect your father, as he settles into the nursing home and gets accustomed to strangers coming and going at all hours, has returned to working on the one project that, as long as you have known him, has always interested him most: his dying. He wanted to die; all this unusual activity simply distracted him from his purpose for a while.

One afternoon, you go to see him, and you find him raving, shouting, babbling on and on, spewing out more words, though broken and jumbled, than he had in years. You know then it is frustration, not pain, he has been raging against. He is frustrated by his inability to die.

"Jesus Christ!" he bawls at the end of one string of complete nonsense. The tumor has not interfered with his ability to swear. The speech therapist will later tell you cussing is more basic than language. As glad as you are to know your father has been left with that much at least, hearing him cursing so prolifically is still a shock. Your father was raised to be a gentleman, and you cannot ever remember him swearing around ladies, not ever.

Except for the single, malicious tumor growing inside his head, your father seems more or less healthy in every other respect. His blood pressure is normal, his heart goes on beating, strong and regular. His overall condition is better than when the paramedics first brought him into the hospital. You remember reading in college about the Fates, those weaving sisters of Greek mythology who measure out the threads of each person's life and clip them at the end of his or her allotted time. Your dad must have more time coming to him — time he doesn't want, but can't figure out how to get rid of.

You ask what is expected to happen in Dad's case and are told the tumor will probably keep growing until it interferes with his respiration and he becomes unable to breathe. You sign a "no CPR" request at the nurses' station and go down the hall to see him.

Whoever dressed your father that morning put him in the one cheery shirt you brought to the nursing home, red polyester with white polka dots. He tries to talk, but it is all nonsense to you. You ask him questions, but his attention wanders. You can't get him even to nod or shake his head in reply. He is eating his lunch, spilling food on himself. You remember how much he'd always enjoyed a good meal, and you pity him for his one remaining life pleasure. You start to cry.

"I'm sorry, Dad, I'm sorry," you blubber. "I'm so sorry things turned out like this."

"Dum-dum-da, da-dum-dum-da, dum-dum-da, da-dum-dum-da... ."

Startled out of your tears, you stare at your father. It is "Le Marseilles," the French national anthem, your father is singing to you.

"Dum-dum-da-da, da-da-da-dum... ."

You join him in a last verse of universal, all-purpose song lyrics. When you finish, your father looks up at you, surprised and pleased.

"Ha-ha-ha-ha!"

He laughs with his mouth wide open. Without his dentures, it is a toothless, formless laugh, but nevertheless happy in the moment. He reaches out with his good arm and gives your nearest knee a clumsy pat. When you lock eyes, you see his eyes are blue. A funny thing, because only recently you noticed his driver's license says they are gray. You wonder how the DMV could have been wrong all those years. Your father's eyes are blue, pale and clear. Just the same as your own.

That night at home — his home that now is yours as well — you search through the sideboard drawers where you know he keeps his photo albums. It takes a while, but at last you find the one you want. The photos are more than forty years old — brittle, thin, black-and-white snapshots turning brown at the edges, curling and cracking. Pictures of your father in Belgium during the war. Your father in uniform on a muddy road near Arlon, on the banks of the River Semois. Your father with his division at Bastogne. Your father as he'd been then, young and strong. A liberator. A man with reason to live, a grand and noble purpose — and that purpose fulfilled. Raised as you were on the Vietnam War, you still find it difficult to view war as anything but a senseless, tragic waste for all involved. Yet when you turn the black pages of your father's World War II photo album to look back on the man he'd been then, you see a happy man. A man living out the best years of his life.

Your father knows how to die. Once upon a time so long ago, before you yourself were born or even considered as a possibility, he'd been ready to die, to give his all in the course of doing his duty for his country. Now, once again, he is ready to die. Dying is something he learned about in Europe, an important lesson. What he had not learned was how to go about living till death comes. He had packed his bags years ago, then sat for ages in the station, waiting for the train, which seemed to him long overdue.

Four days later, your father's train arrives.

All evening, you've been agitated, unable to settle down, go to sleep. You take a hot bath, hoping to relax, but it doesn't help. You turn on the TV, but it's all cops and robbers — mindless, action-packed melodrama. Finally, about 1 a.m., you go to bed and lie there in the dark, in your grandmother's old bedroom, with your eyes open, burning holes in the ceiling.

Fifteen minutes later, the call comes: the night nurse telling you your father died at 12:48 a.m.

Irrational as it will later seem to you, you need to go at once and see for yourself. After all, you put him in that nursing home; you have to see that he is decently assisted out of there. You dress as slowly and methodically as if the end of the world had just been announced to you. Your father's car is parked in the driveway, waiting.

Before you leave, late as it is, you call Bill without a second thought. He is groggy, but determined. "Wait. I'll drive you," he says. You hang up and sit down to wait for him.

How strange to be in the nursing home in the middle of the night. How small your father seems in his hospital bed. The nurse who walks you and Bill down the hall from the nurses' station to your father's room pulls back the curtains that had been drawn around him. All that shows is his head, thrown back on the pillow, eyes shut, mouth wide open in surprise. All lines of fear and worry have slipped from his face. His cheeks are smooth and sallow. You reach across the bed railing to feel his hands beneath the sheet. You stroke his forehead. Still warm.

Your escort nurse is bagging his things — his pajamas, his slacks and slippers, his hair brush and reading glasses, the cheery, polka-dotted shirt he'd worn two days earlier when you last visited.

"I was with him as he passed. He died easy," she tells you without looking up from her chore.

"Thank you," you reply and mean it. It comforts you to hear it. You know your father spent so much time alone in the course of living, it is good to think he'd had company to attend his dying, to wish him well as he departed. Bill excuses himself, says he is going down the hall to the nurses' station to ask about death certificates and other business. You sit down next to your father and wait for the mortuary's pick-up man — basically, a cab driver whose customers never tip.

Here is Dad and yet not-Dad. You'd been nervous about seeing his body without the life in it. But this wasn't so bad, this wasn't so bad after all. It is quiet tonight in the nursing home, and a strange sweetness hangs in the air. You stare, curious, at your father's little yellow head so still upon the pillow, and it seems as if you and he are no longer so separate as you had been while he was alive. You wonder if all human consciousness is a collective thing, like a bright and rushing stream. Perhaps each individual represents only a small measure of that stream, a bit of essence collected for a time in a vessel. Here before you lies one such container. The contents you'd valued and loved had been released, poured back into a rill of unencumbered consciousness to be purified downstream.

You are numb, still in shock, the next day as you take care of post-mortem business at the mortuary, the cemetery, the Social Security office, the Veterans Administration, the Department of Public Health. Your father's files at home turn out to be a masterpiece of organization; you are grateful, for once, for his military sense of compulsive order. From the mortician, however, you learn that a recently concluded grave diggers' strike will delay putting Dad's remains to rest. You giggle nervously to think of all those dead folk, like customers in a bakery, waiting to be taken on a first-departed, first-interred basis.

The mortician is a young man who exudes more good cheer than you would have imagined was possible for one in his profession. Encouraged by your suppressed hysteria, which he clearly interprets as a sense of humor, he tells you about his decor at home: the salt and pepper shakers shaped like tombstones, the embalming jar he'd converted into an aquarium. He tells you the worst thing that has ever happened to him in the course of carrying out his professional duties: an unsuspected pacemaker in a client's chest blew out the wall of his cremation chamber. You quickly reassure him your father was not so equipped.

You shrug as you write out the checks. Seven hundred for the cremation. Five hundred more to have his ashes placed in an urn in the niche that holds *his* parents' ashes. The situation reminds you of that old joke about the bad play — the one to which no admission is charged, but you must pay to leave the theater. You had no idea it cost so much to get out of this world. But, what the hell, you think, it isn't like you are up for doing the job yourself, to take your dad home in a shoebox and bury him in his own backyard like a pet hamster. And it isn't as though you will ever have to do this again for him.

By the day's end, you are not only numb and in shock — you are mostly nuts. You leave the cemetery and wander outside. This last block of Piedmont Avenue in Oakland is lined with headstone masons and florist shops. Even outside on the street, the heavy, cloying scent of day lilies hangs in the air. Unable to trust your driving abilities at that moment, you leave your father's car where you parked it inside the cemetery walls and wander down the avenue as far as MacArthur and Broadway, near where your father was hospitalized.

Generally, you are easily intimidated by the winos and burnt-out beggars who lurch out of doorways to hit you up for spare change. That late afternoon, however, you look each one squarely in the eyes and say simply, "Not today, brother." And each one retreats, seeming to glide away as if carried on a conveyor belt. You feel protected by armor made of a peculiar energy. And though you are not aware of doing anything out of the ordinary, crowds part before you and people on the street move swiftly out of your way to allow you to pass unimpeded, unmolested.

54.
Bill Gets a New Home

In retrospect, taking Juli on an overnight camping trip as a setup to proposing marriage was a crazy way to try and pin down your relationship. But, ultimately, it worked.

After Juli's father went into the hospital, then hospice care, you started spending weekends at her place and she started spending a few nights during the week at yours, especially when she had temp assignments in the City to get to early the next morning. You couldn't let the woman you intend to marry deal with an upheaval of that magnitude alone and unsupported. A couple weeks after her father died and on her invitation, you packed up what little you own, bid your roommates farewell, and moved in with her, leaving behind your Baghdad-by-the-Bay, your city of Hopes and Dreams.

While Juli's contemplation of your marriage proposal seems to have gotten lost in the crisis of her father's death, at least now you are living together, a domestic situation that hadn't been part of your life since years and years ago when your wife of less than a year left you for a mutual friend. Of course, unlike your belated triangle with Juli and David, the mutual friend who'd charmed away your ex hadn't bothered to wait till you split up. Even so, the parallel between your past experience and this present one still troubles you on occasion. Consequently, now more than ever, you are glad you checked with your old friend before making a move on his ex. If your former mutual friend had checked with you before appropriating your wife, you might have accidentally run him over. Or her. Or, more likely, driven yourself off a cliff. But, once again, everything has come down in harmony.

The house belongs to Juli now. A whole house! Her father left her some money, too. Not enough to make her wealthy forever, but certainly enough for her to quit taking on temp assignments in the City. You urge her to do just that.

She keeps saying she wants to write; you keep telling her now she can afford to. With you making good money and living here for free, it's no problem for you to cover all your other shared daily expenses. You watch Juli weighing her need to feel independent against her desire to do what she most wants to do in this life. You are relieved to note she has lately been calling the agency less and less to announce her availability for assignments. Last week she worked only one day.

Juli's been in a whirl of activity since she laid her father to rest. Getting rid of most of what belonged to him and to her grandparents as well — more than half a century of junk — then deep-cleaning every square inch of the filthy old place. Every room is stained with nicotine from all the smoking her father and grandparents did for sixty years — walls, curtains, upholstery, carpeting. Even the pages inside her father's old address book stink. Juli spends her free days tearing up everything, and whatever she can't tear up and throw away, she hoses down with bleach. One day you come home to find her standing in the bathtub with a coffee mug of Clorox in one hand, an old, wrecked toothbrush in the other hand, scrubbing the grout in the backsplash. She's thorough, that one.

You get a little concerned, though, the day she calls St. Vincent de Paul and arranges for them to come and take away the three big, overstuffed armchairs in the living room and every bed in the house.

"Whoa," you tell her, "think what you're doing."

"I *am* thinking of what I'm doing. That's why I'm doing it."

"But the chairs, the beds — what have they ever done to you?"

"Please don't ask me that question unless you have a couple of days to listen to the whole story."

"Okay, but what are we going to sleep on?"

"We'll buy a new bed, just for us, brand-new with no history. In the meantime, we can sleep on one of the mattresses on the floor — my grandmother's, I guess. At least, it doesn't have pee stains."

"How about the air mattresses I got for camping?" you suggest.

"Great idea. I just want all those other things out of here — they're haunted."

Even though you don't agree with her decision, you respect her process, doing whatever she needs to do to work through her grief for her father and turn his home into hers. She seems fine in that area. Nevertheless, ever since you moved in with her, you have observed there's a big difference between friends who do sleepovers and friends who live together as well as sleep together.

For one thing — and it took you weeks to find this out — Juli was mad at you because you were the one to suggest she ask Mrs. Mitkin to look after her father while you took her camping. It wasn't your fault Mrs. M failed to meet the responsibilities she agreed to. And you hadn't realized Juli, from the start, never liked Mrs. M, nosy gossip that she is. If only you'd known how intensely Juli felt about her neighbor, you would never have suggested bringing her into the house.

You know Juli doesn't *really* blame you for her father's accident, but you can't help wondering what really happened with Mrs. M. You know Juli's father got his dinner, because Juli later found his plate and silverware unwashed in the sink. But you have to ask: why didn't Mrs. M help him back to his room in the basement after she gave him dinner? Or could it be that he made a second, unexpected trip upstairs that evening and couldn't get back down again safely? But if he *did* fall on his way downstairs after dinner and Mrs. M wasn't there to help him, then why didn't she find him in the morning when she returned to bring him his coffee and toast? Or *did* she ever come back in the morning? There was no sign he'd had any breakfast. Was it possible he'd tried to get his own breakfast and, in the process, had fallen? And whenever it was he fell, you wonder how she never heard his moans of distress. You suspected she might be a little hard of hearing, but since his moans could be heard from the front porch, you have to assume she never even came that close.

What happened here the weekend of your camping trip was a mystery you have yet to solve. Twice so far, you've gone over to talk to Mrs. Mitkin: once to let her know Juli's dad was in the hospital (also, incidentally, to introduce yourself, so she wouldn't wonder who this strange man was, coming and going at all hours), then again to tell her that Juli's dad had died. She seemed genuinely stricken to hear this, and it made you wonder if, at some point in the past, she hadn't taken more than just a neighborly interest in him.

But you haven't outright asked Mrs. M for her perspective of the events of that weekend, when it seems she somehow failed her charge, because you weren't yet fully aware of Juli's outrage. Besides, events from that point on seem to have progressed just as they were intended and as they inevitably must evolve. Juli had been trying for months to get her father into the hospital. But only because, after her father's fall and removal to the ER, doctors were able to scan him for damage *and* figure out what was really wrong — a huge brain tumor. As it turned out, nothing could have saved him. And though Juli was still too angry to go over and question Mrs. M or even take back her father's house key, you also hadn't asked for its return, because at the time, you didn't consider it your place to do so. Now your living here with Juli changes that.

Every time you've talked with Mrs. M, you notice, old as she is — eighty-something is your best guess — she never fails to look you up and down in that openly appraising way some older women have. Clearly she never needed Women's Lib. She could have taught classes on the subject. But you can deal with it. You weren't in Social Services all those years for nothing. At least, she always acts glad to see you.

Relative stranger though you are, she invites you right into her house, sits you down, and starts talking at you. You let her run on for several minutes before you hold up your hand for silence — a trick you know works for you with Mrs. M because you're a man, but wouldn't have worked for Juli, because it never works for women with other women. Before the old lady can get cranked up again, you get down to business:

"Mrs. Mitkin, I need the key to Juli's house, and I need to know if you know anything about how Juli's dad ended up on the basement floor for hours before we called the paramedics. What can you tell me?"

"Not a whole helluva lot. And I don't have that key, I give it back."

"You gave it back to Juli? When did you give it back to her?"

"Not the daughter. The father. I give it back to her father."

"You did? When did you do that? *Why* did you do that?"

"He wanted it back, so I give it back. That night, right after I give him his dinner."

"But he couldn't speak at that point. How did you know he wanted the key from you?"

She shrugs and cocks her head at an angle before answering: "Sign language, young man. He holds up his own key ring, shakes it, sits the keys on the table — y'know, he only had the one good working arm — puts out his hand and makes the 'gimme' sign." She extends her own hand, palm up, flat and raised, then opens and closes it several times. You get the point.

"And when did this happen?" you ask, fascinated by this glimpse of Juli's father as a competent, self-possessed human being laboring as best he could under a terrible disability.

"Oh, 'bout halfway through dinner. I'd come in, thinking I'll need to take his dinner down to him. Or maybe help him get upstairs — I'm stronger than I look. But when I come in, he's already sitting there at the dining table, waiting, all dressed up in clean PJs and his bathrobe. I nuke his dinner for him, then sit down opposite to keep him company while he eats. He's spilling on himself, but still getting half into his mouth. Then, all at once, he puts down his spoon, looks me straight in the eye, and reaches across the table to pat my hand."

At this point, Mrs. M pauses to illustrate her story by patting her own hand before going on. "I was so struck, it shut me up, and we just set there a moment, staring at one another. Then he pulls back, feels around in his robe pocket, shows me those keys of his, gives them a shake, and makes the gimme sign."

"So you gave him back his key, just like that? What about helping him back to bed? Or giving him breakfast the next morning?"

"Well, I figured he got up the stairs on his own, he most likely could get back down on his own. And he wasn't going to starve if he didn't get his toast for one morning."

"And later on you didn't hear any strange sounds coming from next door?"

"'Course not! I'da been over in a shot with the police breaking down the door."

"How's your hearing, Mrs. Mitkin?"

"My what?"

"Your hearing, Mrs. Mitkin!"

"Just kidding!" she chortles at her own old person's joke. "My hearing's perfectly fine, young man."

"Did you feel a little bad that he wanted his key back?"

"I guess. Maybe I did, a little. But mostly I just thought he was a proud man who didn't want me seeing him like that."

"Mrs. M, you're probably right about that."

"He was a good, kind man, it's a wonder he never remarried."

"Depressed, though."

"What?"

"I said: Juli's father seems to have been terribly depressed most of his life."

"You got that right."

And so later over dinner, with Juli sitting in her father's place at the table, and you sitting right where Mrs. Mitkin must have sat that last night, you tell Juli what Mrs. M told you. And the first thing she says is, "She's lying. If she gave the key back to Dad, where is it? I've got his key ring — that was in his bathrobe pocket, and the spare key's not on it."

You point out there's no way her father could have put a single key on a split ring with just his one good hand, so most likely he pocketed it. And maybe the key flipped out when he fell? Or maybe he'd been holding it loose in his hand? If so, if he *had* been holding the single key loose in his hand, then he couldn't also have kept a good grip on the bannister. Maybe *that* would explain why he fell.

You point out it's mainly because she doesn't like Mrs. M that she assumes her neighbor lied to cover up why she didn't do the job she promised she would. It occurs to you this woman you are living with now, the woman you still hope to make your wife, has been lied to and let down by people close to her *a lot* in her life. You wonder if you will ever really have her complete trust. Because you certainly don't have it yet.

Which reminds you of the other area in which Juli seems to be lagging: working through her anger and grief over her ex-husband, your ex-friend. Even though it's been a good two years since they split up and another year since her actual divorce, she still rags on him more often than is strictly good for the mental health of either of you. And usually this happens right after she's snapped at *you* for something you've done or failed to do that reminds her of something David did. Or failed to do. Like, when you come in late and you forgot to call.

Clearly, on some level, she is still angry and bitter. And those feelings are keeping her as much connected to David as when she was married to him. Once, when she was fuming over some past sin he had committed, you tried pointing out how all that anger was only hurting her. The man himself was having a perfectly happy life elsewhere. This she did not want to hear.

"No fair!" she replied.

"I'm sure he'll bring a shitload of karma down on his head eventually," you replied, deftly sidestepping the logical, but personally perilous observation that life is *not* fair. "It's for your own good that you find a way to forgive him and to let him go. You don't have to forget everything he did. You only need to get to a place where you don't care about it anymore, where it doesn't bother you."

At which point, you raised both your hands in a Buddhist mudra that's supposed to ground and calm one — the tips of your thumbs and index fingers touching, your other fingers straight, but relaxed, like two loose "OK" signs. You put on your best guru voice: "Attachment is the source of all suffering. So you must de-tach, my child."

"Easier said than done," she responded, sounding unconvinced.

"Well," you continued in your normal voice, "try to think

of it this way: your life would not be as it is now if David hadn't jilted you."

"Yeah," she said, "I totally see that. Now you've enlightened me, I'll be sure to call him up and thank him for trashing me. And, while I'm at it, I should probably make it a point to call your ex-wife and thank her as well for trashing you."

"I don't think you need to go that far."

"Maybe we could get a guest spot on *Donahue*, even. Demonstrate how evolved we are."

"Right."

You saw she had no intention of giving an inch. At that moment. But, in the following weeks, you would notice she's no longer ragging on David as vigorously she used to do. So you hope, perhaps, she is at least thinking about forgiving him. Or thinking about trying to forgive him.

And soon after your talk about Mrs. M, Juli went down into the basement, moved boxes and old stored furniture, and crawled around on her hands and knees, searching till she found the spare key, the one Mrs. M had indeed returned to her father that night. Even more to her credit, Juli showed you the key, acknowledged it had probably ended up on the floor pretty much the way you'd theorized, and admitted she'd been wrong to accuse her neighbor of dereliction of duty just because she doesn't like her.

After so much enlightenment, maybe it's too much to hope for, but you'd also really love it if she'd quit smoking.

55.
Juli Gets a New Life

Growing old hadn't slowed down Mrs. Mitkin one bit. Or if it had, then you cringe to think what she was when she was young. Say, in the 1920s. The thought of Mrs. M as a flapper seems bizarre at first, then totally right on. You wonder how all those flower children of the 1960s will seem in another forty, fifty years.

Sometime after your father died, you noticed Mrs. Mitkin was out three nights a week, dressed in her old-lady finery, polyester prints and bright costume jewelry. Several nights a week, she went to a Bingo parlor or played bridge at the senior center; on Sundays, she went to church. You suppose she must have met Henry at one of those get-togethers. And after Henry started coming over, she calmed down some. You'd run into her on the street, and she'd hold you for only five or ten minutes before declaring, "Gotta get." She was hurrying home to Henry.

Henry, like your dad, was at least fifteen years her junior. Which made you wonder if Mrs. M hadn't had designs on your father. Clearly, her taste ran to younger men. Henry worked at a local chemical plant. You guessed he must've been exposed for years and years to a lot of strange substances, because he was the slowest fellow you'd ever met. He'd get started on a sentence, break off in the middle, completely lost, then stand there, looking blank. As a result, he hadn't much to say. And if he sat down for more than five minutes, he fell asleep. But he was a big, good-natured man who grinned while Mrs. Mitkin followed him around, carrying on and on about everything and everyone.

One afternoon, Henry was out in front of what was now your house, working on his car. He bent over, and when his pants rode down, you got a good look at what kind of underwear he had on: shiny red bikini briefs. You were surprised. You'd always thought of Henry as your basic cotton, Fruit-of-the-Loom kind of guy. But when you mentioned this to Bill, he rolled his eyes in the direction of Mrs. M's house and said he had a pretty fair notion of where Henry's red bikini briefs had come from.

About a week later, Mrs. Mitkin came barreling out of her house and cornered Bill between your back gate and the garbage can. She kept him standing there with a trash bag in his hands for fifteen minutes. When he returned at last, empty-handed and red-eared, you asked him what all the fuss had been about.

"Mrs. M says, just because Henry's car is parked out front all night, we shouldn't get the idea they're sleeping together."

"She said that?"

"Well, actually, she didn't say 'sleeping together.' She said 'shacking up.'"

"And what do you think?" you asked.

"Well," he said, "I think they're sleeping together."

A few days later, as you and Bill were leaving the house on a grocery run, Mrs. Mitkin and Henry drove up.

"Getting married!" she yelled.

"Really?" you said. "That's wonderful."

"That's right," she said. "Wedding's next month. You're invited!"

The wedding flyer was stuck in your front door screen when you returned. An hour later, Henry brought over mail he said had been misdelivered to Mrs. Mitkin, but which you suspected she had borrowed out of curiosity from your mailbox.

"So, you're really getting married, are you?" you asked him.

Henry stared at his feet, then glanced up with frightened eyes. He looked more miserable than you ever imagined he could look. "I don't want to get married," he said, "but I don't know what to do, all the invitations are out."

Bill had joined you at the front door. He shook his head and offered an opinion on the subject: "If you don't want to get married, Henry, don't get married. Just say no."

You've noticed that Bill, with his years of working in Social Services, tends to oversimplify the dynamics of human relations. Nevertheless, you are coming to appreciate he is more often right than not. On the other hand, you also knew, only too well, that saying no to Mrs. Mitkin was more than most folks could manage. You doubted Henry could do it. He walked away, confused, without saying goodbye.

A week later, when you were still exclaiming over how

Henry had been railroaded into matrimony, Bill ran into Mrs. M on the street. Uncharacteristically, she did not stay to talk his ear off.

"She says the wedding's off," Bill relayed to you. "I didn't ask for details, and she didn't offer any. She says she's got forty people to call and un-invite, so she had to 'get cracking.'"

Another couple weeks passed before you realized you hadn't seen or heard Mrs. Mitkin for many days. You hadn't seen Henry either. Henry, who for months had been a daily — and nightly — fixture at Mrs. M's house, was suddenly, completely gone, and her drapes were closed. Days came and went.

Then one Saturday morning, Mister Willy, the amiable, toothless fellow who cut her lawn, turned up to do his mowing. He mowed up a storm, but Mrs. Mitkin, who to your knowledge had never missed an opportunity to lecture him on the right way to edge her lawn, didn't show herself. You thought then of your father — how for years he'd sat in the dark, with the curtains shut, staring at the television — and it frightened you. You were relieved Henry had found the gumption to break off their engagement, but what about Mrs. M? You went next door to check on her.

She answered her door promptly, then went and sat on the living room floor, surrounded by a mandala of travel brochures.

"Going somewhere?" you asked.

"Caribbean cruise," she snapped. "Something I've always wanted to do. Monty, that old miser, never took me anywhere." Monty had been her first and, as it turned out, only husband. She wasn't about to get stalled out by a lot of tight-fisted, lead-footed old men.

"Would you like us to pick up your mail while you're gone?" you offered, searching for a way to be kind.

"Nope," she said, "Henry's doing that, thank you."

Not long afterwards, you were coming home from a jog on one of those warm, late-summer evenings when the sky displays luminous patterns of pink and blue, and you saw Henry's car out front. While turning off the sprinkler, you heard Mrs. Mitkin and Henry talking and laughing, sitting on her porch. When you went out again later to shut off the sprinkler, you met Henry on the sidewalk.

"Henry!" you said. "Nice to see you. We were afraid we wouldn't be seeing you anymore."

"Oh, no," he said, giving you one of his real slow smiles. "Just 'cause we ain't getting married don't mean we can't still be best friends."

"I guess not," you said, thinking things had turned out pretty well, after all. A few days later, Henry loaded Mrs. M and her luggage into his car, and this turned out to be the last you would ever see of her. She died at sea — a heart attack took her quick with no time for suffering or second thoughts. And though she had been well past eighty, her passing away surprised you. As Bill put it, any woman who can set herself up for a jilting at that age, then sail off to the Caribbean to recover, achieves a kind of immortality.

You've read that, when someone close to you dies, you may hallucinate him later, imagining you hear his voice or see him on the street. This turned out to be true for you with Mrs. Mitkin. Every so often, you'd be out back and could swear you heard her nagging after Henry or yakking on the phone or shouting to be heard over Mister Willy's power mower. Once, the voice you heard turned out to be Mrs. M's daughter, a tall, sour-faced, older woman who must've looked like her father, but who sounded like her mother. The rest of those times, it was just your imagination.

You never hallucinated your father, however. He was dead, you knew he was dead, and there was no part of you that wasn't convinced of this fact. By the time Bill had been living with you for six months, this house, which had belonged first to your grandparents and then to your father, was more or less completely yours. You'd let your father go.

One small thing about him, however, continued to trouble you for a while: his brain tumor, the secret malevolence that had sprung up in his head and grown there till it crowded out the man himself. The whole business scared you, because, you suppose, children always imagine that, when they go, they'll go like their parents did. In the matter of dying, the younger generation looks to the older one for advice on how to go about it.

It took you months to realize that you die like your parents only if you live as they did. In that regard, each person is given a choice. Just because your father never made up his mind to live his life didn't mean you have to do the same. This is why you finally took the plunge: quit smoking and started jogging. You figure the couple hours in aggregate each day that you once spent smoking cigarettes could be better spent in working out. At age thirty-four, you bought your first pair of running shoes — shiny gold Nikes.

And when Bill asked what you intended to do with all that money, once your father's estate was settled, you told him you thought it was time the two of you took a vacation together, a real serious vacation. You had some idea you wanted to go to Europe, to Belgium to see Arlon, the River Semois, and Bastogne. That would be great, he agreed, but he didn't think he could get more than two weeks off this first year of his new job.

"That's okay," you said, "next year's soon enough. Or the year after that. This year, maybe, we'll take a cruise on the Caribbean."

"Well then," Bill replied, "let's consider making it a honeymoon cruise. After all, just 'cause we're best friends don't mean we can't still get married."

56.

Why Sasha Can

T onight there is no question in your mind: you have Made It! You are Inside in the biggest way possible. When you look up, the lights you see overhead aren't stars, they're kliegs. Stars don't give a flying rat's ass about your petty problems; klieg lights have eyes only for you.

You look up to the scaffolding, over to the double sets of stage curtains and backstage techs scurrying around, down to the scarred, stained floor with its old tape marks looking like bandaids — and you pronounce it *good*. Actually, any night in your performing life that you are *not* freezing your butt off is good. If you were still relying on your juggling skills to put you over, you'd also be celebrating the absence of heavy winds in this huge auditorium.

Yet here you stand: no costume, no clown gear, just your comic-*cum*-storyteller's Ninja uniform of black shirt and pants. And, most importantly, no security props at all, aside from your lucky red nose concealed within your pants pocket. Anytime during a performance when you fear you could lose it (your nerve, that is), all you have to do is reach into your pants pocket and squeeze your lucky red nose. No one in the audience can hear its reassuring little squeak.

You guess management must have opened the doors already, because you notice people are drifting in now to take their seats. This will be the biggest house you've ever played to. There's even a third balcony, and the back rows against the wall are too far away and too shadowy for you to see very well. But those TV cameras are plenty close, and you could just hug yourself, knowing you will be seen by the world and saved for posterity. Tonight won't be your last twenty minutes of fame, you can feel it.

Your storytelling approach to standup (or vice versa) is turning out to be the purest form of entertaining you could have imagined. You are learning how to create whole new worlds with only words, gestures, expressions. People are saying you are a "physical comedian." The freedom of needing nothing outside yourself, of being sufficient unto yourself — the freedom to *be* yourself — jacks you up every time you step onstage. Of course, every time you step onstage, there is that initial fear that you will surely die a thousand deaths in the next 1,200 seconds. But you've given up trying to dampen down the fear. Instead, you use it. The terror and the rush, followed by a warm, soothing shower of thousands of clapping hands.

Even your father, the General, has lightened up on you since you lost the makeup. When you played D.C., Georgetown, he actually came to see you, sitting stiffly at attention throughout your set. But afterwards he came backstage to see you, and he hugged you for the first time you could remember since you were a kid. You wonder if maybe a small part of the problem had been his fear you'd get white pancake on his expensive business suit.

A large part of the problem, though, was gone: your stepmother had walked out on your father a couple years earlier.

"So, Dad, does that mean you're batchin' it for now?"

"That's right, Alex — I mean, Sasha. I need to get clear with myself before I get involved with anyone else again. I'm in AA now."

"You are?" This is not a father you recognize.

"You betcha. Sheila did me a big fat favor by walking out. It really straightened me up when she left. We both owe her a lot."

"*I* owe her? How's that?"

"Son, *she's* the one who insisted I send you to the Academy. Otherwise, I probably would have killed you, I was so out of control."

It was a visit that took a lot of sting out of your childhood, and it wasn't until after he'd left that it occurred to you to wonder how he ever found out that you'd be performing so nearby him.

Now tonight, in your back pocket, you are carrying his approval in the form of a telegram he sent you this morning: "Remember, son: it's kill or be killed." You smile at your dad's attempt to be funny. You suspect, on some level, he may be serious.

So, these days, you must admit: you are a happy man. You are fulfilled in your choice of professions. And, like your father, you're back to living alone. You never rented out your attic after Jujube moved away — you don't want anyone else over your head. Sometimes you climb up there and lie in the space where she used to sleep. Sometimes you wonder if you shoulda ... but no, those rebounders are always trouble.

You might have tried to resume negotiations with her, so to speak. But too late: she has that scruffy hippie guy living with her. When you found out you were hired for this job, you rang her up to tell her. After all, she got you your first standup gigs and the rest was history.

"Jujube! Howzit?"

"Sasha? It's been ages. How are you?"

"Ready for my closeup, Mrs D." Then you launched into the convoluted tale of how you completed your transition from clown to comic. When you told her about the Bakersfield gig you did in your underwear and socks, you were gratified to hear her snorty pig-laugh over the phone.

"Nothing funnier than the sight of a man in just his shorts and socks," she said. "I mean, I'm assuming they were boxers, not briefs."

"That's right," you said. "Clean boxers, even. And lucky for me I discovered the comic value in minimal costuming. So, Jujube. I'm doing this show in L.A. It's not actually standup or a comedy competition or any such thing. It's a storytelling festival, a PBS special of some kind. Anyway, it's going to be televised, and even though there's no winner exactly, I heard some casting people will be there looking for a couple performers to play small roles in an upcoming movie starring ... wait for it! — Robin Williams, ta-dah!"

"I thought you despised actors and acting?"

"I still do. But the pay, Jujube! Movies pay, and, as committed as I am to being independently funny onstage, I want to be able to continue to afford myself and the living standard to which I've grown accustomed."

"Still street performing?"

"Some. Just to keep my hand in, along with a few primo spots in the pier's stage schedule."

"Miss those daily hats?"

"Money for nothing? You betcha. But now, I hope, I'll have residuals to look forward to. No more stacking quarters in the dead of night, like some bank teller on after-school detention. My legacy has begun, Jujube! Just picture it: years from now, it's 3 a.m., and you have insomnia again, so you flip on the late-late-late-late-night movie, and there I'll be — forever young and virile and pulling in the bucks."

"Definitely something to look forward to, thanks."

"Well, and here's something else for you to look forward to: I have this one comp ticket left for this big show in L.A. — if you can get your ass down here."

The call had fallen silent at her end, and you thought for a moment maybe you'd lost your connection.

At last, she speaks: "Sasha, that's so good of you. But I can't afford to fly down for an evening. Besides, I'd need two comps. Bill and I are living together."

"I thought you were living with your father."

"I was. I mean, I'm still living in his house. But he died."

"Oh. I'm sorry. Guess that means now, when it's time to take out the trash, there's no question about who's gonna do it."

She laughs. "Yeah, something like that."

"Lissen, Juju, your asshole ex called me to find out where you are. I didn't tell him, but do you want me to?"

"Oh hell, no. I am so done with him. As far as I'm concerned, he never happened."

"That's the spirit!"

"But, say, about your show: I guess I'll have to catch you on TV. You said PBS, right? Sasha, I'm really glad things are working out so well for you. Really glad. You know, even though I'm not there, I'll always be your biggest fan."

"I know you are, Jujube. And you'll always be my toughest audience. Every time I walk onstage, I'll be playing to you. And giving thanks there's no possible way you can heckle me across the airwaves."

And that was it, the last time you talked to her. When you got the details about the live telecast, you stuffed them into an envelope and mailed them to her. But it was clear she was out of your life, and it felt less cozy, having no one to brag to or to share your triumph with.

"Hey, Mr. No-Pants," you hear a husky feminine voice at your elbow. You look down and see a tiny Asian gal with a giant nose ring — Min from last year's bar gig in Bakersfield. "Like your new digs?"

"Yeah, I was just checking the setup. Whatcha you doing here?" When you met her in Bakersfield, you assumed she was just a small-time club owner trying to class up her dive bar.

"My father owns this theater. I produce for him. I got you this spot."

"Uh, thank you very much," you respond with your best Johnny Cash impression.

"No need to thank me. I only pick the best. Just don't show me up for lousy judgment in slipping you into tonight's lineup — give me the performance of your life."

"Planning on it."

"Oh, and this is TV, so try to keep your pants on," she says, leans in with her rack, and reaches up to stroke your shoulder in that way she has. You shiver. "Nervous?"

"Who, me? Naw. ... I mean, yes! Terrified. I've never played to an audience this big."

"You'll do fine. Just remember: This. Is. TV. You can't resort to cuss words for any cheap laughs. No matter how desperate you think you are. Got it?"

"Got it," you respond, shamefaced.

"I'm sitting front row center. So, look for me there and anchor on my light." She tilts her head flirtatiously, frames her face with her two open hands, palms forward and thumbs extended, then flashes you a bright TV smile. "Hope you're not a spitter." Whereupon she turns to scamper away, but freezes on one foot, like an animé character, when you call her back:

"Min, wait a sec! Got a question."

"Yeah?"

"Um, you ever been to New Orleans?"

"Louisiana?"

"The same."

"No, why?"

"I'm driving down next week. A friend of mine there did me a favor, and I need to pay my respects. I could really use a road buddy, if you'd be up for that."

"An adventure? I like it. We'll talk after the show tonight."

Then she's gone, and you are left to gawk after her. But you have a big grin on your face.

Moments later, you hear the call for places. As you trip downstairs backstage to wait for your signal, you hear the announcer on the overhead and a cheer goes up from the audience.

57.
Ms. Juli Regrets — Nothing

Y ou and Bill watch Sasha's PBS special at your father's house in what is now your living room, on your TV, on your floor, curled up with bed pillows and blankets borrowed from your grandmother's mattress, which sits on your floor in the bedroom you now share with Bill. So much of the haunted, tainted furniture that was in this house for so long has already been carted off to St. Vincent de Paul's, never to be seen again. You are remaking this place anew.

Sasha's time onstage was only seconds under twenty minutes, and lots of other storytellers are also presenting tonight. But he was so good that, later on, you won't remember anyone who came before or went after him.

Only once had you seen him perform in public without all his makeup, fancy threads, and heaps of gear. And, while that night at the pier had earned him a well-stuffed hat, the gig itself had been a failure, in your view. Because, as far as you were concerned, just saying "fuck" every few moments onstage doesn't qualify as legitimate humor, even though the audience laughed its ass off.

Now here Sasha was on the small screen, as you had always predicted: better and funnier for being himself and not resorting to any cover or distractions or cursing. Yeah, baby! you thought, reaching up for an invisible pull cord to give two short blasts on an invisible train whistle. You knew it: it's not his "mask of character" nor even his demonstrations of clowning skills his audiences want — it's him. Everything else had just been getting in the way. Now that he is willing to show himself and be himself, he will forever be the People's Choice. Wherever he goes in this world, he will always be loved.

"Yeah, he's brilliant, alright," Bill delivers his assessment during a fundraising break. "And he's funnier than he used to be. Not so much what he says — but the way he says it! He could probably just walk onstage in his underwear and stand there, saying nothing, and still be hilarious. He just has this ... crazy charisma. I remember back when he was performing at the pier, he was funny then, too, but he was a real asshole. Now he seems almost ... sweet. Like a mischievous little kid. I can see why you think so much of him." Bill kisses the top of your head as he struggles to his feet, swathed in blankets like swami robes. He grabs a pillow before shuffling off. "I could do without the red rubber nose, though."

"He only brought out the nose at the very end to make a point with that last story and finish up the set. I think he was getting nervous about ending well. At least, he didn't say any FCC-forbidden words," you explain, feeling compelled to defend your former flatmate.

"Good thing, 'cause they woulda for sure have bleeped him out. Which makes for a crappy end of a set. I'm going to bed. Gotta get up early-early for work."

"'Night, sweetie," you call to the retreating back of your live-in guru. "I'll be along shortly." Then you lie down to stare at the smoke-stained ceiling that still needs repainting and to think about Sasha, his performance, his life, and how, ultimately, you could never, ever have fit into it.

When Sasha phoned to invite you to fly down to L.A. and attend this show you and Bill had just watched on TV, it was the first time in many months you and he had been in touch with anything more than a postcard from Plano. And, as much as you appreciated his offer, it bothered you that the two of you didn't have much to say to one another that wasn't about his career. You asked the questions, your usual tactic for holding other people at arm's length; he answered them and inquired only superficially about how you were, what you were up to. For all he knew, you could have just finished copyediting Stephen Hawking's *A Brief History of Time* or be training for the Summer Olympics in Seoul.

You were supposed to be friends. You'd moved out of his attic in large part so you would be able to stay friends and not get to a place where you wanted to claw off each other's faces. But what kind of friend experiences a major life change, as you did when your father died, and says nothing about it? Okay, you *did* mention it to him eventually, but only at the point where the subject couldn't be avoided. Before that, it never even occurred to you to seek out Sasha for emotional support. It was Bill you called when you needed that.

No need to search your soul for why. You know, in your gut, that while Sasha likes you just fine, he doesn't care all *that* much about whatever major life changes you may be having. What he really cares about is himself. You he cares about only insofar as you may affect him. Not that this makes him much different from most men.

Which is why you and he share only the common language of his career, his dreams and aspirations. He wanted you with him, so you could support him with your abilities. But about *your* dreams and aspirations? Not so much. You suspect, if ever you'd discussed this with him, if ever you'd been able to discuss anything of importance with him, he'd have told you your dreams and aspirations — like your orgasms — are *your* responsibility.

Before Women's Liberation arrived on the scene more than a decade ago, women were sex objects. (Big social advance: now men, too, can be sex objects!) They were also wives and mothers and housekeepers, teachers and nurses and ballet dancers. Then Women's Lib made it possible for you to be used by men in other ways, other new professional ways. Of course, it's harder to use someone who doesn't offer herself. *Why* did you offer? You clearly thought you needed to offer yourself to someone. You needed to belong, if not *to*, then at least *with* someone.

After months and months away from the man, you see you never could have been anything more to Sasha than a complicated appliance or a finely honed tool, his very own "amazing" Ginsu kitchen knife that could slice, dice, and cut anything put before it ("But wait! There's more!"). Sasha was into you, alright — but only to the extent he needed to be in order to persuade you to be into him. No wonder Kitty declared him a "sadist" who tries to make every girl love him, but who only loves those who don't love him back.

Your maternal grandmother would have said, when it

came to marriage, you "got out while the getting was good." But your big failed marriage to David still led straight to your little sad crush on Sasha. Sasha needed and wanted your professional support — and he was willing to dangle the possibility of a romantic relationship in front of you in order to get it. David had been your boyfriend before you married him and became his de facto publicist and foster mother. Did he pretend to be your loving husband after he'd lost interest in order to retain your services and support? No way to know. But both relationships, with David and with Sasha, seem to have had a lot of bait-and-switch about them.

Sasha could give you free rent in exchange for your labors. Being a kept woman was a far better deal than David had offered. However, to get you to buy into him emotionally and really support him wholeheartedly, Sasha needed to offer you a different kind of currency. You are reminded of every boy who ever told any girl, "I love you," simply to get her to put out. Did Sasha ever say those words? No. But with his longing looks, his lavish compliments, his tales of other devoted showbiz couples in history, he made you think that's where he was headed. And, naïve ingenue that you are, you fell right in, face first. How exciting it was! But he didn't love you; he only loved your professionalism — what you could make of him.

Before that, you'd had this "husband" who never came home, yet claimed he didn't want to lose you. You were so angry with him. Yet you kept excusing him, taking him back, accommodating him. Now that you see how much easier it is in every way without him, you can't understand why you worked so hard to hold onto him.

Q: What did these two men have in common?

A: Dreams for success you were eager to be part of.

Q: Why did you give yourself over to their dreams so completely?

A: Because you already believed the dreams you once held for yourself were impossible to achieve by a young woman with "no special great talent."

In Sasha's case, it's clear now he's able to get exactly where he wants to go all on his own with no help from you.

In David's case, you are sorry to realize, you probably hurt him more by trying to make him stick to a dream you have come to realize he most likely wanted to let of. Oh, yeah, and also by always covering for him and not allowing him to suffer the consequences of his own misbehaviors. Every time he screwed up, you made it good. If it hadn't been for you, maybe he could have failed in his twenties instead of in his thirties. Then how much more time he would have had to get himself turned around and go off in another, better direction.

You were furious — still are — that he would marry you, but refuse to give you even a decent amount of honesty and disclosure. You realize now he simply wanted to shut you up and keep you coming back to give more. It bothers you that his reasons for trying to hold onto you make infinitely more sense than your reasons for trying to hold onto him. When it comes right down to it, you forced yourself on him. (Just as you did with Richard.) Shame on you for rewarding this sick man every time he screwed up. You ought to have let him fail on his own, pick himself up again, and earn his manhood.

Tonight, lying here on the floor in front of the TV and listening to Bill's snores off in the distance of what used to be your grandmother's bedroom, you wonder what your relationship with Bill means. He says he wants to get married — to you. Does he have any idea what he's getting into? Obviously not.

Bill is decidedly outside the usual pattern of your choosing: a man with no dreams of stardom, no aspirations for special accomplishment — a regular guy with straightforward needs and uncomplicated desires. You wonder: maybe he's too Zen for you and not twisted enough to interest you over the long haul? In any case, he has no fantasy-train you can climb aboard and help him choo-choo to interstellar success.

And you can't use him to sublimate your own creativity, either, letting your own aspirations run to waste. He doesn't want anyone to help him advance his plans or pay the rent or even make him look good in public. He doesn't want an appliance or an audience or someone who will make him behave himself. He is willing to fit himself into your life just as much as he wants you to fit into his. He is looking for a best friend, a partner in life. He is looking for someone he can call Home.

With a man like Bill ... or, rather, with Bill, you would be responsible for achieving your own goals, for turning your own dreams into reality. You would be responsible for your own creative and professional orgasms.

Or not.

He would help you if he could, but it would be through secondhand gestures, like making coffee for you when you're on deadline or going for Chinese takeout when you're on a roll with your writing and don't want to stop to cook dinner.

Is it possible for you to stay interested in a man like this? You are willing to find out.

58.
David and the 12 Steps

After your arrest for what they called "indecent exposure" in connection with the young ladies at Mercy High, you finally have to admit: maybe you *are* powerless over pussy and that, in your relentless pursuit of pussy, your life has become unmanageable.

It was then you first learned to appreciate your S.A. sponsor, Albert, because he really truly saved your ass, made bail for you, got you sprung, and never even afterwards fingered you for the cash he knew you didn't have. Besides, who else were you going to call for help? No one.

Following your release, Albert brought you back to his shitty basement apartment on Potrero Hill. And there you *try* to explain to him (the two of you sitting at his red-speckled, chipped, Formica-top, kitchen table, drinking pallid coffee and smoking Kool cigarettes, one after another) you *weren't* "exposing" yourself per se. You were just ... looking. And you had to adjust your clothes somewhat in order to ... you know, reach your ... yourself.

Ordinary and downright boring, Albert is nowhere near hip. And though he is a straight man in San Francisco and might have been expected to possess a certain caché for being a sexaholic-in-recovery, he seems like a man who would be totally resistible to women. On the other hand, you must acknowledge: he has a real talent for listening without betraying any apparent judgment.

At this point in the ongoing tale of woe that is your life, he lights a fresh cigarette off the still-glowing stub of the one he's just finished. He expels a lungful of smoke and grinds out the used-up butt in the huge metal ashtray that sits between you, looking like a spaceship that crash-landed on Planet Garbage. For the past hour, he's been nodding and grunting assent throughout your self-pitying, self-justifying monologue, without ever once interrupting you.

But now he purses his big lips, rolls his eyes in that comic way he has, and says, "So, bro, you're not an exhibitionist — you're a voyeur. A Peeping Tom of little girls coming out of church. That's *so* much better." You don't correct him over the fact of Mercy being a school, not a church.

Still, he leaves it at that, doesn't chew you out further, only adds, "Don't you think it's time you got serious about yourself?"

And so it is, at long last after a couple months of attending the biweekly meetings of your local chapter of Sexaholics Anonymous, you take the first step of this twelve-step program. Until then, you'd only been mouthing the words, like you always did whenever you were required to say the Pledge of Allegiance at a high school assembly.

Taking the next step proves harder: that business about

there being a Power greater than yourself that can restore you to sanity, blah-blah-blah. Apart from the mystery of how you can ever be "restored" to a mental state that, insofar as you know, you have never once in your life enjoyed, even if there *were* such a "Power," then where the hell was *It* when you needed *It*? Like, say, back in Nam, where every waking moment you were so afraid of dying you could hardly breathe. Or much, much earlier in your life, back in rural Florida in 1950, after your biological father dumped your mother, and your mother dumped you on your cretinous relations, abandoning you for three long years while she went in search of a new host to attach her drunken, parasitical self to. Or a couple of years later, when your new stepfather taught you what your dick was for by demonstrating with his own on you. So much for any hope of intervention from any so-called Higher Power.

Then Albert says, in his sponsorly way: "Okay, let's just *pretend*. What if there *were* such a Higher Power who *does* care about you and who *is* both capable and willing to restore you to a sanity you have never previously in your life enjoyed — what *then*?"

"Okay," you tell him, "In *that* case, I *might* be willing to lean on such a Higher Power."

"Good enough," says Albert, slapping the Formica tabletop with the flat of his hand for emphasis. "Let's suppose, then, this is your understanding of Him — so, on *that* basis, could you turn over whatever's left of your sorry-ass-WILL and pathetic-excuse-for-a-LIFE to Him, placing yourself in His care?"

"Yeah, sure," you reply with a shrug. "Whatever."

For decades now, you've gotten away with your bullshit.

Your friends didn't guess what you were up to. Your ex-wife never had a clue. You didn't catch any diseases. No angry husbands or boyfriends intervened by kicking your rear end for you. You had come to believe you were invincible and that the ordinary consequences of one's actions did not apply to you. How wrong you were!

Now you see: you have angered the gods, your Higher Power, whatever. You realize Albert is telling you: you will *have* to suck up and get Him back on your side before you will be allowed to take the next step.

A couple nights on Albert's scratchy sofa, and you return to your squat at the co-op. The few stoned-out artists you pass in the dark, dank hallway show no signs of having been aware of your absence. Kinda like Barbra toward the end. You pick your way to the cavernous, post-industrial studio left vacant by little Mary's artist friend who never did return from her hostess job in Asia. Based on experience with the Boom-Boom girls, you have a pretty fair idea of where she ended up. But, according to Mary, the place is paid for through the end of the year, so what the hell.

Back "home," you yank off your boots, toss them one after the other across the room, and stretch out on the mattress-on-the-floor bed apparently favored by all artist-types. You already know this next twelve-step step will be harder still: to make a "searching and fearless moral inventory" of yourself. You've scored plenty in your life — easily, hundreds of times — but so what? What's the big deal? "Free Love" was where it was *at* in the '60s and '70s when you were coming (so to speak) into your manhood. Your sexuality was your own business, your own private business. Besides, with the regrettable exception of little Mary McGowan (she of the delectably tender thighs and cotton-clad cunt under her crisply pleated, uniform skirt), they were all, so far as you knew and/or can recall, Consenting Adults.

But when you think back on your time with Barbra and, earlier, with Juli, you must acknowledge that a considerable amount of lying and subterfuge did go on. And, you suppose, this didn't exactly qualify as "moral" behavior on your part. And, you admit, you *did* engage in a certain amount of theft of money and drugs (and, once, a beautifully crafted, silver hash pipe) from friends and associates on certain miscellaneous occasions. Although this only happened when you were in real, serious need of said substances. And, regrettably, some lying or, at least, obfuscation had understandably accompanied some of these ... borrowings. (The hash pipe had been a legitimately accidental pocketing. You just never got around to giving it back.)

Forcing yourself to recall (insofar as possible) these times, which you were able to do only with the greatest difficulty by listing as many encounters as you could, year by year, was ... discouraging. In the past, such personal stats would have been cause for justifiable masculine pride and bragging rights; tonight they just seem stupid and crass. Not to mention, a big waste of time and energy.

Forcing yourself to recall HOW YOU GOT HERE makes you realize: it's *all* your fault. Your whole life, you've been blaming others for your behavior. *They* made you do it. You were only doing what you had to do in order to survive. Your father left you. Your mother was a slut. Your stepfather raped you. You had to work since you were fourteen. You entered life with the entire deck stacked against you. If only you'd been raised in privilege, like Barbra or that faggoty friend of hers or even your smart-ass connection Sasha, how much better you would have turned out. That's what you thought.

Now you wonder.

You rummage around the studio till you come across a newsprint pad containing gesture drawings of naked people — what could be more appropriate for your purposes? Flipping through the pages, you think maybe a few are of Mary. Which causes you to speculate on the exact nature of her relationship with the Unknown Artist Formerly Living Here in a way that causes you to press your hand hard to your bulging crotch and consider unzipping your fly....

But no, you have work to do. You dig through an old cigar box full of short, fat, moldy crayons until you find one big enough to write with. Then you get down to business.

And so it is, by identifying the exact nature of your wrongs over the preceding two decades, you discover you have in fact admitted them to (a) yourself, (b) "another human being" — that is, your sponsor Albert — and even (c) that Higher Power (a.k.a. God), however you pretend Him to be.

The next step, number six, is easy: to be "entirely ready to have God remove all these defects of character." Yeah, you are up for that, alright. Ready and willing.

Having humped six of twelve steps, you experience a brief moment of elation. But when you review the remaining steps, you discover that, in order to fulfill the seventh, you will have to ask "Him" (or It?) to remove your shortcomings. This must be the suck-up step, you think. Worse, you see you are expected to be humble about it. Which is such a bitch, because, the way you figure it, if this Higher Power created you in the first place, then He's the One who made you like this. In short, if you're a jerk, so is He.

A week later, lunching with Albert in the overheated, stuffy Chinatown restaurant where he is standing you to yet-another $2 meal, he reminds you: even if you can't observe the spirit of the rule, you can at least observe its letter. Fine, you tell him, frustrated with how your "recovery" is going. Then you make ready.

"Dear God!" you exclaim loudly with eyes turned to the cafe's filthy asbestos-tiled ceiling. "I *humbly* ask you to remove *all* my defects of character!" Three Chinese guys sitting at the next table cease shoveling noodles into their faces and look over at you. You give them your best U.S. Marine Corps whaddya-think-you're-looking-at? stare that sends them diving back into their bowls. Gooks.

Albert rolls his eyes at your less-than-humble tone, but all he says is, "Guess that'll have to do."

But late that night, lying in the dark on your fetid squatter's mattress, spread-eagle like Jesus on the cross, you try again, this time with real feeling. You close your eyes and speak your words to a shadowy ceiling crisscrossed with industrial pipes:

"God, please, whatever the fuck you are, if you are there at all, if you even give a shit, please, *please* do your thing on me! I beseech you!"

Originally, it was the free donuts and coffee, plus the unparalleled opportunity to enjoy an insider's view of perpetually horny women, that drew you into Sexaholics Anonymous. Though, fortunately, you didn't need to travel very far to get to meetings, because they are held twice weekly in the co-op's community space. Starting day one, you were annoyed by how Albert fastened himself onto you. Now, as you approach your eighth step — the one where you are expected to make a list of all the persons you've harmed *and* become willing to make amends to them all — you realize you would *never* have gotten this far without Albert's persistent prodding and unrelenting support. Frankly, you would probably still be in jail.

You begin recording your year-by-year list of "wrongs" committed, scrawled on 18 x 24 sheets of newsprint alongside sketches of nudes, by writing in as many names as you can recall. You are surprised it troubles you there are so many women whose names and even faces and bodies you have no distinct memory of.

"Not bad," Albert says on your next get-together after you hand him the newsprint pad to examine.

"My list or the art?"

"Both," he says. "But you know what you have to do now, don't you?"

"I hate to think."

Which is the moment when you first face the fact you are expected to make "*direct* amends to such people wherever possible, except when to do so would injure them or others."

Which is the moment when you first understand that, sooner or later, you will be expected to contact both Barbra and your ex in order to offer those amends.

Which is the same moment when you first realize you are terribly afraid to do this.

Frankly, you don't know whether all this amends-making is even possible anymore. After the Mary incident, when you were too fucked up to go home, you drove to the flat of your old friend and most reliable connection, Sasha. Miraculously, he was home, and he let you crash on his living room couch. A good idea, since that couch was so much nearer the bathroom than anywhere else in the place. The next morning, you felt bad about keeping Barbra's car out all night, so you called her. She didn't pick up, so you left a message on her answering machine. It was the best you could do.

It was late afternoon by the time you drove back to Ocean Beach, used the remote widget to get into the garage under her condo, and parked in her stall. You used the elevator code to ride up to the third level, only to find, sitting on the landing next to her front door, two big black plastic garbage-can bags that turned out to be filled with your clothes and miscellaneous junk.

A note scribbled on a lined notebook page was taped to one of them. When you leaned in closely enough to read the note, you saw it was unsigned. However, you definitely recognized the handwriting as belonging to Leena, that skanky Euro-ho in film school at UCSF, the one who cleaned houses for a living. The sentiments expressed in this brief missive also confirmed its authorship:

"You bitch, he's mine now. If this doesn't kill you, I will. I know where you live."

Ah, Leena. Short for Magdalena. Whatever. You'd met her months earlier in your neighborhood bar. She smelled like Pine-Sol and rotten old mop heads, but you'd enjoyed sticking your "broom handle" to her twice a week, in between her cleaning gigs. Usually you fucked her in her car parked at Ocean Beach. But once, just once, she insisted on doing it in a bed. And what choice of beds did you have to offer to the young lady?

Barbra was at work that day, making her retail rounds. Though she was not due back for hours, it occurred to you she could very well show up unexpectedly. But just contemplating the danger of possibly getting caught *in flagrante delicto* gave you a hard-on. With Leena hanging from your elbow, you fumbled the front door key into the lock, recalling occasions when you'd done the very same while living with Juli. Just the pressure of such dangerous liaisons got you off like nothing else. Once you managed to work the door open and slam it hard behind you, you grabbed Leena's hand and raced down the hall with her.

In the bedroom, she plopped down onto the bed, dug into her bag, and pulled out a camcorder. "Let's play Porn-Star!" she'd suggested.

Even at the time, you didn't think that would be such a good idea. But there you were: in your girlfriend's bedroom with this strange, volatile female and your giant woody trying to bust out of your jeans. And she *swore* she only wanted something she could play later for the sake of self-gratification, on those future occasions when you couldn't be with her. How could you be so selfish as to deny her this small favor?

Now, you realize, reading this *death threat* (for god's sake!), the crazy bitch must have written down your address so, later on, she could blackmail you or Barbra or both. Why, oh why, didn't you think to suggest going to one of *her* clients' homes?

But that was then, this is now. And *now*, when you try your key in the door, it doesn't work. So you hammer on the door, you yell Barbra's name, setting off a round of imperious yapping from Oskar, Mrs. Schmidt's vile little dog, across the hall. You figure Barbra has to be in there, hiding in her condo — after all, you've had her car out since yesterday afternoon.

After ten or so minutes of this intermittent, futile exercise, you shoulder your two garbage bags with the intention of leaving to return straight to Sasha's. The heft of all your worldly possessions makes you briefly consider the possibility of using Barbra's car awhile longer, since you are still holding onto the key. But, for all you know, there may already be a warrant out for your arrest on the charge of car theft, so the last thing you need is to get busted for that, especially so soon after having plugged a sixteen-year-old. And she could hardly make the charge stick if she has not only the car, but the car key back as well. So you've got to give her key back. Somehow.

You set down the bags and pound some more on door. "Barbra! Barbra! I know you're in there — I have your car key! Please let me give it back!" But there's no answer, so maybe she's not home. Probably out with her fag friend.

You consider places you could leave the key where she would find it. Not here at the door, hanging on the knob or sitting on the floor — someone would be sure to swipe it. Which would be even worse, because they'd probably swipe her car as well, and then *you'd* get blamed. Not her mailbox — there's hardly a slot in those safe deposit box-style mailboxes that the postman opens with his master key. Maybe you could leave it with one of the neighbors — Mrs.Schmidt across the hall is home, she's always home. And though you can tell she doesn't much care for you, at least she knows who you are and she certainly knows Barbra. So, Mrs. Schmidt it is.

"Mrs. Schmidt! Mrs. Schmidt!" you call while knocking

more politely on her door. Instantly, Oskar recommences his shrill barking. Now, *there's* something you won't miss.

"Who is it?" old Mrs. Schmidt demands to know through her closed door.

"It's me — it's David. From across the hall. Barbra's ... boyfriend."

"What you want?"

Oskar, who'd fallen silent for a couple moments, starts in again, and you hear Mrs. Schmidt shush him. "Good boy," you hear her tell the dog, "that bad man cannot come in."

"Please, Mrs. Schmidt. I have Barbra's car key. I just want to leave it with you, so she'll be sure to get it back."

"Leave by door."

"What?"

"I said: Leave key by door. Then go away!"

"Okay. And you'll bring in the key and give it to Barbra as soon as you can?"

"Yes. Now go away."

So, you "leave key by door, then go away." And as you stagger down the building's hallway toward the elevator, straining to keep a garbage bag on either shoulder, you hear a door squeak open, then slam shut, assuring you Mrs. Schmidt has retrieved the key.

Back on the street, you hump your load to your friendly neighborhood bar, quickly survey the place to make sure Leena isn't there, and ask Sam the bartender to call a cab to come pick you up. It costs you your last five bucks to get yourself and all your worldly possessions to Sasha's. When you arrive, it's clear he isn't pleased to see you. But he grants you a month to get your shit together.

You spend a couple weeks of that month calling Barbra from Sasha's phone several times a day, leaving messages on her answering machine — apologizing, explaining, pleading with her to let you come back. But she never once picks up, and she never returns your calls. You even ride the 5 Ocean Beach MUNI line out to her place, in hopes of reasoning with her in person. Though you have accepted the fact that your key to her condo no longer works, you are determined to camp on her building's front step till you can catch her either coming in or going out.

It's early evening when you get there, about the time you remember she used to come home. Already it's pretty dark, so you don't notice right away the realtor's "For Sale" signs — one out front and another upstairs in her third-floor window. You'd waited an hour when her neighbor Mrs. Schmidt arrives with her annoying, diminutive black dog. She trudges up the steps to let herself in. You give her a friendly smile and stand aside to let her access the gate. Oskar snaps at you, but misses.

"Evening, Mrs. Schmidt."

"Same to you, young man."

"Glad you came along when you did. I seem to have misplaced my gate key."

"I don't think so."

"What?"

She presses open the gate and steps inside, yanking little Oskar along with her. Then she turns and slams the gate in your face.

"But, Mrs. Schmidt, please!"

Safe behind the security gate, she looks you straight in the eye in a way that makes you understand you aren't fooling anyone, least of all her. Then she says:

"She already moved. So forget it. You dirty piece of shit."

You catch the bus back to Sasha's.

You realize keys have become a big problem in your life when, at the end of a month, Sasha, true to his word, demands his key back. And when you ask for an extension, he turns you down. You point out that, since Juli moved out months ago, he has plenty of space, and since he's gone so much on gigs these days, you could take care of the place while he's away. He gives you a look that says plainly, "Just who in hell d'ya think you're kidding?"

But he also gives you another twenty-four hours. Which is the point at which you go down into the Mission District, down to the co-op artspace where Mary first took you, and you use her name to wheedle a couple of pothead artists into letting you into the building, so you could swipe the spare key under the fire extinguisher in the hallway. Then you return to Sasha's, swipe two joints from the stash box he keeps under his bed (along with twenty bucks in quarters from the five-gallon, glass water bottle he uses to store his street-performing small change), re-bag your stuff, and head off into your future. No point in arguing.

So unfair, though. Because during your month at Sasha's, you *had* in fact made a lot of progress toward getting your shit together. You did spend a couple weeks laying around, smoking Sasha's dope, feeling sorry for yourself. But then you made yourself as presentable as you could manage, traipsed down to Time-Life Books, and got back on the boiler room roll call. When you applied, they warned you: it takes at least a week to work back into the schedule. But you knew, from past experience, someone was always quitting. So you felt confident it wouldn't be long before your name came up. Only three days later, it did. You receive your first weekly paycheck the same day Sasha throws you out.

In retrospect, however, his throwing you out was maybe the best thing that could have happened, because it led to your coming here to the co-op. And here, at the co-op, someone is always working on something, 24/7, making some sort of crap and calling it "art." Which means: you need never be alone. Literally, never. Even better, while investigating the resources of the co-op's shared "community spaces," you stumble into one of their biweekly S.A. meetings. They welcome you right in, of course, so you help yourself to two glazed old-fashioned doughnuts, along with a cup of coffee (black, two sugars), and you accept a folding chair.

An hour and a half later, the meeting is over, and you leave, amazed to realize so many others— men *and women* — struggle perpetually with the same forces you yourself are unable to resist. But these Tuesday and Friday evening get-togethers seem to inspire a communal sense of optimism. You figure, if these losers can claw their way up out of the pits they've dug for themselves, then maybe the process offers some hope for you as well. Anyway, it's no worse than your average acting class. Maybe, you think, you can work on your performance skills here as well.

Besides, these meetings seem like a great place to pick up women. If nothing else, you know for sure this harem is comprised of self-selected individuals inclined to put out with little regard for standard overtures. But, that very first evening, Albert catches you chatting up one of the evening's speakers —

a mamacita with breasts clearly intended for a woman twice her size. And Albert sets you straight: no hanky-panky with fellow addicts. That, he explains, is *why* you all are here.

Which is how Albert became your sponsor in the first place and started *trying* to patiently walk you up the steps toward "sexual sobriety." As a compromise, ever since that night, you've fueled your nightly whacking sessions by spending mornings before you start work hanging out in front of the Ferry Building and ogling the female joggers as they go jiggling by along the Embarcadero. This routine motivates you to get up early, takes the edge off your anxiety, and enables you to face the day with relative calm and focus. There was one woman yesterday — some dumpy white chick with really short, punky hair, nothing special to look at, but her Wonder Woman T-shirt and gold lamé running shoes made you chuckle. At least, she had a sense of humor about herself.

Okay, now here you are, still needing to work your eighth step. But even just finding all the people you are supposed to apologize to seems an impossibility. Who knows where Barbra went after she sold her condo? Is she staying with "Mr. Ben Dover"? Or one of her sorority sisters? Did she leave town and move back in with her parents? You know some of her past business clients, like that human warthog who owns the House of Shields, but you also know you are still considered *persona non grata* there and in every other such establishment since Barbra quit covering your tabs. No point in trying to track her down that way. It could be unexpectedly dangerous for you.

Sasha was one apology you were able to make, and he accepted your attempt to make amends, especially after you gave him back some of the money and dope you'd borrowed on a long-term basis. Nevertheless, he made it clear you won't be moving in again with him. And he made it clear he has no intention of revealing the current whereabouts of your ex, who, like Barbra, has also gone missing.

Juli. All things considered, you guess you should definitely think about possibly making amends to her. But how can you do that if you can't find her?

You remember she used to work somewhere near the Embarcadero, at that snooty publishing company where you first met Barbra at a holiday party several hundred years ago. But you think she quit that job or something.

You supposed, at first, she must have gone to live with your old friend Bill, since he'd so touchingly asked for your permission to do her. But, though Bill's roommates claim he moved out a while back, they either won't or can't tell you where he went. You've wandered around the Mission, looking for his parked van, Vermin, and even dropped into his old office at Social Services, but he, too, seems to have vanished from the City.

Or if your ex-wife isn't living somewhere with your old friend, then you suspect maybe she's living with her depressed old alcoholic father across the bay in Oakland. Only you have no idea of where that might be, exactly. You always steered clear of her folks, not wishing to draw fire, should they have retained any residual protective parental instincts toward their grown daughter. You suppose her mother still lives in Oregon — for all you know, Juli could have moved out of state.

So, you aren't anticipating any opportunities to contact and make amends to Juli any time in the near future. But it's just as well. Despite Albert's insistence that you *need* to complete your eighth step, you'd just as soon *not* be in touch. Because, frankly, you are conflicted. You still feel it was your personal right to maintain sovereignty over your own sexuality. Even though you also have to admit that, having married Juli, she probably had some reason to expect a certain level of honesty and disclosure from you. Which you most certainly did not give. Not hardly.

All of which leaves you … where? In the months that have elapsed since Barbra disposed of you, you've come to grips with the truth that no one wants you. Once upon a time, you had all kinds of friends — at least, you *thought* you did. Now you have no one. Can it be you did not recognize the full extent to which those men you considered friends resented your prurient interest in their wives, girlfriends, and roommates? Aside from Sasha and Bill, it'd been a long time since you had any male friends you could turn to — men whose female companions you hadn't tried to fuck, whose bathroom medicine cabinets you hadn't raided for prescription drugs, whose wallets you hadn't checked for a dead president or two while they were in the next room. You see now your drug habits formed the foundation of your relationship with Sasha, while Bill had gone on being your friend for ages, mostly because he had no girlfriend or accessible cash or drugs to tempt you.

In a funny way you hadn't realized before, Juli had been your best friend in the world for a long time. At least, she had tried to accept you for who you are and encourage you to be your best self. While your old buddy Bill, when he saw you were sinking lower and lower, had in fact *tried* to extend a hand to pull you out of the quicksand of your addictions. Your two best friends in the world. No wonder they are together now.

Tonight is a big night for you. For the first time, you will be standing up in front of your S.A. group and saying those cringe-worthy words:

"Hi, my name is David, and I am a sex addict."

Of course, the assembled group responds with the standard "Hi, David!" so you pause. And while paused, you glance over at Albert and see he is nodding encouragement. Go on, son, go on! So you add, with a deep sigh for greater dramatic effect:

"And a narcotics addict. And an alcoholic. And an addict to pretty much anything and everything else in the world that a human being can get hooked on — that's me, alright."

Which draws a huge, sympathetic laugh that spurs you on to bad-mouthing yourself for another fifteen uninterrupted minutes. This is your first time onstage in over two years. It feels great. Not having any lines to memorize makes a big difference.

Afterwards during the break, you are on a natural, post-performance high as various fellow addicts come up to congratulate you on your personal journey. One in particular is that Chicana gal with the big tits, the one Albert steered you clear of weeks ago.

"You were wonderful tonight!" she gushes at you. "Did you really wake up in a bathtub in Los Angeles one morning and not remember how you got there?"

"Sure did," you answer proudly, just as you are biting into a glazed doughnut. "Ouch!"

"What's the matter?" she asks.

You feel around inside your mouth with your tongue until

you come upon the problem. "Oh, fuck," you reply. "I just lost one of my front caps." You suck the loose cap clean of chewed doughnut, spit the cast ceramic into the palm of your hand, and hold it up close to examine it. She leans in to look.

"Lemme see where it goes," she says. "In my other life, I'm a dental assistant."

You hesitate, swallow what's left of the doughnut that dislodged your tooth, then give her a wide-gap, shit-kicking, country-boy grin, missing front tooth and all. She laughs.

"Real cute, buckaroo," she says.

"Great. Any idea what can I do about this?" you counter.

She offers a nonchalant wave that ends with her sweaty fingered hand landing on top of your fist enclosing your fake tooth. She proceeds to massage your hand with steady, persistent pressure.

"No problem, cowboy," she says, "I can re-seat that cap in two minutes and get you all fixed up this very night. Your place or mine?"

"Oh, *your* place," you reply. "Definitely, your place."

59.
Juli Does Lunch

Today you have a date with Kitty. Amazingly, you haven't seen your old friend in nearly a year, and you wonder if she's changed much. On the last occasion you spent time with her, you were living with Sasha — correction: *at* Sasha's. You never lived *with* him.

Then last week, out of nowhere, Kitty calls you. You are surprised she has your number at your father's house, because you are certain you never gave it to her. But when she tells you she's sorry about your dad dying, you assume she must have gotten in touch with Sasha, the last number she would have had for you. You make a mental note to verify this later.

You agree to meet for lunch in the City. Kitty suggests Clown Alley — dead-cheap and within smelling distance of Raker & Ho. You reject the idea — you've come to hate that place and all your bad memories associated with it. Instead, you pick Pier 39's Eagle Cafe, with its good memories of Sasha. Kitty hesitates, then assents. The Eagle Cafe it is.

Ringing off, you felt a wave of anticipatory grief, remembering how close you and Kitty used to be. Years ago, you'd chat on the phone for hours, just to have the company. Even after you and David got married, she'd come over, spend the evening with you, crash there. Even early on, because David was home so seldom, your friendship never intruded on your marriage. Though, now you recall, it didn't exactly go well when he did come home. You still resent his using you as his resident pimp.

You review your memories, searching for the turning point when you and Kitty started being distant with one another. You think it was when she admitted she'd taken over your job at Raker & Ho. Okay, it wasn't *your* job by then — you'd been laid off. (Okay, fired.) You couldn't do the job at that point, your head was too messed up. Besides, you didn't even want the stupid job; all you wanted was the paycheck. Also, not to mention, you would rather not have been treated to the humiliation of being let go. All the same, you still feel Kitty should have checked with you before taking the position. It wasn't like the job had been offered to her coincidentally and — oops! she accidentally took it. No, in her usual, go-getter, proactive style, she'd called them up right after you got canned and went for an opening she knew damn well was available.

Which still surprises you, mainly because, of all people in this world, Kitty was the last one you'd have imagined would "sell out" to the "good ol' eight-to-five." Her term, not yours.

These are your thoughts in the Embarcadero BART station as you ride the escalator up to street level, wait for the light, then slow-run your way across the street and past the Ferry Building (ignoring the dirty old girl-watchers who hang out there). You cruise along the Embarcadero, past rotting, broken piers and cavernous, waterfront warehouses, covering the full length of Fisherman's Wharf before turning to head back the way you came, passing all the street performing pitches once again. By the time you meet up with Kitty at the Eagle, you will have gotten in at least a couple of miles, nearly double that distance when you get back on BART after lunch. You have decided you are training for next spring's Bay-to-Breakers Race.

You've given yourself most of the morning to pull off this run. And you need that time, because you haven't been running for all that long, only a few months, and you are S-L-O-W. Real slow. Like, 300-pound, pro-football player slow. In your mid-thirties, you are making a late start on trying to live a healthy life. Frankly, you never used to care whether the bad habits that shaped your lifestyle in aggregate were destined to shorten your life. Now you have multiple reasons to want to live long and prosper. But, to be realistic, you are an outa-shape ex-smoker, so you realize you'll have to work hard against your past choices that put you on the road to a destination you no longer care to visit.

As you approach the entrance to Pier 39, you get chills, remembering all the evenings you used to hang out here while Sasha performed. It occurs to you to take a turn around the ground level, about mid-way back where the small, elevated stage is, just to look over the old place. But then you think: what if I run into someone I know? One of the other street performers ... or even Sasha, slumming for an afternoon? You think he is in L.A. these days, but there's no point in taking chances. Life is too short to risk getting upset unnecessarily.

So, instead you turn off the sidewalk toward the pier, run up the first flight of wooden stairs to the second level that you come to, and dip straight into the Eagle Cafe. In the ladies room, you shut yourself in a stall, hang up your backpack, peel off your Wonder Woman T-shirt, and change into the sweatshirt you've been carrying in your pack. All the rest of your sweat-soaked running clothes — sodden sports bra, long damp tights, heavy socks, gold lamé Nikes — will be fine throughout lunch and on the way home. You still have another two and a half miles to cover, after all. You remind yourself to eat a light lunch so you don't end up puking into the gutter on your way back to BART.

Standing at the sink, you wash your hands and splash your face with water to rinse the salt crusts off your eyebrows. You glance at yourself in the mirror and run your fingers through your new short haircut, before heading out to the dining room to wait for Kitty. Once again, you are glad of your punky new cut. Bill, old hippie that he is, looked heart-broken when he saw you the first time shorn of your long, smooth, shiny locks. But you love having your hair so short you don't even need to carry a comb.

When Kitty arrives, she is late and wears an odd expression. You stand to hug her, then pull back to assess her. She looks tense, agitated.

"You okay?" you ask. "You have such a funny look on your face."

"I just had the weirdest experience. I hitched over to get here, and the guy who picked me up made me give him my socks!"

"Hmmm, paunchy white guy in his fifties, maybe? driving a big, black Camaro?"

"Yeah. How'd you know?"

"The 'Sock Pervert.' Been there, done that. So, what happened?" You feel proud of having once made that same guy pay you for your socks.

She shrugs and raises her foot to show you: penny loafer, no sock. "It's okay, they weren't my favorite."

"How come you're hitching rides, anyway?" you ask. You think: she's got a job — can't she afford the bus?

"Only an hour for lunch. You remember."

"Naw, you're good. You can stretch it to two, easy, if you eat lunch at your desk couple days in a row." Kitty laughs at your advice, then quiets down and takes a good look at you.

"Boy, you've certainly changed, haven't you?" she says. "Looking good, by the way. Best I've ever seen you. This new short cut — very contemporary in a rebellious sort of way."

"Thanks. Only thing easier would be bald."

She laughs, and you think to yourself that Kitty, on the other hand, appears rather shop-worn. Never a health nut to begin with, now she is looking just plain tired.

"And you're also not smoking anymore, are you?" she asks.

"Nope. Quit. Finally had enough. But it worries me at times, because I'm discovering, if I can't smoke, then there are way too many people I can't stand to be around. Also, I'm afraid, if I can't smoke, then maybe I can't write. I mean, I always smoked while I wrote."

"And how far did you get with that?"

"Not very."

"And how's it going now?"

"Actually, better. Surprisingly better."

"So what are you doing instead?"

"Instead of smoking, you mean? I'm jogging, if you can believe it. I figure, if I could spend an hour and a half of every day sitting around, breathing smoke, I can spend that same hour and a half running around, breathing air and working up a sweat. You know: circulation."

"What a concept! Are you training for Bay to Breakers?"

"Dunno. I think I could do the distance now, but I'm not so sure about the Hayes Street Hill."

"Well, keep it up, you'll be in great shape."

"Hope so. Working on it, anyway."

"On the subject of work: the Twins are just the same, still playing good editor-bad editor."

"Tweedledee and Tweedledum?"

Kitty nods vigorously. "But some things at work *have* changed: remember that guy in Acquisitions, Loren McMaster? Well, he died. Had AIDS. Some anorexic, plastic-looking chick in leather pants and four-inch heels came in to let everyone know."

"Sounds like his girlfriend. I met her once, years ago, at a Raker & Ho's 'Christmas-in-January' party. Skinny bitch, dressed to the nines, big hair lacquered into place, applies her makeup with a trowel?"

"That would be the one. But girlfriend? Don't think so. He was totally gay. Didn't you know that?"

"Maybe he went both ways?"

"Naw, I think she was, like, a sister or a cousin or something. Or maybe she was his attendant — she said she was training to become a nurse. Anyway, she's living in his old condo. She brought in a manuscript for a book he'd finished writing just before he passed."

"No kidding. I thought he was just an editor. I didn't know he wrote, too. What's the book about?"

"No one knew he wrote. But what's it about, you ask? Well, it's about a young guy from rural California — his father's a farmer or rancher, something American Gothic — and he goes to UC Berkeley in the late '60s, where he discovers and comes to terms with his true sexual orientation, then moves to the City and gets a high-level job in a publishing house, which sends him to the Big Apple several times a year on business (and on R&R, which he enjoys very much) until he gets sick and dies of AIDS."

"Sounds eerily familiar. Autobiographical, d'ya think?"

"Could be. Anyway, his book is a series of stand-alone short stories that, taken together, make up a kind of memoir-novel about the gay scene in San Francisco and New York City in the 1970s and early '80s. Talk about being 'acquisition-ready.'"

"Hmmmm. So, I guess, this is how you're so sure he was gay?"

"Well, duh."

"I remember he was terribly G.Q. Must've owned a thousand ties. The whole time I worked there, never saw him wearing the same tie twice. Nice guy, though. It's a shame. His book any good?"

"It's a complete first draft, somewhat revised, I'm guessing. But yeah, it's pretty good. Real good, actually. Kind of a love letter and tribute to all his gay pals and their courage in coming out. I think we're going to pick it up. Reading it made me sorry I never got to know him. He went out on sick leave right after I started, and we never saw him again. But, what I really want to tell you is, a lot's changed with scheduling since you were there — they want production to pump 'em out harder and faster. The place is getting to be a regular puppy mill for books."

"Yeah?"

"Yeah. So, the thing is, there's a job there, waiting for you. If you want it. The Twins are each getting their own assistant. No more sharing."

"You want Tweedledee or Tweedledum?"

"Tweedledee, of course!" You both laugh at that. Tweedledee was the nice one. "But I'd be willing to switch, if it would bring you back." Kitty waggles her eyebrows meaningfully. "Or we could flip a coin and take our chances."

"I don't know, Kat. I haven't had to work since my dad passed, and I'm liking it."

Kitty sighs. "I bet," she says. "But at least think about it, okay? The place is awfully lonely. And you must get lonely sometimes, too, all by yourself without your dad to keep you company." She pauses to give you a moment to consider her invitation in light of its potential for future camaraderie. You do not break the silence by offering the truth of your situation. Then she resumes, brightly:

"Besides, if you don't come back, we're probably going to hire this guy who's been temping for us — Kevin, tré gay in that verbally abusive way of your standard-issue vicious queen. Never shuts up. But, tell me: now that you have all this free time on your hands, are you finally making progress on your book?"

"Funny thing you should mention that. Lately, I've been

waking up with ideas and actually going to the trouble of scribbling them down."

"Good sign."

"I think it means I finally have something to write about."

"Even better. So, tell me."

You laugh that your old friend would actually ask you to violate one of her own cardinal rules of fiction writing: never talk away the energy you need to actually write the book — keep it to yourself, at least until you finish the first complete draft.

She correctly interprets your chuckle. "Sorry," she says. "No, never mind, don't tell me. I don't want to be responsible for making you to lose your steam. But promise me something."

"Sure. What's that?"

"That you'll let me read it when it's done, and if I like it, which I'm sure I will, then promise me you'll let me flack it from inside Raker & Ho. You know, nobody gets in there anymore without an agent. I could be your agent."

"I promise. And thanks for the offer. I'll take you up on it … in a few years. But I'm curious, how did McMaster's cousin, whatever she is, manage to get inside with his manuscript?"

"Combination of factors: he was one of our own and highly placed, she had other paperwork — HR-related stuff — that was needed, and, it seems, our resident drag-queen temp was an old friend of McMaster's. He actually crashed the weekly staff meeting to talk up the book. I think the new acquisitions guy told him yes just to shut him up."

"Good thing, then, the book seems like it'll be worth all the trouble. But, hey, what about you? What're you working on nowadays?"

"Nothing," Kitty admits. "Nothing since I started working. I just can't do words all day, then do more words all night."

"Yeah, I know the feeling."

"But at least now I understand why all those evening commuters on the bus look so tired — they're *tired!*"

"I hear ya."

Kitty cocks her head and gives you that special look you know heralds a confession. You raise your eyebrows encouragingly.

"Okay, okay, you know me too well," Kitty acknowledges, "so I'll just say it straight out: I really *hate* working at Raker & Ho. I hate being an assistant *anything*. I hate giving away all my best writing moves to make other people look good, as if they were real writers and not just public figures being paid to crank out some shit that will be mostly reworked in-house. I know I could do a better job of writing most of the manuscripts they shove at me. Hell, I *do* do a better job of re-writing some of them. It's getting so I don't have any enthusiasm left at the end of the day for my own stuff."

You are surprised to hear your old friend sounding so frustrated and bitter. You try to console her.

"Maybe you're just off the track of your natural biorhythm? You said yourself how tired you are."

"God, yes! That place runs totally in opposition to my internal clock. Sometimes I have to stay up all night in order to get to work on time in the morning. Then every time the phone rings, I lose my place in whatever fecal manuscript I'm working on. Plus, the people who work there are boring and gray. Oh, except for Kevin the Temp, of course."

"And this would be the very environment to which you

were trying to talk me into returning?"

"Yeah, well ... there *is* a position open, and you already know what you'd be getting yourself into. I just thought it would be a lot more fun if you were there, too." Kitty paused to let this sink in, before going on: "But you know what the worst thing is?"

"No, tell me."

"Not only do I not seem to care about my own literary output, but I find these days I'm just not enjoying the *process* of writing."

"Whoa! That's different. For you. Me, I *never* enjoyed the process. And I always envied you for starting as soon as you were old enough to hold a pencil and because it was always your favorite thing to do."

"Yeah," she says, wistfully, "it was."

"Maybe you just need a career change to get your mojo back?" you suggest, hopefully. "You could teach."

"Oh, because 'those who can't — teach'?"

"No, of course, not! We already know you *can*. Write, I mean. What about being a writing coach? You've been coaching me for years."

"I could do that. I'm kinda doing it now. Or maybe I'll quit Raker & Ho and run away to join the circus. I could do with some new experiences. Speaking of which: you — you're really getting on with your life. Told you you'd be better off without that two-timer."

"Right you were. What amazes me is someone I once thought I was so close to could go back to being a complete stranger to me. Maybe we were always strangers, and I just didn't realize it."

"How many people can say that!"

"Who knows? It's been more than two years already. My life is completely different. If I saw him on the street, I'm not sure I'd recognize him."

"Sounds like you've managed to 'forgive and forget'?"

"Forgive? Yeah, I guess so. Forget? Not so much." You sit up and do your best Eastern European accent, complete with imaginary monocle: "'We forget nothing!'"

Kitty laughs. "What's that from?"

"*All Quiet on the Western Front*, I think."

"And you're not seeing that clown-guy either?"

"Oh, Kat, Sasha and I were never *that* way."

"But you hoped."

"I spoze. Maybe." You shrug as if that part of your life meant nothing to you. "But it's just as well things worked out like they did. There was never any future there for me."

Then Kitty fixes you with an intense, soul-drilling look. "You know, you've really, seriously changed," she says.

"What?"

"Changed. You're just not the same person you used to be."

You laugh in discomfort at her pronouncement. "Well, I should hope so!" you respond. "You think it's easy for a couch potato to quit smoking and take up regular health-promoting exercise?"

"No, not just that."

"What, then?"

"You're a lot more serious than you used to be. But you've lost something, too."

You'd been on the verge of saying something vague and

platitudinous about how everyone changes over time. But Kitty had managed to capture your curiosity, while simultaneously annoying you.

"Oh, really? That's interesting. Just what is it, d'ya suppose, I've lost?"

Kitty cocks her head and appraises you briefly in that presumptive way she has. Then she declares: "Trust. You're not so willing to trust people as you used to be."

You nod your head in that noncommittal way you have. "Trust," you echo. "Yeah, I'll have to give that idea some consideration."

At the end of your lunch, you and Kitty argue briefly about the check. She had the Bloody Mary; you had the virgin, making a tacit point about your commitment to your new healthy lifestyle. Then you grab the check, and she gives up without so much as a show of struggle, consoling her conscience by leaving the tip. After all, with your inheritance, you can afford it now. Besides, you know they don't pay much where she works.

"Oh, hey," Kitty says, "I nearly forgot to tell you: we're putting out a collection of mostly previously published short fiction by our old nemesis, Dr. B."

"Yeah? So, what's his stuff like?"

"Like if Hemingway had turned to ethnography instead of pursuing literature as a competitive sport. I just wrote a celebrity endorsement for the back cover — wanna hear?" She leans back in her chair and closes her eyes to read from her mind-screen: "'A ripe, yet bitter cassava for the ethnic cultural stew of world literature.'"

"I get it!" You laugh at the "quote" and reply with one of

your own: "'Tales of rural poverty borne with equanimity by Third World victims of an oppressive colonial society.'"

"Say, that's pretty good! Let me get that down. I'm still working on the cover blurb." She whips out a tiny spiral notebook and scribbles out what you just said. "Thanks, I needed that!"

"*De nada.* Never actually read him, but I'm well-acquainted with the genre. I always find it sad that the same people being immortalized in these sentimental tales will most likely never read about themselves, since those stories are typically written in an academic style of little interest to regular folk living their tiny lives, especially when published in some snooty literary quarterly to assuage the editor's White Liberal Guilt over having been born into the same imperialist society that oppressed the 'characters' of the stories."

"Exactly! I mean, who the hell were these stories written for? I can't tell. Were they written for the semi-literate characters who populate their pages — in English, by the way, not the local language? Or were they written for the East Coast Literary Establishment that doesn't give a flying rat's ass about that whole ethnic scene, except to demonstrate how evolved and egalitarian they are?"

You nod, happy to have an opportunity to knock your old prof who nearly succeeded in killing off all your literary ambitions. "But, you know," you go on, "back when I was taking Dr. B's classes, I was afraid to read his fiction. I thought if I did, I'd be too intimidated by his genius to turn in any assignments."

"Oh, you *should* have read it! You would have found his work highly instructive in how to get an easy A in his class.

That's what his Young Turks did, I think: read his stuff, then wrote their own pointless, over-intellectualized stories in his same impenetrable style. And, needless to say, all those Turks had the advantage over us of being able to write with their dicks. Of course, he loved them!"

"You're saying you find his work, um ... boring?"

"Absolutely! And, as we know, to produce a work of everlasting boredom is the greatest art-crime of all."

"Well, it is, at least, a venial sin."

"However: I did find one story in this otherwise dismissible collection that was different in tone and, at the same time, disturbingly familiar: a surreal piece about a crib-death. When you were in Dr. B's class, didn't you turn in a story about an infant who strangles in its bedclothes?"

"Sure did. Got an A on it, too. But that was years ago. How did you—?"

Kitty laughs. "'We forget nothing!'"

"These short stories, they're all reprints? You recall what year that particular short story was first published?"

"'Few years ago, I'm pretty sure. Early '80s."

"So, well after I turned in my story to him?"

"Just about. And you never published your story, did you?"

"No, of course not, it was shit."

"Perhaps not as much shit as you thought."

"Oh well, you can't copyright titles, you can't copyright literary premises, and, if memory serves, there are also only seven major plots."

"Which is why you are planning to entitle your novel, *Gone with the Wind?*"

"No, actually, I thought I'd go with *The Holy Bible.*"

When Kitty stands to make her goodbyes, she leaves you with a sage declaration: "Just remember what Bette Davis said: 'Living well is the best revenge.'"

You watch her walk away, sockless in her penny loafers. You reflect upon the fact that you never got around to mentioning how Bill is living with you now. Never once did you even so much as say his name or allude to his presence in your life. Now you wonder why. And as you jog back to the Embarcadero BART station, you think: maybe you'll tell her the *next* time the two of you meet for lunch.

60.
Juli Works Her Plan

And just where the hell have you been?'"

You'd expected Bill more than two hours ago, and as soon as he walks through the door, you set upon him, stopping him in his tracks. The happy face he'd brought along with him gets scrunched up. He cocks his head to look quizzically at you.

"You certainly have a unique way of expressing your love and concern," he replies.

"I'm sorry. You're right," you admit.

Then he laughs. "'You're right' — I love the sound of that! Even though I know you say it only to distract and appease me."

"Yeah, well, you're 'right' about that, too. But, please, I'm not kidding about the 'where-you-been' part. So far as I know, you got off work hours ago, and you promised you'd call if you were going to be late."

"True. Now I'm the one who's sorry. I just forgot. Besides, I'm all out of quarters for the pay phone. Let's talk about it over dinner."

"I haven't started anything yet — you weren't home."

"That's okay, tonight I'm taking you out. I hope you haven't forgotten: it's our six-months of 'shacking up' anniversary."

Before the wine arrives at your table, you have already apologized three or four more times for your earlier assholism. You remember that famous movie line, "Love means never having to say you're sorry," and you think this must be one of the stupidest, most misguided statements ever made. Since you and Bill started living together, never a day goes by when you don't find yourself apologizing for something. Tonight your acts of contrition include biting your tongue to keep yourself from commenting on the change of clothes Bill selected for your fine-dining experience, his favorite Grateful Dead T-shirt. You remind yourself that, at least it's clean, you mended the hole in the armpit, and this restaurant is in Berkeley.

Bill shrugs off your transgression. "I guess quitting smoking is making you feel a little edgy. And living in your father's house probably isn't helping — the whole place still reeks. Maybe we need to take up the carpets, too. Even after all that shampooing, I can still see the dog-pee stains in the living room."

"It's not just quitting smoking that set me off, Bill. You have no idea how many nights, during the time David and I were supposedly together, I sat around, alone and waiting. I'm sorry, but in my cosmology, just the fact of waiting means something bad is happening for me somewhere."

"Not anymore," he declares. "You'll see. Try to be a little patient and go with the flow. I mean, just allow things to work out, so then they will."

"Right," you reply with a touch of sneer. "'Be here now.'

Which is a lot easier for me if you also manage to 'be here now.'"

Though you have come to equate being patient with a capacity for enduring pain, tonight as you watch yourself with Bill — sitting side by side in the restaurant booth, enjoying your dinners, chatting like a normal couple — it feels like you are viewing the happy ending of some bullshit Hollywood romantic comedy movie. Or maybe you've stepped into a parallel universe where, for a change, your life is actually working.

"How was your day?" he asks. "What did you do, while I was toiling away, sending scientists into the wilderness?"

"Went into the City, went for a run, had lunch with Kitty."

"Really?" He sounds surprised. "I didn't think you and she were still friends."

"No, we are. It's just been a while. A *long* while. But she called and suggested lunch, so I thought what the hell."

"Where'd you go?"

"Eagle Cafe. Pier 39."

"Oh yeah, great old place. Getting kinda expensive, though. Did she pick up the check?"

"No, I did."

"She's working, you're not."

"Yeah, I know. But I can tell you for a fact: she isn't making enough to eat at the Eagle. Don't you want to know what we talked about?"

"Girl-talk? No thanks, I'll pass."

"No, really, you'll find this interesting. My old job at Raker & Ho is opening up, and she wanted to let me know about it."

"I thought *she* had your old job. Is she leaving?"

"No, they're creating a new position to bump up production. Two parallel jobs. Each production editor now gets her own assistant."

"So, the two of you would be working together? Is that a good idea? She doesn't seem like a very trustworthy colleague."

You are surprised at the edge in Bill's voice when he talks about Kitty. But you remember he and Kitty often ran into one another when you were living in the City with David. After all, he was David's good friend, as she was yours. Or so you thought. It just hadn't occurred to you the two of them might also hold opinions about one another — opinions that might not be all that mutually flattering. You realize this is probably one of the reasons you somehow neglected to make any mention of Bill to Kitty over lunch.

"Naw, she's alright. Woulda been nice, though, if she'd told me before she cut me out of my old job. But I think she was just embarrassed."

"About selling out? Or about professionally side-swiping a friend?"

You grin at his analysis. "Bit of both, no doubt. But not to worry: I have zero intention of going back there to work. I have other plans."

"I thought as much. Let's go home, and I'll show you why I was so late tonight."

He parks his still-newish car in front of your house and opens the hatchback of its capacious rear end to reveal the mini-fridge-sized box containing his six-month anniversary present to you.

"I'm going to need your help getting this into the house," he says.

"A microwave oven? A set of encyclopedias? A litter of puppies?" you guess, judging by the dimensions and weight of the box.

"You'll see," he teases smugly. "Just keep a firm hold on your end there, I'll deal with mine."

Sitting on the recently cleaned, but still dog-stained, living room carpet, you and Bill extract the contents of the box from its packing materials: a tiny desktop computer, a Macintosh SE — about a foot and a half tall, grayish cream-colored, with a small, square screen and two built-in slots for disks. Right below the screen on the lefthand side is a rainbow-colored logo of an apple with a bite taken out of it. You smile to yourself, thinking this could be a symbol for the biblical Eve, the moment after her fall from grace.

"The salesman told me there's a new model coming out soon, but this one is still their top of the line, tried and true. He said it has a 40-doobie drive and can hold a bunch of rams. Dunno what sheep have to do with it, but I got you the extra-wide keyboard and a mouse, too — the whole menagerie."

You are speechless at the sight of all this cutting-edge equipment. To think you have your very own desktop computer!

"Thank you," you say simply.

"Happy six-months-of-living-together-in-sin," he replies. "Now you can write your Great American Novel. But you'll have to figure out on your own how to set it up. I suck at technology."

"No problem, I'll manage," you tell him.

"I know you will," he says.

"I have something for you, too, you know." You think

smugly about the tall, shallow box you carefully hid a couple weeks ago downstairs under your dad's old carpentry table.

"Yeah?" he says, looking pleased. "I love presents."

"Wait a minute." You get up to run through the house, then pick your way cautiously down those hazardous backstairs to the basement. The box you retrieve isn't particularly heavy, but it's large and awkward.

"You can see why I didn't wrap mine, either."

You watch as Bill opens his present — which turns out to have been double-boxed for protection — then sits looking at the handcrafted, Canadian-made, acoustic guitar.

"It's beautiful —."

"Rosewood. Smell it."

"But —."

"But, what?"

"But I can't play this."

"Of course, you can't right now. But you'll learn. You love music. You love music played on the guitar. Don't you want to learn?"

"I guess. Just never thought about it before. I mean, the only music lessons I ever had were when I was a kid and my mother forced me to take piano. She wanted me to grow up to be just like Liberace."

"Liberace! Guess she didn't know he was that way?"

"What, gay, you mean? Absolutely not. My mother is a proper Victorian lady, raised by my grandmother, another proper Victorian lady. Back in those days, they didn't have gay people."

"So, how long did you play?"

"Oh, a couple years into grade school."

"Then you stopped?"

"Yeah. It was kinda bad. My piano teacher put me in this big music contest in my school auditorium. It was a citywide contest, with a whole tableful of judges and a couple hundred students and teachers and parents in the audience, staring at me, waiting. I was supposed to have memorized the piece. But I didn't want to do it, so of course I fucked it up so I wouldn't have to do it."

"How did you manage that?"

"When the big day came, I couldn't remember how to play the piece. Even though I'd practiced and practiced, for weeks, and thought I had it nailed. But as soon as I sat down and started to play — I started twice, by the way — my mind went blank. Nothing. I had to get up, excuse myself, and leave the stage."

"How awful. You must have been so humiliated."

Bill nods, then shakes his head at the memory. "I went right home, refused to ever take another piano lesson, and never played again. I'm probably too old to learn now."

Where had you heard *that* before? "Bill, you're never 'too old' to learn. Anyway, you don't want to spend your whole life just being in the audience for someone else, do you?"

Bill looks at his new guitar with an expression of dismay and longing. "What? Like, I could be *The Bill Show*? I'm not sure I'm cut out to be any kind of musician, even a bad one."

"Better to do something you love badly than not do it at all," you respond, quoting Kitty. "I also got you this book on *How to Play Guitar*. Oh, and a tuning fork. The guy at Sherman & Clay said you can use the dial tone from the phone to tune by, but I didn't understand his explanation of how to do it."

"Well, thank you, this is so sweet of you," he says, pocketing the tuning fork and thumbing through the book's pages much too quickly. He sighs as he gets up and kisses you on top of your head. "I'm going to put this instrument some place safe, so it won't get damaged."

"Put it some place handy, where you can get to it easy," you call after him. "The guy at Sherman & Clay said to always keep it in sight. That way you'll remember to practice. Now I'm gonna to take *my* present downstairs and figure out how to put it together."

An hour later, you are sitting at your dad's old dressing table in his basement bedroom, your computer is set up, and you feel ready to rock and roll. You glance over at your dad's wall clock to check the time, so you can coordinate the time on your computer. Then you smirk at yourself when you recall that particular clock is *always* set to 7:22 — the time of Abraham Lincoln's death. Besides, what difference does it make to the computer or anything else what time it is? The time is *now*.

You hit the switch to power up and are gratified to hear an electronic ta-dah! tone. You push a disk into one of the slots and start downloading texting software. You create a file and open it. You are glad now that Raker & Ho installed that first computer in the lunchroom so long ago. You only wish you'd paid more attention to it back then.

Up to this point, you'd been humming along with purpose. Now you are paralyzed by the sight of the blank, glowing screen before you. This is nuts, you think. For months, you've felt your book, all angles and sharp, hurtful corners, twisting around inside you, tearing you up with its efforts to get out. Tonight, though, you feel strangely still within, your book quiet and in hiding, crouched just out of sight.

What if you can't do this? What if, in fact, there's *nothing* inside you? But that's ridiculous, because of course you know there's a whole world, a whole lifetime, "in there." Your past few years alone could fill a summertime beach read to overflowing.

You start typing, just to put something, *anything*, on the screen:

> *Why, sir, I trust I may have leave to speak;*
> *And speak I will. I am no child, no babe.*
> *Your betters have endur'd me say my mind,*
> *And if you cannot, best you stop your ears.*
> *My tongue will tell the anger of my heart,*
> *Or else my heart, concealing it, will break;*
> *And rather than it shall, I will be free*
> *Even to the uttermost, as I please, in words.*
> *. . .*
> *Love me or love me not—.*

A knock on the door stops you mid-speech.

"Who is it?!" you call.

"Coffee!" Bill shouts from the other side of the door.

"Coffee who?"

You turn to watch the door open, and a large mug of coffee appears at the end of an arm, followed by the man himself. "Coffee delivery for you — to fuel your enterprise, m'lady." He sets the hot cup down next to the keyboard. You thank him and push it away several inches, alert to keeping the steaming liquid at a safe distance from your new electronics. Then, because there is nowhere else to sit since you had your father's old army cot taken away, he stands there. Clearly, he wants to visit. The coffee, besides being a kindly gesture, was an excuse to interrupt.

"I see you've managed to connect all the widgets. I knew you'd do it," he says. "So, how do you like your new working tool? How's the writing coming?"

You turn to him, laughing nervously. "Honestly? Right now, I feel a little intimidated. Even the thought of writing something important has got me spooked. For one thing, it seems really weird not having actual words on paper, nothing I can hold in my hands. I mean, what if this thing dies, and all my words get stuck in there?"

"Better stuck in there," he says with a nod toward your hard drive, "than stuck inside *you*. But that reminds me of something the sales rep told me to be sure to tell you: 'There are two kinds of computer users in the world — those who've lost data and those who are going to lose data.' You're supposed to save, save, SAVE! That's why you have those extra blank floppies."

"I'd still feel better if I had a printed-out manuscript to work on. At least for revisions and edits. I used one of these desktops a little bit at Raker & Ho, and it's really hard to make changes on the computer, the screen is so small."

"Then I guess you're going to need a printer right away. Next month for that, okay?"

"Thank you. The computer is wonderful, insofar as I can tell. Only I can't really tell, because no words are coming yet."

"Looks like you got something up there," he says, pointing to your test text.

You glance back at the words suspended on your glowing screen and shrug. "Oh, *that*. That's just some random Shakespeare to get me going. Something to prime the pump."

"Okay, so, what's the problem?"

"Same old thing: not a lot to say."

"I can't believe that. After everything you've been through with your dad and with David and with moving out of the City after years of struggle. Don't they say, 'Write about what you know'? I think you're supposed to draw material from your own life experiences. You certainly have plenty of those."

"Yeah, sure. But my 'life experiences' have been so ... ordinary and stupid, I don't think anyone would be interested."

"I'm pretty sure it's not the experiences themselves that matter, but the conclusions you draw from them. You just have to learn to trust yourself."

"Maybe I just need to learn more words."

"That much, I am certain, is not your problem and never will be."

"Okay then, the right words. The right words in the right order."

At which point it occurs to you: what if you say the wrong thing in your book, and everyone ends up mad at you? You try to prepare Bill for this possibility. "I hope you realize, if I *do* write about 'what I know,' you'll most likely end up as a character yourself."

"Great! But you have to make me heartbreakingly handsome, six inches taller, and the hero of your book."

"That can be arranged."

"Can't hardly wait. Probably my one and only shot at immortality."

You both laugh at that, then stare at one another until Bill breaks the silence:

"Well, it's clear, at least, you have the makings of a plan. And you have certainly made a cozy place here to carry it out. Great start. But tell me...."

"What?"

"You miss San Francisco? I remember, when we first met, you were so starstruck with the City, you seemed entirely willing to inhabit all those roach-ridden, rotten dives, just in order to be there and feel part of the whole scene."

"You, too."

"Naw, not the same. I was only there because the people I knew and the things I wanted to do were there. For you, it was the place itself. That whole 'Baghdad-by-the-Bay,' 'Cool Gray City of Love' mythos. Like the song: 'I left my heart—'."

"'— in San Francisco.' Yeah, I guess so. But people can fall out of love with places, too. Besides, that's my *old* life. You know: the one that didn't work out. My new life, it's right here, right now. Even though living in my dead father's dead parents' house, after being out of college and married and on my own for the better part of a decade, kinda feels like backtracking. But maybe I can figure out where I went wrong."

You laugh to keep the conversation light, to make it sound like you're joking. But Bill doesn't return your tease. He looks at you thoughtfully until you feel uncomfortable and have to raise your mug to thank him again for the coffee. He correctly interprets your gesture of dismissal.

"Well, I'll let you get on with your Great American Novel," he says, kissing you on the top of your head and making for the door.

"Bill?" You stop him before he can escape. When he turns, you set your coffee aside, open your arms, and wave him into them with both hands. He steps into your embrace, bending to receive your kiss. Then you lean back and set your hands on his shoulders in order to look into his eyes. You need to tell him, to thank him for all he is and all he does. Really, truly, deeply thank him so he *knows* you really, truly, deeply *mean* it.

"Bill, thank you. For everything. I so appreciate it ... I so appreciate *you*. I'm sorry for my ... intermittent bitchiness. I'm just not used to anyone having my back."

"That's alright," he says. "If you're happy, I'm happy."

As he shuts the door behind him, you turn again to the glowing screen where Shakespeare waits, patiently standing in for you.

Trust yourself, he says. What a concept! With your track record, how *can* you trust yourself? But trust seems to be the theme of the day. Kitty brought it up as well.

You think back on your conversation today with Kitty. It was your first talk in ages with your old friend. Or maybe it was your last one. This business of "trust" and her remark about the critically injured, if not deceased, state of your trust galled you. Why should it be in any way remarkable that someone who's been through all you've been through would be changed by the experience? Was change such a bad thing? Kitty seemed to imply you've become a lesser person. If anything, you feel you are simply a whole lot less gullible than you used to be.

What is "trust," anyway? Belief in another person? Being able to predict how they will behave? You've already proven you suck at predictions. And David demonstrated absolutely that he could not be trusted. Except that was on him, not on you.

And what about Bill? If anyone in your life has proven trustworthy, it's certainly him. You smile to hear him plunking on his new guitar upstairs — sounds like he is trying to tune the strings. You hope you weren't too pushy with your choice of an anniversary gift, having blithely assumed he would enjoy being able to play, just because you know he loves listening to others play. Having naïvely assumed he would feel himself capable of learning as an adult, just because you have always assumed you were capable of learning anything new at any age.

An ability to learn new skills has never been your problem. Your problem is exactly what Bill said it was: trust in yourself. And tonight, unfortunately, you feel in short supply.

You hear the phone ringing upstairs, and you glance at the extension phone sitting on the floor, jacked into the wall on the other side of the room. You are surprised it didn't ring. But then you remember you turned off the ringer, so you would be certain you wouldn't be bothered down here. A minute later, you hear footsteps overhead and creakings along the basement staircase, followed by Bill's knock on the door and the swoosh of the door opening.

"I know you don't want to be interrupted, but it's your mother on the line, calling from Oregon. I figured you'd want to talk to her."

"Yeah, okay, thanks."

You go sit on the floor next to the phone, pick up the receiver, say hello.

"Juli, honey, so good to hear your voice! How are you, dear?" You hear a click on the line, telling you Bill has hung up the receiver on the main phone upstairs.

"Oh, Mom, I'm fine, just fine." You remember her lack of response, months and months ago, when you called her to tell her that your father, her ex-husband, had died. And you recall, with a flare of resentment, how she showed no interest in getting your stepfather to drive her down to attend the memorial service you'd arranged for him. But you suppose the life they'd shared for a few short years had happened too long ago to matter anymore, that she'd said all her goodbyes the day she packed up everything they'd had together, including you, and left him an empty apartment. "How about yourself?"

"Same as ever, dear. I was just calling to let you know your stepfather and I are driving down in a couple of weeks to visit some old friends of his, so that would be a dandy time for us to get together for lunch."

"And shopping, I suppose?"

"Of course, shopping!"

"Well, just remember, Mom, I'm not living in San Francisco now. I'm in Oakland, at Dad's old place. So, we can meet in the City for lunch, but you won't be able to just walk up the hill and drop all your packages off with me like before."

"Oh, that's right: I forgot you moved. How is your father's old house? I remember those back stairs were something awful. You'll be careful, won't you?"

"Mom, you know I always am."

"Was that your new boyfriend, Bob, who answered the phone?"

"Bill, Mom. Yes. That was him."

"And is he living there with you now?"

"Yep, it's been six months. So far, so good."

"Isn't he the one who asked you to marry him?"

"Same one."

"So, are you sure that's such a good idea, letting him live there?"

"Whaddya mean, Mom?"

She doesn't answer immediately, and you know she is trying to find a way to voice her maternal concern tactfully. "Well, I mean, if you're already giving away the milk, what reason does he have to buy the cow?"

You laugh at your mother's less-than-flattering metaphor. "I don't know, Mom. David bought 'the cow,' but then he turned out to be lactose intolerant."

She sighs at your response. "Well, at least, you're not still living with that ... clown person."

"Mom, I was never living *that* way with 'that clown person.'"

"I'm glad, because you know, honey, you can do so much better than that."

"Anyway, it's not Bill's fault we're not married already. He keeps asking, and I keep stalling."

"Stalling, why?"

"Mom, what I went through with David, I can't go through that again. It'd kill me. I need to wait till I'm absolutely sure Bill and I are right for each other."

No use arguing with your mother, so you don't bother adding, if there's one thing your so-called marriage with David taught you, it's that marriage is a pit-trap, and climbing out is a lot harder than falling in. Especially if you are trying to escape while stuck full of sharpened sticks.

"Well, just don't wait too long to give him an answer."

You punt the conversation back to its original subject: "So,

Mom, you're coming down in a couple of weeks? Maybe you could call me right before you leave home, so I'll know when to expect you, and we can plan where we want to meet?"

"I will, honey. And maybe, when we do meet for lunch, you could take my packages home with you on BART and keep them safe for me for a while? Just this once."

You have to laugh, really. Your whole life has changed, but Mom is always Mom — forever thrilled you should experience all the successes in life she never enjoyed, forever addicted to healing her wounded spirit with retail therapy.

"So, Mom, lissen, I need to let you go now. I'm in the middle of some writing."

"Oh, I'm so happy to hear it. I wasn't sure you still cared about that."

"Yeah, Mom, it turns out I do."

"I don't think I ever mentioned it before, but I used to have literary aspirations myself."

This is news to you. "You did, Mom? Well, what happened? How come you never did the writing you wanted to do?"

"Oh, honey," your mother responds with a chuckle, "because I had *you*, instead."

No pressure, you think as you say good-night to your mother. You had no idea you were responsible for fulfilling the artistic dreams of two generations. Or, for that matter, that she'd ever had aspirations beyond being first in line when Macy's opens its doors on a White Sale Day. You feel curious what it was she wanted to write about, but it's getting late tonight, and you have your own work to do.

Moreover, her advice — about not making Bill wait too long on his marriage proposal — left you unsettled. Because you must admit: waiting has always been the leitmotif of your life. Waiting to see. Waiting to begin. Waiting till it (whatever "it" is) is over. Waiting till you have something to write about. Waiting for some man to decide what he wants to do about you, so you can decide about yourself. Waiting for the curtain to rise on your life's play. You must have thought you were still in rehearsal, when in fact the show opened years ago and it's almost time for intermission.

Bill has never really understood why you kept stalling him on this business of getting married. But he also doesn't care, because some supreme self-confidence (verging on delusion) enables him to simply assume you will eventually see the light and give in.

"Look," you told him the last time he offered his proposal, "I'm not so sure I even want to be married again."

"You've never been married."

"Huh?"

"You've never been married. It's only a marriage if the two people both want to be married to each other."

"So, you mean, *I* was married, but *he* wasn't, so it wasn't a real marriage?"

"Exactly."

The idea caught you by surprise. Still does. For a moment, you were at a loss for reply. What if your marriage to David wasn't something you had to recover from, because it had really only happened in your mind? It would be as though the marriage had never been consummated on a spiritual or any other level, other than physical. That would make you some sort of virgin, you think. And Bill would be your first husband in the truest sense. But you have to be certain.

"Bill," you said at the time, "I hope you know how much I care about and respect you."

"I'm hoping we can find ways to eventually bump that up to love."

"Love? Oh, you had that ages ago. Respect is much, much harder to come by."

And trust, you reflect, is the most elusive of all relationship sentiments to secure, because it is faith, not feeling. But, apparently, this man has earned himself a perfect relationship score.

Bottom line: you feel safe with him.

You relax. Your marriage now seems inevitable, a foregone conclusion. No more of that "Open Marriage" bullshit, however. Never again. Next time, you want a Closed Marriage. And no more divorce, either. Never again. Next time, you'll be a widow. One way or another.

The blinking cursor on the screen in front of you is a reminder that you have come to this time and place in order to get everything out. You must get it all out or else your head, your heart, or both will blow up. You cannot spend the rest of your life perfecting other people's words, letting your own words dry up and die within you.

You speak sharply to your worst fears in order to silence them:

"Everyone, now, just shut up! Didn't we recently complete nearly ten years of the most god-awful research imaginable? It's time for us to write up the results of our study. Let's do it!"

In that moment, your mind is a sterile landscape, unencumbered by any words or images, and all you feel is a sudden, unexpected desire to smoke a cigarette. Which frightens you.

You think: what would Kitty do? And right away, from the depths of your mind, you hear her advice:

"Just start anywhere. Pretend you're writing in your journal. Then you can't fail. Try it — it works!"

So you touch your fingers to the keyboard, you gently close your eyes, you mentally chant your new mantra again and again, "Must trust myself, must trust myself," and you begin to type....

1.

Why I Must

The first night my newlywed husband failed to come home as promised and didn't call, I was a young wife, sick with worry. Years later, I would think: that man had better be dead, because nothing short of actual death is going to get him off the hook tonight.

Midnight, Daniel had said. But already it was well past that. What to do? At one in the morning, I cranked down the oven so my casserole wouldn't incinerate. At two, I turned off the stove entirely, pulled the casserole, covered it with foil, and slammed it into the refrigerator. At that point, I thought: I can reheat. But, by three, the oven was cold, and I found myself wandering aimlessly through our tiny, cramped, downtown apartment.

Passing through the living room again, I lit yet-another cigarette. I had already broken into my second pack of the day by the time I got home. Now the big glass ashtray on our coffee table was overflowing with butts. Supplicant to the Deity of Addictions, I carried the ashtray to the kitchen, as if it were an offering, and dumped the mess into the garbage. Now that I'd purged all visual evidence of the hours I'd spent alone that evening, I could pretend to myself I was making a fresh start. I could deny my true situation: that last call at the bar was nearly an hour ago, yet still there was no sign of the man I'd married not quite five years ago.

When we moved to San Francisco from the East Bay so Daniel could follow his dream of becoming an actor, I was already aware that the theater could be a demanding mistress. After all, I'd had that experience in the years before Daniel came into my life: my steady in high school and college had been an actor, too. But I really didn't understand how insistent the bitch would be. I'd imagined that living together, then getting married, would make a difference. And it did — for a while. But these days, it seemed, Daniel was spending all his waking hours with *her*, not me.

And what happened after work that day had left me feeling more insecure than ever: that young woman at the bus stop, the pretty stranger who asked me if I was Daniel's wife. I told her:

"You must have me confused with someone else. I don't know any Daniels."

"I really think we've met before. After an A.C.T. show. Jessica, isn't it?"

"My name's not Jessica. Besides, I'm single."

Her smile melted away. She frowned. "Oh well, then. I'm the one to be sorry. I apologize for interrupting."

"No problem," I replied, "I have a common face."

My bus arrived just in time to save me, and I boarded it with a sense of relief. I worked my way down the aisle along the sticky overhead pole and found a not-too-disgusting seat at the back next to a greasy tinted window. When I glanced back at the bus stop already receding from view, I saw that woman staring in my direction. I turned to face the front.

I'd surprised myself with my spontaneous lie. I thought of myself as a person who was always truthful. Yet, though I hadn't planned it, the lie had come to me. Unbidden. To protect me. I had refused to yield the truth to this stranger whose relationship to me — and to my husband — was unknown. Later that evening, as I stood in my kitchen, fixing a dinner no one would eat, a feeling came to me: it was the beginning of....

The End

This book was written for
John Gee the Great
(Very Best of All Bears!)
and presented to him
on the occasion of
our 38th wedding anniversary:
April 1, 2022.
Really, truly, deeply.

With everlasting gratitude to
Linda Jay,
my dear friend and esteemed colleague
for half a century.

And with special thanks to
Toni Pebbles
Andy Couturier
Mary Petty
Elaine Bond
Kelly Snider.

Why You Must is the largely fictive work of Susan Gee Rumsey, an expatriot San Franciscan who wrote a love letter to her future, then waited forty years to mail it. (*Photo by Amy Ukena.*)